W9-BXA-391

PRAISE FOR *HERESY*

"*Heresy* is realistic, involving, and carries a real sense of danger. The mystery is well thought out and presented."
—*Statesman Journal* (Salem, Oregon)

"Newman deftly illustrates the complex family and religious intrigues of the time and shows the real action—and the humor—behind convent, tavern, and cathedral doors."
—*Mystery Scene*

"The author mixes moral complexity and careful research to tell an entertaining tale."          —*Publishers Weekly*

"A satisfying journey through medieval France."
—*Kirkus Reviews*

"Newman's facts are, as always, meticulously researched, but she weaves them into the book in such a way that the reader is neither overwhelmed nor bored."
—*The Tennessean*

"The story is complex, multilayered, and impeccably researched. It is easy to be drawn into this remote landscape and to be reminded that, while the technology has changed, the human heart has not."          —*Contra Costa Times*

# Heresy

## A Catherine LeVendeur Mystery

### SHARAN NEWMAN

**TOR®**

A TOM DOHERTY ASSOCIATES BOOK
NEW YORK

This is a work of fiction. All of the characters, organizations, and events portrayed in this novel are either products of the author's imagination or are used fictitiously.

HERESY

Edited by Claire Eddy
Maps by Allison Newman

A Tor Book
Published by Tom Doherty Associates, LLC
175 Fifth Avenue
New York, NY 10010

www.tor.com

Tor® is a registered trademark of Tom Doherty Associates, LLC.

ISBN: 978-0-7653-0247-2

First Edition: December 2002
First Mass Market Edition: March 2007

Printed in the United States of America

P 1

*To*
*Mary Martin McLaughlin*
*magistra, domina et semper amica*

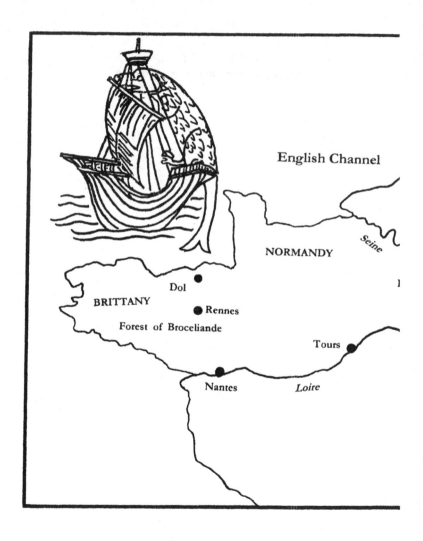

English Channel

Seine

NORMANDY

Dol

BRITTANY

Rennes

Forest of Broceliande

Tours

Nantes

Loire

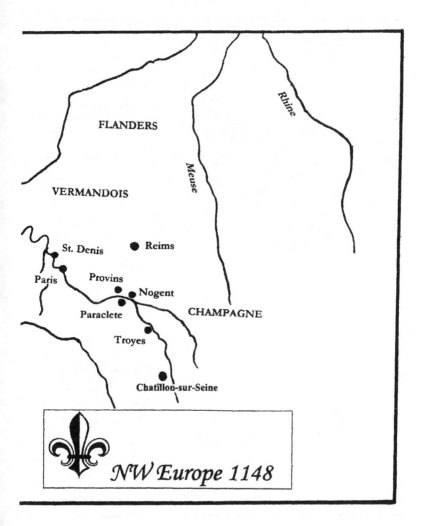

FLANDERS

Rhine

VERMANDOIS

Meuse

St. Denis

Reims

Paris

Provins

Nogent

Paraclete

CHAMPAGNE

Troyes

Chatillon-sur-Seine

*NW Europe 1148*

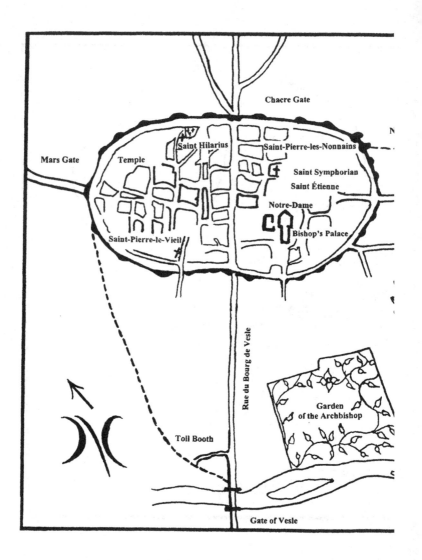

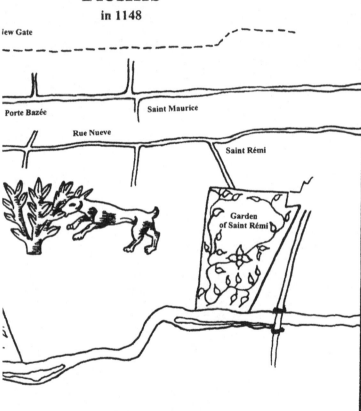

# Reims

in 1148

lew Gate

Porte Bazée

Saint Maurice

Rue Nueve

Saint Rémi

Garden
of Saint Rémi

# Acknowledgments

While I do my best to do the research for all my books myself, the fact is that I always find I need help. The following people have given it to me freely and I am very grateful to them. Any mistakes are in spite of their help and all my own.

Professor Penelope Adair, Pan-American University, and Professor Karen Nicholas, SUNY Oswego, for sharing with me their research on Sybil of Anjou and for many great meals and conversations.

Katherine Christensen, Department of History, Berea College, Berea, Kentucky, for suggesting sources for the Council of Reims.

Professor Marcia Colish, Oberlin College, for her insights on Eon de l'Etoile and the Council of Reims. I'm sorry Peter Lombard wasn't a larger part of this book, but he may turn up in the future.

Dr. Christopher Crockett, for helping me track down some of the bishops who attended the council, especially from the region around Chartres.

Professor David Crouch, Hull University, England, for bringing me up to date on the English bishops and for confirming my research on Marie, Abbess of St-Sulpice and daughter of King Stephen.

Dr. Betty Donoghue, for always being there for me and also for double checking my copy edit.

Mandan Noelle Khoshnevisan, M.A., for being my Stanford Library connection and finding an assortment of maps of twelfth-century Reims.

Dr. Mary McLaughlin, for allowing me to read her work in manuscript, for many spirited discussions on Heloise and for the translation of Abelard's letter at the beginning of chapter four.

Professor Constant Mews, University of Victoria, Monash, Australia, for allowing me to use his translation of the letter of Hugh Metel to Heloise.

Professor Cary Nederman, Texas A&M, for sending me his monograph on John of Salisbury in manuscript, as well as passing on a thesis on Gilbert de Poitiers by one of Professor Mews's students, Claire Monagle.

Dr. Martin Orvitz, pathologist, for giving me the finer points of throat cutting.

Jeffrey Russell, professor emeritus, University of California, Santa Barbara, for setting me to search for Eon, the Latin correction (especially the epigraph to chapter twenty that I had completely botched), as well as general advice and emotional support throughout.

The entire staff of the Department Archives of Ille et Vilaine, Rennes, for guiding me through the archives, letting me fondle twelfth-century charters and enduring my demands for more information.

# Heresy

# Prologue

The forest of Broceliande, Brittany. Sunday, October 26, 1147.

*Eodem anno perfectus est Ierosolimam Conradus rex
Romanorum et Ludowicus rex Francorum cum inestimabili
multitudine plebes christianae, sed transgressi fines Greciae
seducti sunt a Grecorum rege, quasi ad terras pugnae, ubi
periit eorum maxima pars inedia et fame. . . . Obscuratus est
sol 7Kal. Novembris, die dominica, circa horam diei sextam.*

In this year Conrad, king of the Romans, and Louis, King of
the Franks, reached Jerusalem with an innumerable multitude
of the Christian people, but when they crossed the border of
Greece they were tricked by the king of the Greeks as if to a
battleground, where the greater part of them died through
starvation. . . . On October 26, a Sunday, about the hour of
sext, the sun was eclipsed.

*Annales Rodenses,* 1147

*T*he woman ran through the woods, slipping on rain-damp leaves, tripping over roots. Soaked and mud covered, she picked herself up each time, oblivious to bruises. She could hear them crashing behind her, with horses and hunting dogs. She knew she hadn't a chance to escape, but desperation made her keep running. Her lips moved in an endless prayer. It had no form; it was simply a plea for help.

"Blessed Mother, save me. Saint Margaret, save me. Saint Ursula, save me. Saint Eligius, save me. Someone, anyone, please!"

Cecile had always heard that the forest was infested with bandits, with demons, that it had a landscape that varied between worlds. One could go into the fog or cross a stream and find oneself in another time and place. None of those things was as terrifying as the men who were chasing her now. She splashed down an icy rivulet in the hope of putting the dogs off her scent. As she climbed out on the opposite bank, an apparition appeared before her. It was a man clothed in a shimmering assortment of linen robes with silk and gold designs embroidered all over them, in a sort of patchwork as if he were garbed in a dozen albs and altar cloths. In his hand he held a long staff that was bifurcated at the top like a pitchfork. He held it out to her.

Cecile hesitated a moment. Was this Satan? Did she have to choose now between death and damnation? She heard the cries of the hunters, ever closer. Fear made the choice. She grabbed the staff and held on for dear life as the man pulled her up to the bank.

"Come, my child," he said, giving her his arm to lean on. "I shall protect you."

Up close he was less demonic. The hand on her arm was re-assuringly solid. She glanced over her shoulder. "Hurry, they're almost here!"

"Don't worry." The man smiled at her reassuringly. "They have no power in my realm."

He led her into a thicket of brambles and, to her surprise, got down on all fours, crawling through a rough path between them.

On the other side was a cave opening.

"In here. Quickly!" he ordered.

"It's too late," she said as she followed him. "The dogs have crossed the stream."

"My father will not let you be taken," the man said.

"No, I must go." She pulled her hand from his. "I cannot let you be killed, too."

The shouts of the men were clear now as she stood at the mouth of the cave. With the calmness of despair, she turned back to face her pursuers.

And into a strange greenish twilight. The tenor of the voices changed as the men reined their horses to point at the sky.

"What is it?" Cecile cried.

"The power of my father at work." The man took her hand again. "Come with me while their wits are still befuddled."

They entered the cave, which turned out to be nothing more than a tunnel through to an area that had been cleared of trees to make room for an assortment of crude huts. There were more people there, men and women, all dressed as outlandishly as her rescuer. All were pointing at the sky in amazement.

"Master, what is happening?" they called to the man with the staff. "Have we sinned against you?"

The man held up his hands. "Be calm, my children. You have no need to fear. I asked my father to darken the sky so that this poor child could be saved from her persecutors. It will pass in but a few moments."

There was a terrifying moment of pure darkness and then the shadow passed from over the sun. As the light emerged again, Cecile dropped to her knees.

"My lord!" she exclaimed. "I have no words to thank you! Those men would have killed me."

The man placed a hand on her head. "You have found a haven here. No one will harm you as long as you are under my protection. All my children have come here to escape those who would enslave them. You are free to join us."

Cecile looked around. Under the bizarre assortment of clothing, she saw that the people were thin, some bent by work, others wasted by disease. During the eclipse they had clung together. Now they were all staring at her and her savior.

"Your protection is most welcome, but I can accept it only for a short time. It is essential that I find a way to return to my home," Cecile explained. "But I would know who has called upon the Lord to perform this miracle for someone as unworthy as I. If it is in my power, I wish to reward you."

The man stood before her, the fresh sunlight illuminating his face. He clasped his staff and reversed it so that the two prongs dug into the earth.

"I wish no reward." He smiled on her. "It is my father's work that I do. My name is Eon, child, and I am the son of God."

# One

Paris. Wednesday, 6 the ides February (February 10), 1148.
Feast of Saint Scholastica, virgin and scholar.

*Denarii salute mei, per vos ego regno,*
*Terrarum per vos impero principibus.*
*Quod probor et veneror, quod diligo atque frequento,*
*Gratia vestra facit que michi magna facit.*

Money, come to me. Through you I rule;
Through you I command the rulers of the earth.
You whom I extol and revere, love and seek out,
Your esteem creates that which makes me great.

*Petri Pictoris*

*T*he black mud of the streets of Paris had become black ice. The few people insane enough to be out slipped and tripped as they made their way down the slick paths. The ice was doubly dangerous because of the hard chunks of the normal street detritus frozen into it: straw, excrement, rats half chewed by dogs, bits of broken crockery. The dung collectors couldn't be bothered to chisel out most of the leavings and were concentrating instead on the open spaces in front of the bishop's palace and the Grève, where the peddlers set up their stalls and would pay extra to have the ground cleared. So amidst the hard chunks there were also occasional steaming piles. The oaths of those who slid into these could be heard ringing through the crisp afternoon air. The beggars had left the streets and were huddled in the church porches, praying for soup and beer. Even thieves were scarce, having taken their business to the warmth of the taverns.

Catherine stepped carefully through all this in her high wooden sabots, mindful of the fact that she was once again pregnant and that her balance wasn't that good even in her normal state. The wind funneled down the narrow street, catching at her cloak. She pulled it around herself more tightly, her basket of dried fish and herbs tipping as she did so. She snatched at it to prevent everything falling and barely escaped falling herself.

It was the coldest winter in her memory. The weather of the past few years had been dismal, too cold in the summer and damp with many crops failing. Now famine was all around them and illness rampant as people weak with hunger found they had no strength to survive the winter agues. Added to everything else, the news from the king's expedition to the Holy Land was bad.

The army had left in the early summer of 1147, blessed by the pope and Bernard, abbot of Clairvaux. Swords and armor shining, banners waving, King Louis and Queen Eleanor had led an army of pilgrims to free the city of Edessa from the Moslem invaders. Along with them had gone half the lords of France, Burgundy, Champagne, Flanders and Lotharingia. They were supposed to have met up along the way with Conrad, emperor of the Germans, and his army. But almost from the first, things had gone awry. The Germans and French had argued with each other and among themselves. The emperor in Constantinople hadn't welcomed them as expected, and Christian towns had been pillaged on the route. One lord had even ordered the burning of a monastery in retaliation for the murder of one of his soldiers by local townspeople.

Then, last fall, there had been an eclipse of the sun. There were many who feared it was a sign that the expedition to the East was also to be eclipsed by the powerful Seljuk Turks. But the thing that angered those in France the most was the way King Louis kept sending back for more money. Hadn't he taxed them enough to finance the journey? Didn't he know how bad things were in his own country? What business had an anointed king leaving his land in the first place?

Catherine worried about all these things as she made her way back to her home. It seemed to her that ever since this expedition had first been preached, life in France had worsened. She wasn't the only one who was starting to believe that God wasn't happy with the Christian King Louis or his people.

When she arrived at the gate of her house, Catherine felt a deep relief. However dreadful things were outside, she knew that within there was love and warmth and peace.

Peace, of course, could be defined according to many criteria. As she entered, Catherine deducted "tranquility" from the definition. The great hall where they ate, worked, played and fought was currently being used for all these activities. Her six-year-old son, James, was chasing the dog around the room. Or perhaps, Catherine reconsidered, the dog was chas-

ing him. Dragon might have been slowed down by the weight
of four-year-old Edana. She was clinging to the dog's back
with her arms around his neck. From her happy squeals and
his barks, neither appeared to be in danger.

Catherine's husband, Edgar, and her cousin, Solomon,
were seated at the table near the fire. There was a pitcher of
spiced beer on the table that was rocking perilously as the
men alternately pounded the table to emphasize the points in
their argument. Neither seemed aware of the rowdiness of the
children or the noise.

"I'm home!" Catherine called.

"Why should the emperor help the king?" Solomon shouted
at Edgar. "Those *desfaë* 'pilgrims' have ravaged his towns and
destroyed his truce with the Arabs."

"He had no business making truces with infidels!" Edgar
shouted back.

"You'd rather Roger of Sicily ruled all of Europe?"
Solomon countered. "Manuel's empire has Saracens on three
sides and a Norman adventurer on the fourth. He can hardly
fight Roger if he has to spend all his time wet-nursing idiotic
defenders of Christendom! Even your pope agrees with me on
that one."

That was undeniably true. Pope Eugenius had been counting on the help of the German king, Conrad, to defend Italy
against Roger of Sicily, whom he privately considered a far
more serious threat than the Turks. He was not pleased that
Conrad was still in the Holy Land.

"So why are you arguing against Roger?" Edgar shouted.
"He's the most lenient of all the Christian kings where Jews
are concerned. You should be glad no one's helping the pope."

Solomon paused, realizing that he had just argued himself
onto the wrong side. It wasn't easy being a Jew in a Christian
household, or a Christian country.

Catherine took advantage of the slight lull to announce herself again.

"Edgar, are you sure we want one more person in the house
to add to this cacophony?"

Edana fell off the dog; James tripped over her. Both children started howling. Before Catherine could get to them, Edgar and Solomon jumped up and came to her, each stopping on the way to pick up a child.

"You're frozen, Catherine," Edgar chided. "I knew I shouldn't have let you go out today. Come over here and get warm. Do you want some beer? I'll heat it again."

He let Edana slide down his leg and then pulled the poker from the fire. He had to set it on the edge of the hearth to wipe it off with a cloth before putting it in the pitcher, where it sizzled. No one offered to help him. Even the children knew better than to suggest there was anything Edgar couldn't do with only one hand. Neither of them could remember him with two, but Catherine still had nightmares about the moment when he had stepped between his father's sword and the man it was aimed at. The blade had slid through Edgar's wrist with barely a pause, leaving his left hand in a lake of blood on the floor.

Catherine shook the memory away and returned to the present.

"I needed to get out," she said. "The midwife said that I should keep busy as long as I can. And I wanted to stop by and see how Luca was doing. Her new baby isn't well."

"Catherine," Edgar said firmly, "I'm sure Luca is doing everything that can be done for her family. A baker always has bread, at least."

He exchanged a glance with Solomon over her head. They were both remembering Catherine's long convalescence after the winter death of her last child. Grief, along with Catherine's belief that some sin of hers must have been visited on the baby, had made it worse. The men were agreed that she mustn't be allowed to dwell on such things, particularly now, in the early months of the next pregnancy.

"Of course," Catherine said. "Luca takes excellent care of her children. And of our family, as well. She sent us some *gastels* made with dried apple and honey."

"Really?" Solomon began to search the basket for the package of cakes.

"Solomon!" Catherine laughed. "You're as bad as the children. Go on, there's enough for all of you. Now, did something start your argument, or were the two of you just bored?"

She looked up at Edgar, who tried to avoid her eyes.

"Nothing, really," he said. "Solomon feels that King Louis should never have left for the Holy Land."

"He has much company in that position," Catherine said. "I thought you shared it yourself."

Edgar shrugged. "It is a noble cause and he might be succeeding if it weren't for the wiles of the Greek emperor."

Catherine spoke before Solomon could restart the quarrel. "I don't know how many of the stories we've heard from those who've returned are true, but it does seem to me that the emperor could have been more welcoming to the armies. And yet, Roger of Sicily shouldn't have taken advantage of the situation to attack the emperor."

"I heard that Emperor Manuel was the one to declare war on Roger," Edgar insisted.

"It doesn't matter who's at fault, Edgar," Solomon said. "It still means that almost all of our connections to the Arab traders have been cut off. With Roger and Manuel at war and the Spanish rulers pushing the Arabs farther and farther south, everything that gets through to France is three times as dear. And Abbot Suger isn't going to pay more for his incense because we tell him that his precious King Louis has made it impossible to conduct trade."

Now that the subject was money, Catherine felt on more secure ground.

"There must be a way we can keep the cost down," she said. "Either that or trade things that the armies will need. Wool, for instance. Scotland isn't at war with anyone at the moment, are they? Our connections there are solid. Why don't we let the abbot have his incense at the agreed-on price and then prevail upon him to buy blankets from us to send to the king."

"That might help," Edgar said. "Except for the fact that the king is already heavily in debt to the Knights of the Temple. Even if we made the deal, it's likely that he wouldn't pay us. No, Solomon and I can think of only one way to ensure that this family doesn't starve. Spain is still our best source for the luxury goods that will bring the highest return. I think that he and I should leave soon so that we can be back before the fairs in May."

"Oh, Edgar, no." Catherine tried to keep the panic from her voice. "You promised to let Solomon do the traveling."

Edgar sat down on the bench next to her and put his arm around her.

"I know I did, *carissima*," he said. "But I also promised to take care of you and our children. If I must go to Spain to do so, I will. We can't afford to pay so many others to bring us goods. There's no profit."

There was silence. Even the children were watching Catherine carefully. She could feel the anger and fear rising.

"Will someone put that damn dog out!" she exploded. "How can anyone think with that barking? Martin!" she called their one serving boy. "Tie Dragon up in the yard. James, he's your dog. Go help Martin."

"Yes, Mama." James rushed to obey. The tone in his mother's voice subdued his usually contrary nature.

"Solomon," Catherine continued, "take Edana into the kitchen. Samonie can watch her. Then come back. We all need to discuss this."

"Of course, Catherine." Solomon was as wary as James. "I won't be a moment," he promised Edgar.

"Afraid to be alone with me?" Catherine asked her husband when the others had gone.

Edgar smiled. "Never, beloved," he said. "I stand ready to face the force of your wrath. I know I deserve it."

Catherine slumped on the bench, her elbows on the table.

"No, you don't," she muttered. "You just expect me to be unreasonable because of the baby."

He leaned over and turned her face to his.

"You know how much I hate to leave you," he said softly.

She would rather have stayed angry. Now there was no wall to stop her tears.

She was still mopping up her face with her sleeve when Solomon returned.

"If I could go on this trip alone, I would," he told Catherine.

"But with the Spanish emperor's armies everywhere now, we need a Christian, especially an Englishman, in the party. Now that the English have arrived to help fight the Saracens in Spain, Alfonso looks very favorably on the English."

"I know that, Solomon," Catherine said. "It's childish of me to try to keep the both of you tied to my skirts as if you were no older than James. But there are so many signs of doom these days. Storms and sickness, war and revolt. Every day we hear of some new disaster."

Edgar wrapped his arms around her.

"Spring will come, my love," he said. "It always does. You're the one who usually tells me not to be melancholic. And this child will be born strong and healthy to create as much chaos in the house as his brother and sister."

"Am I superfluous here?" Solomon asked, after watching them a moment longer. "If so, I have work to do to prepare for our journey."

Catherine looked up from Edgar's chest.

"Go if you need to, Solomon," she said. "I'll have resigned myself to this by the time you return."

Muttering something about the likelihood of that, Solomon took his leave.

Edgar waited until he heard the door close, then returned to the discussion.

"Would you have me send Solomon alone at a time when Jews are so vulnerable?" he asked. "Too many of these pilgrims see no difference between a Saracen and a Jew. Killing the infidel is all they care about."

Catherine shook her head. "If only he would convert. What have we done wrong that he can't see that the Messiah has come? Aren't we good enough Christians?"

Edgar laughed. "I know that I'm not," he admitted. "I think we'll just have to keep trying to set a good example and hope that one day Our Lord will open Solomon's heart to the true faith."

"I suppose a miracle is all we can hope for," Catherine sighed. "I still feel so much guilt because our example couldn't keep my father from returning to Judaism after having been a Christian for forty years. I don't want to drive my cousin away. As long as Solomon remains our connection to the Jewish communities, there's still a shred of hope that Father will come back."

Edgar held her closer. "I don't know why Hubert left the faith. Some things are not meant for us to understand. But I do know that if we reject Solomon he'll never be converted. Nor, I might add, will we be able to continue in this profession. Solomon is too tactful to admit it, but I'm still his apprentice when it comes to trade."

"And the apprentice must accompany his master," Catherine sighed. "But be careful, *carissime,* and come back soon."

Edgar kissed her. "I promise I'll be home to hear our new baby's first cry. Will that satisfy you?

"No," Catherine said. "But it will have to do."

After spending all winter in the forest, Cecile thought it was odd that not one of Eon's followers had bothered to ask her where she had come from or why the men had been chasing her. Of course, everything about Eon and his people was odd. They seemed unaware of how bizarre they were, dressed in swaths of fine material they had stolen from local churches, pieced together with rough wool. They called themselves by strange names, like Prudence and Wisdom. She saw no sign of either in the rough encampment. But they were kind to her. They fed her and shared their shelter. Not one of the men, including Eon, ever suggested that she should repay this generosity with her body. In that, these mad peasants were more noble than the men she had fled. Cecile knew the horror that she would go back to if the count's men ever found her. This place was strange, but it was safe.

There was only one man among the group who seemed unaffected by the universal adoration of Eon. He called himself Peter. It was some weeks before she gathered up enough courage to ask him how he had become one of Eon's followers.

"The others are all people who have been damaged," she said sadly. "Beaten, starved, driven from their homes. Anyone who took them in would be treated as their savior. But you are no more like them than I am."

Peter smiled at her. "Eon knows why I'm here," he said. "He knows I have no desire to harm him or his people, so he tolerates me."

Cecile thought there would be many reasons for tolerating Peter. He was well built, tall and slender with a strong face and dark brown eyes. He had a hawklike nose that would have been overpowering in a lesser setting. If any man in this place could tempt her, it would be this one.

"Then you don't believe Eon is the son of God?" she asked.

His eyebrows rose. "Do you?"

Cecile shook her head. "I think he is a dear deluded man who has been good to me, but nothing more. His speech isn't that of a peasant. I don't understand why his family hasn't come to take him home where he can be cared for."

"They have," Peter explained. "But he refuses to leave, and his people threaten to kill anyone who tries to take him by force."

"But they have no weapons!"

"That's true, but Eon's cousins don't really want to hurt anyone," Peter said. "They asked me to stay until spring to make sure he doesn't do anything that would cause him to be taken by the authorities. His followers haven't raided a village or hermitage since I joined them. They trap their meat and rely on donations for the rest. I had hoped that if things got bad enough I could convince him to come with me back to the monastery his family placed him in. But his madness is too entrenched and the local villagers too kind. They have little enough for themselves and still they give him bread. I worry about him. I can't stay much longer and I don't know what will happen if he's left to his own devices."

"You're leaving?" Cecile looked up at him in hope. "When?"

"Within the week," he said. "My mother expects to hear from me soon, and there's been no way to get a message out all winter. I have family near Nantes who will send her word that I'm well."

Cecile put both hands on his arm. "Please," she begged, "take me with you! My family must believe me to be dead by now, or worse, still safe in the convent. No one knows what's happening there. I shouldn't have stayed here so long, but I was afraid."

From her wide eyes and shaking hands, Peter deduced that Cecile was still afraid. He had watched her since she arrived. Her gentleness with the inhabitants of Eon's village touched him. She was obviously a noblewoman, but he suspected that she had been abused as evilly as any of the serfs who had come to Eon for protection.

He had also suspected from her demeanor that she might have been in a convent. He had hoped it wasn't true. She said her prayers in Latin but he had told himself that many noblewomen knew Latin. There were other clues, but Peter had ignored them all. Being with Cecile had given him dreams he had never hoped to have.

With a vicious wrench, he brought himself back to her story.

"What is happening in your convent?" he asked. "I thought that most monastic houses were visited regularly by the bishops. Surely any serious irregularities would be noticed and corrected."

Cecile looked at him in amazement. "The bishop knows all about it, but he can do nothing, even if he wanted to. The count of Tréguier has thrown the canons out of the abbey of Sainte-Croix and installed his mistress and her friends there instead. They say that the former abbot, Moses, has left to take his complaint to the pope, but we had heard nothing from him when I escaped."

"Then the matter will soon be resolved," Peter told her soothingly. "Perhaps it has already. I still don't see why you were there. You are a professed nun, aren't you? Sainte-Croix is a male monastic house."

"Oh, yes," Cecile said. "I was at the convent of Saint-Georges-de-Rennes. That is until Count Henri decided to move some of us to his . . . his brothel. The abbess protested, of course, but we had no defense and so we had to go. At first we thought it was only to prove to anyone who asked that Sainte-Croix was really still a religious house. We assumed we would be allowed to continue our devotions as before. But then"—she swallowed—"we realized that his men had no re-spect for our vows or our persons."

"I see." Peter's dark eyes softened with pity. "And so you fled."

She nodded. "I have taken a heavenly bridegroom and will not submit willingly to any man. I told them that. They didn't care. I prayed and pleaded, but Christ didn't help me. I must have sinned greatly to be punished so."

"That's not true," Peter said sharply. "Augustine said so himself when he wrote to the consecrated virgins who had been raped by the Goths. He said that in the eyes of Heaven, they were still virgins for their souls were pure."

Cecile looked up at him, her mouth open as if breathing in hope.

"Saint Augustine said that?" she said. "He must have known." She sighed. "I'm glad that this wasn't brought upon me by my own actions, but I don't understand why God let it happen to me at all."

"Oh, Cecile," Peter said. "I'm neither a saint nor a philoso-pher. I have no idea. But He did help you to escape, after all."

That's so." Cecile was as comforted as she could be. "But not for long. I thought no one would notice I was gone until night. But someone betrayed me, and I hadn't gone half a league when I heard the men coming after me. They hunted me as if I were a wild beast or a criminal."

She shuddered. Peter laid his hand on her shoulder. He wanted to do more but understood now that there was no hope. He could only be her friend and protector.

"I promise to take you with me and see to it that you are re-stored to your convent or your family," he said. "If Saint-Georges isn't safe, I can take you to my mother. She is abbess at a convent in Champagne. It's time that you returned to the monastic life. I promise, we'll leave tomorrow."

In the county of Champagne, miles away from Brittany, Heloise, abbess of the convent of the Paraclete, had been awake since the end of the night office. The other nuns had gone back to their warm beds to rest until dawn, but Heloise used this time to work, pray, and sometimes to remember.

She was drafting replies to the many letters she received, but for some reason her mind kept drifting to her son, Astrolabe. It had always pained her that she had given him into the keeping of his father's family almost as soon as he had been born. But then it had seemed the only choice. Peter Abelard was a great philosopher and scholar. At the time Heloise had believed that it would have been wrong to burden him with a child. And she had loved Abelard too much to leave him. His sister, Denise, had raised Astrolabe with love and a stability that neither Heloise nor Abelard could give him. But Heloise loved him, too, even more now that Abelard was dead. Astrolabe was the tangible result not just of her sin but also of her passion. Of the errors she had committed in her youth, Astrolabe was not among them. She and Abelard had both agreed on that.

Astrolabe normally visited her a few times each year, but there had been no word from him since before the feast of the Nativity. His last letter had said he was going to visit a friend in northern Brittany who needed his help. What sort of help, Heloise wondered. And why was it taking so long to accomplish?

She tried to concentrate on the letter to Mahaut, Countess of Champagne, whose son had gone on the expedition with the king. The subject of the countess's concern was a conflict over a donation made by one of her vassals to another convent. The children of the original donor claimed that they hadn't been consulted before their land was given to the nuns, and they wanted it back. Heloise was used to being consulted in such matters, but worry over her own son made it hard for her to write naturally, even on a neutral matter, to Mahaut whose own child was in so much greater danger. Did Mahaut lie awake nights wondering if her eldest son would ever return?

She was deep into the letter when she caught a movement out of the corner of her eye. Startled, she turned quickly on her stool, nearly tipping it over.

"Mother! I'm so sorry!" The girl dropped her dark cloak, revealing that she was wearing only her shift and wooden sabots.

"Margaret!" Heloise hurried to wrap her again in the cloak. The room was cold. The abbess didn't give herself any more creature comfort than she allowed the other nuns. "What are you doing up at this hour? Does Sister Emily know you're not in your bed?"

"No, Mother. I didn't want to wake anyone." Margaret shivered, but Heloise felt that it was more from fear than the cold. "I had a horrible dream! I tried to put it out of my mind with prayer, but it wouldn't go away. I got up to use the latrine and saw a light in your window, so . . ."

Heloise smiled. "Your sister-in-law was not above interrupting my work, either. You and Catherine may look nothing alike, but you do have some of the same traits."

Margaret looked down. "I wish that were true, Mother. I'm not the scholar she was, nor am I as brave."

Heloise stroked the white scar across Margaret's cheek. "You have more reason to be cautious than she ever did, and a healthy fear is not a bad thing. And as for scholarship, it's true you're not as adept at rhetoric, but your diligence is marvelous. You've made great strides in your Hebrew studies. Soon you'll be beyond me. We may have to send you to a teacher in Troyes."

She had been trying to distract the girl from her dream, but something she had said caused Margaret to gasp and start trembling.

"Mother, can dreams be a prophecy?" she asked, tears forming at the corners of her eyes.

"Only to prophets," Heloise answered. "Do you suspect you've been granted such a gift?"

Margaret took a deep breath. "Of course not." She tried to smile. "It's only that it was so intense, the flames and the shouting."

Heloise sat Margaret down on her bed. "Very well, tell me what you remember and I'll do my best to explain it."

"It was confusing," Margaret admitted. "There was a huge

crowd of people, ugly people, with faces twisted so that they seemed more to be beasts. They were screaming something; I couldn't understand it. Then I saw a man being dragged through them. He was bound, and those he passed spat on him or kicked him. He was brought up to a platform and then the voices became clear. They shrieked 'Burn! Burn! Burn!' "

"Perhaps it was a vision of the Passion of Our Lord," Heloise suggested gently. "We are sometimes given such dreams to remind us of our faith."

"No," Margaret lowered her head and whispered. "At the end, as they tied him to the stake, I saw his face. That's what frightened me into waking."

She raised her face, tears streaming. "Mother Heloise, it was Solomon!"

Now Heloise understood. Catherine had confided to her that one of the reasons Margaret was at the Paraclete was that she had developed an unsuitable affection for Edgar's partner in trade. Solomon felt an avuncular love for the girl, nothing more, Catherine had assured her. Even if he wished to marry Margaret, it was impossible. Firstly, Solomon was a Jew. But even if he converted, such a liaison would never be permitted. Margaret was too wellborn for a match with someone outside the nobility.

Margaret understood this. She had obeyed the decision to send her to the Paraclete with only mild protest, and she appeared to be adjusting well to the pattern of life in the convent, happy to spend her time in learning until her family settled her future. But Heloise knew from bitter experience how ungovernable the heart can be.

"My poor child," she said as she smoothed Margaret's hair. "It was a dreadful dream but nothing more. It was brought about solely through your concern for your friend added to all the talk of heresy and the resentment toward the Jews that King Louis's pilgrimage has caused. I'm sure Solomon is fine."

Margaret looked up at Heloise. The tears were ebbing but the grief remained. Heloise held her until a deep sigh and a hiccough indicated that Margaret had calmed down. The abbess stifled a sigh of her own. At fifteen, Margaret couldn't know how many times the heart can break and mend only to break again. And had to. Just as well, she thought. Otherwise the convents would be so full that there would be no one left to propagate.

"Thank you, Mother." Margaret got up. "I apologize for disturbing you. I'll confess it in Chapter and take whatever penance you set."

"That won't be necessary, my dear." Heloise kissed her and led her out. "You came to me with a spiritual crisis. It's my duty to help you, even in the middle of the night. Now, try not to wake anyone else on your way back."

Heloise returned to her letter to Mahaut. It was made even harder now. Margaret's face kept interfering. The countess had taken an interest in Margaret, who was the count's granddaughter, her mother having been the product of a youthful affair between Count Thibault and a noblewoman of Ponthieu. Countess Mahaut was tolerant of something that had happened well before her marriage to the count and had become fond of her husband's granddaughter.

Heloise guessed that she and the count had an eye out for an alliance that would be beneficial to Margaret and the county of Champagne as well. It shouldn't be difficult to find a good husband for the child. Her father was a lord in Scotland, far enough away to be ignored, but still noble, and Margaret was becoming more beautiful every day. Her skin was so pale that the scar across her cheek was hardly noticeable and her eyes were large and of a deep brown. Her hair was the color of red gold much fancied by poets.

And unlike her brother's wife, Catherine, Margaret was mild and dutiful. Heloise had no doubt that she would obey her family's wishes as was proper.

So why did Heloise's heart sink at the prospect?

She looked down at the letter. There was no way she could concentrate on it any further. Finally she went and stood before the crucifix on the wall, praying fervently for wisdom and a peaceful mind. But behind that prayer was an even deeper one.

*Astrolabe, my son, are you safe? Why is there no word from you?*

# *Two*

The forest of Broceliande, Brittany. Friday, 4 ides February (February 12), 1148. Feast of Saint Rioc, a Breton boy who was good to his mother.

*Haeresis Eunitarum intra Britannias pullulat. Horam Princeps erat quidam perversi mentis, Eunus nomine: qui cum esset idiota. . . . Hic nefario ausu, absque sacris ordinibus Missas celebrabat indigne, ad errorem et subversionem perditorum hominum.*

The heresy of the Eonists increased among the Bretons. At this time, the leader was a certain man of wayward thinking, named Eon. With wicked audacity, he unworthily celebrated Mass, although he was not in holy orders, leading to error and subversion among the ruined people.

*Continuatio Gemblacensis*

*P*eter?" Cecile shook him awake. "Something's happening in the forest. We need to get away now, before anyone comes."

Peter looked at her blearily. The sky was barely grey. It must lack an hour until dawn. The man next to him had snored all night and he had just managed to get to sleep at last. "What is it?" he asked her.

"Gwenael was out gathering wood. She came running back because she saw a huge troop of men on horseback below in the forest."

"A hunting party?" he guessed. "They won't come this way. It's too steep and rocky."

"They might if they are hunting us." Cecile pulled him to get up. "Gwenael says they carried swords, not bows. Please! We can't be found here."

Around them others were stirring. There was a growing sense of panic among the Eonites as the news spread. Eon emerged from his hut and, helped by his acolytes, climbed to the rickety roof where he stood and faced the people.

"Fear not!" he cried, raising his arms. "My father shall protect you. The minions of the devil have no power here!"

His followers surged toward him in the hope that the closer they came to Eon, the safer they would be.

"They have no weapons," Peter said. "They'll be slaughtered."

"So will we be, if we stay." Cecile pulled at his arm. "Please, come with me. We must leave now!"

The man hesitated.

"I have to stop this," he said at last. "I can explain to these men that Eon is harmless."

"Peter, you can't explain anything to men with swords," Cecile pleaded.

"I have to try," he answered. "Which way are they coming from?"

Mutely, Cecile pointed south. By now they all could hear the jingle of harness and the shouting of the men.

"Cecile, hide yourself," he begged her. "When it's over you can tell them that you were a prisoner. Forgive me."

Peter ran toward the break in the woods through which the riders were pouring.

"Stop!" he cried. "These people aren't dangerous! They have nothing worth stealing. Who is your commander? Bring me to him!"

Cecile ran after him, grabbing at his cloak to drag him back.

"Are you mad?" she cried. "They'll trample you!"

"Cecile! Go back!" Peter pleaded with her.

"I can't let you be killed!" she shouted.

Then she looked up at the approaching riders.

"Oh, sweet Virgin, it's him!" she screamed. "Peter! It's me they want, not Eon! Don't let him take me! If he does I'll never escape again!"

The horses bore down on them. Peter put his arms around Cecile to shield her. Then something struck his head and he fell.

When he awoke, he was on the floor of a cart, his arms tied. His head ached horribly and his tongue was swollen with thirst.

Beside him was Cecile. She was still unconscious.

At least that was what he thought until he saw the blood clotting on the deep gash in her throat.

"Cecile?" He stared at the blood. Slowly the horror came to him.

"Cecile!" He reached for her with his bound hands, trying to hold her. The cool blood was sticky on his fingers, on his face as he bent to touch her cheek with his lips. She was stiff as ice.

Frantically, he began working at his bonds. He was astonished when, with almost no effort, they came apart. Someone had cut the ropes nearly through. Why? There was only one answer: to incriminate him in Cecile's death. What other reason could there be? There was no one who knew him here, no one who would want to save him.

It was clear to him that the man Cecile so feared had taken her life. A white rage swept over him. For the first time in his life, he would have joyfully run a sword into a man's heart. He looked about for a weapon. There was nothing. Not even the knife that had cut Cecile's neck. It didn't matter. He would charge the guards like a mad bear and kill them all.

The rational part of his mind asserted itself at once.

He would be brought down in a matter of minutes and hanged from the nearest tree. And whoever murdered Cecile would never be brought to justice.

There was only one hope. He had to get away at once and find help, before his captors found out who he really was.

Peter knelt by the body of Cecile. He made the sign of the cross on her forehead and said a quick but fervent prayer for her soul. Then he kissed her lips.

Finally, he climbed out of the cart, crept past the sleeping guard and vanished into the misty forest.

A week later, Solomon was having a relaxing meal at the home of his friend Abraham, the vintner. It was rare that he was able to have food cooked according to the Law, and he was making the most of it.

"More?" his hostess, Rebecca, asked.

He nodded, mouth full, and she signaled the servant to offer him the platter.

Solomon gave a huge sigh of contentment. Even with Catherine and Edgar he always felt slightly on edge, as if at any moment they would try again to convert him. Here they only nagged him to marry one of the lovely pious girls they seemed to know in abundance. It was little enough to pay for being allowed to be himself for an evening.

Rebecca smiled in a way that told Solomon she knew what he was thinking.

"You could eat like this every night, you know," she said.

"Is that an invitation?" Solomon grinned at her. He capitulated. "Who do you have in mind for me now? I thought we'd been through all the girls of Paris."

"We have," Rebecca said. "But I have a wonderful niece, almost eighteen. She lives near Reims. Her father has vineyards that produce the most delicate wine. She's quite lovely, blond as the English. We can arrange to have her visit this summer, or perhaps you'll be going that way?"

Solomon shook his head. "Spain. Edgar and I need to arrange new contacts there. All these Christian wars have destroyed decent trade."

"Be careful down there," Abraham spoke for the first time. "The Saracen parts of Spain are becoming almost as dangerous for us as the Christian ones. The new Saracen leaders aren't as soft on Jews as the old ones."

"I know that well." Solomon finished the bowl of spiced chicken and leaned back on his cushioned chair, a cup of Abraham's best wine in his hand. He twirled it, the silver filigree shining in the lamplight. He regarded his friends with sadness.

"Where is there a place where we don't have to be wary?" he asked them.

Abraham refilled his wine cup.

"At this table, my friend," he said. "And don't think we didn't notice how you turned the conversation away from the possibility of having such a home and table of your own."

Solomon laughed at that. "I've begged you to stop thrusting these poor women at me. Have you no pity for them? Think what you're asking them to take on."

"The opportunity to turn you back into a good, observant Jew?" Rebecca replied. "Any woman would consider it a worthy challenge. And," she added considering him in the candlelight, "without meaning to give you cause for pride, you do bring other advantages to a marriage."

"Rebecca!" Abraham feigned shock.

"I suppose you're referring to my ability to acquire perfume and jewelry for less than the market price?" Solomon teased.

"That reminds me," Abraham shifted the talk again. Solomon had made it clear that he still wasn't interested in a good match. Abraham would respect that, although he knew Rebecca would return to the subject if she saw an opening. "While you're in the south, keep an eye out for the silks that the Sicilians looted from the Byzantines last fall. You might get a good price for them."

"More important"—Rebecca was serious now—"the Sicilians also kidnapped the silk weavers, some of them Jewish. No one has learned where those poor women have been taken."

Solomon agreed, grateful that they were no longer discussing his marriage prospects. "I'll be alert for both silk and information," he promised.

Soon after, he took his leave and, carrying a small closed lantern, made his way as quickly as he could from the Île de la Cité to the bridge leading to the Grève. He was walking the narrow passage between the buildings that lined both sides of the bridge when he felt someone come up behind him. He swirled around, shining the lantern into the surprised face of a young man.

"Who are you?" Solomon demanded.

The man stepped back, trying to get out of the light.

"Sorry, sorry . . ." He waved his hands, showing they were empty. "Are you Solomon the Jew?"

"I repeat," Solomon said firmly, "who wants to know?"

"I was told to look for a tall, dark man with a beard and curls who walked through Paris as if he owned it," the man replied. "I'm supposed to be careful not to make you angry."

"That much is correct," Solomon admitted. "Who sent you, then?"

The man looked sharply right and left, then up to the overhanging balconies.

"Could we go back to the Île?" he asked. "I don't know who's listening here."

"So that your friends can attack me?" Solomon said.

"No, no, no!" The man stepped back another pace. "I told him I wouldn't be able to get you to come. But he begged me to try. A friend of yours is in trouble. He told me you were his best hope."

Solomon rolled his eyes. "You can't expect me to be taken in by that one."

The man bit his lip. "He told me, what was it? He told me, 'It makes sense that the son of a heretic should feel safest in the home of a halfhearted Jew.' "

"*Edondu!*" Solomon's face changed at once. "Why didn't you tell me straight out? Where is he? What's wrong?"

"I escaped with him." The man turned, assuming Solomon would follow him. "They came for us, saying that we were heretics. My master had told me that Peter wasn't one of us. He tried to explain to the soldiers, but they didn't believe him. So my master told me to free him and see that he got safely away. I had a small knife in my shoe. First I cut my ropes and then his, but someone saw me. I had to run a long time before I could look for Peter. At least he got away before they discovered that Cecile was dead."

"Whom did you escape from? Where? Why?" Solomon lowered the lantern to light the uneven ground. "Who is Cecile?"

"He'll explain," the man said over his shoulder. "It's not far. The owner of the Blue Boar gave us a room to hide in."

Solomon followed cautiously. It sounded as if the person in trouble was his old friend Astrolabe. But if so, why hadn't he gone directly to Catherine and Edgar? Even more, what kind of trouble could someone like Astrolabe get into? Heresy? Murder? That was ridiculous! Unlike his argumentative father, Peter Abelard, Astrolabe was the most inoffensive man imaginable. He had once lamented to Solomon that all his father had given him was his looks, and the resemblance made it all the harder to convince people that he was neither a philosopher nor a theologian.

Despite his confusion, his natural wariness made Solomon take notice of the man seated near the doorway of the Blue Boar. He was hunched in his cloak like a beggar, but Solomon saw no sign of infirmity or starvation. As soon as they entered, the man leapt up and left.

Perhaps it was just someone who suddenly remembered that his wife had told him to be home by Compline, Solomon thought. But he took note of it, just the same. No action could be considered totally innocent in these days.

The tavern was low-ceilinged and dark with only a couple of oil lamps on the table that served as a bar. The air was pungent with smoke from the charcoal brazier and the odor of the bodies of the drinkers. Solomon sniffed and regretted it at once. Someone had been sick in the corner by the stairs.

The man led him up two flights to the alcove under the roof. As they entered, the sliver of candlelight was extinguished. In the brief moment before the light had vanished, Solomon saw a man with tangled hair and a several weeks' growth of brown beard.

"Astrolabe?" he asked in astonishment. "What's happened to you?"

There was a rustle as a spill was lit from the brazier and taken to the candle.

Astrolabe looked up at him. He was dirty and gaunt. His clothes were stained. His tunic had been ripped and the tear closed by a pin. "Solomon, you have to help me. If this gets out, the truth won't matter. The scandal alone could ruin my mother's life."

Solomon had to bend almost to his hands and knees to reach the pallet where Astrolabe sat. With some difficulty, he managed to make himself comfortable. He could tell that this would be a long story.

"From the look of it, your life is in more danger of ruin than hers," he said. "Very well, I'm ready. Start from the beginning."

Astrolabe sighed and began. "I never should have told Eon's cousin I would help him—"

"Wait," Solomon interrupted. "This sounds like a story that will need beer."

* * *

Not far away, in the chapter house of the cathedral of Notre-Dame, another man was listening to the opposite side of the story.

"Our orders were to capture the heretics who had been pillaging the area between Rennes and Nantes," the soldier said. "It wasn't hard to find the group and bring most of them in. The archbishop of Tours was pleased, but I can't believe they're the right ones. Oh, there were a couple of rough characters, but most were peasants, runaway serfs, a few tradesmen. They put up almost no resistance. And their clothes! I felt like an idiot treating them like dangerous criminals. But then, on the second day out, we found the dead woman. She had been knocked out in the raid so we had put her and another wounded man in a cart. The next morning when I came to check on her, I discovered that her throat had been cut from ear to ear. The man had escaped."

Canon Rolland nodded. "A heinous crime indeed. Are you sure the man in the cart with her is the one who killed her?"

The soldier shrugged. "Who else could have done it? We have a body and an escaped prisoner. What would you assume?"

"The same as you, I suppose," the canon said. "Wasn't he searched for a weapon at the time of his capture?"

"I don't know," the soldier said. "None of the heretics seemed to have much more than a rusty meat knife. But it's strange about the murdered woman. This Eon says that she was a saint, sent to them by God. He's mourning her as a martyr. So if she was so holy to them, why should one of Eon's followers want to kill her?"

"You believe the rantings of a mad heretic?"

Canon Rolland was a large man. He leaned over the table where the soldier sat, causing the soldier to reach for his knife without thinking. Although he was well trained in fighting, the soldier had the sense that this cleric was dangerous. He wished he had more than this short knife with him. He stood to face his questioner.

"The others all give the same story," he said firmly. "She appeared during the eclipse last year. They say that she was being pursued by demons but God and Eon saved her. She was special to them. They also say that her speech was Norman and that of a lady. They believe we killed her. If their curses had any merit, I'd have a tail, no nose and several horrible diseases by now."

The canon pursed his lips, nodding. "A ruse to put you off, I'd guess. She may have been a captive of these outlaws, whatever they say. This man who escaped could well have been ordered to kill her to prevent her from telling the bishop the truth about them. Would you know this prisoner again?"

"Perhaps," the soldier said. "I don't know. They all looked so preposterous in their stolen robes."

Rolland sighed at that. "The murderer must be found," he said. "This woman died a Christian martyr, I'm sure. Her killer must be brought to justice. But that job is for others to perform. My greatest concern is not crimes against the body, but against the soul. This man may have taken one life, but he threatens the eternal life of many more now that he is free to corrupt others with his poisonous beliefs. The tongue of a heretic is much more dangerous than his knife."

This brought an image to the soldier that he tried vainly to ignore. In his experience, a sharp blade was always to be preferred as a weapon. After all, it is hard to preach after the tongue has been removed.

The canon was pacing now. "Heresy. I foresaw this. King Louis went off fighting distant heathens and left France open to the real Enemy. As the devil lurks in the darkness, so heretics mask themselves as true Christians. How can decent people recognize them?"

The soldier thought of suggesting that the canon go to Brittany where there seemed to be heretics preaching at every crossroads. They were easy to spot. The Eonites were barely a whisper in the roar of unorthodox beliefs. But he kept silent. Increasingly all he wanted was to get out of the presence of this man whose steady gaze from bulging blue eyes was unnerving him. He did venture one suggestion.

"Perhaps you could take the matter up with the bishop of Paris?"

The canon nodded very slowly, looking him up and down. "Perhaps I shall."

The soldier felt as if the man were measuring him for his coffin. It was with great relief that he left the chapter house and fled into the night.

When he had left, another man came out from where he had been hiding in the shadows. He was much smaller than the canon, with weepy grey eyes and a drooping nose. He was wearing the robes of a monk.

"I told you how it was with the heretics," he said. "Do you believe me now?"

"I'm more inclined to," the canon said, "but I need proof. Do you think you can get it, Brother Arnulf? You have only a month before Eon is taken before the pope."

"That will be enough time, with your help," Arnulf answered. "If that soldier can identify the heretic who killed the woman, then we shall see that he has the opportunity to do so."

"Do you really think this murderer is the son of Peter Abelard?"

Brother Arnulf nodded. "The description fits. The other heretics say his name was Peter and that he wasn't from the villages from which Eon drew most of his followers. My informant said that he had been seen in the area of Broceliande last summer. Those heretics couldn't have survived without the help of someone of intelligence. Eon hasn't the sense of a suckling pig."

"So you think it was Abelard's son who murdered the woman?" the canon asked.

"Why not? Perhaps she knew who he was and threatened to betray him."

The canon smiled. "That's more than I could have hoped for. If I couldn't be revenged on that bastard Peter Abelard, I can at least have the joy of seeing his son hang."

"Astrolabe, I don't understand," Solomon said a few hours later. "You say this woman arrived in the midst of the eclipse last year and it wasn't until a week ago that you found out who she was?"

"It was like that there," Astrolabe explained. "Eon's followers believed that they had become new people. He changed their names. They left the past behind. No one asked anyone, including me, where they had come from or who they were."

"And this woman, you say she finally told you that she had been a nun at Saint-Georges-de-Rennes?" Solomon was puzzled. "Did she say where she had come from before that, who her family was?"

"Normandy, I think. She was an orphan and had been placed in the convent by her guardian, Thierry of Flanders," Astrolabe said. "I think she had a sister who is now the heiress of the family land."

"So who do you think killed her, and why?"

"I don't know, but I'm sure it was one of the men in the raiding party," Astrolabe said. "She recognized one of them. I suspect that he was one of the followers of the Count Henri who abducted and raped the nuns."

"But why did you run when you found her body? Surely once you explained who you were and told your story to the bishop, you would have been released," Solomon said. "Eon's family could confirm that you were with Eon on their behalf."

"Solomon, I thought you of all people would understand," Astrolabe said. "First of all, the real murderer was among my captors. Second, I am the son of a condemned heretic, caught with a group of heretics. What chance did I have to get the truth to anyone who would believe me?"

Solomon nodded. He had once been accused of murder simply because he was a Jew and nearby; Edgar had convinced the authorities to release him. Without his help, Solomon might now be no more than bones and ash.

Astrolabe swallowed and leaned closer to Solomon.

"I must find the one who killed her," he said, his voice shaking. "Cecile was so kind, so beautiful. She had been abducted from her convent and raped. I said I would keep her safe. But the monster found her. I was useless, Solomon. I tried to stop them with words. Why did I think that would work? When has it ever?"

Solomon gripped Astrolabe's arm in pity and surprise. Astrolabe had been in love with the woman, a professed nun! It was the last thing he would have expected. But Solomon knew well the futility of trying to govern the heart.

"Even with a sword, you could have done nothing against so many," he told Astrolabe.

Astrolabe shook his head. "I should have tried. Now all I can protect is her memory. I will find the one who killed her."

Looking around, Solomon noted that there was no food in the room and wondered if Astrolabe had enough money for soup. He should have got some when he had gone down for the beer.

Astrolabe continued. "The worst of it is that poor Cecile's death is so involved with Eon that the real killer may never be found," he said in disgust. "I don't know exactly what's behind his capture, but I believe that it has little to do with orthodox teaching and a lot more with power. Poor Eon isn't a heretic; he's a fool. No intelligent person could believe a word of his nonsense. Someone is using him, as that person wants to use me."

"Well, that may be, but I still don't know why you're sitting here freezing when you could be sleeping by a warm fire at Edgar and Catherine's," Solomon told him. "Do you think they would turn you out now? Astrolabe, now of all times, you need friends. Christian friends."

Astrolabe shivered. "I couldn't. Catherine and Edgar would do everything they could to help me, regardless of the cost. I didn't want to risk exposing them."

"What?" Solomon stared at Astrolabe. The cold in the pit of his stomach was not caused by the icy room, but sudden fear. "What do you mean?"

"Solomon, how long have we known each other?" Astrolabe asked. "It's true that I haven't the learning of my parents, but I'm not blind or stupid. I am aware that Catherine's father is also your uncle. Hubert was born a Jew, wasn't he? He either pretended to be a Christian or truly converted. Now they say he's gone away on a pilgrimage, but if he has, I don't think it's a Christian one."

Solomon stood upright with a jolt, hitting his head on the roof beam.

"*Dame!* Have we been that careless?" he asked.

"With me you have," Astrolabe admitted. "You and Catherine look too much alike, and she favors her father as much as I do mine. That alone is suspicious, but you've all slipped in your conversation when I've been there. I'm not the only one who has wondered. I know that you've all been in danger more than once because of rumors that Hubert was too involved with his Jewish partners, even that he was a convert who had returned to Judaism. I learned enough Hebrew from my mother to understand when you called Hubert 'uncle'. This is not the time to bring more trouble upon you."

"Catherine and Edgar are good Christians," Solomon insisted. "Hubert left Paris partly to protect their reputations. They aren't judaizers."

"That's obvious," Astrolabe said soothingly. "I've seen how hard they both try to convert you. And, no, I'm not horrified that you and Catherine are cousins. My father and mother both taught me that Jews must be led to the True Faith, not pushed."

"People of that mind seem to be fewer every year," Solomon grunted.

"Exactly. And that's why I can't draw Catherine and Edgar into this." Astrolabe seemed to feel he had made his point, but Solomon was still doubtful.

"I don't think they would see it that way," he said. "And it seems to me that you'll need to get word to your mother at the Paraclete, if only to tell her that you're safe. Since Edgar's sister is a student there, it would be natural for them to send a message."

Astrolabe was quiet a moment. Solomon presumed it was because he was about to agree.

"There's something more," Astrolabe finally said. "Calot, the man who found you for me, escaped shortly after I did, in the confusion after finding Cecile's body. He told me that there had been a man the evening before who had particularly

studied my face and searched my clothes while I was unconscious in the cart."

"Are you sure?" Solomon asked. "Do you think he knew
you? Then why didn't he identify you?"

"Calot is sure," Astrolabe said grimly. "And I don't know
why. Perhaps he was waiting until he could denounce me pub-
licly. My first thought when I escaped was to vanish, go south
perhaps, where no one could find me, but that would mean
that Cecile's murderer would go free. Also, if my name were
connected with this, even if I were safe, it would cause a scandal that could destroy my poor mother."

"It seems to me, you idiot, that so far you've worried about
everyone except yourself," Solomon said. "I still don't know
what you want me to do, when you reject any thought of letting
your family or other friends know what's happened to you."

He started to put on his cloak. "It's late and I don't want to
be challenged by the watch, if any are insane enough to be out
on a night like this. You can come with me or stay here. Don't
deceive yourself that no one knows about your being found
with heretics. If one person recognized you, then word has
probably already reached Paris, or the Paraclete."

Astrolabe's face was a mixture of fear and relief.

"You may be right," he said after considering this. He gave
a twisted smile. "In that case, I would be a fool not to take the
help of my friends."

"Sanity at last!" Solomon gave a sigh of relief. "Now put on
your boots and let's go home. What about your friend? Where
is he?"

"Calot? He only came with me as far as Paris," Astrolabe
answered. "He is continuing on. He has friends somewhere
east of here."

As they left, Solomon told himself that this was a simple
matter, though tragic. It would be easily resolved. Heloise had
the connections to be sure that Astrolabe was exonerated,
even if the real murderer were never found. Yet, as they
crossed the bridge and headed to the house on the Grève, he
had a feeling between his shoulder blades that there was

someone following them. Each time he turned, there was no one. But the streets were full of shadows, and in each one Solomon sensed an evil presence, preparing to attack.

The day was barely grey when Catherine woke. She lay for a while, listening for sounds of activity in the house. All was quiet and she settled back against Edgar, resting her cheek on his back, enjoying his warmth. But soon she realized that she couldn't stay in bed any longer. She slid from under the covers, trying to keep the cold from getting in to wake Edgar, felt for her slippers and made her way down to use the latrine next to the kitchen rather than add to the chamber pot.

She picked up a spare blanket from the chest on the landing and wrapped herself in it. The air was freezing. She thought of going up another flight to check on the children, who were probably both curled up in bed with Samonie, their only real servant. But her primary need won out. She fumbled across the hall and down to the kitchen.

It was only on her way back that she noticed that the trestle bed had been set up. There was someone in it, snoring lightly. It didn't sound like Solomon, who normally slept up in the storeroom with the silks and spices.

She tried to think. Could Samonie have let a friend in after the rest of them had gone to bed? Not likely. Catherine tiptoed over and lifted the covers.

Her shriek of surprise and delight wakened the rest of the household and caused Astrolabe to leap out of bed, knocking Catherine onto the straw on the floor.

"Saint Brigid's sacred girdle! Are you all right?" Astrolabe helped Catherine to her feet.

"Of course." She brushed straw from her shift. "I just can't believe you're here! How did you get here?"

"Catherine! What's wrong? Why did you scream?" The voices came from the stairs as Edgar and Solomon rushed down to her. Edgar's face lit with relief when he saw she was unhurt and even more when he recognized Astrolabe.

"You look like you've spent the winter in a cave," he exclaimed. "Have you decided to turn hermit?"

Solomon came up behind her and put a hand on her shoulder.

"I found him and brought him home," he said. "Can we keep him?"

"Of course," Edgar said. He looked out the window. "It's nearly dawn. We may as well see if there's something to eat, before we find out what brings Astrolabe to us in such a state."

"No need, Master Edgar." Samonie appeared at the kitchen door carrying a pitcher, followed by her son, Martin, with a tray. "The children are both still sleeping, but I heard the noise and knew I'd be needed. I've never known a disturbance in this house so dreadful that, sooner or later, someone didn't send for food."

"With the things that have disturbed us in the past, we always need fortification," Edgar said. "Thank you, Samonie. Now, first we eat. Then we'll decide what to do."

Astrolabe felt that for the first time in weeks, he was back in the sane world.

# Three

Paris. Wednesday, 13 kalends March (February 17), 1148. Feast of Saint Silvan, Merovingian bishop, whose biography was ignored due to bad writing but recovered through the excellent editing of Leutwithe, abbess of Auchy, who corrected the style, saving the sense and details. Such editors should always be canonized.

*Quoniam pro multis, qui increverunt, enormitatibus propellandis, et quae Deo placitura sunt confirmandis proxima Dominica qui cantatur: "Laetare, Jerrusalem" . . . in fiducia Spiritus sancti concilium celebrare decrevimus, fratres nostros archiepiscopos, episcopos et alios ecclesiarum praelatos de diversis mundi partibus duximus convocandos.*

Therefore, on account of the many evils that have been cropping up, and so that things can be established in a way pleasing to God, We have decided to hold a council on the next Sunday on which "Laetere Jerusalem" is sung, and we have, trusting in the Holy Spirit, summoned our brother archbishops, bishops and other prelates of the church from many parts of the world.

Pope Eugenius III
Letter 321, Oct. 11, 1147

$C$ atherine came down the stairs, balancing a basket of clothes on her growing stomach and trying to look around it so that she wouldn't trip.

"Mistress, will you please sit down and let me do the work?" Samonie begged her. "Your husband would kill me if he knew I let you do so much. Think of the baby."

Catherine put down the laundry at the bottom of the staircase.

"I do forget," she said. "Now that the sickness has passed, I seem to either be terribly sleepy or so full of energy that I can't stop moving. I don't remember that with the others. Remind me to look up this phenomenon in Soranus if I ever get to a good library again."

"Certainly, Mistress. I'll be sure to do that," Samonie said with a noticeable lack of respect. She had known Catherine too long. "But for now could you perhaps do something less strenuous, like mending Edana's shift? I swear she tears it every day."

"That she does," Catherine admitted, taking the small shift from the basket. "I don't know if it's because she wants to do everything James does or because she's rowdy unto herself."

"The latter, I'm sure." Samonie picked up the basket to be sure Catherine didn't try lifting it again.

Catherine watched her, noting how tired she looked.

"Samonie, we can't continue doing all the work ourselves," she said. "You're worn out with the cleaning and cooking and caring for the children. And now I'm of little help. There must be someone else we can hire who would be trustworthy."

"I don't see how. You know how people gossip," Samonie replied. "And don't think there are any secrets you could hide from a nursemaid."

Catherine shuddered at the thought of what her children blurted out even when cautioned to be on their best behavior.

"I've sometimes wondered how I could stop you if you decided to betray us." She spoke without considering Samonie's reaction.

It was immediate.

"How can you even think such a thing!" she exclaimed. "After all we've endured together. All this trouble with Master Astrolabe has unhinged you. I can't think of another reason for you to wound me so!"

"Samonie, I'm so sorry!" Catherine got up at once to embrace and reassure her. "I didn't mean it. I know you'd die for us; you've proved that."

They both turned quickly at the sound of the front door shutting.

Edgar and Solomon entered.

"We left Astrolabe with the monks at Sainte-Geneviève," Edgar said. "They won't betray him. Many of them were students of his father. Solomon will bring him back here once we've thought of a way to help him."

But he seemed preoccupied with something other than Astrolabe's problems. He looked around the room. "Where are the children?" he said with a touch of panic. "You didn't let them go out, did you?"

"They're with Martin, playing in the storeroom," Catherine said, puzzled. "It's too cold for them to be out."

"Thank God." Edgar pulled with his teeth at the fingers of his glove.

"Edgar, what is it?" Catherine was becoming concerned. "Solomon, what's happening? Are we being invaded?"

"In a way," Solomon said. "We were at the *parleoir des bourjoies* on our way back from the monastery. For once no one was talking about trade. Archer's oldest child just died from the spotted sickness; two more are sick. They aren't the only ones."

"No!" Catherine said. "It can't be! It's too early in the year. We never worry about the spotted sickness before spring."

She felt suddenly breathless. Gasping, she clung to Samonie.

"Saint Fustian's iron nose ring!" Edgar burst out as he rushed to her.

Everyone stared at him.

"Damn it, Solomon," Edgar continued. "Why did you have to tell her like that? Catherine, sit down. Samonie, fetch her some wine."

Solomon knelt by the chair. "I'm sorry, Catherine. I didn't think. I'm sure James and Edana are safe from contagion."

"No," Catherine was shaking. "They were at Archer's last week, playing with his children. They all seemed healthy then. It's horrible how quickly it strikes. Oh, dear! James won't understand when I tell him Ermon won't be able to see him anymore. Poor little boy. Poor Archer! Edgar, we have to protect our children. Where's my thread?"

She started to search through her sewing basket. Edgar gently stopped her.

"I don't think we have to do that yet," he said. "I'll go to Saint-Julian tonight and give a candle for their safety. Only very ill children are measured. We shouldn't do it unless it's necessary."

Catherine forced herself to appear calm, knowing that Edgar was more concerned about her than the children at the moment. He was right, of course. It was only when there was nothing else to be done that one measured a sick child with string and vowed to use it for a candlewick, for a candle the height of the child, to be given to the saint who would intercede for its life. They hadn't done it for baby Heloisa. Catherine had been ill, too, and the baby died before anyone knew how bad it was. Both Edgar and Catherine had felt guilt along with grief. They had promised themselves never to neglect the saints again.

"If the sickness is in the air of Paris, how can we keep James and Edana from breathing it in?" Catherine asked the world. "They already wear bags of herbs and charms at their necks, but so did Archer's children."

"Solomon had an idea," Edgar said. "It was Astrolabe who made him think of it, he says. It's only a short trip to the Paraclete. You'd be safer there. Heloise would take you in for an emergency like this, and you could come home when the danger is past."

"At this time of year?"

"Hear us out, Catherine," Solomon said. "We could send you by mule cart, and Astrolabe could go with you among the guards. No one would notice him then. He may feel that he should keep his troubles from his mother, but we know that she is the logical person to solve them."

"Even if the roads are clear, a cart would take at least five days," Catherine argued, but they could see she was prepared to be won over. She trusted Sister Melisande, the infirmarian of the convent, to care for the sick far better than any doctor in Paris. Of course, she hoped the nun's skills wouldn't be needed.

"Even a week on the road would be fine," Edgar said. "There are enough monastic houses along the way where you could find hospitality. I'd give you something to donate to each in return for shelter."

"It would be good to see Margaret," Catherine admitted, "and Mother Heloise as well. But you and Solomon will come too, won't you? You have to stop at Troyes before you leave for Spain, and the convent is on the way."

"We discussed that," Edgar said. "We have matters to finish here, but if we leave a few days after you do, we should overtake you before you arrive."

"It would be easy to fix a cart to be warm enough for all of you," Solomon added.

"It's not the cold," Catherine said. "It's the bumps in the road. Riding in a cart is almost as bad as being in a boat."

"I know." Solomon patted her back. "But you can at least get out and walk a bit. I didn't mean to frighten you, but we think it would be better if you all were out of the thick humors in the city. It will only be worse when the cold ends and the rains begin."

Catherine nodded. She didn't need to be told that. She had spent most of her life in Paris and loved it, but disease always came with the spring rains and then again at the height of summer. To have such an illness hit during the winter was terrifying. How much worse would it be later? A few days of discomfort was little enough to endure for the lives of her children. And it would be a good way to get Astrolabe out of the city unnoticed. Catherine didn't like what Solomon had told her about his sense of being watched. She trusted him not to imagine such a thing.

"Very well," she said. "How soon can we leave?"

They sent a messenger to the Paraclete that morning, warning Heloise of the impending visit. With panic nipping at their heels, they managed the arrangements and packing in only three days.

The morning before the departure, Samonie's son, Martin, came to Edgar who was working in the storage room.

"Wool, pelts, amber," Edgar checked the stock. "But the silk and spices are not sufficient. We must do more trade with the south. Well, we'll do the best we can for now. What is it, Martin?"

"I was wondering," Martin said nervously. "You've not told me what I'm to do yet."

"I thought you would go with your mother and Catherine," Edgar said in surprise. "They'll need your help."

"No they won't," Martin said. "They have the guards to carry things and the nuns and lay brothers to help once they reach the convent. I thought that you would want me to go with you."

"With us?" Edgar considered. "I must admit that it hadn't occurred to me. You would be useful and I promise to take you some other time, but not now. Actually, if Catherine agrees that you don't need to go to the Paraclete, I'd prefer that you stayed here. Keep the house open. If messengers come for us, send them on, that sort of thing."

Martin's face fell. "I'm being left behind?"

"You're almost sixteen now," Edgar said. "I think you're old enough for this responsibility. If you handle it well, then Solomon and I might well think of having you come with us on the next journey. But if the prospect of staying alone unsettles you. . . ."

"No, no, not at all," Martin assured him. "I'll be fine. And I'll take good care of your property. I promise."

"It won't be for long," Edgar said. "It should be safe in a few weeks for everyone to return, and then, of course, you'll be indispensable."

Martin submitted, but Edgar could see that he was still disappointed. Staying in Paris while everyone else went traveling must gall the boy, but that didn't matter. It would be useful to have someone to make sure no messages went astray. More important, Martin would be safer in Paris than on a trip to Spain. He had already had the spotted sickness and survived, so he was safe from the disease. But Samonie still grieved for the death of Martin's sister. Edgar didn't want to risk her losing another child. He knew the pain too well himself.

The cart was balanced on two wheels and drawn by a stout mule. It was covered by a canopy on a frame that protected Catherine and the children from the worst of the wind and snow. Edgar had seen to it that the interior was lined with furs, cushions, featherbeds and blankets. Catherine privately wondered what all these would look like after a few days of two active children and a dog, but her concern made her hold her tongue. Ripped bedclothes were a small price to pay for the well-being of James and Edana.

Another cart had been loaded with their baggage, including folding chairs and dishes. One couldn't expect Heloise to provide everything for them.

The guards were the best to be found. Edgar and Solomon had promised them their usual pay twice over to deliver the family safely to Heloise. Astrolabe rode among them, complaining that his chain mail chafed but otherwise indistinguishable from the other men.

Despite the urgency, Catherine was reluctant to set out.

"Samonie, did we leave milk souring in the pantry?" Catherine almost turned at the door. "Martin may not think to check it."

"No, Mistress. I scoured the kitchen well and checked the larder." Samonie nudged her toward the cart. "There's nothing that will draw vermin. In this cold, it's not likely that anything will spoil, in any case. And Martin will certainly take care of things. I trained him myself. Let's hurry. We want to be out of the gates when they open at dawn, don't we?"

"Yes, it's a long way and the days are still so short." Reluctantly, Catherine allowed Samonie to lead her to the cart where Edgar and Solomon waited.

Edgar held her a moment before helping her into the cart, where the children were already settled.

"Rest as often as you need to," he told her. "You mustn't let yourself get overtired in your eagerness to arrive."

"I promise," she said. "You and Solomon will be right behind us, won't you?"

"No more than three or four days," he said. "I'm sure we can overtake you. But don't dawdle in this weather just for us, either."

Catherine smiled. "You should decide, *carissime*, if you want our travel to be fast or slow."

"Safe and uneventful, that's all," he said. "May the Virgin and all the saints watch over you."

He kissed her for rather a long time, Solomon thought, in view of the cold and the many years they'd been married. At last Edgar released Catherine, who wiped her eyes and let the men lift her into the cart.

"Good journey!" Solomon called as they started off.

"See you soon, Papa!" Edana's voice came from the depths of the cushions.

James's voice rose above hers. "But, Mama, why can't I ride a horse, too?"

The dog began to bark.

Solomon turned to Edgar.

"I think that, for the sanity of your wife, we should try to follow as soon as possible."

Margaret was in the chapter house sitting near the fire while she worked on embroidering an *alpha* and *omega* on a wall hanging for the dormitory. Her stitches were not the quality of a well-brought-up young woman, and she had already pricked her finger with the needle. Her face was almost as red as her hair with the effort of doing the job properly.

She was concentrating so hard that she didn't hear Sister Emily enter. The gentle hand on her shoulder caused her to start and poke the needle into her finger again. She jerked her hand away from the embroidery frame to avoid getting blood on the cloth.

Emily laughed. "I used to find Catherine in here poring over a book instead of sewing," she said. "At least you make the attempt."

"I'm afraid I've forgotten all that my mother taught me," Margaret confessed. "Since she died, I've not done more than help with the mending. Perhaps there is some other task I could do to honor Our Lord."

"Any service done in His name is to His honor." Emily smiled again. "The work is judged according to the heart of the worker. But I bring you a respite. Mother Heloise wishes to see you."

Catherine would have asked why, but Edgar's sister only smoothed her skirts and followed Emily across the cloister, shivering in the thin winter sunshine.

They went to the guest house, not the abbess's room. Margaret noticed the tired horse being led to the stable and wondered who had arrived. Her first thought was that Solomon had come, but she knew his horse and she also knew that he had been discouraged from coming to see her while she was a student at the convent. Her second thought was that something terrible had happened to someone she loved.

Margaret had reason to expect bad news. She had received enough of it in her life.

So she was relieved to see the smile the abbess gave her when she entered. Sister Emily left quietly, leaving Margaret with Heloise and the messenger.

"Come in, my dear," Heloise said. "This man brings us word of an army on the way to invade us."

Margaret looked at the messenger in alarm. Then she recognized him as someone Edgar had hired before to carry missives and her heart leapt. She had to restrain herself from hugging him.

"Catherine is coming!" she shouted with joy.

"And the children," Heloise said. "And, I believe, a dog."

"Dragon," Margaret nodded. "James won't be parted from him."

"Your sister-in-law seems to see my convent as a refuge in all matters," Heloise commented. "I suppose it's a compliment to my influence that she turns to me in times of trouble."

"My brother, is he all right?" Margaret asked at once.

"So I understand." Heloise indicated that the man should repeat his message.

"My master sends his greetings to the Abbess Heloise and begs you to keep his family for a few weeks until the danger of spotted sickness has ebbed in Paris." He bowed to Margaret. "They left the morning of the feast of Saint Sebastian. They should arrive by Saturday."

"Oh, that's wonderful!" Margaret clapped her hands like a child. "Isn't it, Mother? We have space for them, don't we? The children can sleep in my bed, if necessary. I don't mind the floor."

"I don't believe it will come to that," Heloise said dryly. "The guest house is fairly empty this time of year, although I expect a visit from Countess Sybil in a week or two. But I think we can accommodate all of you, especially since Catherine is bringing her own beds."

She turned back to the messenger. "You said there was something else?"

He bowed again. "Yes, my lady abbess. Lord Edgar told me to tell you that Lady Catherine was bringing you a gift that he hoped would make up for any inconvenience you might suffer."

"What sort of gift?" she asked.

"I wasn't told, my lady," he answered.

Heloise shook her head. "I can't imagine what they think I might need," she muttered. "Thank you, sir. Please go to Sister Thecla, the portress. She'll see that you have food and a bed."

When he had left, she looked at Margaret. "Perhaps you'd like to turn the embroidery over to Ida and help Thecla prepare the room for your family?"

"Yes, Mother." Margaret could barely contain her excitement. "Thank you, Mother. I've missed them so much! Oh," she paused. "I didn't mean that I've been unhappy . . ."

"Of course not," Heloise sighed as she sat back down to work. "Even the hermit saints must sometimes have longed for those dear to them, despite the tranquility of their caves."

Margaret ran out. Heloise went back to her room and her letters. Sitting at the desk, she sharpened her stylus and pressed it into the wax, softening it first with the warmth of her hand. She swallowed hard as she forced herself to concentrate on the work. But at the back of her mind there was the constant yearning.

*My son, my dear Astrolabe, where are you?*

At that moment, Astrolabe was sitting quite comfortably in a tavern just outside the town of Provins, about halfway between Paris and the Paraclete. He and Edgar had agreed that the guards shouldn't think he was anything but another man hired to protect the family. Therefore his first few days had been spent in establishing himself with them. He blessed his uncle and cousins for having given him rudimentary training in arms and, more important, the proper vocabulary to hold his own in their banter, which was often only a thinly veiled challenge.

Solomon had also tried to prepare him.

"First of all, you can't call yourself Astrolabe," he had said. "Even if they've never heard of you, they'll laugh themselves off their horses when they hear it."

"You think I don't know that," Astrolabe had responded. "I've had that name all my life, remember?"

"And I'm surprised you haven't changed it before now," Solomon had replied.

"I have been known to call myself Peter," Astrolabe admitted. "I hope it doesn't dishonor my father. I was given the name Peter Astrolabe, but no one ever called me by it."

"I'm sure he'd be proud," Solomon said. "Especially if it keeps you alive. Very well, can you act menacing?"

Once Astrolabe had stopped laughing at that, he had assured Solomon that he thought he could grimace and scowl with the best of them.

Solomon had had his doubts, but so far on the trip the other guards seemed not to have guessed that Astrolabe was really a clerk in minor orders and an escaped prisoner wanted for heresy and murder. What surprised him was how comfortable it was to be Peter again. Perhaps Solomon was right. It was wonderful to be able to say his name and not wait for the stare, either of recognition or confusion. What had his parents been thinking of?

"More beer, Peter?"

Astrolabe looked up. He hadn't been paying attention to the conversation. Godfrey, one of Edgar's regular men, was picking up the pitcher. "If so, it's your turn to pay."

Astrolabe nodded and fished a silver bit from the bag at his belt. Godfrey caught it and stumbled to the bar.

Astrolabe leaned back against the wall. He scratched at a flea bite on his neck. He hadn't shaved in almost a month now. The beard was another curtain to hide behind. He liked it. In his thick woolen shirt and leather braies and tunic he felt that if anyone noticed him at all, it would be only to mark him as a man to be avoided.

It felt good.

The beer came and Astrolabe emptied his bowl. He belched with gusto and laughed at Godfrey's convoluted story about a woman he had known in the south.

"I tell you," he insisted, "she had vanquished whole armies without ever setting her feet on the floor. The first time I was with her I was sure I'd be sucked into that dark cavern and be lost."

He stopped to refill his bowl and noticed smugly that the room had gone quiet as all the drinkers waited to learn how he'd survived.

"I don't mind saying now that I was terrified," he grinned.

"This great wide road opening before me, ready to devour any who dared descend into it. Too late I remembered the pathetic pilgrim I had met on the road the day before. He was all that remained of the last force that had stormed her deceptive gate. The bells were even then tolling for the rest. I pleaded with the blessed Saint Maurice to help me."

"And what could he do?" A voice jeered from another table.

Godfrey turned to face the man. "Why, remind me that I was a soldier, as he had been," he said. "What does a good fighting man do when faced with a superior force?"

He paused only long enough to take another drink.

"Why, attack from the rear, of course!"

The room erupted with guffaws and foot stamping. Godfrey leaned over to Astrolabe.

"That should get us at least another pitcher free!"

Yes, Astrolabe decided, this wasn't a bad life at all. He had drifted too long, in minor orders as his parents had wished but unable to get a benefice that would support him. Why not do something else for a time?

The door to the guest house opened and Samonie entered. The man nearest grabbed her around the waist.

"My own prayer answered!" he cried. "Godfrey, is this your slayer of nations?"

He tried to kiss her, but Samonie had been in this position before, not always unwillingly. Smiling, she ducked her head and brought it up hard against his chin.

He loosed his hold for a moment, and before he could recover enough to strike her, Samonie had spotted the guards. They were all on their feet at once, and the man decided the *jael* wasn't worth his life. He left, grumbling and rubbing his chin.

"Why are you out so late?" Godfrey asked. "We thought you were all asleep at the monastery."

"Obviously." Samonie's scorn included Astrolabe. "I came to make sure that you weren't all drinking away the evening so that you'd be good for nothing tomorrow. My mistress is too much of an innocent to suspect that the men her husband paid to protect her were spending their time getting drunk and whoring all night."

Godfrey loomed over her, but Samonie didn't budge. Astrolabe felt both ashamed and embarrassed. Didn't Samonie know how it would look for them to be tongue-whipped by a serving woman in front of the whole room? He stepped between them.

"We were only drinking new beer," he told her. "You should trust Edgar's judgment. None of these men have failed him yet."

"Because they always had a man in charge of them." Samonie wasn't about to back down.

Astrolabe laid his hand gently on her crossed arms. "Catherine doesn't know you're here, does she?"

Samonie shook her head and lowered her voice so that only he could hear. "I wouldn't bother her now, with her worry for the little ones and that sick from the ride and the one inside her. And you, sitting here swilling with the rest of them! Shame on you!"

Astrolabe saw that the room was happily viewing this new entertainment. If something weren't done soon, one of the other men would make a comment and there would be flying chairs and broken heads as well as the watch called in. Why didn't Samonie understand what she was doing?

"You're right," he said, looking to the other men to support him. "As the newest man here I should have been left behind in case I was needed. Allow me to walk you back to the monastery and stand guard at your door tonight."

As he spoke he guided her toward the door. Samonie was surprised at the strength of his grip on her arm. As he led her out, he turned to the other men and winked.

The roar of laughter was clear through the closed door. Astrolabe hurried her down the path before she could decide to make another sortie against the guards. They were soon on the empty road between the town and the monastery. It was black as pitch. Astrolabe wondered how she had found her way without a light, and why.

"Now, why did you really come all this way alone?" he asked her. "And in your slippers."

Samonie pulled her hood more tightly over her face. She turned her head to look up at him.

"There's a man staying at the monastery, a monk."

The howl of the wind blew her next words away. Astrolabe leaned down to catch them.

"I didn't see him for he's not staying in the guesthouse but with the other monks. One of the lay servants told me that he was asking about anyone who might have known Peter Abelard." Samonie tried to see his reaction to this, but the night was too dark.

"I thought you should be warned," she added.

Astrolabe wasn't sure what to answer. It wasn't that unusual for men to seek out those who had known his father. After all, he had been a famous philosopher and teacher. There were many who still believed that his work had been condemned unfairly. Even Pope Eugenius wasn't ashamed to admit that he had studied under Peter Abelard.

On the other hand . . .

"Why do you think this has something to do with me?" he asked. "Most of those who study my father's work don't even know that I exist."

Samonie tried to answer, but the wind was too cutting. She started to walk more quickly on the uneven path to the monastery.

"There was more . . ." she began.

Suddenly she gave a cry as she slipped in her thin shoes and crashed onto the hard, rough ice.

"Samonie!" Astrolabe knelt to help her. "Are you hurt?"

There was no answer. Astrolabe felt her neck and face for some sign of life. She was breathing; he exhaled in relief. But his fingers touched something warm and sticky at her temple. Cautiously, he sniffed. Blood. He had to get her back to the monastery at once.

Samonie was heavier than he would have guessed. She was slight of build, but years of hard work had made her body solid. He wasn't sure he could manage to carry her all the way.

Each step seemed to take forever. Astrolabe eased forward. He wished he were wearing sabots instead of riding boots. No wonder Samonie had fallen. If he weren't careful, they would both go down. What could have been so important that she would come out in the middle of the night without bothering to dress for the weather?

There was a man coming toward him, carrying a lantern. Astrolabe called out.

"Here! Watchman! *Avoi!* I need some help!"

As the man came closer, Astrolabe realized that he wasn't a town watchman but a monk. Or a man in the garb of a monk, he thought. Brigands weren't above dressing as clerics. But it was too late now; the man was coming toward them.

"The lady fell," Astrolabe explained when the light of the lantern hit them. "Can you help me get her someplace out of the cold? She's staying at the monastery guesthouse, but I don't think I can carry her that far."

He couldn't see the man's face but was uncomfortably aware that his was illuminated clearly in the light. The cleric said nothing, but the lantern swung around leaving Astrolabe blind for a moment.

"Follow me," the man said. "I'm a stranger in this place, but there is a cluster of peasant homes not far from here. I passed them on my way. They can shelter her while you go for help."

He led Astrolabe in silence until they saw the group of huts, huddled close together next to the road. The cleric strode up to the nearest one and pounded on the door.

"Open up!" he ordered. "Travelers seeking aid!"

The words didn't matter, Astrolabe realized. The cleric spoke with the authority of one who expected immediate obedience.

They heard the latch being drawn and a frightened face looked out. Astrolabe moved into the light. His arms were aching.

"The lady is hurt and needs care," he explained. "I will pay you for your kindness."

"*Stultus!*" the cleric muttered, adding in Latin, "Now they know you have money."

Astrolabe stiffened but made no response that might indicate he understood. Why should the cleric have supposed that a common soldier would have Latin?

The door opened a little more, revealing a frightened face that was probably female.

"We have nothing to offer, my lord," she said. "We're near the end of our winter stores. But we can give you a place to lie and fresh water."

"That's all we need."

Astrolabe pushed his way in and searched for a place to set Samonie. The light had gone again. He looked back at the door and discovered that his guide hadn't followed them in.

"May Saint Lawrence roast him alive!" he cursed as he fumbled in the dark.

He felt a hand on his arm.

"There's a place in the straw," the woman said. "We have sheep to warm us."

Astrolabe already knew that by the smell. He was relieved that the winter famine hadn't forced these people to sell or slaughter their animals. The hut was warm.

"My friend is hurt," he explained again. "She hit her head on the ice. I need enough light to judge the wound and water to try to revive her."

"We have no oil for a lamp and the fire is banked for the night," the woman explained. "I crave your forgiveness, lord, but I will fetch a cup of water."

It would have to do. He laid Samonie in what appeared to be a clear patch of straw and heard someone scrabbling to get out of the way.

The woman must have had wondrous vision, for a moment later Astrolabe felt a cup being pressed against his arm. He took it gratefully. Then he wet the edge of his sleeve and washed Samonie's face, splashing the water on her cheeks. She stirred but didn't wake.

He leaned back on his heels.

"I must go on to the monastery for the cart," he said into the darkness. "I shall see that you are rewarded if you attend to her while I'm gone. I'll return before the bells ring for matins."

"They've already rung, my lord," a child's voice spoke.

"Prime, then," Astrolabe said. "It's only a short distance and I can do it easily with no burden. Make certain that she rests easily."

"We're good Christians here, my lord," the woman told him. "We shall do our best to see that she is comfortable."

Astrolabe thanked them and, after some fumbling, found the door. Once outside he marked the place by the empty dovecote leaning on its pole by the stone fence. The clouds had blown away and the stars gave enough light for him to find the path. Although he'd only been a few moments inside the hut, he saw no glimmer of the lantern carried by the cleric, although the road was straight back into the town.

Astrolabe felt a frisson at his neck that had nothing to do with the cold. He crossed himself hurriedly, murmuring a prayer to Saint Anthony to protect him from spirits and demons.

# *Four*

A monastery near Provins. Very early on quinquagesima Sunday, 9 kalends March (February 21), 1148. Feast of Saint Pepin, duke of Brabant, mayor of the palace under King Dagobert, whose main claim to sanctity seems to be that he defended the poor against the nobles and that his daughter became Saint Gertrude, abbess of Nivelles.

*Fugiunt arietes, immo et pastores Dominici gregis; remanent oves intrepides. Arguit Dominus tamquam infirmam carnem, quod in articulo etiam passionis suae nec una hora cum eo potuerunt vigilare. Insomnem ad sepulcrum illius noctem in lacrymis feminae ducentes, resurgentis gloriam primas videre.*

The rams, or rather the very shepherds of the Lord's flock, flee; the ewes remain undaunted. The Lord reproved the former as weak flesh because they could not watch one hour with him at the time of his passion. It was the women, spending a sleepless night at his sepulcher, who deserved to be the first to see the glory of the risen Christ.

Peter Abelard,
De auctoritate vel dignitate ordinis sanctimonialum

*C*atherine had already been wakened by the sound of the monks chanting matins and by the kicking of her son. James didn't appreciate being cooped up in the cart all day and took it out on her by night. She realized at once that Samonie was gone but assumed she was in the latrine.

After a few moments, Catherine realized that she had to go, too. All her pregnancies had given her a very weak bladder. Edgar had once threatened to design her side of the bed with the chamber pot already installed. Catherine had not thought it a matter for humor and he didn't tease her about it again, although it was now he who slept next to the wall so she could come and go in peace.

Catherine felt for the chamber pot, not wanting to leave the children alone. There didn't seem to be one. She resolved to speak to the monastery porter about it in the morning. But that didn't help her problem now.

It was while she was sitting in agony, wondering if Dragon, the dog, was enough to guard Edana and James while she was down the passageway, that she heard the ringing of the entry bell beneath her window.

Who could need admittance at this hour? she wondered.

She tried to see through a crack in the shutters, but they were barred fast.

And what was keeping Samonie so long?

With a growing sense of disquiet, Catherine found her shoes and belt and put them on. She was sleeping in shift and hose already. She quickly pulled the long *bliaut* over them and went to the door.

"Catherine!" Astrolabe stopped himself from knocking on

her face instead of the door to her room. "I came to tell you that Samonie is hurt. I left her with some peasants, the porter is sending two of the lay brothers and a donkey to fetch her here."

"What?" Catherine stared at him. "How did she get . . . What were you doing with her?"

"That isn't important now," Astrolabe told her. "She came to the tavern for me. Something about a visiting monk who has been asking questions. Do you know anything about it?"

Catherine shook her head. "And I didn't even notice she was gone until a moment ago. What is this all about? Is she badly hurt?"

"We won't know until she gets to the infirmary here," Astrolabe said. "Her breathing was regular when I left. She said there was a cleric here, asking about my father. Did you see him? Do you know why that should have worried her enough to come fetch me?"

"I can't imagine," Catherine said. "There are a number of monks of other orders staying here. But I haven't spoken with any of them. What could this be about? Samonie has kept things from me in the past, but I thought we understood each other now."

"Mama, I have to make pipi," Edana's plaintive voice came from the bed.

"Of course you do," Catherine sighed. "And so do I."

She went back and picked the child up. Edana slumped half asleep across her shoulder.

"Astrolabe," Catherine said, "I don't know what's going on here, but will you stay with James while I take care of this? Then I can try to concentrate while we wait for the monks to return with Samonie."

When she returned, she tucked Edana back in, lit the oil lamp and sat down opposite Astrolabe.

He told her the whole story, including the spectral cleric who had helped him.

"Do you think he could have been the same man who was asking for me?" he asked. "All I know is that his accent was Norman."

Catherine was torn between worry and anger. "I don't know, since you couldn't describe him. And I never heard him speak. Oh, Samonie! What could she have been thinking of?"

The monks arrived soon, with Samonie on the donkey, shaky but awake. Catherine sent Astrolabe down to see to her.

He found her sitting on a bench in the entryway. His questions faded as he saw the gash on her temple.

"God's eyes!" he exclaimed. "What could you have fallen on?"

Samonie touched the cut gingerly. "I don't know, but my head feels like I've drunk a vat of wine on an empty stomach."

She squinted at him, trying to bring him into focus.

"I came to with my face in a sheep's bottom," she said calmly. "What exactly was I doing with you?"

"You don't remember?" he asked.

She started to shake her head and winced. "No, I only remember that I went out looking for you. I must have found you. Did I say why?"

"You were just about to when you fell," Astrolabe explained.

"Did I?" she asked. "How stupid of me."

She started to rise but fell back again as one of the monks returned with a bowl of warm water and a bandage. Astrolabe waited quietly while he ministered to her. When he had finished, the monk helped her to stand.

"Can you get her up the stairs to the guest room?" he asked Astrolabe. "We have no place in the infirmary for a woman. I believe that all she needs is rest and time to heal."

"I can travel tomorrow, can't I?" Samonie asked worriedly.

"In your cart, perhaps," he said. "But the blow might well cause you nausea for a few days and headaches for some time after. You are all welcome to stay until you're more fit."

"No!" Samonie answered. "We must continue."

She looked up at Astrolabe. "I only wish I could recall why it's so important, but I know that I should send you all on without me. You need to keep going! Someone . . . something about a heretic. I'm sorry, I can't remember any more."

She shook her head emphatically, then winced at the pain.

"Samonie, let me help you to the room," Astrolabe said

soothingly. "Catherine is waiting for us. We can get you to bed and discuss it in the morning, which is almost here."

He yawned. Samonie was instantly apologetic.

"Of course," she said. "I'll go at once. And I've kept Mistress Catherine up as well. If only I knew why."

Her distress was so obvious that Astrolabe ignored his irritation with her and took her up to the room.

Catherine was waiting.

"Samonie!" she cried. "I've been so worried. Here, come lie down. The children have kept the bed warm. Astrolabe, thank you."

She noted how drawn he seemed.

"Would you tell the other guards that we'll rest here one more day?" she told him. "We could all use some time out of that cart, and that will give Solomon and Edgar a better chance to catch us up."

Astrolabe saw no reason to protest. He looked at Samonie, who still seemed perturbed by the idea, but made no comment. She was already sagging onto the bed. He bade them all good night and went to look for a corner where he could snatch a few hours of rest.

Catherine bit her lip in worry when she saw the shape her servant was in.

"I'll put you on the outside of the bed," she told Samonie. "And I'll take the middle. Then I can check you from time to time."

Samonie nodded, too exhausted to do anything but obey.

They arranged themselves, pushing the sleeping children closer to the wall. It would be colder for them but safer. Catherine feared that, in her present state, Samonie might overlay one of them and smother the child without waking.

Catherine closed her eyes.

Questions piled up in her mind. Why had Samonie gone out? Why had she needed to find Astrolabe? Was someone following them? Were they in danger? Most of all, she wondered, what was keeping Edgar and Solomon?

Her mind speculated on these for some time, the answers

becoming more and more implausible until, at last, she fell asleep.

The monk Arnulf stomped his boots on the stone outside the tavern. It had taken him the rest of the way from the cottage to regain his equilibrium. What was that guard doing with the woman from Paris? He had guessed her to be loose legged when he had first spotted her at the monastery, but he was amazed that she would have gone out for a topple so late and in such weather. He sincerely hoped she wasn't badly hurt and wondered what she and the guard had been doing when she had hit her head. Something sinfully acrobatic, no doubt, he thought wistfully.

He entered the tavern, reeling at the sudden gust of heat, sweat and beer. In one corner was his friend from Paris, Canon Rolland. When he saw the cleric, the canon got up and climbed the ladder to the sleep loft above. The cleric followed.

"Did you spot him?" he asked Rolland. "He wasn't at the abbey."

"There was no one with the guards," the canon answered. "Perhaps he didn't come with them after all."

"I tell you my information is that a man left from the Blue Boar with the Jew and entered the house of Edgar, the English merchant," insisted Arnulf. "I was sure they had smuggled him into the cart with the family. I wish you had been the one to ask at the monastery."

"You should be able to spot him," Rolland said, "if he's really old Peter Abelard reborn. You knew his face well enough."

"That I did," the cleric answered. "And hated it. But I saw no ghost of Abelard wandering the streets tonight. Only that servant woman out whoring with some soldier."

"We've missed something," Rolland insisted. "He's either with them or with the merchants. We must find him before he gets to the Paraclete. Once under his mother's protection, we won't have a chance to have him condemned."

"Not even for murder?" Arnulf asked.

"Idiot! Once it's known who he is, the worst that would happen is that he'd be given a heavy penance, a pilgrimage barefoot or something." Rolland lowered his voice. "But if we can prove he's a heretic, then he'll never have peace again, even if he doesn't burn. The scandal will ruin him. Oh, it will be such a joy to shame that Astrolabe even more than his cursed father did me."

He drank his beer, grimacing as if it were vinegar. Arnulf moved away from him a bit. There was something about the bitterness of the man's anger that unsettled him. It was important to Arnulf that Astrolabe take the blame for Cecile's death. But there was no need to be so passionate about it. Murder and heresy were not to be made instruments of revenge.

Nor, he reflected, could they be allowed to go unpunished because the criminal's mother was friends with half the nobility of Champagne and his father had taught half the bishops. It would have been better if the man had been no one of any importance. Still, Arnulf reflected, the choice had not been his.

Far to the north of the Paraclete, another friend of Heloise was awake in the dark winter morning. Faintly she could hear her new baby crying, but that didn't concern her. The wet nurse would be feeding him in a moment. Sybil, countess of Flanders, had more serious matters to worry about. Her husband, Thierry, had also gone to the Holy Land, leaving Sybil to run the country, care for their four small children and deliver the fifth safely.

No sooner had he left than their old enemy, Baldwin of Hainaut, had attacked the country. Sybil had immediately been faced with the task of raising and directing an army. She had managed to arrange a truce for the last month of her pregnancy, but no sooner had Peter been born, even before she had been churched, than Baldwin had made more incursions. Sybil wasn't surprised. A man who would break an oath made to the pope wouldn't be intimidated by one sworn to her.

Normally, the absence of the count would not have been a disaster. Sybil had allies of her own. But most of the lords had

left with the king. Her brother, Geoffrey of Anjou, was fully
occupied with seeing that his son, Henry, inherited the duchy
of Normandy and the throne of England. That left few whom
she could turn to in her need.

And now word had come that the count of Tréguier had
dared to remove Cecile of Beaumont from her convent. Sybil
had not yet told Cecile's sister, Annora, who was living in the
castle under Sybil's protection. She had sent one of her men
to Brittany to find the count and see that the girl was returned
at once to her proper cloister. It angered her that this was necessary at a time when she needed every one of her knights.

Sybil was proud of her army and the loyalty of her men.
They had fought off Baldwin's attacks and even taken the battle into his own territory. Nevertheless, Baldwin had sworn to
keep the peace while Count Thierry was on pilgrimage, and
he had broken this vow. It was up to Pope Eugenius to see that
he was punished. To acquire papal help, she needed the support of people of undoubted piety and wisdom.

She had decided to present her case before the pope, his
cardinals and the bishops of Europe when they convened at
Reims next month. The ignominy alone might be enough to
convince Baldwin to withdraw his forces, although she would
prefer more concrete aid. But first she would go to the Paraclete. Heloise would know whom to approach and how. She
could also lend her voice to the demand that Henri of
Tréguier be punished for violating the sanctity of the convent
of Saint-Georges-de-Rennes.

If Pope Eugenius couldn't convince Baldwin to stay in his
own land, then she had only one other recourse. Sybil would
take the drastic step of unleashing the full force of the censure
of all the women religious she knew. She had friends or family in all the great convents of Christendom. All those women
had fathers, brothers, sons and nephews who listened to them.
And they would all counsel these men to protest Baldwin's
aggression and Henri's blasphemy.

Having made her decision, Sybil returned to her bed. In his
keep, miles away, Baldwin whimpered in his sleep.

\* \* \*

Solomon regretted suggesting that they make haste on their journey. The roads were deadly for two men going this quickly on horseback. He expected any moment to be thrown as his poor mount went down on the icy trail.

"Edgar, there's no point in pushing us like this," Solomon complained. "We left Paris too late to catch up with the cart. They'll all be nice and warm at the Paraclete by now."

"All the more reason to get there soon," Edgar answered, panting. "Catherine will worry until she sees us."

They were riding as quickly as the road allowed, too quickly for Solomon.

"Look, *vieux compang,* it's cold enough to freeze the balls off a pagan statue," he said. "Even Jupiter would cover himself against this wind. And what will Catherine say if you show up with all your parts iced over and ready to break?"

"She'd be furious and tell me that there were some things she couldn't live without," Edgar laughed. "Very well, we'll stop at the next town."

"Sooner, Edgar," Solomon begged from beneath the wreath of scarves he wore. "I can't feel my nose at all and am all too aware of the rasping of the saddle on my ass. And the light will be gone soon."

They had come to a rise in the woods. Edgar stopped and scanned the horizon before they descended again. He rose in the saddle, exposing his nether region to a chilling blast.

"I can see smoke rising over there," he pointed to the north. "It may be a village or a company of *ribauz.* Do you want to risk it?"

"Right now I'd rather have my throat slit than continue freezing. At least I'd die in warm blood," Solomon answered. "Besides, a lot of the *ribauz* are no more than charcoal burners or peasants driven from their land. I don't mind paying well to share their fire."

"Be on your guard all the same," Edgar said. "We're no match for a troop of desperate men, even if we're better armed."

"At least we haven't much to steal," Solomon said philosophically as they made their way in the direction of the smoke. "It was a good idea of yours to put all the money under the straw in the cart."

It was farther than it had looked from the road to the source of the fire. Edgar had begun to fear that they had passed it among the trees when they came upon a trail that seemed more worn than the deer runs they had been following so far. About a hundred yards later, they entered a clearing.

"Amazing!" Solomon exclaimed. "We seem to have chanced upon a rich hermit!"

Edgar was also surprised to find, instead of some rude lean-tos, two well-built houses on either side of a small stone oratory. There was also what looked like a grain shed behind one of the houses.

Solomon made for the nearest house, but Edgar held him back.

"There's something odd here," he said. "Listen. No chickens clucking, no dog. Not a sign on the ground of sheep or goats. No pigsty. What sort of hermit doesn't even keep a goat?"

"Why don't we ask him when we get inside," Solomon suggested. "Perhaps he gave everything away to the poor. Do you think he'll let us stable the horses in his church?"

"He'll have to," Edgar said. "There's no place else."

Solomon accepted that. Every now and then Edgar got a tone in his voice that reminded one that he had been born a nobleman, not a merchant. If the owner of the oratory refused their request, Edgar would simply order him to obey. Usually, people did. The worst thing was that he seemed totally unaware of it. As a Jew, Solomon had been forced too often to seek protection from lords who had no intention of ever letting him forget that his safety depended on their power. The mere sight of them made his bile rise. Edgar was his best friend. Solomon didn't want to be reminded that he came from this same stock.

Of course, he sighed, he was more than willing to use Edgar's assumption of authority when he needed it.

"Shall we get down and knock on the door," he asked, "or wait until spring thaws us?"

Edgar dismounted and approached the nearest house. Before he raised his hand, the upper half of the door opened to reveal three frightened faces, two women and a man.

"We mean you no harm," Edgar said quickly. "My companion and I seek shelter for ourselves and our horses for the night. We have food we can share with you and coin to pay for your trouble."

The three looked at each other and shut the door. Edgar heard a low, intense conversation.

"I don't think we need to worry about this lot," Edgar called back to Solomon. "They seem to be trying to decide if we plan to slit their throats, not the other way around."

"Well, tell them to be quick about it," Solomon answered.

The door opened again, this time all the way. The man stood there alone.

"You are welcome to our poor shelter," he said. "We have no space for horses, but"—he swallowed—"you may use the chapel. There is some straw and water, but we have no hay to give them."

"Thank you," Edgar said. "My friend and I will attend to them and then join you, unless you'd rather we stayed with our animals?"

The man's face showed that he would much prefer that.

"No, of course not," he answered, aware of the rules of hospitality. "Please return to share what little we have, my lord."

The door shut on them again. Through the wood, Solomon and Edgar could tell that the argument had started again.

"Two women and one man." Solomon tried not to smirk. "Being a hermit is suddenly much more appealing."

"They may be brother and sisters," Edgar suggested, annoyed at the slur.

"Even more interesting," Solomon said as they entered the oratory.

The small building had two slits for windows on either side. In the far wall was a larger window, crudely covered with boards. It was nearly dark and the men could see little as they unsaddled the horses and rubbed them down. Solomon went out in search of a bucket and a source of water.

The hermit was waiting for him.

"I'm sorry we don't have more to offer," he said, handing him the water bucket. "We have few visitors and almost none on horseback."

Solomon thanked him and brought the water in.

"These people are hiding something," he told Edgar.

Edgar had made one pile of straw for the horses to nibble on and was spreading more against the far wall. "Such as . . . ?" he asked.

"How can I tell?" Solomon snapped. "They won't let me see it. But I want to know what they have in that other hut. I'm sure I heard movement in there before the man stopped me."

Edgar was tired and worried about his family. There was something strange about the hermits, but they didn't seem threatening. He laid his bedroll on half the straw pile.

"Unless it's a feather bed, I don't care," he said.

Solomon wasn't satisfied. He wasn't convinced of the harmlessness of these people. The hermitage could be a blind, drawing travelers in so that they could be robbed or murdered in the night.

He doubted he'd sleep. But first, he had a more pressing need.

"What do we have to eat?" he asked Edgar. "From the look of this place, gruel is all they can offer."

"I've cheese and dried meat in my pack," Edgar said. "They probably won't touch the meat, but the cheese should be welcome. We can spare it."

But when they returned to the house, they found their gift rebuffed.

"We are fasting this month," the older woman told them. "We have only grain and water. You are welcome to that."

"You don't mind if we eat our own food, do you?' Edgar asked.

In the flicker of the small lamp, Edgar could see the yearning of the younger woman for the cheese and meat, but she set her lips and shook her head when he offered it to her again.

They tried to make conversation, but the three hermits gave only short answers. Once they had eaten, the three bowed their heads and recited a *Nostre Pere*, then they bid them good night. Edgar nudged Solomon when he saw that each went alone to a narrow pallet against the wall.

"Makes our packs and blankets look luxurious, doesn't it?" he said as they returned to the oratory to sleep.

"I'll never understand you people," Solomon said as they unrolled their blankets. "Why should the Holy One give us bodies if he meant us to abuse them? But as long as it's dry and out of the cold, and we are undisturbed I've no complaints."

They were awakened the next morning by the chanting once again of repeated Our Fathers. Solomon felt that their hosts had deliberately increased their fervor to a level that would make sleep impossible.

When Edgar and Solomon came out, the three were waiting by the door.

"We know you want to be on your way," the man said. "Please take what you need." He hesitated. "There's a broom by the door. If you could remove the evidence of your animals?"

"Certainly." Only the manners required of a guest kept Edgar from losing his temper. He told himself that these were holy people who had removed themselves from the world and that he was an intruder. He told himself this several times.

The men were soon on their way. Edgar looked behind and saw that the door to the hut was once again shut. He could almost believe that the people had never existed. There were stories about odd beings in the forests. He enjoyed them on a warm summer night in the comfort of Paris. He didn't care to see them come to life.

"Strangest hermits I ever came across, even if they didn't try to kill us," Solomon echoed his thoughts. "Do you think they're holding the young one against her will? She'd have eaten the cheese if the others hadn't been there. Pretty, too. Or she would be if she were better fed."

"She didn't seem any worse off than the other two," Edgar said. "They probably thought we were devils come to tempt them. Still, I've never seen a less welcoming group. No wonder they have so little, if they greet everyone like that."

They rode for a while in silence.

"I would still like to know what was in the other hut," Solomon said after several minutes of brooding.

Edgar shook his head. "Why? What has it to do with us?"

"Nothing, I hope." Solomon urged his horse forward. "But there was something alive in there. I don't like the feeling that, whatever it was, it now knows my scent."

The hermits had waited behind their barred door for some time after Solomon and Edgar left.

"Do you think they suspected anything?" the elder woman asked.

"Of course not," the younger answered. "We didn't preach to them. We're cowards, you know."

"There's a time for bravery," the man told her. "I'm not eager to burn, are you?"

"Our poor friend must be," the elder woman said. "We should have brought him in with us last night, no matter the danger."

The man shook his head. "We're just lucky that he saw them coming in time to hide."

"He had had no business becoming involved with those Eonites," the older woman said as they left the hut.

"It was a family matter," the man said. "I think he is leaning toward joining us at last after his experience there."

He tapped on the door of the other hut. "Are you all right? It's safe to come out now."

There was a rustling as a bedraggled, shivering man came out from under the pile of straw that had kept him from freezing. He limped to the door, his feet cramped with the cold.

The older woman gave him little sympathy.

"Maybe now you'll learn that we are your only family," she said. "Here, I brought barley in hot cider. Eat."

At her castle in Flanders, Countess Sybil was preparing for her journey somewhat differently than Catherine had. She wasn't concerned with places that would take her in. As the wife of a pilgrim and as the daughter of King Fulk of Jerusalem, she knew that no monastery would dare turn her away.

But that didn't mean she had no worries.

"Annora," she called to her friend, "has word come yet from the lord of Guînes?"

"Nothing," the lady Annora answered. Her grey eyes reflected Sybil's disquiet. "I've heard that he has been having trouble with the lord of Ardres. Do you think it might keep him from sending the help he owes you?"

"Those two have been fighting over the same worthless piece of land since they were children," Sybil spoke sharply. Part of her anger was at the lords, part at herself for not having the courage to tell Annora that her sister was still missing. "They can go back to it once this danger is over. Annora, I must have more men to fight Baldwin, or there will be nothing left of Flanders by the time Thierry returns."

"You've done all that could be expected of you," Annora said. "It's hard to raise an army when all the important vassals of the count have gone with him to the Holy Land."

"And when those who remain prove themselves to be oathbreakers," Sybil said grimly. "I've fortified the towns as best I can. Now the pope has insisted that the bishops and abbots come to Reims to debate church policy. Has it never occurred to him that I need those men to preserve order?"

Annora knew she wasn't expected to answer that. She was younger than Sybil and still somewhat in awe of her. She had been sent to Flanders to stay with the countess when her sister Cecile entered the convent. When her father had died, he had left it to Sybil to find her a husband who would be an advantageous alliance with both Flanders and their small lordship in Normandy. Annora had made no objection. She was grateful that someone was watching out for her interests. Her only request had been to be allowed to examine the candidates for her hand before negotiations began.

She pushed a blond braid out of the way of the embroidery she was working on and made gentle noises of agreement as Sybil continued her plaint.

"One would think that all the prelates of Christendom would be prepared to excommunicate Baldwin." The countess was preparing a list of items to take. She wrote with such force that she scraped the board beneath the wax and had to stop every few minutes to resharpen the point of her wood stylus.

"But no." Her knife whittled the wood furiously. "Instead they worry about the color of a cleric's coat or whether consecrated nuns are wandering about the countryside unescorted." She stopped, aware that she had almost said too much. Better to wait until Cecile was found. She continued. "I tell you, Annora, the next time anyone preaches to raise an army to fight the Saracens, I'll leave Thierry at home and lead it myself."

"Like Queen Eleanor?" Annora asked with a smile.

Sybil's sniff expressed completely her opinion of the piety of the French queen.

"Went to buy silk, she did," Sybil continued. "What sort of woman takes her jewelry casket with her on a pilgrimage? She'll return more laden than she left, I've no doubt."

"I know it's sinful of me, but I wish I had someone to bring me trinkets from the East," Annora said. "Apart from Cecile, all I have is a cousin who is a monk and another whom we haven't spoken to in years. Our family has sadly diminished."

Sybil looked at her kindly. "Well, I shall do my best to assure that you are not the last. Even with these other worries, I do not forget that you need a good husband."

They were interrupted by the arrival of Sybil's chamberlain, Eustace of Gramene.

"My lady," he bowed. "We've made arrangements for your stay in Reims. I've told them to expect you just before *Laetare* Sunday, when the council is set to begin."

"Excellent," Sybil told him. "That will give us time to consult with Abbess Heloise and, perhaps, Countess Mahaut as well. Annora, how many servants will accompany you?"

Annora looked up, startled. How many should she take? What would be expected of her?

"My maid, of course," she said slowly. "And my groom. Father Gundrum is my usual confessor here, but I would imagine that we'll have no shortages of priests."

"That I am sure of," Sybil answered. "That number seems quite reasonable. Very well, Lord Eustace, can we be ready to leave in time to arrive at the Paraclete by the kalends of March?"

"There will be no difficulty at all," Eustace answered. "The weather has kept Baldwin from anything more than occasional sorties. Lord Anselm and Count Ingram can contain him until your return."

"I suppose I should be grateful that the baby came in the winter, or I might not have managed to arrange the truce," Sybil commented. "Odd that a man who would violate a sworn oath would also agree to keep his troops at home so that I could give birth."

"His unpredictability is all the more reason why we need whatever sanctions we can get to demonstrate to him the consequences of his actions," the chamberlain said. "My only concern is that you are too soon out of childbed to undertake this journey."

Sybil lifted her chin. "It is my duty to protect Flanders," she said. "I have placed myself in the hands of Our Lord and His Mother. They will take care of me as long as I trust in their mercy."

Eustace smiled. "Of course, Lady Sybil. But I shall accompany you in case they need an earthly instrument for their work."

As the countess turned away, Eustace gave Annora a wink.

# *Five*

Near Nogent-sur-Seine, a few miles north of the Paraclete. Tuesday, 8 kalends March (February 23), 1148. Feast of Saint Serenus, martyred because he wouldn't let a Roman matron stroll in his garden.

*Le ior de la cendre, fait l'en l'entreual apres chapista: et apres midi la procession; et chante'n R. Afflicti et V.: et l'oroison de la messe: et trouveroiz ce ou darrenier dou messsel en i fueillet darrien, et ausins a toutes les autres processions fors dou dymanche et de morz.*

On the day of the ashes, have an interval after chapter and, after sext, have the procession and sing the response "Afflicti" and verse [Domine Deus Israel] and the prayers of the Mass. And you will find this at the back of the missal on the last page and also those for all the other processions for Sunday and for the dead.

The Old French Ordinary for the Paraclete

*C*atherine walked alongside the cart. Her stomach couldn't take the jolting any longer. Edana hopped happily beside her, and James was riding in front of the guard, Godfrey, asking him question after question about his military exploits. Godfrey was making up fabulous tales about the dragons he had slaughtered and the Saracen giant he had toppled in single combat. When James seemed doubtful, the other guards insisted to him that they had been there and that all the stories were true.

"Godfrey is the greatest warrior since Roland," one of them said without a smile. "Except for me, of course."

James tried to stand up in the saddle so that he could study this new hero.

Catherine wondered if the nuns would be able to endure the energy of her vivacious son.

The road was wider now, and they were going through more villages. Astrolabe and Godfrey assured her that they would be at Nogent before nightfall. Tomorrow they would cross the Seine and from there follow the River Ardusson all the way to the Paraclete.

Samonie poked her head through the curtains on the cart.

"I'm coming out to join you, Mistress," she said. "I'm feeling much better, but the stench in there is making my head ache again."

Catherine laughed. "I wondered how long you would last with only the dog to keep you company."

"That dog has slept more of the journey than I have," Samonie complained, climbing over the rail and dropping to the ground. "And he snores."

"Dragon does not snore," James shouted. "He roars!"

James commenced to demonstrate, raising himself up again in the saddle and pawing the air.

"Be careful, James!" Catherine cried.

"I have him, lady," Godfrey laughed. "You seem to be more a lion than a dragon, young man!"

His laugh faded as he turned and saw what was behind them. James looked over his shoulder.

"Is it Papa?" he asked.

"No," Godfrey answered. "My lady, get back in the cart. All of you. I don't like the look of them."

Catherine, too, had hoped that the rapidly approaching horsemen were Edgar and Solomon, but she knew the way they sat their horses, and these men, even at a distance, were nothing like. The question was, were they rushing somewhere important or were they coming to catch up with and attack them?

Astrolabe got down to help first Catherine, then Samonie, into the cart. He handed them the children.

"I'm sure there's no danger," he told them, "but we must be cautious."

"Of course," Catherine answered. "So must you. Tell Godfrey to have the other guards pull their hoods down to shadow their faces. You mustn't chance being recognized, especially dressed like that."

The driver stopped the cart as the riders drew near. Astrolabe and the other two guards positioned themselves around it, prepared to draw their swords. Godfrey held up his hand in greeting.

The two men slowed and then stopped.

*"Dex te saut!"* Godfrey called. "And good journey on this grey day."

"God save you, as well," the larger man answered. "A strange time of year to travel with your family."

He nodded to where Edana's face peered over the edge of the cart. It vanished at once.

"My master's family is fleeing illness in Paris," Godfrey answered.

"They may be going into greater danger," the man told him.

"We are chasing heresy in Champagne. One heretic, especially, who escaped from my lord the archbishop of Tours."

"You've followed him a long way if you've come from Brittany. But why here? Would he not have headed to Gascony or Italy, to the refuge of his fellows?" Godfrey asked.

The man shook his head. His hood fell back, revealing a strong, lined face with protruding blue eyes. His short, tonsured hair was dark blond. Godfrey knew him from the tavern in Provins. "Not this one," he said. "He seeks refuge closer to hand. Don't fool yourself, good man. There are heretics even in Champagne. Those who follow the false preacher Henry, and those who deny the efficacy of the sacraments and the humanity of Our Lord."

"Is the man you seek one of these Henricians?" Godfrey asked.

"No," the smaller man spoke. He was also tonsured with a fringe of dark hair that was already thinning, despite his youth. His long nose twitched as he spoke. "He follows a mad cutthroat named Eon. Just as bad. Another Breton. The place breeds troublemakers. This bunch has been roaming the forests despoiling churches and robbing priests and hermits."

He spat in the road.

"They sound as lawless as they are misguided. We wish you speed and luck in your search," Godfrey said.

He signaled the driver to start off again. Astrolabe kept his head down. He didn't recognize the big blond man, although he seemed familiar, but the other man's voice was that of the one who had led him to the peasant's hut the night before. How had they managed to follow him so far without knowing how he was traveling? He wondered if they were playing with him. All he could do was keep his face shadowed and pray that they would be on their way.

But the men didn't move.

"You must see that we are men of the church and unarmed," the first cleric said. "So we can only ask your permission to look inside the cart."

He moved toward it.

Godfrey and his men moved to block him, but their intervention wasn't needed.

"That will be quite enough!" Catherine rose from the cart like Venus from the sea. Her veil was askew and her *bliaut* stained by paw prints, but her wrath was divine.

"How dare you keep my children sitting here on the road like common peasants?" She leaned over the edge of the cart, gripping the rail. The round of her stomach was clearly visible. "How do we know you're clerics? Searching for heretics! A fine excuse to rob us!"

The clerics backed away.

Godfrey stared at her. "My lady . . ." he began.

"You are not to be blamed, Godfrey," Catherine said. "It is these *stulti* who should apologize at once. Heretics! Why should heretics travel on the open road? We are respectable people from Paris, not Breton *indocti*. Perhaps you should return to Tours and continue your work there."

Astrolabe coughed. Catherine stopped.

"My lady," Godfrey spoke again. "I don't know what you're telling them and I don't think they do, either."

"Oh dear!" Catherine said, realizing. "I was very angry. I didn't think."

"I understood you quite well, my lady," the blond cleric said. "And, as a canon of Notre-Dame, I ask myself how a respectable woman from Paris learned such fluent Latin."

Catherine flushed, still angry. "Paris is a center of learning, as you may have noticed." Her tone implied that the cleric hadn't benefited from it. "Many women attend the lectures of the Masters. The queen herself speaks Latin with ease. I've heard her. I have often listened to the scholars debate. Therefore, I assure you that I know what orthodox teaching is. Now, you will go on your way and allow us to continue on ours. My children are cold and tired and we wish to make Nogent by nightfall."

The blond man opened his mouth to argue again, then shrugged, bowed and slapped his reins to make his horse move on. The second cleric followed him, looking back over his shoulder in puzzlement.

"They were at the tavern last night," Godfrey said. "I knew them at once. Do you think they didn't remember us?"

"They certainly will remember us now," Astrolabe said from behind Catherine.

"No," she answered. "They'll remember me. You were just a blurred face in chain mail."

"They couldn't have thought that we would turn Astrolabe over to them, if he had been in the cart," Godfrey said after thinking. "They could see we were armed. If we had really been heretics, we could have killed them and left their bodies by the road. I believe that they meant to warn us not to harbor him. Perhaps we should not stop at Nogent tonight."

"But where?" Catherine asked. "Samonie is still weak and the children . . ."

". . . will be fine," Samonie finished. "So will I. If we ride with the guards, the mule will have less to pull. We may be able to go around Nogent and arrive at the Paraclete before compline."

"You mustn't risk yourselves for me," Astrolabe insisted.

Catherine bit her lip. They would have to make the river before sundown. If they did, then the rest of the trip would be short. If not, they might be forced to spend the night in the forest. Should she risk all their lives, including the one within her? But what was the risk that they would reach Nogent to find soldiers ready to take Astrolabe into custody? How could she face Mother Heloise if she let that happen?

"We shall go on," she decided.

They turned south on a trail that would take them to a ferry across the Seine.

And so, when Edgar and Solomon arrived at Nogent that afternoon, they found no one who could tell them what had happened to their family.

"We can't have missed them on the road from Provins," Edgar said for the tenth time. "Godfrey wouldn't have let anything happen to them. He's completely dependable."

"You've convinced me of it," Solomon said, although he

was equally worried. "There must be someplace that we haven't asked yet."

"But where?" Edgar looked around as if a new monastery might pop up in the landscape.

Solomon didn't want to suggest it but he did anyway. "If one of the children fell ill, they might have been stopped outside of the town. They wouldn't be allowed to bring sickness in."

He knew that Edgar had been thinking this as well.

"Yes, if we can find no one in town who has seen them then we'll have to retrace our route."

Edgar fell silent and didn't respond to any more comments from Solomon. He was impatient to be on their way. Where could Catherine have gone?

They came to an inn on the far side of town. Solomon dismounted and questioned the innkeeper, who was trying to chip the ice off the path to his door. Edgar stayed on his horse.

"We haven't time for beer," he reminded Solomon.

Solomon grunted a noncommital reply. He approached the innkeeper, who looked up hopefully. He was disappointed to find that all the stranger wanted was information.

"No, I haven't seen them," he answered, puffing as he worked. "What's so special about these people, anyway, that so many are looking for them?"

"Edgar," Solomon said, "I think that, after all, we need to stop long enough to talk with this man. And in that case, a warm spiced beer wouldn't come amiss."

Heloise had just come from Vespers. The sisters were all in the refectory, eating their evening bread. Only one meal a day was served in the winter, but they were allowed a bit more in the evening to see them through the Night Office. Heloise usually ate hers alone in her room. As she crossed the cloister, she noticed some commotion at the gates. She hurried over, ready to call on the lay brothers if there should be any trouble.

Sister Thecla met her halfway.

"It's only Catherine," she assured Heloise. "The poor thing

was so eager to be home with us that she pushed them all to travel after dark. Most foolish, even with the guards."

"Are they all right?" Heloise asked as she continued to the guesthouse.

"The serving woman has a cut on her head from some accident," Thecla answered. "I've sent for Melisande to tend to her. She should look at Catherine as well. I'd say she's about four or five months with child."

"Again?" Heloise shook her head. "That one was certainly not meant for a life of celibacy. I'm sure it's just as well she never made her profession with us. And her children?"

Thecla smiled. "You won't believe how they've grown. Both look healthy and very lively."

"We should send someone to tell Margaret they've arrived," Heloise said.

"I'll go myself, in a moment," Thecla assured her. "Don't you want me to send Catherine to you later to greet you?"

"No, I'll meet them at the guesthouse. Catherine must be exhausted from the journey."

"That she is." Thecla grinned to herself. "Where shall I put the guards?"

"Where you always do," Heloise answered. "Is there a problem with them?"

"No, not at all," Thecla answered, her face alive with suppressed delight. "I just wanted to be sure."

Heloise followed her, wondering what could have made the usually reserved woman so elated.

They entered the guesthouse. Catherine stood to greet the abbess. Heloise started to go to her, arms outstretched, when she noticed the guard standing to one side.

She stopped, all the blood draining from her face.

"My Lord!" she cried. Then she looked again.

"Oh, Astrolabe, my dear son!" she exclaimed, throwing herself into his arms. "Whatever are you doing with a beard? You look so different! Oh, I've been so worried about you. My very dear Astrolabe!"

She released him at last and held him at arm's length, gazing at him hungrily.

"Oh, my precious," she breathed. "What has happened to you and when did your beard start to go grey?"

By the next day the ice had melted at last, leaving grey drizzly weather that chilled the bones worse than the cold. The Paraclete, built near the river, was enveloped in morning fog through which the bells rang the hours of the Office, guiding travelers to the convent by their sound.

James and Edana regarded the place as a second home, where the nuns spoiled them dreadfully. No one complained when they came in covered with the thick green mud of the area. They were slipped honey cakes in the kitchen by the cooks and sugared walnuts in the scriptorium by Sister Emily, who received a box from her mother every winter.

But Catherine drew the line at their attempts to join the nuns and students as they processed around the cloister and into the oratory for Ash Wednesday services. She stood them next to her in the little church and made sure they followed the Mass as far as they could, repeating the responses even though they didn't understand them. They lined up with the townspeople to receive the ash cross on their foreheads, a reminder of the reason for the forty days of fasting to come.

Afterward Catherine discovered that the two children had decided that the one cross wasn't enough. They had gotten a piece of charcoal from the brazier in their room and happily drawn x's all over their bodies.

"They look like plague victims," Catherine grumbled as she poured water over James, who was standing naked in a tub protesting the removal of his artwork. "Stay still, James! You've been very naughty."

Next to her, Emily was washing Edana and trying not to giggle.

"You'll have to explain to them about ostentatious piety," she said. "No, Edana, the cross the priest put on stays until tomorrow."

"So I can show it to Papa?" Edana asked.

"Yes," Catherine said. "As soon as he arrives."

If he arrives, Catherine thought. She should have sent one

of the guards on to Nogent to wait for Solomon and Edgar. What if they were wasting time going back over the route, looking for them? She scrubbed James's legs harder and then his cheeks. He lifted his chin and set his lips, not willing to admit that she was hurting him. *Oh dear,* Catherine nearly laughed. *Who is he being now, a martyr being gnawed by lions or a hero facing an army?* She wiped the soot off more gently.

Margaret had dutifully walked in the procession and attended Mass, but when the other nuns and boarders went back to the dormitory to pray or study, she had gone to the guesthouse. Astrolabe found her sitting at the window, watching the empty road.

"They'll be here soon," he assured her.

Margaret looked up at him with a rueful smile.

"I know," she said. "And staring at the road won't make them arrive any more quickly. I'm glad you're here, of course," she added. "I was so surprised to see you dressed like a guard. I hardly knew you."

They stood together in silence for a while. Margaret seemed so frail and lonely that Astrolabe was tempted to put his arms around her and tell her to cry until she didn't hurt anymore. But he didn't want to insult her with pity so he simply stayed near.

"Astrolabe," Margaret said after a while, "Catherine said that it wasn't right for her to tell me your secrets, but will you tell them to me? Someone said you were rescued from a band of Breton heretics. That can't be true, can it?"

"Oh, dear." Astrolabe shook his head. "I appreciate Catherine's unusual discretion, but I'd rather you understood the truth than add to your worries with rumors about me. Come over here and sit down. I'll tell you all about it. You can still see the road from the bench.

"It all started when I went to visit my aunt Denise in le Pallet." He began the story as he had to Solomon, Edgar, Catherine and his mother. But somehow telling Margaret was easier, and he found himself making it more a story and less a defense.

"One day," he continued, "an old friend came to see me. He comes from Dol and has a small holding there. He told me that he needed help. A cousin of his had invented some sort of strange belief and then hidden himself in the forest of Broceliande. He had begun preaching and had gathered a group of followers who were causing trouble."

"Why didn't the bishop of Dol stop him?" Margaret asked.

"I asked that," Astrolabe told her. "He said that the bishop had his hands full with more serious heresies, bandits and lords who were flaunting his authority. No one cared about Eon."

"That's a funny name," Margaret said.

"It's an old Breton one, but that was what caused all the trouble." Astrolabe smiled. "His family knew he wasn't very bright and sent him to a monastery where they thought he would be safe, not likely to come under the influence of anyone unscrupulous. Well, one day he was listening to the monks praying and heard the words " '*per eum qui venturus est judicare vivos et mortuos, et seculum per ignem . . .*' "

"Through him, who shall come to judge the living and the dead and the world through fire," Margaret translated.

"Right, but poor Eon was entranced by the word *eum*. He thought they were saying his name so he asked what the passage meant and someone told him. He must have brooded on this for a long time because eventually he decided that he was the one the prayers were talking about and that he must be the son of God."

Margaret gasped. "But surely the monks would have explained it to him!"

"I don't know if they even knew." Astrolabe shrugged. "By the time I became involved, he had wandered off in the forest. When I found him, he told me that his abbot had given him permission to become a hermit, but I can't believe that."

"And you say people believed his fantastic claim?" Margaret was finding this hard to credit.

"Oh, yes." Astrolabe looked out the window again. "Out there people are starving, you know. Some have lost their land and been forced to sell their freedom in return for food. Others have gone into the forest to avoid tithes they can't pay.

They're angry and despairing. Eon has a certain charisma, I'd say. He truly believes himself to be divine, you see. He treats these dispossessed with tenderness and respect. He makes them feel human again. He reminds them that they have souls.

"They say he raided villages and attacked hermits," Astrolabe continued. "That's nonsense! If you had seen that poor bedraggled troop of his . . . Margaret, a few peasants with hoes and pitchforks could have driven them off."

"Then why did the archbishop of Tours send men to capture them?" Margaret wanted to know.

Astrolabe shook his head. "If I understood that, I wouldn't be so worried."

Margaret put her hand on his. "We'll find out. Mother Heloise won't let anything happen to you. Neither will my brother. We know you've done nothing wrong."

"That gives me great comfort." Astrolabe looked down into her trusting face. He wondered how a girl who had seen her mother killed and who had later been horribly beaten by a mob could still have such an air of innocence and faith. In many ways she shamed him.

He thought of Cecile. Despite the evil done to her, she had not given in to despair either. For a moment, her face floated before him. He had to blink to keep back tears.

At that moment, Margaret glanced out the window, gave a cry, leaped up and ran from the room.

"Margaret!" Astrolabe called. "Your cloak!"

He grabbed it and followed her.

The horsemen spotted her running toward them. One of them dismounted and strode toward her, holding out his arms to her.

"Oh, Solomon!" she cried, clinging to him. "We've been so worried!"

"There, there." Solomon released her at once and set her down. "We were only delayed because of a problem with the arrangements for our journey south. You shouldn't have let yourself get so agitated."

"I don't notice any concern about me," Edgar said, coming

up to hug her. "But I'm only your brother. I notice that my wife isn't waiting at the gate for me either."

"The last I saw, she was trying to get your children into a washtub," Astrolabe said. "Welcome. I have much to tell you."

Edgar nodded. "We have had some interesting experiences as well. I notice you haven't been shaved yet."

"I thought I'd ask your opinion first," Astrolabe said. "It may be better that I remain a guard for a time."

Edgar raised his eyebrows at that but, at that moment, Margaret remembered familial duty and with an effort switched her attention to her brother.

"Are you really going to Spain?" she asked after she had kissed him. "If so, I have a shopping list for you."

"I thought you might," Edgar grinned. "I'm glad to see you, too. Now, will you find someone to see to our horses so that I can go see what havoc my children have wrought on this peaceful convent?"

Canon Rolland and Brother Arnulf also participated in an Ash Wednesday procession. The faithful wound through the streets of Nogent. There were more penitents this year than usual, thinner, more ragged, apprehensive.

Rolland watched them with a speculative expression.

"These people are fearful now," he told his friend. "They look at the world around them and see the hand of God raised in punishment. Today they believe their misery is their own fault. But tomorrow they'll start wondering what they could have done to deserve to watch their children starve. Then they'll realize that it's their leaders who are to blame. God isn't interested in the rabble, but in punishing the kings and bishops who are leading them into Hell."

"And when they realize this, then what?" Arnulf asked.

"Then . . . well, that is the question, isn't it?" Rolland said.

"Do you have an answer?"

"Not yet," Rolland told him. "It depends a great deal on what is decided at the council in Reims next month. I seriously doubt that the bishops and abbots will be able to stop their endless squabbling over authority and tithes long enough to face the real threat."

"Heresy," the monk said decidedly.

"Exactly," Rolland said. "It surrounds us. It has become a viper in the bosom of the very highest circles of the church. If we can't bring the faithful back to the faith, if we can't present a unified leadership, then we shall splinter into a thousand sects that Satan will easily conquer."

"That sounds like the end of the world." The monk shivered.

"It does indeed," Rolland agreed. "And I, for one, am not prepared to face it." Come, we have work to do. Back to Paris. Master Peter and Master Adam are preparing to catch a much larger fish than this Breton. You and I have been bringing in the wandering preachers and madmen of the forest. But they have discovered a heretic in bishop's garb. Even so, our information may help the pope to realize the deadly gravity of the situation."

"If he only saw these poor people, that would be enough," Arnulf said sadly. "Their plight only convinces me that my desire to denounce all heretics is necessary, especially when the poison has filtered from one of the worst of them down to the next generation."

"Abelard's son?" Rolland said. "Are you quite certain about him? Perhaps we have let our judgment be clouded by old injuries."

Arnulf stared at him. "How can you even think that? You can't be weakening now. It's Satan working in you. You must find him! Astrolabe is a heretic even the masters of Paris will not touch. It's our responsibility to see that he is brought to trial along with all the others. The Christian world must know that we will protect it from evil, no matter where it is found."

"Of course," Rolland said. "I only wanted to be sure that my revenge would fall on one who deserved it. But it makes sense that the wickedness of Peter Abelard should reside in his son as well. The world thinks all us Bretons are fools or schismatics. I would have helped refute that, but Abelard made sure no one took me seriously. I was the first to know the evil hidden in his heart."

Arnulf moved a step away as if to prevent Rolland from coming close enough to sense the wickedness that hid in his own heart. This one needed careful handling. The monk wondered if he had chosen his associate wisely. Restraint was needed if he was to accomplish his design.

"Papa! Papa!" James and Edana leapt from the tubs and ran across the cold floor to greet him.

"Come back here at once!" Catherine ordered as she and Emily grabbed for them.

"I'll go see if their clothes are dry," Emily suggested and slipped into the next room.

"Oh, Edgar!" Catherine said as she handed him a blanket to wrap around James while she captured Edana. "I'm so glad you're finally here. I'm sorry that we took another route. I know it must have caused you trouble, but there was a problem. It seemed better at the time. Are you very upset?"

"Of course not. You made the best choice." Edgar was surprised that she seemed to think he would be angry. "Who knows what would have happened if you'd gone to Nogent? *Carissima*, do you think I would have let you go with our children and much of our treasure if I didn't believe you would know enough to deviate from the plan when necessary?"

Despite the fact that each of them was holding a slippery, clean and wriggly child, this conversation seemed to Catherine to be one of the most important they had ever had.

"I thought your only concern was to get the children out of the bad humors," she said. "And you couldn't leave immediately."

"Yes, but if I didn't trust you to make decisions and have the strength to carry them out, then I would have taken you all myself and trade be damned."

"Oh." Catherine smiled at him, eyes shining. "You never said that before."

"I didn't think I needed to," Edgar answered.

Then another thought struck her.

"Does this mean you're going to be gone on trading missions as much as my father was?" she asked. "Because if so, then I'd rather you thought I was irresponsible."

"James," Edgar said firmly, "I'm putting you down now. Take your sister and help her into her shift and you get dressed, too. If you behave I'll take you on an elephant hunt before bed."

Catherine waited while James took his sister's hand and headed for the next room, where Sister Emily waited with their clothes.

"Now," Edgar said, "I intend to explain to you why I don't intend to stay away from home a moment longer than is necessary to keep us fed."

"I hate to mention this," Catherine said when she could catch her breath, "but I know Mother Heloise wants to see you. Also, I need to sit down. Your next child is kicking me dreadfully."

That night they ate a stew made from dried fish soaked in water with herbs. It was poured into a trencher of bread. Solomon, Edgar, Catherine and Astrolabe shared it, scooping out the stew with their spoons and then tearing the bread into equal shares.

"At least during Lent I don't need to worry so much about being offered pork," Solomon commented as he finished his piece and washed it down with cold water. "But I'll be glad to head south where the wine flows in all seasons."

"Have you decided to come with us, Astrolabe?" Edgar asked.

Astrolabe leaned back against the wall behind his bench. It seemed to Catherine that he had aged in the past week or so. It wasn't only the beard, which did show grey, but an air about him of sadness. It gave him a *gravitas* that he hadn't had before. It made him seem more like his father in attitude, if not in appearance.

"It might be best if you left the country until after the council," Catherine suggested.

"Yes," Astrolabe answered, "it might. I know Mother would prefer that I not subject myself to a public accusation. I thought so too at first. But I've spent the past few days in serious prayer. Now I believe that it is important for me to face these men."

"But not in chains, like your poor Breton madman," Catherine insisted.

"No," Astrolabe said. "Also, I want to be able to know the names of my enemies before we meet again. I owe it to Cecile to find the man who killed her."

"That's all very noble of you," Solomon commented. "Just how do you intend to do that?"

"I'm not sure yet," Astrolabe admitted. "But I think it will mean that I won't be shaving for a while."

"I have an idea," Catherine said. "The countess of Flanders will arrive soon. She's coming here before she goes to Reims. Perhaps Astrolabe can arrange to travel with her. You seemed to enjoy being a guard."

She grinned at him.

"It did make the conversations in taverns more interesting," he laughed. "And as we discovered, no one really looks at a guard. They only see the weapons."

"Do you think your mother will approve of this plan?" Edgar asked.

Astrolabe sighed and stood. "I won't know until I tell her of it. I should go now, before Compline rings, and find out if she can see me tonight."

When he had left, Catherine found she was too tired to wait for him to return. James and Edana had been put in a trundle bed in their room. Samonie was sleeping in the infirmary where Sister Melisande could tend to the headache she still had from her fall. While she was feeling much too gravid to be appealing, Catherine did long to spend as much time alone with Edgar as possible before he set out for Spain. If it were in bed, that would be even better. She got up.

"Solomon, would you excuse us for the night?" she asked. "You must be weary as well from your journey."

"Of course," Solomon told them. "Edgar, go warm your wife. I'll sit and watch the fire awhile."

He wasn't sorry to see them go. Solomon needed some time

to himself. No one had mentioned that Margaret hadn't joined them for the evening meal. He hadn't asked. He didn't like the aversion in Edgar's eyes when he showed concern for the girl. He picked up a poker and jabbed at the fire. That was all it was, of course. Margaret's mother, Adalisa, had begged him with her last breath to watch over her child. It was his duty to see that she was happy. Poor Adalisa hadn't been. He was determined to make sure that Margaret wasn't married off to some brutish lordling who would be cruel to her, as Margaret's father had been to her mother.

That was all. She was a child for whom he felt an avuncular responsibility. Nothing more. How could there be anything more?

Solomon smashed the glowing coals to ash. Then cursing the lack of beer, he went to bed.

Astrolabe followed Sister Thecla to the outer door of his mother's room. She scratched at the door, and when Heloise answered, opened it and then retired discreetly to her own chamber.

Heloise held out her arms. "My dear boy! I've had so little time to see you! Forgive me. This whole episode has worried me more than I care to admit."

"I know, Mother." Astrolabe kissed her. "I never meant you to become part of it."

"If someone is trying to harm you, then I'm part of it," Heloise said. "For you are part of me."

"I'm so sorry," Astrolabe began.

Heloise put her hand on his mouth. "No, you mustn't be. You were trying to help a friend. You've done nothing to be ashamed of."

She motioned to him to sit on the stool by her chair, where she could have her arm around his shoulder and look into his face. She smiled and then sighed.

"When your father was tried, both times, I was already in the convent," she said. "I could do nothing to defend him. I couldn't even be there to offer my comfort. He came to see me after they had forced him to burn his work at Soissons. I never saw him so discouraged. Not even the attack on his body was as devastating as having his writing condemned."

"I remember how he was after the second trial," Astrolabe said. "I think the despair hastened his death. I find it hard to forgive Abbot Bernard for hounding him so."

Heloise laid her head on his. "There are days when my charity is also strained. But the abbot is a good man, if not always well counseled. Remember that, my dearest."

Astrolabe turned his face to hers. "You know what I've decided, don't you?"

"Yes," she said. "I wish in my heart that you would run from this trouble, go somewhere safe. But we can't let the death of this poor woman go unavenged. From what you've said, her murderer is also guilty of sacrilege and the brutal rape of consecrated virgins. Men like that can't be allowed to roam free. What would we do if he and his friends came here?"

"I hadn't thought of that!" Now that he did, the idea froze his blood. "The Paraclete has always been a refuge. I meant to bring Cecile to you for safety. Then, for her sake, you'll risk the scandal of my being accused?"

Heloise smiled at him, shaking her head. "I'm not afraid of scandal," she said. "Our cause is just. I'm also proud of my son who is willing to face those who would slander him—just as his father did."

"Thank you, Mother." Astrolabe kissed her. "It may be difficult to explain why I was with the Eonites when poor Cecile was killed, but I'm sure I can prove that I'm no heretic. My theology is contained in the Creed. I leave the subtleties to men like Father and Bishop Gilbert. But even if I can clear myself of everything, I feel I owe poor Eon a defense as well."

"If he truly is mad, then he can't be held responsible for his ravings," Heloise assured him. "But those who follow him may not be so innocent."

"From what I saw, they are only poor, ignorant people," Astrolabe said. "Their parish priest has failed to teach them, if they even have a priest."

"Then it is the bishop of the area who is to blame, for not

providing them with one," Heloise said. "I shall write to the abbess of Saint-Sulpice in Brittany for more information. She is Count Thibault's niece. There should be time for a response before the council begins. This time I will not wait patiently while the fate of those I love is decided."

# Six

The Paraclete. Friday 3 nones March (March 5), 1148. Feast of Saint Gerasimus, a fifth-century Christian who became a hermit to escape the lure of heresy. Eventually he attracted seventy followers to live on dates, bread and water while they listened to his orthodox preaching.

*Helwidi abbatissae uenerabili Paracleti, Hugo Metellus, humilis homuncio: in cythara et psalterio psallere Domino. Fama sonans per inane uolans apud nos sonuit, quae digna sonitu de uobis, nobis intonuit. Foemineum enim sexum uos excessisse nobis notificauit. Quomodo? Dictando, uersificando, noua iunctura, nota uerba nouando. Et quod excellentius omnibus est his, muliebrem mollitiem exuperasti, et in uirile robur indurasti.*

To Heloise, venerable abbess of the Paraclete, Hugh Metel, a humble dwarf: sing praise to the Lord on harp and cymbal. Your reputation, flying through the void, has resounded to us, what is worthy of resounding from you, has made an impression on us. It has informed us that you have surpassed the female sex. How? By composing, by versifying, by renewing familiar words in a new combination, and what is more excellent than everything, you have overcome womanly weakness and have hardened in manly strength.

Hugh Metel, letter to Heloise

*W*e'll be back before the feast of Saint John," Edgar told Catherine. "I promise."

Catherine snuggled closer to him.

"You'll find us at home, waiting impatiently. The danger from the sickness should have long passed by then, and we can't impose upon the nuns for long," Catherine said. "I've resolved to be brave about this. So don't do anything to make me cry."

Edgar kissed the tip of her nose, the only part showing outside the blankets.

"I think you just want to go on the journey instead," he teased her. "You'd rather I was the one to stay home with the children."

Catherine moved closer to him. "You may be right," she admitted. "I do enjoy traveling, as long as no seas are involved. Perhaps someday we can go on another pilgrimage. Rome would be nice. James and Edana seem to adore adventure."

Edgar didn't like the way the conversation was going.

"Well, until we find out if this one does"—he put his hand on her stomach—"perhaps you could contain your desire for new sights."

He lifted his hand suddenly and then put it back with a wondering grin.

"The little *orcus* just kicked me!" he said.

Catherine laughed. "Good! I suspect he'll be kicking me for the next four months and I also expect you to be home for his arrival. He obviously needs his father's strong hand."

Edgar smiled. His left arm was under Catherine and, just for the moment, he forgot that there was no hand at the end of it. His thoughts were only on the movements of the child to come.

When she bade him Godspeed, Catherine found it difficult to remember her vow to be brave. After all, she reminded herself, it wasn't as if he were going to fight. All she needed to fear were bandits, accidents and illness.

Margaret kissed her brother good-bye.

"Don't forget the silk," she told him. "Green, but not too dark."

"I'll do my best," he promised. "Solomon will remind me, I'm sure."

"Of course I will." Solomon smiled at her.

Margaret tried to smile back, but her mouth trembled. She started to embrace him, but he stepped back. She looked up at him in hurt and surprise. Solomon's eyes flickered to where Edgar was watching them. He held out his hand to her.

"Safe journey, Solomon," she said, taking his hand in hers. "Take care of my brother. Come home soon."

"We certainly will, loaded with all the rare treasures your heart could ask for," he said lightly.

Margaret bent her head. "One will be enough," she whispered.

Solomon released her hand. She hadn't felt how tightly he had been holding it until she saw the red marks of his fingers on her skin.

The men then made their farewells to Abbess Heloise and to Astrolabe. They checked the packs and gathered the guards. Three of them would accompany Solomon and Edgar, but Godfrey had elected to stay in case Catherine needed him.

The others went back to their work, but Catherine stood at the gate with her arm around Margaret waving until Edgar and Solomon were no more than dots on the road.

Catherine then swallowed hard and shook herself.

"I suppose I should go rescue Samonie from the mending," she said. "Edana tore her shift again this morning. I believe she rips it as soon as she wakens, just to get it over with."

"I promised Sister Jehanne that I would rule some pages for her," Margaret sighed.

They looked at each other.

"Duty," said Catherine.

"Duty," Margaret agreed.

"Of course, we might also take advantage of the fact that the rain has finally stopped and see if we can find any green shoots in the garden to put in the soup tonight," Catherine suggested.

Margaret gave her a grateful look.

They found few greens so early in the year, but by the time they returned to the convent with their baskets, they had managed to control the tears that would start, despite their determination.

Sister Thecla met them on their return.

"Catherine, dear," she said, "the abbess would like to see you. Margaret, I thought you were in the scriptorium."

"Yes, Sister. I'll go at once," Margaret sighed.

Catherine entered the abbess's chamber prepared to apologize for the disruption her family was causing the convent, but Heloise brushed that away. She had other matters to discuss.

"You attended Bishop Gilbert's lectures in Paris, didn't you?" she asked.

"When I could," Catherine answered, surprised.

"Have you read his commentary on Boethius?" Heloise asked.

"No, although I've heard some of the arguments from it."

"Did you understand them?"

Catherine felt herself blushing. "I'm not sure. To me there appeared to be some inconsistencies in his logic, but it's been so long since I was a scholar."

"Then it's time you became one again."

Heloise handed her a book, roughly bound in board. "We've recently acquired a copy. There's time for you to read it before we make our own copy and send it on."

Catherine held her hands out greedily.

"You don't think the debate over this book has anything to do with Astrolabe, do you?" she asked. "Surely Bishop

Gilbert's subtle theology has nothing in common with the beliefs of the Eonites."

"It does seem unlikely," Heloise said. "But I want us to be prepared for anything. People somehow expect Astrolabe to be able to defend his father's theses. Gilbert made it clear that he felt Abelard was the one modern philosopher who must be refuted. Now Bishop Gilbert is being put on trial for his beliefs."

"I remember that the bishop was called before a meeting in Paris last year," Catherine said. "Several of the masters had questions about his understanding of the Trinity as expressed in the commentary."

She rubbed her hand across the cover of the book, as if absorbing the words through the wood.

"Gilbert is to be questioned again after the council at Reims," Heloise said. "There are those who wish to condemn him as Abelard was. Now, I don't know who these men are who wish to harm Astrolabe, but you have told me that they have been asking for him as Abelard's son. My husband made many enemies in his life. Some would be happy to see Astrolabe condemned out of sheer jealous spite. He told me that someone may have recognized him after he was captured with the Eonites. Think how it would please my husband's detractors if his son were to be accused of this heresy."

Catherine reflected that this was the first time she had heard Heloise refer to Abelard as her husband. She wondered if this was how she always thought of him in her own mind.

She opened the book. There were no elaborate capitals and the lines were uneven. One reader had put notes and citations in the margins. This was something intended to be read and studied, not displayed.

"Are you sure you trust me not to be led into error?" she asked Heloise, only half joking.

The abbess's lips twitched. "Not if you are still as stubborn as I recall. Some of this book, I understand, is a reworking of the debates Gilbert had with Abelard. That might interest you as well. See if they reflect Abelard's work fairly and then form such responses as you are able."

Catherine hugged the book to her chest. "I shall do my best

to refute his refutations." She grinned. "Thank you, Mother. I know you are doing this to help me keep my mind from worrying about Edgar and I'm so grateful. I can't think of anything that would distract me better."

"Just be prepared to give me a cogent précis of the work," Heloise told her. "My time won't allow me to study as I used to, and I don't want to be ignorant of the issues involved here. Remember, my son's life may depend on it."

"Oh, yes, of course." Catherine sobered at once. She hoped she could remember how to form a proper argument.

She turned to go, then turned back. "It's odd, you know. Master Abelard warned Bishop Gilbert that if he didn't defend his fellow theologians, he might find himself accused of heresy, too. It's too bad that the master didn't live to see his prophecy came true."

Heloise nodded sadly, then smiled. "I have no doubt that he knows."

Catherine carried the book carefully to the scriptorium, where Margaret was sitting at a table carefully drawing the fine lines on a page.

"I used to find that so boring," Catherine commented.

"I like it," Margaret said. "I can think about anything while doing this."

Catherine decided not to ask what was occupying her thoughts now. She sat down to read the book and soon became totally caught up in the fine points of Bishop Gilbert of Poiters's opinions on the nature of man and God. She didn't notice Margaret leaving for Nones or Sister Jehanne coming in to light a candle just before Vespers. It was only when the light was so dim that she found her nose pressed almost to the page that Catherine came to herself.

She hurried back to the guest house to find that the family had passed the day quite comfortably without her.

"I'm so sorry," she began.

Then she noticed that there were a number of new boxes and bundles in the room.

Samonie explained. "I've moved all our things in here. You

and I will have to share the children's room again, I'm afraid. The rest of the building is completely full. I've also shaken out your best *bliaut* and found your gold and emerald earrings."

"Whatever for?" Catherine asked. "The nuns don't care for that sort of ostentation."

"No, but I won't have you taken for a servant, as you once were in your old clothes," Samonie said firmly. "Tonight you must look like a proper lady. You are dining with the countess of Flanders."

Catherine had certainly met nobility before. It was hard not to in Paris, of course, and the count and countess of Champagne, Thibault and Mahaut, were almost acquaintances since the count was Margaret's grandfather, albeit on the wrong side of the blanket. But it was different to be dining with only Countess Sybil, her chamberlain, her ward and Abbess Heloise.

"I'm going to spill something, I know it," she told Samonie as the maid sewed her into her fashionably tight sleeves. "Loosen the right one a bit, Samonie. I can't feel my fingers."

As they were finishing, there was a knock at the door. Samonie went to open it, then stepped back, bowing.

"Mother Heloise!" Catherine rushed to greet her. "You honor me too much. If you had sent someone to fetch me, I would have come to you. Please come in."

She looked around wildly for a place to sit, but every chair and pillow was covered with clothing.

"I'm sorry," she said as Samonie uncovered one of the cushioned stools. "I wanted to look my best tonight."

"And you do, Catherine," Heloise said, taking the offered stool. "The yellow accents your dark skin and the blue brings out your eyes. However, I didn't come to inspect your toilette. I've been speaking with Astrolabe. He tells me that Annora, the ward of Countess Sybil, is the sister of the woman who was killed in Brittany."

"Oh, the poor woman!" Catherine exclaimed. "Does she know?"

Heloise shook her head. "My son believes that only he and the murderer are aware of Cecile's identity. Therefore, we feel that it is better to keep her death a secret. If it's not public knowledge, then whoever did this might be tricked into incriminating himself."

Catherine wasn't so sure.

"It doesn't seem right to keep such a thing from the woman's sister," she said. "She should be allowed to grieve and pray for her soul. And, if Cecile knew her killer, don't you think he's already had time to prepare himself to act astonished when he learns of her death? He has probably formulated an account that will place him far from Brittany at the time."

"Not if he believes that the blame has been put on my son." Heloise's full lips tightened in anger.

"I know, Mother," Catherine said gently. "I fear that the one who did this is even now trying to be sure that Astrolabe will be the one punished for it."

"I am aware of that." Heloise's voice was steel. "Which is why the villain must be identified before he can do so. I believe that Sybil will aid me in this. But I don't know if we can trust Cecile's sister to wait patiently while we work. Or to hide her grief until the culprit is found. Don't you agree, Catherine?"

Catherine reddened with guilt. Her expression had shown her doubts. "It just seems cruel to keep the poor girl ignorant of her sister's fate," she explained.

"All the sisters here are praying for the soul of Cecile," Heloise said. "She's not being neglected. And it will be much easier for Annora to cope with Cecile's death if we can give her the murderer at the same time."

Catherine nodded a reluctant agreement.

"Will you help?" Heloise asked.

"Of course, Mother." Catherine was surprised that she even needed to ask. "Whatever I can do, although I don't see how I can be of much use, other than giving you my notes on Gilbert's *Boethius.*"

"We never know what will be expected of us," Heloise answered. "Now, shall we go to dine with the countess?"

A small room in the guest house had been changed completely from a utilitarian waiting room to an elegant dining chamber. Countess Sybil had brought her own wall hangings, embroidered with scenes from the life of the Virgin. They now covered three of the walls. Cushions had been placed on the chairs and the table set with the finest linen. There was a gold saltcellar next to the countess and silver cups for the wine. The candles were of pure wax, not tallow.

Catherine stopped at the doorway to adjust her skirt over her round belly. She thought a prayer to her name saint that she not embarrass Heloise. She knew she had a tendency to blurt out her opinions before considering the audience. This would be a good night to learn restraint.

The countess's confessor said a blessing over the food and then left.

"He has offered to hear the confessions of the lay brothers tonight," Heloise explained to Catherine.

"Also, he finds the social requirements of these dinners very enervating," Sybil added.

No one smiled. Catherine wasn't sure if that had been meant as a joke or a criticism. She stifled a sigh but not well enough. Sybil focused on her.

"I see that you are with child," the countess said. "How far along are you?"

"Almost five months, by my reckoning," Catherine answered.

Sybil nodded, appearing to be thinking something else. But she wasn't finished with Catherine.

"Then you're past the dangerous time," she said. "The quickening has occurred?"

"Oh, yes." This was the most active of her children so far.

"Excellent." Sybil said no more but signaled for the servants to pour the wine.

Heloise motioned to have the trenchers brought in.

It was another Lenten meal of fish stew in bread trenchers, and the wine was heavily mixed with water, but it was still much more than Heloise and her nuns would normally eat at this time of year. Catherine wondered if she could save some for Margaret. How much could she tuck in her sleeve before anyone noticed?

Come to think of it, she wondered why Margaret wasn't dining with them. Edgar's sister was much better born than Catherine. She wasn't cloistered and, at fifteen, was older than many married noblewomen. It would have been natural for her to be included.

There was something happening here.

Catherine bent over her meal, trying to look modest and uninterested in the conversation. From time to time she glanced at the countess's ward.

Annora was young but older than Margaret, probably in her early twenties. She was quite attractive: pale, blond, with light eyes that seemed to change from grey to green in the candlelight. She tended to keep them half closed through the meal. Catherine wondered if she thought this made her look mysterious or if she were just half asleep with boredom.

Astrolabe had received the impression from Cecile that the family had a fairly large holding in Normandy. Since Sybil's nephew, Henry, now controlled Normandy, it was natural that she would concern herself with the girl. It was odd that Annora wasn't married by now. No doubt it was another thing that had been delayed by the departure of so many eligible men on the expedition to the Holy Land. It was terrible that she would have to bear the loss of her sister alone.

At the moment the others were discussing the expedition. Sybil was explaining her problems with Baldwin of Hainaut, and the chamberlain, Eustace, was extolling the bravery and skill that Sybil had shown in keeping Baldwin from taking over Flanders.

"I am blessed in the strength and loyalty of my people," Sybil said. "But we should not have had to endure these attacks. Baldwin broke his oath and should have been excommunicated immediately. Yet nothing has been done. I need your help, Heloise."

Heloise did not appear to be surprised.

"Of course," she said. "I shall be happy to do whatever is in my power, but my influence is small."

Sybil gave a refined snort.

"You are much too modest," she said. "You have contacts at most of the monastic houses in the area. I need you to write asking that the abbots and abbesses lend their voices to my request for a condemnation of Baldwin."

"Honestly, I don't know if that will help," Heloise answered. "Even if you get the pope to put Baldwin and all of Hainaut under interdict, it won't matter unless the bishops of Baldwin's own land respect the decree."

"We know that," Eustace intervened. "But we are hoping that an interdict will encourage the count of Champagne to support us as well."

Catherine looked up. Now it was even odder that Margaret had not been included. And certainly Count Thibault wasn't the one Sybil would normally have asked. There were other lords closer to Flanders who had no love for Baldwin. She opened her mouth to say so but shut it at a glance from Heloise.

The abbess looked puzzled. "But Count Thibault sent most of his best men with his son in King Louis's army. He could hardly commit many soldiers to help you."

"It's true that we sent the best of our soldiers and knights to liberate the Holy Land," Sybil agreed. "Including my own husband. That's only proper. I had in mind another sort of support from Count Thibault. Are you acquainted with Raoul of Vermandois?"

"Not personally," Heloise said frostily. "He's been living in adultery with the queen's sister for years now. They aren't likely to visit me."

"There are those who feel that the union has been legitimized," Eustace said. "Raoul's first marriage was annulled by the requisite number of bishops. But he would like his marriage to Petronilla of Aquitaine to be countenanced by the pope. We understand that Thibault, Countess Mahaut, and Raoul's former wife, Elenora, will all be at Reims for the council. I understand that they plan to stop here on their way."

Heloise dipped her fingers in the bowl of water the page was offering. She dried them thoroughly on her napkin before answering.

"Are you suggesting that I counsel them to withdraw their objections to the annulment?" she asked.

Her voice sounded shocked, but Catherine knew Heloise too well. The abbess had been expecting this.

Sybil gestured for the page to offer Heloise the fruit plate, oranges brought at great expense from Spain. Heloise took one and peeled it in a spiral. Catherine exhaled. So did Sybil.

"Elenora has let it be known that she has no feeling left for Raoul and no interest in returning to him," the countess said. "She is provided for with her dower lands, and they were childless. The only obstacle is the affront to the honor of Champagne. Count Thibault was furious that his cousin was cast off so blatantly. Surely you can make him see that he gains nothing by continuing in his opposition."

Heloise finished her orange and wiped her hands and mouth again. She smiled at Sybil.

"You're planning an alliance with Vermandois, aren't you?" she asked. "Is this part of the bargain?"

Sybil gave a look like a child caught with her thumb in the honey pot.

"We have discussed a marriage between my son, Phillip, and Raoul's daughter, Elizabeth," she admitted. "We were also talking about my Margaret marrying young Raoul."

Young was right. None of the children were more than twelve. Young Raoul wasn't walking, yet.

"Two marriages?" Heloise said. "Is Vermandois that important?"

"Of course," Sybil exclaimed. "It's right on our border. And we need the connection to the French crown if we're to survive. Raoul is coregent now, as well as being the king's cousin."

Catherine understood that. She had always been glad that she could watch from outside as the children of the nobility were traded back and forth among families until they needed charts to work out who their cousins were and how many times over. But in order for the matches to be of any use for dynastic purposes, legitimacy was important. For some reason the Flemish were more particular about this than most. They traced both the maternal and paternal lines and demanded that the nobility marry only other noble families. After a few generations, this became almost impossible without resorting to incest. If Sybil's children were to marry those of Raoul and Petronilla, then their legitimacy would have to be beyond question, no matter how exalted their birth.

The candles were burning low. Even though the discussion fascinated Catherine, she found it hard not to stifle a yawn. The baby woke her up each night with more regularity than the bells calling the nuns to prayer. Across the table from her, Annora was also trying to keep her eyes open. The woman had said nothing the entire evening. Catherine wondered why she was even there.

Heloise must have noted their attempts to stay awake. She rose from the table.

"You are a wise woman, my lady," she said. "You can see beyond the immediate. Yes, I shall discuss the matter with the count and countess of Champagne. They may have already come to the same conclusion on their own. And I will give you my support in placing ecclesiastical censure on Baldwin, although I fear it won't substitute for your army."

Sybil rose too, and Catherine gratefully stood up. Her feet felt swollen and numb after sitting so long. It was all she could do to hobble back to her room. While the food had been excellent and the politics interesting, she still had no idea why Heloise had insisted that she be there.

She said as much to Samonie as the maid ripped her sleeves off and unlaced the *bliaut* over her *chainse*.

"The talk was all about the situation in Flanders. Not a word concerning Astrolabe," she complained. "Oh, yes! It's so good to be able to lie down. I had nothing to contribute to the conversation at all."

"Perhaps," Samonie said mildly as she massaged arnica and lavender oil on Catherine's feet, "you were supposed to be listening."

She left Catherine next to the sleeping children while she went to shake out the good robes and fold them into the clothes chest. When she returned, Catherine greeted her with a sheepish smile.

"Samonie," she said, "the king should have counselors as accurate and honest as you. Now I'll spend all night wondering what point I was meant to take note of."

The maid climbed into the bed and over the children to her place next to the wall.

"Don't wake me if you discover it," she said as she burrowed into the blankets.

But both she and Catherine were sound asleep before the bells rang for Compline.

Astrolabe had not slept so well.

"Now that I've seen Cecile's sister I feel less happy about keeping the truth from her," he told Heloise the next morning as they met outside the convent chapel. "As I've thought about it, I've begun to feel that my best chance is to speak out first. I should go to Pope Eugenius and tell him why I was with Eon and what Cecile told me about the situation at the abbey of Sainte-Croix. Abbot Moses will confirm that the count of Tréguier has taken over the abbey. Moreover, the abbess of Saint-Georges should know at once what has happened to the nuns who were taken from her."

He looked down into his mother's eyes and saw her fear for him struggling with the knowledge that he was right.

She put her hands over his.

"Let me pray first," she begged him. "I need guidance before deciding."

Astrolabe nodded. He didn't want to hurt her and he most assuredly didn't want to find himself branded as a murderer and heretic. But he had already made his decision. His mother wanted him to be cautious and safe. His father would have wanted him to be honest and unafraid.

Perhaps he had inherited more from Abelard than just his face.

*     *     *

Countess Sybil was also heading for the chapel. Her face
didn't reflect her usual piety. Heloise had agreed far too easily
to something that must have gone against her beliefs. There
must be a reason. And why was that pregnant woman at the
table? She had no title. Her position at the convent had not
been explained. Was Heloise sheltering a woman who had
been wronged by some nobleman? Not her husband, Thierry,
of course. He was devoted to her, more so than she to him, she
feared. And, of course, he had been gone more than nine
months already. Sybil was sure that she was about to be asked
to bring one of her men to task. She shook her head. If the
woman wasn't wellborn, there was little chance that the man
would acknowledge the child.

If only Heloise would ask something else of her.

It was a relief to everyone when, after Tierce, Heloise summoned them to meet her in the guest house. Catherine was
pleased that this time Margaret was included.

As the day was chill, the abbess seated them all grouped
around the charcoal brazier. As they moved closer to the
warmth, Heloise chose to stand. For once, everyone was looking up at her, even her tall son.

She spent a long moment before she spoke, as if searching
for inspiration to find the right words. Finally, she smiled at
them all.

"Countess Sybil, I know you've been wondering why I
agreed to support a marriage that I believe to be based in sin,"
she began.

Sybil nodded. "I know that political concerns would not be
enough to persuade you," she said warily.

"This is so," Heloise agreed. "I must confess that I need to
ask for your help on a matter I consider much more serious.
After consulting with my friends and my conscience I have
decided to trust you with all the information."

She went over to Annora and took her hands.

"I am so very sorry, my child, to have to inform you that
your sister, Cecile, has been killed in Brittany."

Annora gasped and drew her hands away. "No! That's impossible!" She cried. "Cecile is safe in the convent of Saint-Georges."

Catherine started. What had made the abbess change her mind?

"Astrolabe"—Heloise turned to her son—"please explain what happened."

"Thank you, Mother," he said. "She has the right to know."

He knelt by Annora's stool. "I'm so sorry," he said. "I should have protected her."

She stared at him without comprehension.

"It began last autumn . . ." Astrolabe told the story as gently as he could, leaving out Cecile's torment at the hands of the count's knights; but by the end, Annora was sobbing uncontrollably. Sybil took the girl in her arms.

"Why didn't you tell us at once?" she asked. "This murder is a crime not only against poor Cecile but against the Church as well."

"I confess that I feared for my son," Heloise said. "It is possible that Astrolabe may be accused of this horrible deed. Cecile recognized someone among those who raided the camp of the Eonists. This was no doubt the reason she was killed. But someone also recognized Astrolabe and seems to wish to see him take the blame. I don't know if these people are the same. I do believe that, if he is accused, it will happen at Reims before the pope and all the prelates of Christendom. We must discover the truth before that can happen."

"First we must care for Annora," Astrolabe said firmly.

Heloise nodded and signaled to the page. "Have someone fetch Sister Melisande from the infirmary. Tell her to bring a sleeping draught."

Catherine sat next to Annora so that the countess could release her. She took a napkin and dipped it in the hand-rinsing water, then wiped the hot tears from Annora's face.

"Please forgive us," she said. "I wish there had been some way to prepare you."

Annora shook her head slowly. "How?"

Catherine had no answer.

Sister Melisande arrived, took one look at Annora and assumed command.

"Come, my dear," she said. "You need a warm drink and rest. I'll take care of you."

Annora made no protest as the nun led her from the room.

They all felt uncomfortable when she had gone, embarrassed at their relief at not having to watch her grief.

"Now," Heloise said, "I'm even more determined that the true perpetrator be brought to justice. That poor child!"

"But Mother," Catherine interrupted, "how can we do that? We need to send someone to Brittany to investigate."

"I don't think so," Heloise said. "If the murderer was among those who captured the Eonists, then he will likely come to testify against them at the council. At the moment he may not be aware that we know anything about Cecile. It's essential that this be kept secret until we can find out who really killed her and are prepared to prove it."

" 'We'?" Sybil asked. "Does that mean you plan to attend?"

Heloise shook her head. "It would not be appropriate. Although all the abbots have been summoned, no abbess was. If I came to the council uninvited, it would be just as bad as ignoring the summons. My presence would be a distraction."

"So what do you have in mind?" Sybil asked.

Heloise hesitated. "I need to ask you to provide my son with a plausible reason to be in Reims without being identified," she said. "I'd like you to take Astrolabe with you as one of your guards. With the beard and in chain mail he's not so likely to be recognized. Then he can investigate."

"Of course," Sybil said. "That's not a problem at all."

"There's more," Heloise said. "And I thought more about this than anything else. If there were anyone else, I wouldn't ask."

She turned to Catherine, who looked up at her innocently.

"I also need to send someone who is fluent in spoken Latin but who wouldn't be expected to be, someone who has experience in searching out the truth and who understands the nuances of the debates on heretical beliefs."

Catherine's jaw dropped. "Me? But Mother, I can't! I have my children, the baby coming."

Heloise looked away. "I know, Catherine. It's wicked of me to ask this of you, but I know of no one else I can trust. As for James and Edana, there will be no problem finding people here to care for them."

"But I've never been apart from them," Catherine protested. "They're already confused because Edgar is gone."

"For goodness' sake, young woman," Sybil interrupted. "I left five children in Flanders, including a new babe. My husband is off fighting Saracens. You aren't so far along that a trip to Reims will endanger you. If Abbess Heloise asks it, who are you to refuse?"

"No, Catherine," Heloise said softly. "If you agree, it must be freely. I know what I'm asking of you. Countess Sybil is fortunate that her deliveries have been easy and her children healthy. You have not been so fortunate. I have consulted with Melisande and she feels the risk to you would be small. Still, I will understand if you refuse. I hope that you wouldn't be absent for more than two or three weeks at most. We shall care for your children as if they were the most precious beings on earth."

Catherine looked up. "They are, Mother," she said simply.

Heloise sighed. "I understand. I should never have asked this of you. It was my own selfish love for my son that prompted it. Forgive me."

Catherine rose and knelt rather clumsily before the abbess, raising her hands together in a gesture of fealty.

"My Lady Abbess," she said. "Without your guidance and love, without the direction and understanding of Master Abelard, I would never have met Edgar. My children never would have been born. I owe you more than can ever be repaid. Please forgive *my* self-interest. For you and for your son, who is also my friend, I shall do as you request, without reservation."

"So shall I, Mother." Margaret slid down beside Catherine, putting her arm about her shoulders. "I will be happy to go with my sister-in-law and help her."

"Margaret." Heloise gave her a stern look. "Your brother and your grandfather would flay me with scallop shells if I sent you on this mission. If you are going to submit to my authority as fully as Catherine, then you must remain here."

"Catherine?" Margaret implored.

"Please stay, Margaret," Catherine said. "I'll worry less if I know you are watching out for the children."

"Are we decided, then?" Sybil was growing impatient. "If so, I would prefer to arrange the details later. I have other matters to attend to, and I wish to see that Annora has everything she needs."

"Of course, my lady countess," Heloise bowed. "I shall come with you."

When they had gone, Margaret turned on Catherine.

"It's not fair!" she cried. "I could help you. Why should I be left behind again? Haven't I been good? I came here to the Paraclete. I've studied. I've prayed. When you came, I thought it was to take me home. Now everyone is leaving me again."

Tears rolled down her cheeks, making the scar livid. It was more than Catherine could take. She burst into tears as well.

*"Lacrimae Christi!"* Astrolabe exclaimed, looking from one to the other. "I think I'd rather be burnt for heresy than be the cause of all this woe."

Catherine wiped Margaret's face and then her own with her sleeve.

"Oh, Astrolabe," she gave a shaky laugh, "it's not because of you. I always cry more when I'm pregnant and, as for Margaret, I suspect she is under the influence of the moon."

Margaret blushed. "Yes, that's true. I hadn't thought of that. I'm sorry, Astrolabe. I do want Catherine to go with you and find who killed your friend. I'll be fine staying here with James and Edana."

Astrolabe regarded them both with affection and not a little disquiet. Once again, he wished he had never brought those he cared about into this.

# Seven

The convent of Saint-Pierre-les-Nonnains, Reims.
Thursday, 15 kalends April (March 18), 1148. Eventually the
feast of Saint Idesbaud, almoner of Countess Sybil of
Flanders and abbot of Dunes, whose body was found whole
and fresh 457 years after his death.

*De perquirenda vero pecunia, quam nobis in usus*
*quotidianos penecessariam vestra prudentia non ignorat, vos*
*rogamus, et quanta possumus precum instantia petimus.*

Since Your Prudence is not unaware of the constant need for
money, that it is essential for our daily needs, we ask for as
much as possible and we request it at once.

Louis VII, letter to Abbot Suger,
written from Constantinople, 1147

*I*'ve never seen a place so crowded in all my life!" Annora exclaimed.

She was hanging out of the window of the guest house of the convent, craning her neck right and left. Her blond braids swung and bounced against the stone wall. Below them in the streets of Reims there were constant processions of clerics, bishops and abbots with their retinues. As they passed, laypeople tried to move out of their way, but there was no place to go. A nobleman on horseback tried to push his way through but was effectively blocked by two deacons carrying a miter and cross in front of the sedan chair of the bishop of Vézelay. The swearing from the man on horseback rose to the room above. Catherine listened in awe at his fluency.

"Perhaps we should close the window," she suggested. It had occurred to her that the countess might not approve of her ward observing such behavior.

She regretted this a moment later as Annora closed the shutter and returned to her sewing. For a moment the woman had been animated. Now the grief had returned. It would have been better to let her learn a few obscenities and escape her sorrow for a moment.

They had arrived in Reims two days earlier to find the place already bursting at the seams. Even Catherine felt overwhelmed by the number of clerics present. She understood at once why Abbess Heloise had wanted her there. Latin was the dominant language. It amused her in the shops to hear someone who had been speaking it fluently suddenly drop into stuttering French when faced with the need to communicate with the shopkeeper. It took all her self-control to ignore the lively

and often ribald conversations the monks and clerics thought
were private.

"Annora," she asked, "has Countess Sybil told you if you
are to go with her when she presents her case to the pope?"

"Me!" Annora looked up from her embroidery in panic.
"What could I say to him, except to plead that he find the one
who murdered my sister? No, I'm here only because the
countess thought it safer to keep me close."

She paused, then decided to confide in Catherine.

"I believe she also had plans to arrange a marriage for me
here," she admitted. "But now I don't know. I am not as eager
to wed as I was before."

Catherine came and sat beside her, putting her arm around
the girl's shoulder.

"It does seem wrong to continue with our lives when someone we love is gone," she said. "But it's even more important
now that you have a family of your own to depend on."

"It's not that," Annora said, her voice hard. "Until I know
who killed her, I can't be sure the man I marry isn't his friend,
his cousin or even the one himself who cut her throat."

Catherine's arm dropped.

"Saint Faith's kidnapped corpse!" she exclaimed. "Don't
add to your troubles with such a thought! Isn't that a bit unlikely? There are thousands of noblemen in France. The man
who did this is certainly one of the retainers of the count of
Tréguier. Countess Sybil wouldn't consider having you
marry a common knight. And we only know that he was with
those who came for Eon. He may well not have come to
Reims at all."

But even as she said it, she wondered. She had assumed that
the people trying to condemn Astrolabe had no connection to
the one who killed Cecile, that her death was simply one more
thing they wanted to put against him. But what if the men
hunting for Astrolabe were friends or relatives of this fiend?
Family unity was often more important than justice. Someone
else in the party that captured the Eonites might well have
seen the murder and remained silent, hoping that the blame
would be diverted.

Catherine felt a twinge of guilt. She had her own family secrets to keep.

These speculations she kept to herself. Annora was already devastated by the turns her life had taken in the past year. Her father had died. When the army had left for the Holy Land she had been uprooted from her home and sent to live in a foreign country. The sister she had believed to be safe in the convent, praying for her, had been cruelly assaulted and then murdered. The poor girl must feel that nothing was certain anymore.

Annora was not comforted by Catherine's reassurance.

"You can't understand," she said, pulling away. "You have everything, family friends, beautiful children, a husband who seems to love you, by all appearances."

Catherine blushed and put her hand over her stomach, as if she should hide it. Annora looked away.

"The countess is kind to me, but she is also surrounded by family," she continued. "Now that my sister is dead, I am the last of my line. The husband I choose will have control of our castellany. If he is feckless or cruel, I won't be the only one to suffer."

"You are quite right," Catherine said, abashed. "I only have to think of the safety of my close relatives. You must consider the welfare of your tenants, retainers and serfs, as is proper. It must be a great responsibility."

Annora sighed. "A great burden, rather. Lady Sybil seems to manage so well. She was directing the army against Baldwin right up until she went into labor. Childbirth was no more than momentary inconvenience. I don't think I could be so strong."

"I know I couldn't," Catherine agreed.

The noise from the street below rose suddenly. Both women hurried back to the window.

"Is it the pope?" Annora asked, peering over Catherine's shoulder at the procession.

"Hardly," Catherine laughed. "It's the regent of France, Raoul of Vermandois, with his scandalous wife."

"Now *that* I must see." Annora pushed Catherine aside and leaned far out the window to gawk with the crowd at Queen

Eleanor's adulterous sister, Petronilla, her own troubles momentarily forgotten.

The taverns of Reims were as crowded as the streets, but it was not difficult for two strong men in leather and mail to find a place at one of the tables. Astrolabe stretched his long legs out toward the fire and sighed happily. He had found an ally in his fellow guard, Godfrey. Godfrey had worked for Hubert many years and had willingly stayed on with Solomon and Edgar. He was the son of a blacksmith in a village near Sens. He had grown up as apprentice to his father but soon realized that he preferred wielding a sword to fashioning one.

"I wanted to see more than the forge and the backside of a horse, but didn't fancy binding myself to some lord who would keep me standing a cold watch while he and his well-born men feasted," he explained to Astrolabe. "Like as not, I'd be the first one killed in any brawl. So I kept at my trade until one day a couple of merchants came around looking for men who were honest, could fight and didn't mind travel. I owned up to the last two and I suppose I seemed to them too innocent to be bent. They were Hubert and his partner, Eleazar. Eventually, they trusted me with the secret that they were brothers. Then I could be given messages to carry to both families. Good men, both of them. They treated me well. Solomon and Edgar seem so far to be good masters as well."

He leaned forward, lowering his voice.

"And, as for secrets, how does it happen that a man like you fits so well into this craft? I'd have thought you'd be teaching schoolboys in some monastery."

Astrolabe grimaced. He looked into his beer, trying to guess what was floating in it. Deciding that it was probably not alive, he drained the bowl. He regarded Godfrey's honest, friendly face. It might be that he had found good masters because he was a good man, the kind who could be a friend.

"This isn't something my mother likes to have me speak of," he said quietly. "She and my father were not the kind of people . . . that is, their situation was such that . . . well, anyway, they left me with my aunt Denise in Le Pallet where I was born. My father was the eldest son in a knightly family. I was raised among people who earned their keep and kept their land by fighting. Even though we all knew that my parents would never permit it, they let me train with them."

He shrugged. Godfrey looked at him in puzzlement.

"But your mother loves you; I know she does," he said. "How could she have left you?"

Astrolabe smiled. "She does love me, but not above all. She loved my father first, then God and finally me. I don't mind. If you knew the whole story, you might understand."

Godfrey shook his head. "I doubt it."

They sat in companionable silence, both observing the other inhabitants of the tavern. They weren't the only men-at-arms there. Bishops and abbots were not so unworldly that they would travel without protection, and there were a number of laymen who had come, like Countess Sybil, to plead for help from Pope Eugenius.

At one table there were several men, well into their second or third pitcher, all talking at the top of their voices.

"What language is that?" Godfrey asked. "It sounds like pigs grunting and whistling."

"English, I think," Astrolabe answered. "I don't speak it but I know the sound."

He glanced over at the men, then stiffened and slunk down on his bench. The voice calling for more beer, now in fluent French, was one he knew well.

Godfrey looked over his shoulder at the table of Englishmen.

"A friend or an enemy?" he asked.

"An old friend," Astrolabe answered, "A student of my father's in Paris and a good friend to Catherine and Edgar. I don't want him to greet me here. I should have known he'd gravitate to a tavern and other English."

"Should we go?"

Astrolabe shook his head. "No, that would attract his attention. If he gets up for a piss soon, I'll follow him and warn him not to notice me."

Godfrey considered him. "He might not anyway. Even in the past weeks you've changed more than you think. You stand taller, walk with more confidence. Amazing what you can do when you don't worry about tripping on your skirts all the time."

Astrolabe gave a snort for reply, but he was not displeased.

It didn't take long for the Englishman to rise and make his way out, promising his friends that he'd be back in a moment. Astrolabe got up and went out into the street where there was a dark corner, well used by the smell of it.

There was only one man there at the moment. Astrolabe went over and tapped his shoulder. There was a strangled yelp.

"Saint Oswald's severed head, man!" the Englishman cried. "Don't ever do that! You couldn't find your own corner?"

Astrolabe laughed, "Sorry, John. I wanted to get to you before someone else showed up."

John turned and looked up at him, his face changing from anger to bewildered recognition.

"Astrolabe! What are you doing in all that metal?" he asked.

"It's a long story that I don't want to tell you here," Astrolabe said. "And don't use that name. Call me 'Peter,' please. Can you meet me outside the front of the convent of Saint-Pierre tomorrow morning?"

John looked him up and down. "Peter, hein? Are you planning on abducting a nun?" he asked. "If so, you'll have to find someone else to help."

Astrolabe's face showed horror. "I'd never do such a thing!"

"Don't be so fierce." John backed away from him, unfortunately into the wall. "I was only joking."

"I know, old friend," Astrolabe answered, moving aside to let him out. "But the question hit me in a sore spot. You'll understand when you know the whole story. No, we need go to Saint-Pierre to collect Catherine, who is staying with the nuns."

"What? Why? Where's Edgar?" John was becoming more agitated.

"Tomorrow I'll explain it all," Astrolabe promised. "Will you be there?"

"With all these unanswered questions? Of course I will."

"Good. Now, when we return, pretend you don't know me at all," Astrolabe cautioned.

"I'm beginning to think I don't," John answered as they once more entered the smoky tavern.

At the Paraclete, Heloise had little time to worry about those she had sent to Reims. Beyond the day-to-day management of her convent and its lands, she had a stream of visitors to attend to. Everyone who was going to the council seemed to be using her guest house as a way station.

Sister Emily came to her early one morning with a problem that was unprecedented.

"We have two bishops and an abbot each of whom says that he has the duty to say Mass for us," she said. "They are arguing now about which of them is most important."

Her usually calm demeanor was gone. Her lovely face was flushed and her wimple askew. She was also currently wondering whether to tell the abbess that one of the unruly abbots was her own uncle, Humbert.

Heloise set her jaw. Emily sighed in relief. No one could defeat Mother Heloise when she got that expression. The matter would soon be taken care of without alienating anyone. She followed Heloise out to watch.

The abbess had arranged her face to show nothing but smiling gratitude as she approached the three men. All immediately turned to her with cries of welcome and simultaneous offers to give the service.

"My lords," she said, bowing her head with humility. "I am overwhelmed by your graciousness. We are not used to such exalted personages serving us. I fear that my nuns would be quite undone by your presence. Therefore, I believe that our chaplain, Father Gérard, should be allowed to proceed as usual. Otherwise it will be days before we would be able to settle back into our quiet life."

Emily also bent her head, but to hide her smile. Heloise had said nothing untrue. But she had heard something very different than the clerics had. The nuns were not at all used to receiving communion from someone who thought more of himself than the miracle of transubstantiation. The debate over the relative importance of the three men might well keep the convent in an uproar for days. Emily was not the only one of the nuns with bishops and abbots in the family.

When she had managed to placate the prelates, Heloise went to the chapel for Nones, then to the refectory, the dining hall that doubled as the scriptorium. There she found Margaret among the students sitting, as usual, so that there was shadow on her face to hide the scar.

Shaking her head, the abbess motioned for Margaret to join her.

"There was a courier from your grandfather," she told the girl. "He should be here by evening and has requested that you join him and the countess for dinner."

"Should I change my *bliaut*?" Margaret asked, looking down at her ink-stained overtunic.

"I think that would be appropriate," Heloise said. "Margaret, don't you want to impress Count Thibaut with how lovely and accomplished you've become?"

Margaret knew Heloise was poking fun at her, but she still answered earnestly.

"I don't want him to think that I ask anything from him other than his affection," she said. "I know that my mother was only a bastard child and I have no rights."

"Poot!" said Heloise with feeling. "You are of his blood and acknowledged. That's all that matters. And I happen to know that the countess is also fond of you. So dress yourself to honor them and don't worry so much about what they will think. It's not likely to be anything you might imagine."

So Margaret dressed herself carefully, with many offers of advice from the other students and even some of the sisters. They all assumed the one thing Margaret really feared and were very excited about it.

"Perhaps the count has found an English lord for you," Hevida suggested. "Wouldn't you like to go back home?"

Margaret shuddered at the thought.

"He wouldn't send her there now that the Angevins are going to be the next kings," Emeline sneered. "It's probably someone local, a castellan or someone like that. No one of any real importance."

There was a pause as they all tried to think who in Champagne might be eligible at the moment. With many of the younger men in the army with Count Thibault's son, Henry, there weren't many to choose from.

"Gautier was just widowed," Hevida said thoughtfully. "He has no son. But his daughters do."

"Girls! Stop that chatter at once!" The usually gentle voice of Sister Emily cut through the conversation like a whip. "You are scholars, not peasant women gossiping at the well. Have none of you any work to do?"

The group dispersed at once, leaving Margaret alone, with her belt not hung and her hair half braided. Emily considered her thoughtfully.

"I know they say that red hair is a sign of the devil," she said, "but you make it look holy. Let's make the plaits loose and let a few curls twist like ivy along your cheeks. There. That's better."

Margaret looked at her in adoration. Sister Emily could have married anyone. She was beautiful, with thick blond hair and huge hazel eyes. Her family was related to half the nobility of France. But she chose to spend her life in prayer and study. Only, Margaret reflected sadly, that wasn't what she wanted for herself. The future she longed for was impossible. She knew it. She tried to resign herself to it. Just the same, the speculations of the other students filled her with dread.

Emily finished adjusting her hair and helped her to hang the belt on the loops of her *bliaut*. She knew Margaret's sad history and didn't blame her for wanting to stay with her family rather than be sent away to marry a stranger.

"I'm sure that your grandfather only wishes to see how you are doing," she assured Margaret. "It's unlikely that he would want to arrange a marriage until the king's return with the army. Who knows how many families will lose an heir in this war? No point in setting up an alliance until we know how a man's prospects may change."

Margaret sighed deeply. "It's terrible to be grateful that nothing can be decided until we know who has died or decided to join the church. But I'm not ready for any more changes. I'd rather stay here for a while."

"My dear," Emily laughed. "Even here we are not immune to change. I'm being sent to our new priory at Pommery soon."

"Oh, no!" Margaret cried. "I'll miss you so."

"I'll miss you and the Paraclete," Emily said. "But part of being a bride of Christ is that one must learn to cleave to Him and not to temporal attachments, even to someone as dear as you. Now, hurry along. The count and countess are waiting."

When Astrolabe and John appeared at Saint-Pierre-les-Nonnains that afternoon, Catherine greeted them with delight. She had spent the previous day worrying about what trouble James and Edana were causing and if they were calling for her. Since she had committed herself to this task, it was essential that she not let her longing for her family interfere.

"I need to concentrate on the work at hand," she told them. "John, we haven't seen you in ages! Where have you been hiding?"

"At Celle, near Troyes," John said as he hugged her gingerly. "I haven't been able to find a position yet, so my old friend Peter, who is abbot there, took me in." He looked at her stomach. "I can tell what you've been doing. Where's Edgar?"

"Gone to Spain," Catherine told him. "This expedition of the king has caused trade to be bad everywhere. He and Solomon need to find a way to feed the family."

She turned away to watch a sedan chair going by, its curtains drawn. Astrolabe and John speculated as to who was inside until Catherine could wipe her eyes and blow her nose. Once she had stuffed her handkerchief back in her sleeve, she faced them again with a smile.

"Now, has Peter, here, explained our situation?" she asked, indicating Astrolabe.

John nodded. "I can't believe the Count of Tréguier could get away with such a thing, even in the wilds of Brittany. Kidnapping nuns! Evicting monks! Why has no one sent an army to rout him out? The bishop of Saint-Malo used to be abbot there; you'd think he'd do something."

"I don't know," Astrolabe said. "Perhaps it's too far away for anyone to care."

"If it's that far away, then why is a harmless lunatic like Eon being brought here for trial?" Catherine countered.

John interrupted. "The street is hardly a place to discuss all this. Could we go somewhere else?"

"If we can push through this mob to a baker's, we can get bread," Astrolabe said. "I have some cheese that Mother packed for me. Then we can find a quieter place."

The street was again filling up. There were again too many people on horseback, pushing those on foot aside. Peddlers' cries punctuated the noise, along with the clanking of their packs. Every now and then there was a squawking as an unwary chicken found itself trapped in a sea of feet. The drainage ditch that ran down the middle of the street was clogged with refuse of every kind. The dung collectors couldn't keep up with the supply. Every few moments an unlucky pedestrian would slip and land in the damp waste. Catherine was grateful that Astrolabe and John were on either side of her to keep her upright.

As they came to the square before the cathedral, the crowd opened up suddenly and Catherine found herself nose to nose with a horse at the end of its patience. It curled back its lip and raised its head for all the world as if it were going into battle.

"Saint Vincent, defend me!" Catherine slid backwards to avoid the horse and the cart it was pulling.

John and Astrolabe pulled her in opposite directions to get her out of the pathway. For a moment, she thought she'd be trampled. Suddenly, Astrolabe dropped her arm and vanished into the crowd.

John got her to the side of the square, both of them panting.

"The *deofolcund deor*!" John exclaimed. "Are you unharmed?"

"Yes, thank you," she answered. "Although my bladder seems a bit overexcited. What was it and where did Astrolabe go?"

"Some sort of prisoner's cart," John said, looking after the crowd as it followed behind, shouting and pelting the cart with rotten apples and horse droppings.

Catherine tried to see, but the crush around the cart was too thick. All she could make out were the outlines of three or four men and the shape of the long chains that held them.

John grabbed a passerby armed with a moldy loaf.

"Who are those people?" he asked. "What have they done?"

"Heretics," the man spat. "They say one of them thinks he's the Savior himself, come again."

Catherine looked thoughtful.

"Times have been bad enough, I'd say, for the Second Coming," she commented. "How can we be sure he isn't?"

The man started to swear at her, then stopped, fixed by the earnestness in her deep blue eyes.

"Lady," he said more gently, "even Jesus wouldn't lower himself so far as to come back as a Breton."

Nevertheless, he dropped his bread, wiped his hand on his tunic and went the other way.

"That must be Astrolabe's Eon," John said.

"I wish we could get closer," Catherine fretted. "I want to see what kind of man this is who could fool so many people."

John chuckled. "So you don't think it's possible that he's Christ come again?"

"Of course not. Everyone knows that it won't happen until the last Jew is converted," Catherine reminded him. "And when I left Paris, they were still adamantly going about their business."

"Even if a miracle changed all their hearts, Solomon would still be left," John laughed. "It's almost impossible to convert someone who doesn't care about theology. Solomon only insists on remaining as he is. No one can change him."

Catherine sighed. "I know. Believe me, I've tried. Now, what about Eon? Do you think that Astrolabe's enemy will wait until the trial to denounce him?"

"No idea," John answered, distracted.

Catherine followed his gaze. There was a crush of bishops in the portal of the cathedral. In their midst was a gaunt man dressed in the simple grey robe of a monk. Catherine knew him, Abbot Bernard. She had heard that he was supporting the cause of those who would try Gilbert of Poitiers for heresy. Catherine still believed that it had been Bernard's influence alone that had condemned Master Abelard six years before. And yet, Bernard had also stopped the people of Lotharingia from killing the Jews last year. She had heard so much about him, had seen him more than once, even heard him preach, but still she didn't understand him at all. Some called him a saint; others complained that he thought only of power, wishing to be greater than kings or popes. Some believed that he already was. The current pope, Eugenius, had been one of Bernard's monks before his elevation, abbot of a Cistercian monastery in Italy. Would Bernard's opinion be the deciding one if Astrolabe were accused?

The party entered the cathedral. Catherine wanted to find Astrolabe, but John still stared at the now empty doorway.

"John?" She broke into his thoughts.

"What? Oh, sorry, Catherine," he sighed. "If I could only get a letter from Abbot Bernard, my career would be made. Peter can't keep me at Celle forever, unless I turn monk. If I could just get a position as a secretary to one of the bishops. Any benefice would help. But I need a recommendation."

"John! I didn't know." Catherine was astonished. She was aware that his family had no money or influence, but John was a brilliant scholar. "I'd have thought by now you'd be running the papal curia."

He shook his head. "If not for Peter giving me a place at Celle, I would have starved," he said. "I'm ordained now, you know. I took holy orders last year. I could even be chaplain to some lord. But times are bad."

Catherine couldn't deny that.

John shook himself. "Where has Astrolabe gone to?"

"Call him Peter," Catherine reminded him, looking around. "He disappeared into the crowd. Do you think he tried to follow the cart?"

"Not if he has any sense," John said. "No, there he is, on the other side of the square. What is that he has with him?"

Catherine tried to pick her friend out of the mass of people. Finally she spotted him. He had someone by the arm, a woman, perhaps. The form was clothed in castoff bits of clothing: a man's tunic over a woman's *chainse* and a cloak patched in enough colors to make the person look like one of those who juggled or sang in the streets for their bread.

Astrolabe saw them and started across the square, dragging the ragbag with him. As he came closer, they saw that it was a woman, not old but past her first bloom, her light brown hair streaked with grey. Her narrow face bore lines carved by sun and salt wind, but her brown eyes were clear and intelligent.

"This is Gwenael," Astrolabe said. "She is one of the people I stayed with when I lived in the forest. Gwenael, these are my friends, Catherine and John."

The woman bobbed her head in a barely civil greeting. To Catherine it looked as if once Astrolabe released his hold on her she would take flight.

"What have you told them?" she asked in heavily accented French.

"Everything," he answered. "You can trust them."

Gwenael shook her head. "No one is safe," she hissed. "Let me go, Peter. I must follow my Lord."

Catherine stepped forward, blocking Gwenael's retreat. "They are taking him to the cathedral for trial," she said. "You'll be able to see him soon. Forgive me, but you seem not to have eaten or bathed for some time. Will you let me take you to the convent where I am staying? The nuns will care for you."

The woman's eyes narrowed in suspicion. "Lock me up instead, I've no doubt," she said.

Astrolabe gave her arm an impatient shake. "I said my friends were safe," he insisted. "If you wish to be thrown into prison with Eon, then we'll take you there. If not, then let Catherine see to you."

Tears pooled in Gwenael's eyes and poured down her cheeks.

"I'm not worthy to share his cell," she wept. "I betrayed him. I deserve no bed but the street."

Catherine put her arms around Gwenael and let the woman sob against her shoulder until the wool of her cloak was soaked.

"You must have been very afraid," she said. "Even Saint Peter denied Our Lord when he feared for his own life."

The sobbing increased and they could get nothing more coherent from her, but she did let Catherine and Astrolabe guide her back to the convent, where Catherine took her to the alms gate and gave her into the charge of one of the sisters.

"Will you watch out for her?" Astrolabe asked. "I believe she means to declare herself and go to the flames, if necessary, rather than deny Eon again. From what she told me, she ran when the soldiers came and then followed behind. She walked all the way here, hoping to find him again. Please try to convince her that there's no point in joining him in prison."

"I haven't had much luck in converting heretics so far," Catherine said. "But I'll try. What interests me more is what she might have seen and what form her betrayal took."

"I don't know," Astrolabe said ruefully. "I was unconscious most of the time."

"She may have seen the one who struck you, though," Catherine said. "Of course, the word of a peasant heretic probably won't count for much in a court, but she could help us find him, at least."

"Will she?" John asked.

"I can't say," Astrolabe answered. "Perhaps if Catherine can win her confidence. Like most of Eon's followers, her life has not been marked by good fortune or kindness from those above her."

"Even so, she doesn't seem a fool," Catherine commented. "So how could she have believed that he was the son of God?"

Astrolabe scratched at a flea in his beard. Gwenael wasn't the only one who needed a bath.

"Perhaps," he said after some thought, "Eon made her believe that she had a soul and that it mattered to him that it was saved."

Catherine started to answer, but her words were drowned by the cacophony of the city bells as they tolled None.

"Midday already!" John said in surprise. "And we've not yet broken our fast. Didn't we start out in search of bread and beer? Cabbage pie would be good, too. I for one can't think at all for the roaring of my empty stomach."

"I confess to feeling the need for something as well," Catherine said. "Peter?"

Astrolabe sighed. "Very well. You two find a soft, dry patch of ground over there by the apple trees and I'll see what I can do about food."

"Good," said John, giving him a push toward the marketplace. "Then we can decide how best to save you from joining your friend Eon in chains."

As the bells rang at the Paraclete, Margaret filed into the chapel behind the nuns. She began reciting the psalms, but her heart needed more guidance than they could give her.

The dinner the night before had not been as awkward as she had feared. Her grandfather and his wife had been very kind to her. They seemed pleased with her deportment and proud when Heloise had mentioned her dedication to her Hebrew studies.

"Hebrew!" Thibault had exclaimed. "Do you intend to be an abbess-scholar, like Heloise?"

"Oh, no, my lord!" Margaret had answered too emphatically. "I mean, I have no calling. The contemplative life is not one I am suited for."

"If you become an abbess, my dear," Heloise sighed, "you'll find little time to contemplate anything."

She smiled. "Margaret is a fine student, but she may feel that Hebrew would be useful in her associations with the Jewish merchants her brother deals with."

"Oh, yes." Thibault's forehead creased as he remembered. "Your brother married Hubert LeVendeur's daughter and then took over when Hubert left on pilgrimage, didn't he? Odd thing for a nobleman to do, even if he is English."

"Catherine's mother comes from a good family," Margaret

said. "And my brother is the youngest son. He had no prospects at home."

"Ah, that brings us around to another topic." Countess Mahaut gave Margaret a motherly smile. "Your prospects, my child. Your grandfather and I have been discussing them. We have decided to take you with us to Reims and see what you think of our decision."

And that was why Margaret prayed the next morning as she never had before, as her boxes were being packed for the trip to Reims and her fate.

# Eight

Reims. Friday, 14 kalends April (March 19), 1148.
Feast of Saint Joseph, "husband of the mother of God."

*Ad quod concilium dominus Albero archiepiscopus tam
magnifice pervenit . . . In camerula autem de corio facta,
lineo panno intrinsecus decenter obducta, inter duos
ferebatur equos, quod cunctis visu erat mirabile*

The lord Archbishop Albero [of Trier] arrives at this council
with great splendor . . . In a tented bed made of leather,
padded sumptuously within with linen, carried between two
horses, to the wonder of all who saw it.

*Gesta Alberonis,* caput 86

*D*espite the number of clerics in town, or perhaps because of them, the traditional drinking and carousing for Saint Joseph's Day had started earlier than usual. Countess Sybil had made it clear that no ward of hers would dare leave the safety of the convent on the feast of the patron saint of cuckolds.

"You'd think men would have more respect for poor Saint Joseph," she said. "He was a holy man and a good husband. Why should his feast be an occasion for such debauchery?"

Catherine had often wondered that herself. "Edgar always said that men felt a kind of pity for him. After all, what recourse did he have when his wife had been made pregnant by the Holy Spirit?"

"I think that they just are glad for any excuse to get drunk and beat their own wives." Sybil turned from the window with a sniff.

"Really?" Annora's eyes grew large.

Catherine hurried to reassure her. "Some men do, of course," she said. "Especially when addled by wine. But my husband has never struck me. Count Thierry is also a good man. I'm sure that the countess would never give you to someone cruel."

She looked at Sybil, hoping she hadn't misspoken.

Sybil smiled at them. "Of course not, Annora. I would not allow you to marry anyone who wasn't pious and of good character. You needn't fear on that score."

Annora bowed her head. "Thank you, my lady. I trust you to know what is best for me and for my people."

"Such a good child." Sybil patted the girl's cheek before

she left the room. "Stay in with your sewing today. Tonight we shall dine with the count of Vermandois. Despite the difficulty about his marriage, I think you will find him a most worthy man. He has connections with all the great families of France and, of course, the king has entrusted him with the secular management of his demesne while he is in the Holy Land."

She sounded as if she were reassuring herself more than Annora and Catherine.

Once she had left, Annora ran to the window.

"I'm sure she's right about staying in," she told Catherine. "But it's so exciting down there. I wish I could see it all. In my village it's usually quiet, even on Saint Joseph's Day."

Below them there were lines of men snaking through the street, each holding on by one hand to the shoulder of the one in front. The other hand held a drinking bowl. Some of the men were dressed as women, with exaggerated breasts and false braids swinging over their hips. Catherine wasn't sure how that custom had begun, but it was part of the fun. She remembered watching the men in Paris do the same when she was a child. Her parents had not let her out, either.

"Annora," she tried to catch the girl's attention. "Do you think Countess Sybil means for me to dine with Count Raoul this evening? I don't think it would be appropriate for me to attend."

"Why?" Annora reluctantly turned her gaze from the street performance. "I thought Abbess Heloise agreed that his marriage was probably canonical."

"No, she didn't," Catherine answered. "Just that it was a fact. But I meant that I am only the wife of a merchant. I don't belong at the table with the high nobility."

Annora gave her a long stare. She had only known Catherine a few days but had learned a great deal about her in that time.

"That isn't the sort of thing that you would worry about," she said. "You don't want to go, do you?"

Catherine sat down. Her feet were hurting again. "No, I don't," she admitted. "These are people who are close to the king. My husband and my . . . his partner depend on the goodwill of the king and his advisers. I don't want to risk making a bad impression on them."

"But why should you? You might be able to help your husband."

Catherine shook her head. "No, I tend to forget my place. Or I'll upset the salt on someone. It's better if I remain here. In any case, I'm not sure if I was included in the invitation."

"Well, I'll find out for you," Annora said. "But if Countess Sybil intended you to be present, I think it would be more damaging to refuse."

Sadly, Catherine agreed. She spent a moment feeling sorry for herself, then remembered the Breton woman that Astrolabe had brought to the convent the day before. Even if Gwenael decided to reject Eon and his belief, what had she to look forward to but penury and eventual starvation?

It made her own worry about knocking over the saltcellar appear ridiculous.

It didn't ease the heartache she felt, longing for her husband and children. In that, she and the heretic woman were sisters.

Astrolabe and Godfrey were enjoying the festival with the rest of the men. They were sprawled on a bench watching the lines go by and saluting them with a drink as they passed. Astrolabe was amused at how many of the men wore the tonsure of minor clerics. He wondered if any of them would be bishops one day and if they would look back on this celebration with shame or regret for good times gone.

Gwenael was sitting between them, holding her bowl of beer but rarely sipping from it. She tried to shrink as much as she could against the wall, hiding behind the two guards. Peter was not what she had thought him to be when they had all been living in the forest. She still wasn't sure if he meant to help her or turn her in to be put in chains with Eon and his followers Wisdom, Knowledge and Judgment.

Astrolabe saw her huddling and thought she was cold.

"Do you need another cloak?" he asked. "Is Catherine's too thin?"

Gwenael gaped at him.

"No, my lord," she said. "I am warmer than I've ever been. It was most kind of the lady to let me borrow this. But I must go to my master soon. He needs my help."

"Are you that eager for the flames?" Astrolabe asked her. "After the pope hears the story he may simply send Eon home for his family to guard, but the court won't be as understanding with the rest of you if you persist in your beliefs."

"But this court of bishops and cardinals cannot be respected," Gwenael answered. "Or trusted. They are the Pharisees, the Pilates of our time. How can those men in gold and silk recognize the Son of God? The glitter of their jewels blinds them to the truth. Should I deny my conscience to save my body?"

Astrolabe had no answer to that, although he wanted to tell her yes. He knew that in some cases her evaluation was true. The modern world had as many Pharisees and hypocrites now as in the time of Christ. But he also felt certain the Eon was not the answer. He had to convince Gwenael of that before her master came to trial.

He shifted uncomfortably on the bench. He also was very much aware that his interest in this woman was not as much the need to save her soul but in what she might know that could save his own life.

"You may be right," he told her. "But for now you are of more use to Eon if you are free."

"And I would not like to see you in chains," Godfrey added to her. "Your life has been hard enough."

Gwenael looked at him. He smiled at her. She bent her head again. Every few moments, though, she stole a glance at his face. This man was not like Peter. He spoke slowly so that she could understand. He looked at her as if she were a person and not an object of charity. She found herself wondering how old he was and if he had a wife somewhere.

Immediately she scolded herself. Such speculation was nonsense. She had pledged her heart and soul to Eon. It wouldn't do to trade eternal bliss for a few years of earthly happiness. Of course, unlike many other preachers, Eon had never suggested that the way to heaven was only for the chaste.

The two men on the bench were completely unaware of the spiritual struggle happening in the woman sitting between them. Godfrey took another swill of beer, stomping his feet to the rhythm of the song as the chain of men passed.

"Who's that old goat?" He sat up, causing Gwenael to slide to the ground. "He must be mad to try to pass through with all this going on."

Astrolabe stood to see over the throng. There was a very old man on horseback, surrounded by clerics and a few guards. He appeared unconcerned by the ribald celebration going on around him. If anything, he regarded the men in the street with wry benevolence.

"Saint Peter in chains!" he breathed. "It's Master Gilbert, bishop of Poitiers. How he has aged since I last saw him!"

Godfrey looked at him with interest.

"That's the man all the fuss is about, the heretic bishop?" he asked. "He looks even more harmless than the poor Breton heretic. Hell, he looks about to fall into the grave."

"He must be close to eighty now," Astrolabe said. "But I wouldn't expect him to die any time soon. They say his mind is as sharp as ever, which is much more than most of us can ever hope for. He's probably the most astute theologian in France."

Godfrey watched the old man until he turned at the corner of the street.

"Forgive me if I don't genuflect," he said finally.

Even though she knew she was traveling under the threat of marriage, Margaret found herself enthralled by the variety of the people they were meeting on the road to Reims. There were bishops and abbots from all over, of course, but also all the attendants that men of importance could not survive without. The bishops especially came with their cooks, ostlers, butlers and even laundresses, although even to Margaret some of the last appeared to be rather overdressed for the job.

She was honored that Henry, the bishop of Troyes and

Countess Mahaut's brother, chose to ride with her. He pointed out the people he knew and gave her bits of information about them.

"Over there, that's Thierry, the master who teaches at Chartres." He pointed to a tired-looking man about the same age as her grandfather. "Another Breton, like Peter Abelard. I don't see Bishop Geoffrey, though. They say he's been ill. I don't know who that is." He gestured at another man in a fur cloak and hat. "He seems important, though, doesn't he?"

"You were a canon at Reims, weren't you?" Margaret asked. "You know everyone there, I suppose."

He smiled at her. "Many. I'm eager to see old friends, even more than to debate the canons we will decide upon. But I must be boring you with all this tittle about old men you've barely heard of."

"Oh, no!" Margaret said quickly. "My brother and his wife are very interested in church politics. I'd like to learn as much as I can. But," she added shyly, "I was wondering more about what it is like in Carinthia, where you and Countess Mahaut were born. Do you find it as different in France as I do?"

"As you do?" He gave her a puzzled look. "Of course, I forgot. You come from the savage wilds of Scotland, don't you? Well, my home is more mountainous and we see more Greeks and Russians trading in our cities, but it's all Christendom just the same and so not that strange. Do you find France so alien? You speak the language very well. Better than I do."

"Thank you," Margaret said. "My mother always spoke it with me. She never really felt comfortable speaking English. Perhaps it's strange only because we lived in a small village. There's so much more happening in Paris."

Bishop Henry laughed. "If we are comparing Carinthia to Paris, then I must agree that it is very different."

He spotted two men riding just ahead of them as they approached the gates of Reims. Moving closer to Margaret, he lowered his voice.

"Now those two might interest you," he said. "Canons Cato and Arnold, archdeacons of Poitiers. They're the ones who started this protest against Bishop Gilbert."

"His own canons!" Margaret was horrified.

"There's a story there, I'm sure," Henry said. "I wish I knew what it was."

Margaret had heard something of them. Canon Arnold was said never to have laughed in his life. From what she had seen of Bishop Gilbert when he lectured in Paris, the canon should have been a good match for him. She shook her head.

"I confess that I don't understand any of this," she said. "My sister-in-law Catherine finds it all fascinating."

Bishop Henry's face grew stern. "It is that fascination that leads untutored minds to heresy," he told her. "Be glad that you have a pure and simple faith."

Margaret smiled to cover her annoyance. She had been at the Paraclete nearly a year now, and while her faith was still pure, she hoped, there was nothing simple about it. Heloise would have been ashamed if a student of hers could not find her way through any theological tract. They were expected to be able to recognize rhetorical errors that were often the basis for accusations of heretical doctrine.

Not that Margaret had any particular talent for doing so.

"Oh, look, my lord!" she cried suddenly. "There are fire jugglers performing by the gate. Oh, please let me get close enough to see them better!"

"In this mob, my dear?" Countess Mahaut had come up behind them. "Just thank the saints that you're on a horse. Now, Henry, see that she doesn't get separated from us. Heloise would be furious if anything happened."

Margaret cringed, her hand instinctively going up to the scar on her face. Mahaut saw the movement and was stricken with remorse.

"Thibault," she said to her husband, "perhaps it was a mistake for you to bring your granddaughter with us. The crowds may be too much for her."

Count Thibault studied Margaret, who was now absorbed in trying to see the fire jugglers before she passed into the city.

"Nonsense!" he said. "She's tough, like all my family. There's a lot of my mother in her. Our family doesn't breed weaklings."

That was undeniable. The Norman duke, William the Bastard, had conquered England, and his descendents, Thibault among them, were doing their best to control the rest of the Christian world. Mahaut thought of Thibault's older brother William, the one child who had not lived up to his name. She had never been quite sure what had been wrong with him, only that he had been sent off to Sully with a caretaker wife and banned from inheriting any real power. Most of the family were indeed strong; weaklings weren't given a chance.

That mustn't happen to Margaret.

Looking at the mass of people invading the city, Catherine was grateful that she had a bed. How in the world would enough space be found for them all? And what about food? The last of the winter stores would have to be opened up, if there was anything left in them in this famine year.

"How many will starve because Reims had to provide for the leaders of the church?" she wondered aloud.

"How many have starved already?" came a voice from behind her.

Catherine turned around.

"I'm sorry," she said. "I thought I was alone."

The woman facing her was a nun, but not one of the sisters of Saint-Pierre. She was tall, nearly Catherine's height, and about her age, with a pale face and strong jaw. She seemed vaguely familiar. Catherine noted her long, fine hands unstained by hard work or ink and decided that she must at least be a prioress.

"I apologize for disturbing you," the woman said. "My name is Marie. I am the abbess of Saint-Sulpice, in Brittany."

"Oh, my lady," Catherine bowed. "It is I who apologize. I knew that Mother Heloise of the Paraclete had written to you concerning the situation at Rennes, but I was unaware that you would be here. Do you wish me to move out of this room for you?"

She made as if to do so at once. Marie was not only an abbess but also the daughter of King Stephen of England. That would make her . . . Catherine tried to work it out, the niece of Count Thibault and therefore some sort of cousin to

Margaret. The position of Edgar's half sister was becoming more and more intimidating to her. It wasn't until she had been thrust among all these members of the high nobility that Catherine realized how inappropriate it might be for Margaret to continue to live with her and Edgar.

She must have been staring, for the abbess regarded her with surprise.

"Do I have mud on my nose?" she asked.

"Oh. No," Catherine said. "I'll just pack up my things."

"There's no need for that," Marie told her. "I was only looking for the lady Annora. I understand that she has information on the fate of the women who were taken from Saint-Georges by the count of Tréguier."

"Yes, she does, my lady," Catherine said. "At least, she knows about the death of her sister, Cecile. I'm not sure how much more Countess Sybil has told her about the circumstances."

"I see," the abbess said. "I shall ask Sybil, then. And you are?"

"My name is Catherine," she answered. "I'm just the wife of a merchant. No one, really."

Marie's eyebrows rose. "And yet you are well enough acquainted with Abbess Heloise to know that she has sent me a letter, which I have not yet received. And you are also here under the protection of the countess of Flanders and sharing a room with her ward. Interesting."

Catherine smiled nervously, but the abbess seemed not to be interested enough to pursue the matter.

"Please tell the lady Annora that I grieve for her loss and am here to do what I can to see that Henri of Tréguier is brought to justice."

"Thank you, my lady abbess." Catherine bowed again, overbalanced and fell against the bed. "Oh, dear! I mean, I'll convey your message to her."

Abbess Marie pursed her lips, but Catherine couldn't tell if it was in disapproval or amusement. She nodded to Catherine and left.

Catherine sat on the bed for a moment, unnerved by the encounter.

"Well," she said, patting her stomach, "won't we have a story to tell Papa when he gets home? That is, if he isn't so angry with me for leaving your brother and sister at the Paraclete that he refuses to listen."

Then she started to consider the import of the abbess's presence now in Reims. It appeared that several people intended to force the count of Tréguier to release the nuns of Saint-Georges and to return the monastery of Sainte-Croix to Abbot Moses and the canons. Perhaps that would make it easier to convince everyone that Cecile was murdered by one of the knights of the count.

But Astrolabe wouldn't be completely safe until they found out which one.

The bishop's guards were trying to clear the square outside the cathedral. The beggars were told to go to the abbey church of Saint-Rémi, and most departed without complaint. There was much more trouble from the hundreds of people trying to get an audience before the council.

"Nothing has begun yet!" one shouted at a particularly insistent man. "Sunday after Mass. Come back then!"

"I happen to know that debates have been going on for almost a week now," the man shouted back. "I must get to the council before they decide."

The guard looked at the man. He wasn't a cleric.

"What could they be doing that would matter to you?" he asked. "Your daughter run off with the parish priest?"

"Fur!" the man answered, waving a fox tail collar in the guard's face. "They want to keep the clerics from wearing it. That will ruin me!"

The guard laughed. "Don't worry. The bishops aren't about to give up their fancy dyed-fur cloaks. Now, move along or be trampled by their hunting stallions, another thing they'll never surrender, no matter what the pope demands."

He turned to face another man trying to get to the church. This one was different from the furrier. He was a plainly dressed cleric, not well nourished. The guard felt more sympathetic to him but not enough to let him through.

"There's nothing happening now," he said. "The bishops and abbots are encamped all over the countryside, wherever a room can be found. The one you're looking for could be anywhere."

The cleric smiled. "I'm not looking for a bishop today, thank you."

His smile turned to a grin as he waved at another man who was having more luck making his way through the crowd.

"Over here!" he called. "I've had some luck! Buy me a beer?"

The guard sighed, sympathy ebbing. It would be a long day's work before he could hope for a beer.

"Get on with you, then!" He shoved the cleric toward his friend. He regretted the movement when he saw the size of the cleric's friend and the long knife at his belt.

"Peter!" John greeted him. "I'm glad I found you. A few days in this place and a hermitage will look positively welcoming."

"It already does," Astrolabe answered. "I have a flask right here. Let's find a quiet corner and you can tell me what you've discovered."

They walked down to the city gates. Outside, elaborate tents were going up in the fields. Men were pounding stakes into the ground and roping off areas for horses. Several enterprising meat pie sellers were already setting up a communal stall next to some trestle tables of freshly cut wood. John and Astrolabe sat down at one. Astrolabe brought out the flask, a clay bottle in a leather pouch with a long strap to hang it from.

"That will do for a start," John said, pouring some into his bowl. "But I've enough news for at least another. You didn't bring Gwenael?"

"More beer is always possible," Astrolabe answered, trying to hide his impatience. "Gwenael is with the nuns. She is becoming more nervous about being seen in the streets, she says. What have you learned?"

"Well, the archbishop of Tours is the one who insisted on bringing your heretic here," John began. "He has a plan of his own that Eon is only part of, I suspect. I haven't heard anything about Henri of Tréguier. It may be that people are afraid to accuse him because his mother, the dowager countess, gives so generously to the church. However, I think it more likely that the story simply hasn't spread very far. But Moses, abbot of Sainte-Croix, is here in Reims. He's not only the one Henri threw out of the monastery, he's also the countess's confessor. Therefore, she may have given him permission to have her son excommunicated."

"She must be furious with Henri!" Astrolabe commented.

"She may hope that an excommunication will bring him to his senses," John continued. "Anyway, all of these things are tied up with the archbishop's determination to make the bishop of Dol submit to his authority. Engelbaud of Tours wants to prove that Olivier of Dol is not a good shepherd to the people."

"Perhaps in all of these wranglings, my role will be forgotten," Astrolabe said. "With so many other heretics and rebels to attend to, who would care about one more man?"

John poured another bowl. He shook the bottle.

"Not much left," he said, then returned to the subject. "I don't know. With Gilbert of Poitiers being brought to trial, a lot of people are remembering how your father was condemned at Sens. Some are saying, as I am, that we can't let Gilbert be judged as Abelard was by men with not enough understanding of philosophy. Others feel that this is another example of how dangerous it is to apply learning to faith. They say that scholars are more to be feared than wandering preachers like Eon. You are connected to both kinds of heresy. The murder is simply an added gift."

"How much time do we have?" Astrolabe asked him, signaling for a pitcher to refill the bottle.

"Until Wednesday at least," John answered. "First they'll have to go through all the wrangling about primacy and repeating that priests mustn't marry and nuns should stay in the convent, as if those were new ideas. Then there are divorces to be decided. After that they'll bring out Eon. I haven't heard when Abbot Moses will be allowed to speak. He may even do it in one of the private meetings rather than before the whole council."

"What about Master Gilbert?" Astrolabe asked.

John snorted. "He has to wait until the council is over. Pope Eugenius has ordered some of the bishops to stay behind another week to examine his works for heresy."

Astrolabe grimaced. "Why? They've had almost a year to do that."

"I have no idea," John said. "I wasn't consulted."

"So, if I'm to be dragged into this, when do you think it will be?" Astrolabe asked.

"I'd say with Eon," John answered. "It will give Gilbert's enemies more arrows to shoot. Of course, if they can't condemn you for your association with Eon, they may try to connect you with Gilbert when he comes before the council."

"No, Master Gilbert wishes to dispute my father's work as well," Astrolabe said. "Accusing me in association with him would do little."

"Let's assume that we have four days, then, to find out who wants to see you condemned for heresy or murder." John looked at the assortment of people around them. "It would help if we knew which, or if it will be both. Where shall we start?"

Astrolabe thought about it.

"First we have to find the men who brought Eon and his followers to Reims," he decided. "Then see if Gwenael recognizes any of them. Then we need to find out which of them are also in the service of the count of Tréguier. Then we need to get the man to confess to killing Cecile."

"That all?" John asked. "Then we ought to have a couple of meat pies first."

"And more beer?" Astrolabe suggested.

"Definitely more beer," John agreed.

Catherine was growing restless indoors. She wanted to know what was happening to Astrolabe. What if he had been discovered? If it hadn't been for the baby she would be down in the streets now, finding things out on her own. It was amazing what kinds of information one could pick up with a shopping basket and a willing ear. But she knew she couldn't risk being crushed in the mob. She had miscarried too many times.

"I'll take care of you," she told the baby as it shifted inside her. "I asked Mother Heloise to pray for us every day and I promised your papa that I would do nothing dangerous."

She sighed. Responsibility came with parenthood, but it was galling nonetheless.

To pass the afternoon, Catherine took out her best *bliaut*, with roses embroidered on the sleeves in silk and gold thread, and shook it out, just in case she would have to dine with the upper nobility.

"I don't know what I'm doing here," she muttered as she worked. "Latin is of no use if I'm not near enough to overhear anyone. I can't be of any help to Astrolabe. I should be with my children."

She brushed at a spot of what looked like meat sauce, rubbing the thin wool almost through in her effort to erase it.

Absorbed with her thoughts, Catherine didn't hear the voice calling her until the door opened and Margaret rushed in.

"Catherine!" she exclaimed as she clung to her sister-in-law. "You have to help me. My grandfather wants to send me to be married in Carinthia!"

# Nine

The guest room at the convent of Saint-Pierre.
A few moments later.

*Ibi quidem coram orthodoxa praedicatione tua plebs*
*haeretica stare non poterat; eorum haeresiarches pertimuit,*
*nec apparere praesumpsit. Proinde placuit tibi super*
*haeresibus insurgentibus non aliquo scribere.*

Here the heretics could not stand before your orthodox
preaching. The leader of the heretics was afraid and did not
dare appear. Thus it pleased you to write no further about the
rebellious heretics.

Hugh, archbishop of Rouen, letter to Alberic, cardinal bishop
of Ostia, on their trip to Brittany to root out heresy, 1147

*M*argaret!" Catherine cried. "What are you doing here? My children! Something's happened! What is it?"

"No, no, they're fine." Margaret tried to calm her, even though she was in a state herself. "My grandfather brought me here. I thought it was just to meet people, but the countess and her brother want to marry me to one of their relatives in Carinthia! They think it's wonderful that I already speak German. I wish I'd never learned a word when we lived in Trier! They want me to go back with the Carinthian bishop. Catherine, you must tell them I can't go so far away from home!"

"Of course you can't," Catherine said feebly, trying to take it all in. "Edgar won't allow it, I'm sure. Now, wipe your eyes and tell me slowly what happened."

Margaret sniffed, pulled a handkerchief out of her sleeve and blew her nose. She looked around the room. Although there were a number of boxes and bags around the beds, she and Catherine were alone for now. She sat down on one of the boxes. Catherine sat next to her.

"Now first, tell me how my children are," she said. "Then I can concentrate on this marriage problem."

Margaret nodded, still trying to compose herself. "Both the children are fine. The nuns spoil them dreadfully, or would if Mother Heloise would allow it. James has decided he's in love with Sister Emily. He's even letting her teach him his letters!"

"Wonderful," Catherine said with a touch of envy. "I could never get him to sit still long enough."

"And Edana just plays and lets herself be hugged a lot," Margaret finished. "It's good, you know, for Samonie especially. She's needed a rest. I'm glad you let her stay at the Paraclete."

"There are plenty here who can help me dress," Catherine said. "Then I'm not missed at all?"

"Of course you are," Margaret said. "But James and Edana will survive just fine until you return. It should be soon, don't you think?"

"It will have to be," Catherine told her. "The council hasn't started yet and there are already food shortages. Now, how did you find yourself betrothed?"

"I don't know," Margaret sniffed again. "I had a lovely journey here. Bishop Henry was very kind to me and thought my German was amusing. Then, after we arrived last night, the countess and my grandfather told me that they thought I would be perfect for some relative of hers who is lord of a province or something in Carinthia. They seemed to think I would be thrilled."

Catherine gave her a look. "Did you tell them that you weren't?"

Margaret hung her head. "No, I was too stunned. I just thanked them for their thoughtfulness and went to bed. This morning Countess Mahaut greeted me as if it were all settled."

"Oh, Margaret!" Catherine wailed. "What did you expect? My dearest, you didn't need to throw a tantrum to let them know that the idea of going so far from home to marry a stranger terrifies you, but you have to at least say something. Count Thibault isn't a monster. He wouldn't marry you off against your will."

"I know, but how can I refuse when they tell me what a wonderful thing they've done for me?" Margaret tried to explain. "The count owes me nothing. Countess Mahaut has every reason to resent my existence. Yet they have both been so kind. How can I refuse?"

Catherine saw the problem. "It is generous of them to treat you as if your mother were a legitimate child of Count Thibault. But that doesn't mean you owe them obedience in this. Anyway, nothing can be decided without Edgar's approval. He is legally your guardian."

"I know," Margaret said. "But I thought that, since the count is so powerful, Edgar wouldn't have any say in the matter."

Catherine laughed. Margaret gave her an indignant stare.

"I'm sorry." Catherine managed to appear serious again. "But you should know your brother better than that. You know that look he gets, as if everyone opposing him is not only wrong but also beneath him?"

"Oh, yes," Margaret said. "I tell him he looks like a fishwife presented with week-old trout."

"That's the one." Catherine was relieved to feel Margaret relax. "Believe me, it wouldn't matter if the pope wanted you to marry. Edgar would still give him that look and refuse. He loves you too much and so do I."

Neither one of them mentioned Solomon.

"Now," Catherine said, "as long as you're here, will you have time to help me?"

"If Grandfather permits it, of course," Margaret answered. "Have you found out who killed the poor lady yet?"

"We don't even know if the murderer is in Reims," Catherine said sadly. "Annora never says anything, but I know she's disappointed in us."

"I know that your job was supposed to be to eavesdrop," Margaret said. "But that's ridiculous. You'd have to literally hang from the eaves around here to get close enough. There's no place to stand outside. Now that I've seen the crowds, I don't believe anyone could expect you to find one man among them all. Especially when you don't even know what he looks like."

"That's why I'm still in here," Catherine explained. "Feeling completely useless."

Margaret leaned her head on Catherine's shoulder.

"I'm glad you are," she sighed. "I needed to find you right away. If I hadn't, I might be on my way to Carinthia at this very moment."

"Although," Catherine said slowly, not listening to Margaret, "I should be able to narrow the search down somewhat. We are supposed to be looking for a Breton knight. Except, why would one of Count Henri's men be here? Just because a man was in Brittany doesn't mean he's Breton. Henri could have brought in men from anywhere. And I did see the clerics who are hunting for Astrolabe; we just don't know their names. They are clearly connected with this. There's a chance that they'll turn up here if they intend to be among those who accuse him."

"That's not much to go on," Margaret said.

"I know it all too well," Catherine sighed. "But Mother Heloise expects me to do something and I owe her too much not to try. I can't help feeling that there's something we've all missed. I just wish I knew what to do next."

Margaret suddenly sat up straighter, almost sending Catherine into the pillows.

"Samonie!" she exclaimed. "I almost forgot. She remembered something about the man looking for Astrolabe at Provins."

"What was it?" Catherine asked. "Anything might help."

Margaret spoke carefully, trying to recall the exact words. "Samonie said that she was told that the man said he was but an emissary for a powerful lord, someone who could raise an army to wipe out the heretics in our midst and that Abelard's son was an example of the worst of them."

Catherine gasped in anger. "How dare he spread rumors like that! Oh, the devil knows the best way to poison minds!"

"You don't think the cleric was really an agent of a lord?" Margaret asked.

"I can't think of one who would fit," Catherine said. "Abelard's enemies were not among the nobility. Still, we should keep it in mind. So far, all the threats against Astrolabe seem to come from shadows. If only we could grasp one long enough to find where it comes from."

She put her arm around Margaret again.

"Now, let us try to find a diplomatic way to tell your grandfather that you weren't meant to be a lady of Carinthia."

*"Forligeren feldelfen!"* John swore as he joined Astrolabe and Godfrey. He continued to swear as he sat at the narrow table and thumped his beer bowl on it to attract the notice of the

boy with the pitcher. "Saint Aldhelms's archaic assonance! Oh, excuse me," he added as he noticed that Gwenael was with them.

"Something wrong?" Astrolabe asked.

"King Stephen has forbidden the archbishop of Canterbury to attend the council," John fumed. "I have a friend who is one of his clerks, and I had counted on getting an introduction to the archbishop at least. Now I don't have a straw left to grasp."

"You want to go back to England to live?" Godfrey stared at him in astonishment. "You can't get a decent glass of wine in the whole country."

"The beer is good, though," John said. "And I'd take a position in the court of any bishop, even if it meant going to Spain."

"You still have recommendations from Peter of Celle, don't you?" Astrolabe asked. "Those should get you an audience with Abbot Bernard. If you can get a letter from him, you should have no problem. With all the bishops in Reims for the council, there must be one who is in need of a secretary."

"I don't know." John sat down, shaking his head. "For every bishop, I swear that there are ten office seekers. What *are* you drinking?"

"In a day or two it will be beer," Astrolabe told him as they both stared at the milky liquid in the bowl. "I didn't want to wait."

"With that philosophy you'll never survive in a monastery," John said.

"It hadn't occurred to me to join one," Astrolabe answered as the boy handed John the pitcher.

"Nor to me." John took it and poured himself a bowl of the new beer. "By the way, I heard that there is a large group traveling with the archbishop of Tours, including some who are in charge of your heretic friend."

Gwenael sat up straight at once, emerging from her hiding place between her two guards.

"Master Eon! Where are they keeping him?" she demanded.

"In chains in a storeroom near the archbishop's palace,"

John told her. "As you will be if you don't keep your voice down. Although I'll bet there are many who envy him his bed with the crowds in this town. He hasn't been harmed. What I've been told is that he's being used as bait for a far worse heretic."

He gave Astrolabe a long look over the rim of his bowl.

"They can't mean me," Astrolabe said.

John shrugged. "For all I know they are talking about the bishop of Dol. He seems to be the main enemy of the arch-bishop of Tours. But it's an odd group and not a lot of them Breton. They won't talk freely in front of me. We need a spy."

Astrolabe gave John a look.

"Are you thinking what I think you are?" he asked. "Mother would be furious if we put Catherine in danger."

"But Catherine said yesterday that she wanted to do more," John said.

"But what excuse could she have to stay long enough among the group from Tours to hear anything?" Astrolabe argued. "I won't have her doing kitchen maid's work in her condition. I'd rather go to the flames than face Edgar with that on my conscience."

John was momentarily stumped, then brightened.

"I have an idea," he said. "Let's at least ask her. Catherine has never failed us before."

"That's true," Astrolabe said. "But it was mostly because all we asked of her was a warm meal and a bed."

Canon Rolland had understood that he was the one in charge of finding the heretic. Hadn't he risked his life trying to capture Astrolabe before he could reach his mother's convent? Wasn't he prepared to repeat the story the soldier had told him, that Astrolabe had been seen with the heretic Eon? He was ready to make a public accusation so why were they still sneaking around the back streets of Reims?

He didn't like all this secrecy. He wanted to make his denunciation and return to Paris. But it was becoming more apparent to him that someone else was directing things through the person of his friend, the monk Arnulf. It was Arnulf who had told him that they couldn't enlist the help of the bishop of Paris, or of scholars like Master Peter the Lombard or Master Adam.

"Why not?" Rolland asked. "They both agree that Abelard was wrong in his understanding of the nature of the Holy Trinity. They would believe that his son had also fallen into error."

Arnulf sighed and shook his head. "This is not some quibble among philosophers about subtle distinctions. These Bretons and their friends would destroy all of Christendom and deliver us into the realm of Satan."

He said it so calmly that Rolland wasn't sure he understood the enormity of the statement.

"You can't mean those ragged peasants?" he asked. "Surely the danger is greater if the leaders of the church and the most brilliant philosophers are led astray. If the pope and the council are blinded by dazzling rhetoric to adopt heretical doctrine, that is what will destroy us. The Breton heretics are an annoyance, nothing more."

Arnulf gave him a hard stare. "I understood that you were with us," he said. "You were mocked by Peter Abelard and denied your rightful place among the masters, weren't you?"

"Yes, and most unjustly," Rolland insisted. "Just because I couldn't answer as quickly as some of the others. He was cruel and vicious in his rebuttals to my arguments. He made fun of my accent, yet he called himself Breton, too. But he was only clever, not right. You tell me that his wickedness lives on in his son, and that's all the more reason to make our knowledge public."

Arnulf rubbed his forehead. Privately he agreed with Abelard's assessment of Canon Rolland's intelligence. He forced himself to smile.

"If we denounce Astrolabe without naming his confederates, then we've accomplished nothing," he explained.

"How can we name them if we can't even locate him?" Rolland interrupted.

"Because he's bound to be there to defend this Eon fellow," Arnulf continued. "If he is, we can accuse him and add the murder of the woman to his crimes. If he daren't show his face at Eon's trial, then we can accuse him of the murder. That will bring his friends out to answer that charge. Then we shall have them all."

Rolland shook his head. It was true that he considered matters for a long time before he came to a conclusion. But it meant he was careful, not stupid. He would have to study this plan. But it felt flawed. He didn't like it. After all these years, he wanted to be sure of his revenge.

Catherine had sadly realized that she was doomed to spend this journey associating with the nobility. She wished it weren't the case. She never felt comfortable with people who had their own armies.

"I swear, if I had known what was before me I'd have gone to Spain with Solomon and left Edgar with the children," she told Margaret as she dressed to greet the count and countess of Champagne. "Your brother would know how to treat your grandfather so that you would be saved from the marriage and still not anger them."

"That's not true, Catherine," Margaret assured her. "You won't threaten them. Edgar would. Do you really need the belt? The keys and purse will thump against your stomach."

"That's all right," Catherine said. "It will serve the little fiend right, considering how much he's been thumping me. Can you lace up my shoes for me? I don't know where the maid has gone. I don't think she likes serving me and the lady Annora, too."

Margaret obligingly knelt and threaded the laces through the leather loops. She noted with concern that Catherine's feet were swollen again. This wasn't something she knew much about, but Samonie had impressed her with the notion that Catherine should not be allowed to stand for long.

"Are you sure you want to come down with me?" she asked.

Catherine was about to tell the truth, then she saw Margaret's expression.

"Of course I do," she said. "I'm going mad trapped in this little room all day. And it's not as if I hadn't met the count before."

As they left the room, Catherine noted with surprise that a guard had been posted at the bottom of the stairs. Was it for their protection?

"I really don't see any need to have armed men in a convent guest house," she muttered to Margaret.

The guard stepped forward, his hand held up to stop them. The torchlight shone on his face.

"Astrolabe?" Catherine immediately looked around to see if anyone had heard her. She lowered her voice. "What are you doing here?"

"Making sure you don't get into any trouble," Astrolabe said. "Margaret? What are you doing here? I thought we'd left you with my mother. Is everything all right?"

"Yes, except I don't want to go live in Carinthia," Margaret answered.

"Nor would I," Astrolabe admitted, looking puzzled. He turned to Catherine. "I've been talking with John. We have a plan and need your help, but I don't know if you'll like it."

"Do I have to wear tight sleeves and shoes and stand a lot?" Catherine asked.

"Neither of those."

"I like it already," she said. "What do you want me to do?"

Astrolabe grimaced, then bent down to whisper in her ear.

"Beg in the street outside the house of the bishop of Tours."

Catherine did not have time to react before she was ushered into the presence of Countess Mahaut, Count Thibault and his niece, the abbess Marie of Saint-Sulpice.

She tripped on the fresh rushes on the floor and would have landed on her nose if Margaret hadn't steadied her.

"My dear!" Countess Mahaut cried. "Geoffrey," she signaled the page. "Get a chair for the lady at once! Are you all right?"

Catherine felt her face flame. "I am quite well, my lady countess, thank you," she said. "I'm grateful to you for bringing my sister-in-law to join me. She has told me how much she enjoyed the journey in your company."

Catherine allowed the page to seat her at one side of a long table set up for all the guests. Now that she had managed to be sure all eyes were on her, she was grateful to be ignored for a while.

Astrolabe came and stood at attention behind her. He handed her the scarf she had dropped.

"Did you really slip, or did you do it on purpose to keep anyone from noticing me?" he asked.

"I'll never tell," she answered.

Margaret was seated much farther up the table than Catherine. This was to be expected, but it left Catherine with no one she knew to speak to. At first she felt uncomfortable sharing her trencher with a stranger, but the young man seemed so intent on catching the eye of the woman across from him that she soon realized that he was paying no attention to the food. So she concentrated on getting out as many of the chunks of fish that she could find. If only this were a meat night! Catherine craved red meat and the count's table was one place she might get it.

In the meantime, she studied the people at the table across from her. Of course there were a number of clerics, given the nature of the council and the fact that Count Thibault was paying for the food. She had no trouble spotting Bishop Henry of Troyes, seated next to his sister. Margaret was at his right. She was eating little. Catherine wondered if she could hide away a few crusts in her sleeve so that Margaret could have something when her appetite returned.

At the count's right was Abbess Marie. Mother Heloise had said that she was a highly effective abbess. Henri of Tréguier would have had no luck if he had tried to rob Saint-Sulpice of a few nuns. It was good that she was taking an interest. There were still women at Sainte-Croix who needed rescuing.

There were a number of bishops in attendance and at least one cardinal. Catherine was glad she hadn't had the task of assigning their seating. According to John, the primary reason many of them were in Reims, apart from the pope's order, was to establish their own primacy over other bishops or to defend it against one of the other bishops. The determination of the bishop of Dol not to submit to the archbishop of Tours was not unusual.

It seemed forever before the trenchers were cleared and the washing bowls brought round. Then the entertainment began, a rather lugubrious minstrel intoning the martyrdom of Saint Ursula. Despite having rinsed her fingers and wiped her face, Catherine felt greasy, overly hot and sleepy from the strong wine. It was unfortunate that this was the time that the man beside her should remember his manners.

"Good evening," he smiled at her. "I'm Gui of Valfonciere. It's near Rouen, do you know it?"

"My father was born in Rouen," Catherine answered, trying not to stare at the blob of fish sauce on his chin. "But I have never been there. I live in Paris."

"All the time?" Gui seemed puzzled. "Your family holds land that near the city?"

"As far as I know," Catherine said, "the only land we have is that on which our house sits."

Gui squinted at her over his wine cup. "Then why are you here?" he asked.

A wickedness seized Catherine.

"To eat dinner," she answered. "And you?"

Gui blinked a few times. "I owe service to the duke of Normandy and to the archbishop of Rouen. Archbishop Hugh ordered me to come with him," he answered. "That's him, over there, next to Lady Annora."

"Oh, you know her?" Catherine asked.

"Of course. She's my cousin," Gui answered. "But then, almost everyone is, aren't they?"

He leaned closer to her.

"Are you my cousin?"

Catherine leaned away. "I doubt it," she told him.

Gui shook his head. "Then I don't understand why you are here."

Teasing someone far gone into his cups was losing its appeal. Catherine wished the nobility would rise so that she could leave.

"I am in the party of the countess of Flanders," she told Gui. "She was kind enough to invite me to eat here tonight."

Gui clonked his cup on the table.

"But then you must be someone," he insisted. "Everyone here is important, or a cousin."

"Sorry," Catherine said. "I'm very sure I'm not either."

Finally, Count Thibault stood, signaling that the guests might leave. Catherine knew that she still had to wait awhile before her turn came.

Gui rose when Archbishop Hugh prepared to leave.

"Umm," he looked at Catherine. "Annora doesn't seem to have noticed me. You won't tell her I was here, will you?"

"If you don't wish it, then I won't," Catherine answered. "But why not?"

"Oh, you know how families are," he said. "My father, her father, words spoken in anger, a matter of land donated without permission. That sort of thing. We aren't speaking at the moment."

"Perhaps you could make it your job to mend things between you," Catherine suggested.

"Not with the dragon of Flanders guarding her." Gui stopped, all color draining from his face. "I didn't say that. Yes, my lord. I'm coming at once."

He hurried away.

Catherine was relieved to be done with him. At the moment, all she wanted was to get back upstairs and into bed, even though she knew the room would be crowded with women, most of whom would not be ready to sleep.

Margaret and Annora were by her side as she walked slowly toward the stairs.

"Are you well, Catherine?" Annora asked. "You seem tired."

"I'm fine, thank you," Catherine answered. "The dinner was excellent. The singer was a bit too slow for my taste, that's all."

"You can't expect anything lively in Lent with bishops underfoot," Margaret commented. "At least you didn't have to sit at the high table with everyone looking at you."

"That's true," Catherine admitted. "Which reminds me, I have some sweets for you. I saw how little you ate."

Margaret said nothing but squeezed Catherine's hand.

"I've been given permission to stay with you, if there's room in the bed," she said.

"We'll make room, won't we?" Annora smiled at Margaret.

Catherine stared at her. "Thank you, Annora," she said. "I hope we won't be too cramped."

"It will be nice," the woman answered. "Like when I was a child and my sister . . . my sister and I and our friends would all be put in a featherbed and have to signal when we should roll over together."

Catherine smiled. "Yes, my sister and I used to do the same."

"I wish I had a sister," Margaret sighed. "Not that some of my brothers aren't nice but . . ."

"It's different." Annora finished. "I miss her terribly, you know. Even though I didn't think I'd ever see Cecile again once she entered Saint-Georges, I still knew she was there if I needed her. It's lonely now."

Catherine opened her mouth to mention Gui but remembered his warning. It did seem that Annora had deliberately ignored him at dinner. Still, she was sure he was wrong. Annora would probably be delighted to forget old feuds just to have family around.

Or perhaps it was just that she was missing her own family so much.

Where was Edgar now?

Edgar swore silently at the man across the room, who was snoring loudly enough to rattle bits of thatch down from the roof. He couldn't believe that anyone else was asleep. Yet no one was throwing anything at the snorer. Edgar stuck his fingers in his ears and tried praying that the man would strangle on his own tongue.

But it wasn't just the noise that was keeping him awake. For several days now, Edgar had felt uneasy about Catherine. There was something he should have told her, something he had seen or heard that wasn't right. But he couldn't remember what. He told himself that it was just his worry and guilt at leaving her with another baby coming, but the disquiet wouldn't be quelled.

The next day on the road, just north of Toulouse, he finally admitted his concerns to Solomon. Edgar wasn't surprised at the reaction.

"You're not getting out of this," Solomon said. "Catherine and all the children are safe at the Paraclete. Heloise is not going to let anything happen to them."

"I know that," Edgar snapped. "It doesn't change the feeling. There's something wrong. I know it."

Solomon gave him a sidelong glance.

"You aren't getting like your Uncle Æthelræd, are you?" he asked. "It made my flesh creep the way he could see what was happening miles away. You start in with visions and I might send you home."

Edgar had to laugh at his nervousness.

"No chance of that!" he chuckled. "You're more likely to start having visions than I am."

They rode on for a few moments in silence. The path was steep and slick with spring rain. The horses had to be guided carefully over loose scree. From the woods on their left came a sound of scrabbling. For a moment, everyone froze, hands to swords. Then one of the men whistled and a dog appeared, a fresh rabbit in its mouth. They all relaxed.

"But I know there's something," Edgar continued, "something that wasn't right."

Solomon rolled his eyes.

"I know you," he sighed. "You're going to gnaw on this just like that dog and get far less pleasure. If you ever come up with something, you can tell me. Until then, keep it to yourself. It's nothing to do with me."

Edgar shifted in the saddle. He hadn't ridden so much in years.

"But I think it is," he insisted. "You know it, too. Damn! It's right at the edge of my mind. Think. Our journey to the Paraclete. What happened?"

"You nearly tore the town of Nogent apart looking for your

family." Solomon was tiring of the game. "Perhaps you noticed something odd there."

"Perhaps." Edgar lapsed back into brooding.

After a moment, Solomon moved forward in the line to talk with his friend Isaac of Troyes. Edgar alone was not a stimulating companion.

Catherine woke up the next morning to discover that the bed had not been big enough to hold Margaret, too. The girl was curled up on the floor in Catherine's cloak. As Catherine leaned over the edge of the bed, Margaret opened her eyes and smiled.

"The narrow cots of the convent are looking more appealing," she said. "Although they are cold. Are you going to talk to my grandfather today?"

Catherine nodded and stepped over her, then wove around all the luggage to reach the curtained corner where the chamber pot resided.

"Oh, excuse me!" she said to the woman squatting before her.

"You'd better find another," she warned Catherine. "I've got a dreadful constipation."

There was a rustling around the room as several of the women dove for their medicine chests.

"Olive oil and dust from the tomb of Saint Martin," Annora called from the bed. "My mother swore by it. I know I have a vial here someplace."

There were various other suggestions from around the room, but the one most welcome to Catherine was the location of another chamber pot.

She returned to find that most of the women were now out of bed. The bedding and the portable beds had been folded up against the wall so that there would be space for everyone to dress.

"What have you come to plead for?" one woman asked her. "It must be serious to travel now in your condition."

"It's a matter of duty," Catherine answered.

The woman nodded and didn't press her. Everyone understood duty, especially to family or one's lord.

"I'm here with the countess of Nevers," she said. "Now that her sons have gone with the king and Count William has become a Carthusian, the governance of the county has been laid on her."

Catherine blinked. This last was news to her. She had only met Count William once, and her opinion of him was that he was a wicked, impious philanderer. How amazing that he should decide to end his days at one of the strictest monastic houses. Or perhaps not. The depth of his sins would require some serious repentance.

Annora told of Countess Sybil's problems with Baldwin of Hainaut. Others added their stories.

"Abbot Bernard, when he preached this pilgrimage, said that it was a chance for even murderers and blasphemers to find salvation," one woman sighed. "But it seems to me that only the best men went to the Holy Land and the worst were left behind for the rest of us to cope with."

Catherine listened without making any comment. She realized that, in this room, she was learning more about the situation throughout Christendom than would ever be presented at the council. These women were the ones who had been left with the responsibilities of their fathers, brothers and husbands added to their own. Many were traveling with countesses and vicountesses who were bringing charges against other nobles and also church officials who had appropriated rights. They were well informed about the situation in their lands.

No one said a word about heretics.

# Ten

Near the portico of the church of Saint-Symphorian, not far from the cathedral of Notre-Dame, Reims. Saturday, 13 kalends April (March 20), 1148. Feast of Saint Marcellinus, orthodox Christian martyred at Carthage by heretics.

*Ad ipsos spectat eleemosynarum largitio, quorum est terrena possessio, vel quibus credita est rerum eclesiasticarum dispensatio. . . . Quicquid habent pauperum est, viduarum et orphanorum, et eorum qui altario deserviunt, ut de altario vivant.*

The distribution of alms is the duty of those who possess earthly wealth or those charged with dispensing the goods of the church. . . . Whatever they have belongs rightfully to the poor, to widows and orphans and to those who serve at the altar and thus deserve to live from the altar.

Aelred of Rievaulx, *De Institutione Inclusaum*

*C*atherine bent her head, letting the snarled curls dangle over her face. She stretched out her bare feet. They were filthy with street debris. John had obligingly rubbed muck on them, adding a few splotches to her face for good measure.

"It might help if you had some sores or bruises," he mused. "And a lady's hands are always better cared for than a beggar's. I don't know if this will work."

"Look at my hands, John," Catherine held them up. "I'm not a grand lady. I scrub and prepare food. I'm scarred from slips of the knife and spatters from the pans."

"You don't take care of your nails, either," John commented as he examined her hands. "Amazing! You could pass as a beggar after all."

"Thank you, I think." Catherine bit at a ragged cuticle, adding defensively, "I have a goose grease and rose petal salve for my skin but I never have time to use it."

"You should make the time," John said. "You don't need to do all that work. I don't understand why you don't have more servants. Edgar never struck me as a miser."

"We like keeping our household small," Catherine answered. "Now, am I ragged enough?"

John surveyed her critically. "Yes," he said slowly, "but there's still something wrong. What do the rest of you think?"

Catherine turned to present herself to Astrolabe, Godfrey and Gwenael, who had advised them on where to get worn clothes.

"She looks disreputable enough to me," Godfrey said.

"Do you think her hair is too clean?" Astrolabe asked.

"It's not her hair." Gwenael spoke so softly that the others couldn't make out what she had said.

"Speak up, Gwenael," John said. "On this subject, you are the expert."

"Master John!" Godfrey admonished him.

"I didn't mean it like that," John tried to explain. "Haven't I myself been a beggar at the doors of my friends? It's only through their goodness that I haven't joined the troop at the church door. Gwenael, if you think that Catherine is still not able to appear in need of charity, then please tell us."

Gwenael pursed her lips. "She's grubby enough, I'll give you," she said. "It's not that. But I don't know. The way you sit, my lady, it's too straight, too confident. You don't look as if anyone has ever kicked you or beat you with a stick. You haven't been so hungry that you would eat scraps left for the pigs or boil acorns for soup. Your hands are rough, but your face hasn't been out in all weather. You haven't bent your back in the field for days on end just to lose the crop to a storm or a battle. Your eyes, they still have hope in them."

"Oh." Catherine had no answer for that. Her life had been hard enough, but there had always been love in it and a measure of security. Even when she had been lost in England with baby James and no understanding of the language, she had still known that somewhere she had a home and people who loved her and could afford to feed her. How dare she think she could pretend to be truly in need? Her shoulders drooped.

"You make me ashamed of even attempting such a ruse," she told Gwenael. "I'm sorry."

"There!" Gwenael said. "It's a bit like that. Despair is what you were missing. If you could add some humility and fear, then you'd have it. I know, let me go with you. I won't speak, then no one will note my Breton accent. But I can remind you if you sit up straight or look people in the eyes."

"You're not supposed to look at donors? All these years I've been giving alms and I never noticed that the paupers didn't look at me," Catherine said. "Are you sure?"

"Yes," Gwenael said firmly. "You look at the ground as if about to kiss their feet and mutter, 'Blessings on you, good lady. May the saints guide and keep you,' or something equally grateful. But you never dare to meet their eyes."

"I don't think that this was what Our Lord had in mind when He told us to remember the poor," John said. His clerical garb seemed suddenly constricting.

"That is a difference between us as well," Gwenael added. "I would never assume to know what Our Lord meant. *My* Lord Eon shared with us equally. He made us all feel that we were the same, not only in the eyes of Heaven, but in his eyes as well. They say that Jesus did the same. Is it any wonder I believe Eon to be Our Savior come again?"

John's jaw fell. "Are you sure you are not a theologian?" he asked.

Gwenael drew herself up indignantly. "Of course not. I'm a good Christian!"

"John, we're straying from the matter at hand," Astrolabe observed. "Catherine, will you feel better if Gwenael accompanies you?"

"I confess I would," Catherine said. "I'm very much afraid of being accused of taking alms falsely. I don't think I could bear the shame of it, and how could I explain?"

Astrolabe grimaced. "This was a bad idea from the start," he said. "I don't believe that the possible gains are greater than the risk. What are the chances that you'll hear anything that will be of use to us?"

"It's all we have right now," Catherine answered. "I'm willing, just nervous. Gwenael will keep me from doing anything stupid."

"I will at least try, my lady," Gwenael said. "We should start at the church, where we won't be noticed in the throng. If that works, then we can move to the door of the house of the bishop of Tours."

"Good enough." Catherine stood, putting a hand to her aching back. "Now, if you men will leave, we'll see if we can find a place at the church portico, in the shadows."

*Where I shall pray that no one from the dinner last night recognizes me,* she added to herself, imagining the expression of her trencher mate, Gui, if he should see her in this state.

"We won't be far, if you need us," John said. "I'll keep you in sight every minute."

Margaret had been fetched early that morning by a servant of Countess Mahaut. Fortified by her conversation with Catherine, she had made up her mind to tell the countess that she declined the kind offer to be married. Her resolve lasted all the way to the house where the lords of Champagne were staying.

"Good morning, my child!" Mahaut kissed her. "My brother and I are so delighted that you will be joining our family. We have much to discuss. I want to provide you with an appropriate wardrobe as my wedding gift. You must come with me to my fair at Provins. There are always drapers there with wonderful cloth."

"You are too kind to me, my lady," Margaret pleaded.

"Of course not!" Countess Mahaut smiled at her fondly. "You're a dear child who deserves a secure future. And, of course, this will help cement the alliance between Champagne and Carinthia for another generation. Consider how pleased your grandfather is."

"Of course." Margaret bent her head humbly and fought back tears. "But don't you think I should wait until my brother returns from Spain?"

"Oh, no," Mahaut replied. "That could be months! You want to be settled in before the winter."

The winter! Margaret's heart froze at the thought. Oh, why wasn't she strong enough to let the countess know how she felt?

"Now, my dear," Mahaut continued, "I am going to Mass at Saint-Symphorian. Would you care to come with me? After that I shall introduce you to some of our friends."

"Thank you; I would be honored," Margaret answered faintly.

She trailed after the countess and her court, feeling totally furious with herself. Catherine would be so ashamed of her!

"*Avoi!* Yes, you two *jaels*," the man at the church shouted. "Get away. This is our spot. You want to beg, go somewhere else."

The man's legs were withered and his back twisted. His friend, a boy of about fifteen with a vacant smile, pulled him from one spot to another on a small plank, fitted with crude wooden wheels. Catherine's first impulse was to leave a coin. The second was to slap the man for referring to her as a whore.

Gwenael did neither. She sat on the step next to him and took his hand.

"Good friend," she said gently. "We are not women of the streets but wives of men taken for the king's army. We were left with no way to earn our food but dishonor, and my friend is in no state even to do that. Please let us stay near you, for we are alone and frightened in this city. We are here only because our need is desperate."

"No more than anyone else's," the man grunted. "And what are you doing so far from Brittany, woman? Can't you find alms in the city of Nantes?"

"We've come here to throw ourselves on the mercy of the bishop," Gwenael improvised. "He wouldn't see us at home, but how could he refuse to help us with all his fellow clerics watching?"

Catherine gave a moan that was not entirely faked. Her legs were aching again. She sat on the other side of the man.

"Please?" she asked.

For the first time in her life, she looked straight into the eyes of a beggar.

He blinked first. Perhaps it was the contrast of her deep blue eyes in her thin, pale face and the black hair against her cheeks. Catherine had early learned that her eyes were more eloquent than she was.

"Very well," he muttered. "But you must share what you receive. They'll give me less with you here."

"Thank you, kind good man," Gwenael answered before Catherine could offer to give him all their alms. "We only need enough for bread."

"You'd do better at the convent, then," the man told them. "They give bread away each morning. The coins you get won't go far. Prices are doubling every day the pope and his troop remain in Reims."

Gwenael and the man settled down for a chat about the vagaries of the nobles. With him, she wasn't at all tongue-tied, and soon they were both laughing over a story the man told about a miller in his village, the blacksmith's daughter and a hot horseshoe.

Catherine minded her orders to not look around, so she smiled at the boy who was sitting on the ground digging holes in the soft earth with his fingers. He smiled back.

"What are you doing?" she ventured.

The boy smiled again.

"You'll get nothing from him," the man told her. "He can't speak, nor understand much. But he's a good boy. We get on well together."

Catherine nodded with discomfiture and left the boy to his amusement. Other beggars had arrived at the church, and they too seemed to have their own places and pecking orders. There was some conversation, then they settled into position at their own stations.

"No talking among ourselves, now," the man warned Catherine and Gwenael. "You'll get nothing if you don't pay attention to the grand folks alone. They see us whispering and such and they'll start thinking we're plotting something."

"Oh, surely not!" Catherine said.

Gwenael hushed her with a look.

"Remember, you'll have to do the talking to the lords, my lady," she hissed in Catherine's ear. "Hunch over more, hide your face. If you can't do it, now's the time to say. People are coming for Mass. Those who attend on Saturday are good pickings."

Catherine swallowed. "I can do it."

She held out her hand as a woman and her retinue approached the church portico.

"Alms, good lady," she quavered. "For the love of Christ, help us, please."

The other beggars added their chants to the litany: "Food for my child." "Mercy, please. Enough for an ointment to ease my pain." "For the love of God, the Blessed Virgin, the holy saints, help me!"

It was easy to keep her head down. Catherine had never been so mortified in her life. Every few moments a coin was placed in her hand. She mumbled thanks and handed it to Gwenael. So far she had heard very little Latin. That wasn't surprising. The clergy would all hear Mass in the abbey churches or their rented homes. This was merely a test. She did catch a number of other interesting snatches of conversation. People talked over her head as if she were one of the stone carvings on the tympanum.

"With your coloring, a pale green would be nice for the wedding, don't you think?" the voice was familiar but Catherine couldn't place it. "Here, child, one should never forget the poor at our gates."

A coin was placed in her hand.

"May the saints bless you," Catherine began.

Then she heard a gasp. Catherine ventured a peek around her hair.

Margaret was looking down on her in horror.

"Go. Say nothing," Catherine mouthed, pulling her scarf farther down over her face.

"Margaret?" The countess sounded worried. "Did that woman say something improper to you?"

"Oh, no, my lady," Margaret answered. "I was only startled by her face."

"Not a leper is she?" the countess asked quickly. "They know they aren't allowed here."

"No," Margaret said. "A fire, I think. Horrible."

Their voices were lost as they entered the church.

For the next few moments Catherine didn't have to pretend palsy. Her hands were shaking and her heart thumping. She should have told Margaret what they were planning, but there hadn't been time. Thank the saints that Margaret had been so quick-witted.

As the Mass began, the crowds thinned so Catherine and Gwenael made their way back to where Astrolabe and Godfrey were waiting for them.

"I need to wash," Catherine said shortly.

Astrolabe took off his helmet and hurried to the nearest well.

"We did very well." Gwenael showed Godfrey that handful of silver pieces they had received.

Godfrey looked at them wistfully. "I don't suppose we could take a few for some wine and real meat?"

Catherine had slumped onto a bench set into the wall. She looked so pitiful that a passing monk started to come over to her and ask if he could help. She sat up straight at once.

"Absolutely not!" she said.

The monk, startled, backed away, then turned and hurried down the street.

Godfrey grimaced. "It was only a jest, my lady. I know it would be theft."

"It is theft," Catherine said. "I'll not feel clean until we see that it goes to those who really need it."

Astrolabe soon returned with cold water. Catherine pulled a rag out of her sleeve and tried to rub off the dirt.

"It's just smearing," Astrolabe said. "We should find a bathhouse."

"It's Saturday," Catherine said. "The bathhouses will be full. Even the pope wouldn't get in unless he'd reserved a tub. No, let me change back into my own clothes. I'll return to the convent. They'll have soap and hot water. I can tell them I fell down. They won't find that hard to believe."

"So you don't want to try doing this again?" Astrolabe asked.

"I didn't say that," Catherine snapped. "Tomorrow afternoon, the council will open. All the bishops and their retinues will be present. I'll do better this time, and that will be our chance to catch careless talk. Gwenael, will you accompany me to the convent?"

"I'll take you," Astrolabe offered.

"No, I need to find a place to change on the way and I'll need help."

"Catherine . . ." Astrolabe began.

Gwenael put her hand on his arm. "Not now, my lord. Perhaps you could come by this afternoon. She'll be better then."

She took the bundle that held Catherine's clothes. Leaving the men, they made their way to a shed near the city walls where Gwenael kept watch while Catherine put on her *chainse* and then the linen *bliaut* embroidered in silk. Gwenael helped her lace up the sleeves and adjust the silver ring that kept her scarf in place. Catherine rubbed her face with her sleeve, leaving marks on the linen.

"I suppose I must put on the hose and shoes again," she said.

"I'm afraid so." Gwenael helped her into them.

They wrapped up the begging clothes and set out again. This time Gwenael walked a step behind, as befitted a servant.

Catherine was unnaturally silent. The morning's experience had given her a lot to think about.

Astrolabe turned to Godfrey.

"This was a big mistake," he said.

Godfrey shrugged. "It may have been more than she expected, but she's willing to do it for you. Be grateful."

"For my mother, really," Astrolabe said. "There must be another way to find out who wants to destroy me."

"So name it."

Astrolabe shook his head. "Let's go find John. He may have learned something."

Godfrey brightened. "A good idea. I have a terrible thirst."

Canon Rolland stood in the back of the chapel where the bishop of Paris was saying Mass. It wasn't fair. He should have been the one to assist. He had been in the service of the bishop longer than any of the men up there at the altar, parading around as if they were the holy apostles!

It had always been so. His life had been one of minor achievements with the grand ones always out of reach. It was Abelard's fault. He had been the butt of so many of the master's barbs that the other students had also seen him as a fool. Now those men were bishops themselves. Hell, even Pope Eugenius wasn't ashamed to admit that he had learned from Peter Abelard. What chance did *Rollandus obtusus* have?

Look at Maurice there, Rolland continued fuming. A nobody from Sully, with dirt under his toenails. But now he wore fine leather shoes and silk robes and was allowed to carry the paten.

It really wasn't fair.

Rolland bowed his head and struck his breast as the host was raised. He stayed back, though, as the others went up for communion. He couldn't receive the sacrament with such hate in his heart. He fervently hoped that Abelard was even now burning in Hell and that his son would soon join him there, via the flames of the heretic's pyre.

The thought cheered him.

As he left the chapel, he was spotted by the monk Arnulf, who sidled up to him.

"Have you spotted the heretic yet?" he whispered.

"No, and I don't believe he had the courage to be here," Rolland answered. "He's probably halfway to Spain by now."

"That doesn't mean you can't accuse him," Arnulf said.

"A fine fool I'd look if I did," Rolland snorted, "without anyone to corroborate the story. What happened to your witnesses?"

"You mustn't lose faith!" Arnulf pleaded. "They'll be here. I know that once we bring Eon up before the council, Astrolabe will be there to defend him. We must continue to gather information on this band of heretics and those who are even more dangerous. I'm sure that Astrolabe is really a follower of Henry of Lausanne or even a secret Manichee. If we can just get him up for questioning, I know we can make him confess not only his part in keeping the Eonites free for so long but also his involvement in the other heresies that threaten to tear the church apart."

Rolland envisioned the scene. It warmed him all over.

"Then everyone will have to admit I was right," he said.

"And give you the preferment you deserve," Arnulf said. "You'll be an archdeacon before you know it."

"Perhaps." Rolland dragged himself from his cloud of future glory. "But of course that is secondary to preserving orthodoxy."

"Oh, of course," Arnulf said. "Now, I was at Saint-Symphorian this morning and I'm sure I saw one of the Eonite women begging on the steps."

"Never!" Rolland exclaimed. "She wouldn't have the gall. How did you know her?"

Arnulf rubbed his forehead. The gesture was becoming habitual during his conversations with the canon.

"I saw her before, in Tours," he explained, "at the edge of the crowd when Eon was brought in. She was wearing the same patched clothes as the rest of them. A wonder no one else noticed. I should have denounced her then. She looked so pitiful that I presumed she was harmless. A grave error, I fear."

They had left the bishop's house now and were heading toward the cathedral, where ropes were being strung to keep back those who had no business with the council. No one was quite sure how many bishops and abbots were in attendance, but it was certain that the cathedral would never hold all of the people who wanted in. Rolland knew which side he would be expected to stay on. Places inside were for important laymen and the upper clergy. His hands clenched.

He looked across the parvis at the men who had just emerged from the cathedral.

"Saint Genevieve's shorn tresses!" he breathed. "It's Abbot Bernard and the pope!"

He watched them pass through the crowd, envious of those who spoke to them without fear. Arnulf noticed his wistful look.

"If you do your work well," he told the canon, "you will be the one they honor."

"Yes." Rolland returned to his cloud. "I will."


"Catherine, what were you doing?" Margaret pulled her aside as soon as she entered the room.

"Trying to get information that will save Astrolabe," Catherine answered. "What was Countess Mahaut saying about a wedding robe? I thought you were going to tell her you wouldn't go to Carinthia."

"I couldn't." Margaret hung her head. "I needed you there with me instead of taking alms under false pretenses. Catherine, how could you?"

"Well," Catherine answered wearily, "they told me I wouldn't have to wear shoes."

Margaret gave her a look of disgust. "You can't get away with an answer like that. What do you think my brother would say?"

Catherine grabbed Margaret's arm. "If you don't promise now that he'll never learn of this, I swear I'll let you go off into the wilds of Carinthia."

"Catherine?" Margaret wilted before her anger.

"Oh, Margaret, I'm sorry." Catherine took the girl in her arms. "You don't know what a morning I've had. I'm so ashamed. I would die if anyone knew about this, especially Edgar."

"I would think so," Margaret said. "You still have mud on your face, you know. Let me help you get it off."

"I told the sisters that I'd slipped in the street," Catherine said as Margaret wiped. "They were most concerned."

"As they should be," Margaret said. "There's another dinner tonight, by the way. Countess Sybil is entertaining my grandfather. I believe that you and Annora are expected to attend."

"Sweet Virgin's milk!" Catherine exclaimed. "This is worse than Paris. I thought that at a council everyone would be praying or something."

"Even I know that this is where the fate of whole countries is determined," Margaret said. "I never learned much from my own father, except to stay out of his way, but one thing I'm clear on is that everything in life, religious or lay, comes down to power, and this is where it's decided who wields it."

Catherine looked at her in astonishment. "You have grown up, haven't you? Perhaps you should consider this marriage. You'd make a good countess or whatever it is they have there."

"No, I wouldn't," Margaret answered decidedly. "Now, will you promise to dress decently and be at the dinner tonight to support me in my decision?"

"I will, if you'll help me set up one of these beds so that I can have a nap first," Catherine answered.

She lay down but didn't get any sleep. Between her own thoughts and the women coming in and out of the room, there wasn't much chance of repose. But at least she had her feet up and the baby only kicked now and then to reassure her that it was still alive.

She closed her eyes. There was just too much to worry about. Catherine knew that her first responsibility was to help Astrolabe. She agreed that the clerics would be more likely to talk unguardedly around her, but there must be a better way to find them. The idea of pretending to be a beggar had sounded exciting. Now she knew better.

And try as she might, the concerns of her own family worried her more than those of Astrolabe and Annora. Were James and Edana really doing well at the Paraclete? And if so, why? She missed them horribly. How could they be happy without her? Then there was Margaret. Poor dear. Was nothing in her life ever to be easy? Of course she wasn't going to be packed off to a foreign country like a shipment of spices. But how could they prevent it without alienating the count and countess of Champagne? Their patronage was essential to continued trade. Her family had always received privileges and freedom from tolls within the county and at the fairs. The loss would be devastating for the family finances.

These thoughts tumbled about in her mind as she dozed, becoming blended and confused. She finally awoke with the vague feeling that Annora was to be married in Carinthia, Astrolabe lose his trading privileges and she and Edgar about to be burnt as heretics.

It was not a restful afternoon. But, in that space between sleep and reality, Catherine had an idea.

John had been easy to locate. The tavern had been staked out by the few English clerics whom King Stephen had permitted to attend the council. Astrolabe and Godfrey found him at a round table in the corner chattering away happily in his native language. He broke off the conversation when he saw them.

"How did she do?" he asked, sliding into French effortlessly. "I thought that I should leave when I saw them start back to you."

"A total of six silver pennies," Godfrey said. "I didn't know how well beggars were done by."

"I didn't mean that," John said. "Did she learn anything?"

"Only that a lot of people have been driven from their villages by the famine and that abandoned wives are common," Astrolabe answered, giving him the money. "Can you see that this gets to those in need?"

"Of course." John put the coins in his purse. "So it's no use to try again?"

"Lady Catherine is willing," Godfrey forestalled Astrolabe's objection.

"So she says," Astrolabe admitted. "I wish there were another way. Have you learned anything?"

John shook his head. "That in itself is strange. There's a great deal of discussion about the heretic the archbishop of Tours has brought in but nothing about a woman being murdered. That doesn't make sense. You're quite certain she was dead?"

"John, no one survives a slit throat like that," Astrolabe said with a shudder. "She was cold and drained of blood. I know. Half of it was on me."

He closed his eyes, trying to remember Cecile as she had been in life, not when he had last touched her.

John pretended not to notice Astrolabe's emotion.

"I wonder why you weren't killed, too," he commented.

"I don't know," Astrolabe said, forcing himself to remember less sharply. "I presume the murderer was interrupted or felt that only Cecile was a danger to him."

"It only takes a second to cut the throat of a man already unconscious," Godfrey observed. "And he couldn't be sure that you hadn't seen him as well when Cecile recognized him."

Astrolabe felt his neck. It seemed undamaged. The talk had given him a frisson as if cold steel were tickling him just below his ear.

"Do you think I should worry about being attacked?" he asked.

"Always," Godfrey answered. "But especially now. Someone killed your friend to protect himself. If you are seen as a threat, then what would stop him doing it again?"

The shiver at Astrolabe's neck ran down his spine. He shook himself to expel it.

John put his arm on his friend's shoulder. "We'll find him, Peter. Whatever this monster is planning, whoever is helping him, we won't let him do any more harm."

It was only bravado, but the words gave Astrolabe some comfort.

Another dinner. Huge amounts of food on platters. Heapings of spices that were even more expensive because of the wars. Wine only slightly diluted with water. And all in the middle of Lent.

Catherine sighed. She ate all the meat put before her, reminding herself that it was for the baby, but she had to force herself to finish. Even though she knew that the remains of the meal would be given to the poor, even now lining up at the gate, it seemed obscene to have so much. She felt in the trencher to see if there were any bits of lamb left. Then she realized that her bread partner had eaten nothing.

"Annora," she said, "you should have stopped me. Please, get the page to bring you more."

"I'm not hungry, Catherine." Annora smiled. "I have only myself to feed. You take what you want."

"I feel such a glutton." Catherine wiped her fingers on her napkin. "Are you feeling well? The room is very close."

"That is a polite way to put it," Annora answered. "It's impossible to find a laundress or a bath in this town. We've all, well most of us, tried to counter the problem with scent. Attar of lily and lamb don't mix."

"Would you like to go out for a few moments?" Catherine asked. "I would accompany you."

Annora accepted and they threaded their way through the tables out to the convent garden where cool evening breezes soothed their rumpled spirits and settled their stomachs.

"Have you been out in the town at all?" Catherine asked. "I'm sorry that I haven't spent much time with you. I didn't mean to abandon you."

"Don't fret about it," Annora said. "The countess took me yesterday to visit the Abbess Marie. She is here in place of the abbess of Saint-Georges, where my sister was, to plead for the return of the nuns, you know."

"Why didn't the abbess of Saint-Georges come herself?" Catherine asked. "I had wondered."

"Abbess Adela is now bedridden," Annora explained. "She's terribly old. They say she's nearly a hundred!"

"Ah," said Catherine. "Now I understand how Henri de Tréguier could kidnap the nuns. I couldn't imagine any abbess allowing such a thing. Don't they have a lay advocate?"

"I think it's the same Henri," Annora said. "After all, if he could throw his own mother's confessor out of his monastery, he must be powerful. I wish Cecile had gone to Saint-Sulpice. No one would dare confront Abbess Marie."

"For one so young, she does have a commanding presence," Catherine said.

"Well, she is a king's daughter," Annora said. "It's in the blood."

A vision of Edgar's "fishwife" face passed through Catherine's mind. Yet Margaret showed no signs of aristocratic arrogance. The noble blood must flow more thinly in some, or more nobly.

"My goodness!" Annora exclaimed suddenly. "What was that?"

She turned quickly toward the door to the dining hall, bumping into Catherine.

"What?" Catherine managed to avoid falling. "What is it?"

"I'm sorry," Annora said, puzzled. "For a moment I was sure . . . I must have been mistaken. I thought I saw someone in the doorway. He seemed to be about to come toward us, then I could have sworn something came out of the ground and pulled him down, like a soul dragged into hell."

Catherine crossed herself. "Saint Anthony's dancing demons!"

She headed for the door. Annora ran after her.

"Catherine, where are you going? It was just a trick of the light, I'm sure, someone passing by, not coming out."

"Perhaps," Catherine answered. "But I want to see, all the same."

"Look, there's no tunnel to Hell," Annora said when they reached the doorway. She laughed. "I knew as soon as I spoke that it was but a fancy. I'm unsettled by my loss."

Catherine glanced at her. In the torchlight, her face seemed flushed. Her laugh was high and nervous. She must have seen something. But what? And why was she so eager to deny it now?

Catherine took the torch from its bracket and held it so that she could see the ground.

There was no gaping hole to the netherworld. But the grass had been gouged deeply and recently. She swept the torch in an arc. Something gleamed. She bent and picked it up.

It was a gold brooch, intricately made, with topaz stones. The clasp had broken. Catherine held it up to the light.

There was a red smudge on the topaz. Catherine sniffed it. Yes, there was no mistaking that.

It was blood.

# Eleven

The garden. A few seconds later.

*. . . ecce astitit in visione homini turba daemonum in morem Scotorum sitarcia suas prono, ut assolent, clune portantium.*

A vision of a crowd of demons appeared to this man in the form of Scots carrying their provisions, as is their habit, in a bag attached flat on their buttocks.

Guibert de Nogent, autobiography

*I* told you!" Annora said. "Some poor soul has been swallowed up by Hell. Shouldn't we go for help?"

"Yes, why don't you?" Catherine answered, studying the ground by the doorway.

She continued circling the area with her torch, moving a bit outward each time.

"I can't leave you here alone," Annora protested. "What if it comes back?"

Catherine looked at her. "I'm not afraid of demons," she said. "My faith is strong."

"Well, of course, but . . ."

"Go on." Catherine shooed Annora in with her free hand.

The woman went in, calling loudly for someone to come aid her. Catherine grimaced. She had only a few moments. It may have been a demon coming for a sinner, but there were other possibilities and she felt they should be discounted first.

The ground by the door had been disturbed as if by a scuffle. Likely, she thought, that had been when the brooch had been torn from a cloak or tunic. The plants were flattened farther out as well. Catherine followed the trail, noting more blood gleaming on the flower buds. It ended at a thicket of ill-pruned laurel bushes. Catherine hesitated to try to make her way through them. She stepped back. Already there were cries from the hall, along with some laughter. Annora's tale of demons was not being received with complete seriousness.

Catherine shone the light onto the laurel. There were broken branches and still more blood. She stepped closer.

The bush in front of her moaned.

Catherine jumped back, slipped on the damp grass and landed hard on her bottom.

"Who . . ." She caught her breath. "Who's there?"

The groaning grew louder as the bush began to shake.

*"Maria Virga, ora pro me!"* Catherine shrieked as she tried to get up.

She scrabbled backwards on her heels and elbows. Behind her the voices were growing louder. Before her something was emerging from the laurel.

A blackened hand reached for her.

Catherine screamed.

When she fell, the torch had rolled along the grass to stop, still flaming, between her and the monster. In its light, Catherine saw a shape break from the bushes. At first it seemed short and misshapen, then it rose, stretching out until it hovered over her, blood dripping on her skirts.

*"Pater, Filius, Spiritus Sancti!"* Catherine held her hands up from the ground in an effort to ward it off. "You have no power here! Go back to . . . go back to . . . to . . . Gui?"

She had finally recognized the face under the blood. It was her dinner partner of the night before.

"Help me," the man choked as he fell at her feet.

The next few moments were a confused haze as Catherine felt herself being lifted back to her feet amidst questions and exclamations.

"This man has been attacked." She pointed at the now unconscious Gui. "He needs attention at once. I'm fine. I just need to rest a moment."

There was a ripple in the crowd as Margaret pushed her way through.

"Catherine!" She embraced her tightly. "I knew when they said a woman had been cornered by a demon in the garden that it could only be you. Did you defeat it?"

Catherine opened her mouth to explain. She looked at the chaos around her: finely dressed nobles, guards, servants, everyone talking at once. In the torchlight they all looked demonic.

"Yes," she answered, "I did. Let's go back inside."

She leaned against Margaret. They walked slowly back to

the hall. From the doorway Annora saw them and came to help.

"Did it attack you?" she asked. "Are you hurt? You were right. I should never have left you. I should have had more faith."

"*Harou!*" came a shout from behind them. "Out of the way!"

The women moved aside as four men came through carrying Gui. He was awake enough to keep his arms around the shoulders of two of the men, but his eyes were glazed and his face smeared with blood. Annora took one look at him and shrieked.

"Gui! What are you doing here? What happened to you?"

"Annora," Catherine pulled her back. "He's in no shape to answer you now."

"No, I suppose not," Annora said. "But as soon as he is well enough I intend to find out why he's in Reims. So he managed to escape the monster. I'm not surprised that a demon was lying in wait for him. My father always said he was born to walk the path to Hell."

Catherine sighed. "I don't think it was a demon you saw, after all," she told Annora.

"But there was this big black shape rising from the ground," Annora insisted. "What else could it have been?"

"Someone in a long, black cloak," Catherine answered. "Wearing a gold brooch."

She fumbled at the knot in her sleeve. "I hope I haven't lost it."

"Catherine," Margaret spoke gently, "wait until we get you inside."

"I can't have dropped it." Catherine felt the material until she found the lump that was the brooch. She sighed in relief. "Very well. You're right, Margaret. I really would like to go in, sit down and wash my hands and face."

When they got back into the hall, bright with candles, Catherine looked down at the front of her robe, then twisted as best she could to see the back.

"Oh, Margaret," she sighed again. "I hope Edgar and Solomon have good luck on their journey. Grass, mud and blood! I've ruined my best silk *bliaut!*"

Margaret shook her head. "Edgar won't mind," she said. "It's a small price to pay for routing a demon."

The next morning was the fourth Sunday of Lent, the one at which *Laetare* is sung. More important, it was the official opening day of the council. Pope Eugenius was to celebrate Mass before the proceedings began, assisted by his cardinals.

"There's no way we'll get anywhere near the church," Astrolabe fretted.

"I know," John said. "But for you it will be all right. You don't need to be there today. They aren't going to bring Eon out for another three or four days at least. We still have time to find out who is trying to hurt you."

Astrolabe wasn't reassured. So far they had discovered nothing. John stared into his bowl of watery soup as if it would reveal the future.

"It's no use for me to even try to find a position," he said at last. "The one person I had hoped would help me isn't here. Without an introduction there's no hope. I might as well go back to Paris and tutor rich dullards again. They'll probably all become bishops and I'll die in some dank garret without even a candle to my name."

"More likely in a tavern, crushed by a falling beer barrel," Astrolabe said with small sympathy. "This isn't your last chance, John. You aren't without friends. We won't let you starve."

John gave him a crooked smile. "Thank you. And in the meantime," he said, "you'd rather I worried about something more imminent, like a murder charge hanging over you?"

"Well." Astrolabe shrugged. "If you must have something to worry about, it would be helpful if it were me. You'll find a position soon, I'm sure."

"Astrolabe, I've been studying and teaching for half my life." John stared at the cluster of elegantly dressed bishops making their way to the cathedral, followed by their various archdeacons, deacons, priests, clerks and other acolytes. "I write a fine hand and know the rules of rhetoric inside out. Why will no one take me into his service?"

"I have no idea," Astrolabe said. "I'd accept you in a flash, if I were a bishop."

John laughed at that.

"Neither of us will ever go that far," he said, continuing to watch the spectacle of church authorities passing by. "Say, isn't that the Breton woman you took in?"

He pointed to where Gwenael was trying to cross the square without being trampled or beaten back by the bishops' guards. She waved frantically to get their attention.

The two men directed her to meet them at the far end of the road, where the crowd was thinner.

"What's wrong?" Astrolabe asked at once. "Where is Catherine? She was supposed to meet us this morning."

"Oh, it's dreadful!" Gwenael clasped her hands to keep from grabbing his tunic. "She was attacked last night, with some other people at the dinner. They say a demon was waiting in the garden."

"What?" Astrolabe rubbed his ear. He must not have heard correctly.

"Is she all right?" John asked.

"The midwife was called this morning," Gwenael said. "She's not to get out of bed for a day or two. But they don't think she'll lose the baby."

Both men exhaled.

"Now what's this about a demon?" Astrolabe demanded.

"I'm not sure." Gwenael looked tired and miserable. "I was put to work in the kitchens, carrying out the refuse and scrubbing the pots. I knew there was some commotion but thought it was just the young men, drunk as usual. It wasn't until the servers came that I learned what had happened. Some man was beaten up and left for dead. Catherine found him. She probably saved him from being dragged into Hell."

"But how do you know it was a demon?" Astrolabe asked.

"Everyone said so," Gwenael answered.

"Then it must have been." John tried to keep a straight face. "Everyone couldn't be mistaken."

Gwenael gave him a sharp look. "I know when you're

mocking me, Master John. If all those lords and ladies and bishops say it was a demon, why should I doubt them?"

"What does Catherine say?" Astrolabe asked.

"I wasn't allowed in to see her," Gwenael said. "One of the maids gave me the message to find you. That was all."

"I should at least go and ask after her," Astrolabe told John. "I'll meet you tonight at your English tavern."

"Fine," John said. "I'll see if I can pick up any new information."

Astrolabe looked around. "I wonder where Godfrey has gone. I thought he was going to meet us this morning."

"I'll find him," Gwenael volunteered eagerly. "I know the bake shops he likes best."

"By all means." John winked at Astrolabe. "Remind him that he promised to be at the tavern after Vespers."

She hurried off.

John turned to go, then turned back to Astrolabe.

"If there's anything I can do to help Catherine," he said, "I'm more than willing."

"Of course," Astrolabe said. "But I imagine she has a dozen women all giving her advice at once. I may need you more than she, if Edgar ever learns that I put her in such danger by bringing her here."


"I'm fine," Catherine kept repeating. "It really wasn't that bad a fall. You mustn't concern yourselves about me."

Both Countess Sybil and Countess Mahaut were in the room, most of the other women having been sent elsewhere, at least for the day. Margaret sat on the bed, holding Catherine's hand, more for her own reassurance than anything else.

"It won't hurt you to stay in bed a day or two," Sybil said in a tone that had sent troops into battle.

"Certainly not," Mahaut agreed with the voice she used to pronounce judgment at her court in Provins.

Catherine lay back on the pillows.

"Yes, my ladies. I promise to do so," she said. "But it really isn't necessary for Margaret or Annora to miss everything on my account. All I need is some water and rest."

"There must be something else we can do for you, my dear," Countess Mahaut said.

"Well, if it isn't too much trouble," Catherine conceded, "I wouldn't mind having something to read. I never finished the book that Master Gilbert is being questioned on."

There was a long pause in the room as the countesses looked at Catherine and then at each other.

"I believe I might be able to have a copy located and sent to you," Mahaut told her.

"Perhaps Abbot Bernard can spare his," Sybil said with a wicked gleam. "Or Master Peter the Lombard. I believe he's been asked to provide a list of Bishop Gilbert's doctrinal errors. I'm sure he'd be happy to have you go over the work in case he missed something."

Catherine felt the blush rising. "I didn't mean to show such hubris. A saint's life would also be fine, and instructive, I'm sure."

"Nonsense, child," Mahaut said. "You wouldn't be a protégée of Heloise if you didn't study theological tracts. I'm sure you'll make as much sense of it as any of those Paris masters."

"Thank you, my lady," Catherine said softly.

She felt a tension between the two women that had nothing to do with her. Was Countess Mahaut opposed to Sybil's plans for her children and those of Raoul of Vermandois, or was there some other dispute?

She was relieved when they finally left.

"Margaret, you'll be expected to attend Mass this morning with your grandfather," she reminded her. "I wasn't lying. I am fine, but more than willing to rest awhile. There's no need for you to hover over me. With the count and countess, you may even be able to find a place inside when the council starts. I wouldn't have you miss that. I want you to tell me all about what happens."

Margaret got up with reluctance. "I'll do my best, but you know my Latin isn't good enough for the kind of debates they have. It's a pity they won't speak Hebrew."

Catherine laughed. "That *would* be a scandal. Now go along."

The shutters in the room had been closed so that the sunlight came in only in lines through the cracks in the wood. The noise from the street below was muted. Catherine was alone at last. Finally she could take time to analyze the events of the previous night.

If a demon had come after Gui, there would be nothing left of him, so Catherine rejected that theory. She was rather sorry to do so. It's so much cleaner to blame minions from Hell than to find evidence of Satan working through human beings. But in her experience, that was the devil's favorite pathway.

Therefore, the question was who was the person in the dark cloak. Was he simply a thief? Again she had to admit that very few robbers lurked inside the garden of a convent guest house in wait for drunken revelers. Even fewer had good wool cloaks fastened with expensive gold and jeweled brooches.

The brooch! She had meant to show it to the countesses, but all she had thought of was getting everyone to leave so that she could rest. She hadn't even had time to get it out of the knot in her sleeve, so no one else had been given the chance to identify it. Well, it would have to wait until the evening. Catherine went back to her theorizing.

The unpleasant conclusion was that the "demon" had been hunting for someone in particular. Was it Gui, or had Annora's cousin chanced upon this person unexpectedly and forced him to act too soon?

That was harder for Catherine to decide.

There were a number of important people dining in the hall last night. They all had enemies. There were many people of lesser importance who also might have incurred resentment. Gui had seemed harmless to her, but there had been little time to evaluate him.

Was it a coincidence that he was the cousin of Annora and, therefore, of the murdered Cecile? If so, then she was back where she had started. If not, then could Gui be a threat to the person who had killed his cousin, either by something he knew or something he represented? If she could find the owner of the brooch, these questions could be answered. But who would admit to owning it now?

The lines of sunlight stretched across the bed and across the floor before they vanished.

Catherine slept.

Outside, the chaos began to resolve itself into various processions, all heading toward the cathedral. The princes of the church were first, with their households, then the lords of the land with their retainers and families. Although most people owed fealty to different lay and ecclesiastical lords, everyone knew whose party he should be attached to in this instance. At another gathering, each might well find it proper to follow another lord. So the groups were made up of people from different families, different countries. The archbishop of Reims, Samson Mauvoisin, nodded to his cousin, Guillaume de Passavant, once a canon at Reims but now the bishop of Mans. The adulterer, Raoul, count of Vermandois, was also one of the regents of France and so had a place of importance, near to Thibault of Champagne, the uncle of his abandoned wife. The council was a mirror of the complexity of the tapestry of all of Western Christendom.

Godfrey was watching the procession when Gwenael finally found him. He pointed Raoul out to her as he and Petronilla went past.

"More than ten years now, he's been trying to get a divorce," he told her. "Two popes have denied it. But last year he put down a revolt by the commune here in Reims. Now Bishop Samson believes that his plea should be granted. King Louis made him regent of France, so other nobles will speak for him, like Countess Sybil. If Count Thibault withdraws his objections, the marriage will be recognized by the pope."

"Bastards," Gwenael commented, "all of them. I guess noble blood means that even your sins are different. I didn't know Raoul was the one who had destroyed the commune. That explains why so many people here hate him."

"They do?" Godfrey asked. "Where did you hear that?"

"In the streets," Gwenael said. "I'd say most of the people hate all these pompous nobles for coming here and stealing the food from their mouths. There are a few people who like the council being held here. Some are dazzled by greatness. Some are counting the silver from prices they've tripled. But I can feel the resentment against them everywhere poor people gather. If they'd only let my master preach, he would find a torrent of converts."

"Your master? You still believe in this Eon?" Godfrey couldn't understand it. "He's been captured, dragged miles behind a cart, imprisoned. How can you think he's really the son of God?"

"Of course I believe in Eon, why shouldn't I?" she asked in genuine bewilderment. "It doesn't matter that he's been mocked and scorned. Isn't that what they did to Our Lord the first time?"

Godfrey didn't answer. Gwenael watched the procession. The glitter of gold chains, silver crosiers studded with jewels, richly caparisoned horses and even more richly dressed men seemed to overwhelm her with anger.

"Very well," Godfrey said at last. "I see your point. So, which apostle are you?" He laughed.

Gwenael's face changed. She looked away from Godfrey, lips trembling.

"Judas," she whispered. "I must be Judas."

The portress at the convent told Astrolabe that Catherine wasn't allowed to see anyone, by order of the countesses and the abbess. He had expected this and left a message that he would return tomorrow. On a whim, he asked if the man who had been attacked were able to receive visitors.

"He isn't here," she told him. "They've taken him to the house of the Templars. You can ask about him there."

She shut the gate firmly.

Astrolabe wondered if the man had been a knight of the Temple. He realized that he'd forgotten to find out his name, if Gwenael even knew it. He decided to pay a visit. The Temple was on the opposite side of town from the cathedral so he was soon away from the crowd.

As he approached the gate, he put on his chain mail helm again just in case someone there might be able to recognize him.

The guard was a man of middle age wearing a brown cloak. He relaxed when he saw Astrolabe and gave him a nod, as one fighting man to another.

"God save you," Astrolabe greeted him. "My master has sent me to inquire as to the state of the man who was attacked at the convent of Saint-Pierre last night."

"Oh, you mean Lord Gui," the guard said. "I wasn't here then. They took him to the infirmary."

"Is he one of yours?" Astrolabe asked.

"Nah." The guard scratched under his mail. "He's a Norman, they say. But the new dukes of Normandy have given generously to the Temple, and we have the best physicians for treating wounds, so we got him."

"A stroke of luck for him," Astrolabe commented. "I don't suppose he's able to see anyone yet? My master wanted a report on the extent of his injuries."

"No idea. I'll send a boy to ask." The guard whistled and gave the order to a child not much older than James.

"You didn't tell me who your master is," he said to Astrolabe.

"Count Thibault." Astrolabe gave the first name he could think of and hoped that the man didn't have a brother among the count's guards.

"Why would he be caring about a Norman lord?"

Astrolabe shrugged. "He didn't confide in me."

The boy came running back to say that Lord Gui was awake and would see the messenger.

Gui was lying on a narrow cot in a long room. There were a few empty beds around him. At the other end of the room was the infirmarian's work space, a long table and shelves filled with boxes and pots. Dried herbs hung upside down from the ceiling. On the table lay a terrifying array of pincers, cups, knives and other medical instruments.

"Who the hell are you?" Gui greeted him, squinting through blackened eyes.

"My name is Peter," Astrolabe said. "I've been sent to see how you are."

"Not by my cousin, I suppose." Gui waved a bandaged hand toward a chair. Astrolabe took this as an offer to sit.

"Annora thinks I'm a minion of the devil. Her father saw to that."

"No, it wasn't your cousin," Astrolabe said. "The word is, though, that your master came for you last night."

"My what?" Gui rubbed his face. There were long scratches across it.

"Didn't a servant of the devil come at you with its claws?" Astrolabe asked.

"Most certainly," Gui answered, "but it came in human shape. At least, I think so. Truth be told, Peter, it's not too clear in my head. I remember feeling a bit gone with wine and thought I'd just water the plants. I took a step outside and, well, the next I knew I was on the floor in the hall with half the nobility of Christendom staring down at me."

"So do you think it was a demon?" Astrolabe asked. "Or a human enemy."

"I don't know what it was," Gui said wearily. "It felt like a bear. Didn't anyone else see it?"

"From what I understand, only your cousin," Astrolabe told him. "She said she saw a black shape rise from the ground and envelop you."

"And of course she would imagine it to be a creature of evil," Gui said.

"Is there anyone who would wish you ill?" Astrolabe asked.

"Besides Annora and her sister? No."

"Her sister?" Astolabe was alert at once.

"Cecile, but she's off in a convent in Brittany so I doubt she attacked me." Gui grimaced. "Could I have a drink from that cup? The infirmarian said I could have some whenever the pain was too much."

Astrolabe gave him a sip of the potion. Gui leaned back.

"Why should your cousins dislike you?" Astrolabe asked.

"My father and theirs fought for twenty years over a piece of land that they both said came to them from their mother's dower," Gui said. "The judgment finally went to my family. They accused us of buying off the arbiter."

"Did you?"

"It was an archdeacon of Rouen," Gui said, as if that answered the question. "My father probably just gave him a higher price. Then, when he died, Annora's father got the decision reversed."

"Families are always arguing over such things," Astrolabe said. "Why should it cause such hatred into your generation?"

Gui suddenly closed up.

"What difference does it make? It has nothing to do with what happened to me," he said. "Who did you say sent you here?"

"Countess Sybil was concerned." Astrolabe hedged the answer.

"Annora's keeper, I see." Gui's voice was becoming faint. The potion was taking effect. He roused enough to mumble, "Tell her I'm not dead yet. She can send brutes or monsters from Hell and she still won't get it. I'll give it to the monks before I see it in her grasp."

Astrolabe tried to calm him. "I'll tell her anything you like," he promised. "It's nothing to me."

"Something to me," Gui said indistinctly. "Everything to me."

Astrolabe left soon after, stopping to tell the infirmarian that he had given Gui more medicine. He gave the guard a wave as he passed through the gate but didn't stop for another chat.

Gui's revelations had put another worry into his mind. What if the person who killed Cecile hadn't been one of the men who had raped her but a relative? All he really knew was that she had spotted someone she recognized and feared among those who had captured Eon and the other heretics. What if that person thought Gui was a threat to him as well? Could someone want to get rid of all that remained of the family?

He remembered Cecile in the camp of the Eonites. She was so gentle with those frightened people. They believed God had led her to them. Perhaps she had believed it, too. She had been an angel, soothing their pain. Astrolabe had been as much in awe of her as anyone. He wished now that he had spoken to her more instead of only watching from afar.

Did her death really have anything to do with the men who had been asking for him in Provins and Nogent?

Did it matter? She was dead and he had not been able to prevent it.

What if by speaking out he could protect Annora and Gui? What right had he to protect himself if it left them in danger? Was there anything he knew that could save them, anything that might have saved Cecile?

His mind a whirl of guilt and doubt, Astrolabe fervently hoped Catherine could see him soon. He needed her common sense to help him decide what to do.

Brother Arnulf was worried. Canon Rolland had been avoiding him. Now that he was back among his fellows from Paris, the canon was wavering at the role he had to take in the plans for revenge on the son of Abelard. This wouldn't do. Arnulf needed Rolland to back him up. No one was going to pay attention to a simple monk. The soldiers from Brittany would testify again that they had seen Astrolabe among those they had taken in the forest. But unless he could be found for them to identify, it would be easy to disprove the accusation, especially since he had apparently been using a false name. Rolland had to be pressed to step up the search.

Astrolabe was in Reims, Arnulf was sure of it. None of that family would ever run from a confrontation. That was what had made old Abelard so many enemies, including Rolland. He'd checked with one of the servants of Count Thibault, and they all said that Astrolabe hadn't been at the Paraclete. So where was he hiding? Who was helping him? This was a matter of heresy even more than murder. Keeping a criminal from justice was a serious offense. Only a powerful lord would dare give him protection. Arnulf had asked everywhere, but no one knew of a minor cleric recently added to the household of one of the lords and brought to Reims. Could he be masquerading as a monk?

Arnulf scrutinized every face as he worked his way through the crowd.

"What are you looking at?" a gruff voice demanded.

"Nothing, lord." Arnulf cringed. "Bless you."

The man wasn't Astrolabe, for certain. He was short and hairy, with a bull's neck. He gripped Arnulf by the neck of his cowl, pulling him almost off the ground and cutting off his air.

"I've no use for your kind." The man's breath came hard against Arnulf's face, onions and beer. "Remember who feeds you and keeps the Saracens from overrunning us all while you sit and pray."

"Oh, I do, lord." Arnulf smiled.

"Don't forget it." The man dropped him and moved on, followed by his guards.

Arnulf tried to appear as though nothing had happened, but he couldn't ignore the smirk of a cheese peddler who had watched the whole exchange.

"What did you do to rile him so," she asked. "Offer him your ass?"

"Hardly." Arnulf tried to piece together the tattered bits of his dignity. "I was merely in the way of his wrath."

"I'd stay out of it from now on," she suggested. "That's the seneschal of Baldwin of Hainaut. I don't think he cares much for stray monks."

Arnulf nodded. Countess Sybil's enemy. And now his. He was already wondering how he could put this to good use.

"Have a nice bit of cheese?" the woman asked hopefully. "Just the thing for Lent."

He brushed her aside and went on. He had to find Rolland.

Astrolabe thought he would be early at the tavern, but he found Godfrey already there.

"You didn't bring Gwenael?" he asked.

The guard shook his head. "I insulted her savior." He grimaced. "She's not speaking to me."

Astrolabe shook his head.

"We've got to convince her not to try to free Eon," he said, "or she'll be condemned along with him."

"I know," Godfrey said. "I'm worried that she's going to give herself up for his sake. She seems to think she's betrayed him by escaping. What is there about this man that would inspire such loyalty?"

Astrolabe thought a moment.

"There is a charisma about Eon," he said at last. "Perhaps

it's the madness. He's taller than the average, and not bad fea-
tured, but he makes you think he's more. Beyond his kindness
to these poor souls, he does seem to possess a spark. When he
preaches, I believe they really see the glory he describes. Of
course his power must be demonic, but I can understand the
allure, even though I don't feel it myself."

"I don't want to see Gwenael burned," Godfrey said.

"I don't want it to happen to anyone," Astrolabe said firmly.
Godfrey looked up with hope.

"Do you have a plan to save them?" he asked.

"I'm sorry," Astrolabe said sadly. "At the moment I don't
even have a plan to save myself."

# *Twelve*

The old cathedral of Reims. Laetare Sunday, 12 kalends April (March 21), 1148. Equinoctium, Feast of Saint Benedict, reluctant organizer of monks.

*Archiepiscopus itaque Lugdunensis eccelsie, . . . protestus est Rothomagnesem, Senonensem, et Turonensem archiespicopos et provincias eorum sibi et ecclesie sue jure debere primatus esse subjectos. . . . Bituricensis autem Narbonensem archiepiscopum et episcopum Aniciensem et abbatem Castridolensis vendicavit [etc., etc.].*

The archbishop of Lyons . . . claimed that legally the archbishops of the provinces of Rouens, Sens and Tours should be subject to him and his church by right of primacy. . . . The archbishop of Bourges also asserted a legal claim to authority over the archbishop of Narbonne, and the bishop of Le Puy and the abbot of Bourg-dieu [etc., etc.].

John of Salisbury, *Historia Pontificalis*

$\mathcal{M}$argaret was regretting her good fortune at having a place to stand in the cathedral. Countess Mahaut had a folding chair that she could lean on, but her shoes weren't meant for standing on cold stone floors, and the debates, even when in French, were boring.

Margaret knew in principle that it was terribly important which bishop was subject to another. Lands, benefices, tithes and respect all depended on it. But none of these affected her. She had no rights to the tithes. For those who paid the tolls it didn't matter who got the money in the end. All the arguments of the various bishops sounded the same to her. They must have to Pope Eugenius as well for he disallowed every challenge. Even so, the debates and the protocol lasted for hours. It was nearly time for Vespers when she finally escaped from the cathedral.

Catherine was awake and ready for information when Margaret dragged in to check on her.

"Really, Catherine," Margaret insisted, "it was very tedious, even with the shouting."

"You mean they had to shout to make themselves heard?" Catherine asked. "I'd have thought people would be better behaved than that."

"No." Margaret sat down gratefully. "Of course there was the constant murmur of voices, but mostly the bishops made themselves heard over that. I suppose it comes from preaching. They seemed to go on forever. The archbishops were making their demands and the other bishops and abbots refuting them. That was easy enough to follow. I was nearly asleep, even standing up, when Albero of Trier got up to speak."

"I remember him from when we lived in Trier," Catherine said. "He seems to have spent most of his years in the see fighting with someone. What did he want?"

"I couldn't understand all of his argument," Margaret said, "but it got the attention of everyone else. He seemed to feel that Reims should be subject to Trier. Something about first and second and ancient Roman rights. That's when all the shouting began."

Catherine stared at her, then began to laugh. "You must be joking!" she exclaimed. "He said that right here in Reims? And I thought I was cursed with hubris! He must think that because Trier was Belgica Primae in the days of Rome, he can have control over the area that was Belgica Secundae. Tradition usually carries some weight in these debates, but to go back a thousand years! And then to make such a statement in the city one wants to control. I wish I could have seen the reaction to that!"

"It was so loud that it woke me up," Margaret said. "I nearly fell onto Countess Mahaut, I was so startled. The French bishops were barely kept from coming to blows with the Lotharingian ones. And in church, too!"

"Well, the first day of the council doesn't sound tedious to me at all," Catherine told her. "Did you find out when they are going to bring Eon in for trial?"

"Not before Wednesday at the earliest." Margaret was pleased to have come by the information. "Tomorrow they say the pope is going to excommunicate all those who were ordered to attend and didn't come. That should be more fun."

"A good excommunication is always interesting," Catherine said. "Are there many bishops missing? It seems to me as if every cleric in the world is here. One wonders who is tending to the business of their sees."

"Well, King Stephen only let a couple of the English bishops come," Margaret said. "And there's only one here from Spain that I know of. I don't know about others. I asked about the Bretons, and someone told me that the bishop of Dol didn't come to answer the claims of the archbishop of Tours."

Catherine shook her head. "The bishop of Dol is the one

who should have handled Eon in the first place. Astrolabe would never be in such trouble if the bishop had been at all effective. Nor would Henri of Tréguier ever have gotten away with appropriating a monastery. I wish I had him here. He's the cause of all this mess. If he'd done his job, I'd be back at the Paraclete with my children and not cooped up in this tiny room."

"I hadn't thought of that," Margaret said. "Maybe there is a reason for all those arguments about superiority. I thought it was just about money."

"Well, that's a lot of it," Catherine sighed. "But a strong bishop can keep the nobles in line. Just as a strong king can prevent the church being appropriated for private gain."

Margaret yawned.

"Don't worry," Catherine said. "My political lecture is over."

"I'm sorry, Catherine," Margaret said. "I suppose I should try to understand it better. If you want to know the finer points of the arguments, you should ask John. I saw him by the door as we went in."

"I will, as soon as I'm let out of this bed," Catherine said. "I'm sure the baby took no harm from my fall. He's as lively as ever."

"Or she," Margaret commented.

"Or she," Catherine agreed. "The midwife says I'm carrying him high and that means a boy, but I never noticed the difference."

Margaret yawned again. "Excuse me."

Catherine smiled, "No, excuse me, my dear. I've kept you too long. You need to rest. Are you expected to dine with Count Thibault tonight?"

"No," Margaret said. "They are eating with the abbot of Clairvaux. I wasn't invited."

"Then get yourself something from the kitchen," Catherine said. "Come back soon. I've kept the bed nice and warm for you."

Godfrey and Astrolabe were well into the beer pitcher by the time John arrived.

"Did you get in?" Astrolabe asked. "What happened?"

John took out his bowl and reached for the pitcher. He cut a chunk of cheese from the square on the table. Once he had wet his throat, he stuffed the cheese in his mouth. The other two waited impatiently for him to swallow.

"That's better," John sighed at last. "I didn't dare leave for fear of losing my place. I thought I'd die of thirst. Don't worry, you missed nothing of interest. I spent most of the time looking around to see who was present."

"Did you see anyone wanting to hire a clerk with a taste for beer?" Astrolabe asked.

"Not that I could tell," John said. "For once my primary interest wasn't my lack of a position. But I think I spotted the cleric who was chasing you. A big man, you said, blond, with a Breton accent and protuberant blue eyes?"

"That's right," Godfrey said. "I'd know him if I saw him again."

"He's a canon of Paris," John told them, "called Rolland."

"Paris?" Astrolabe said. "What would he have to do with the capture of a heretic in Brittany?"

"Nothing, I would say," John answered. "But when I saw him, I remembered him from my student days. He was one of those who wanted to learn from your father. Failed completely. He hadn't the stamina. He was always sensitive about his origin. Seemed to think that Abelard should be more understanding since they were fellow Bretons."

"Ah." Astrolabe took some of the cheese. It crumbled in his fingers and left orts in his beard. "My father was not kind to those who couldn't keep up with his lectures. And he didn't come from the area where Breton was spoken. He thought the language barbaric and the people the same."

John snorted. "Having felt the sharpness of his tongue myself, I'd say Abelard was vicious to those he scorned. He could mock a man down to a puddle on the ground. He could also be tremendously kind to those who endured, but Rolland never saw that side of him. He didn't last long."

"But what has he to do with Eon or with Cecile's death?" Astrolabe asked.

"I don't know," John admitted. "But he must be involved somehow. Why else would he be hunting for you if not in connection to this Breton business?"

"Perhaps if we could find the man who was traveling with him we could find out," Godfrey suggested. "He did his best to stay hidden in his cloak and hood when they stopped us on the road, but I had the impression he was a small man. Now that we know where Rolland is from, I can go to the places where the Parisians meet and watch for him. I would bet that our silent stranger is the one who brought the news from Brittany and convinced the canon to help him. Sooner or later, he's certain to contact Rolland again."

"Would you mind?" Astrolabe asked. "Spying on the Parisians might take away from your time helping Gwenael."

"I don't 'help' her that much," Godfrey answered with a smirk. "Truthfully, I find her adoration of this false messiah disquieting. She resists any attempt to make her see reason. I'm out of my depth here. Perhaps Master John could convince her that she is in danger of losing her life as well as her soul."

"I could try," John said doubtfully, "but I have little hope. I don't have the persuasive power of Abbot Bernard, for example."

"I'm sure that when Eon is brought before the council, he'll recant and go back to his monastery," Astrolabe said. "Then Gwenael will see that she's been deluded. At that point, she'll be ready to accept your help."

Godfrey was doubtful. "Perhaps if Abbot Bernard preaches to her and her fellow Eonites she'll be converted. But I can do nothing while she's in the grip of this madman," he said. "And I don't choose to join her in heresy. So, Master John, Master Astrolabe, in the meantime, I am at your service."

Behind them someone made a sudden gagging sound, spraying his beer across the table. The men looked around. A man in a monk's robe was scurrying out, his hood pulled over his face.

Godfrey paled. "Peter! I'm sorry! How could I have been so careless? I'll see to him."

He got up at once and went out after the monk. Astrolabe rose to go with him.

John stopped him.

"We don't want to make any more of a scene," he warned. "The man may have simply choked on a twig in the beer. There are enough of them."

"Perhaps," Astrolabe said. "But I've been far too complacent. I thought the beard and the mail would change me too much for anyone to recognize."

"Believe me, I'm surprised that your mother knew you," John said. "Someone who had only seen you once or twice certainly wouldn't."

Astrolabe gave a crooked smile. "Peter the guard has become more natural to me than my old self. I hope I don't have to give him up yet."

John nodded. He gave a worried glance toward the door. "Godfrey is taking a while. Perhaps we should go after him now."

Arnulf paused outside the door of the tavern. He was so excited that he almost danced in the street. At last! He had to find Canon Rolland and tell him the good news.

As he headed down the road, he heard the sound of boots coming quickly behind him. Arnulf quickened his pace. So did his follower. Arnulf tried not to panic. Clearly the men at the other table had noted his abrupt departure. He had to get away, but how?

The street was dark enough but so narrow that it would be impossible to duck into a doorway without being noticed by someone passing. A man could touch both sides with his arms outstretched.

Arnulf began to run. His only hope was to make it to one of the squares before his follower. Then he would have his choice of routes. He slipped on something and stayed upright only by grabbing onto the first thing his hand touched. A horrible clanging started right next to his head. He had pulled on a bell chain outside a shop.

The shock of it propelled him forward, but he knew his pursuer was gaining on him. There would be no chance of escaping. Still, fear pushed him on.

Panting, he burst into the square. He skidded to a stop and nearly laughed in relief. The space was full of monks, processing through the town, chanting Compline.

Arnulf vanished among them just as Godfrey emerged. The monk, mindful of how he had been delivered, stayed with the procession until the end. Then he set out to find Rolland.

Godfrey met John and Astrolabe on the way back to the tavern.

"I lost him," he admitted. "He may have run because he thought I was a brigand, but we should assume that someone now knows who you are. How could I have been so stupid?"

"Never mind," Astrolabe told him. "We've all become careless, especially over our beer. At least we already know the name of the other cleric. If our monk has gone to Canon Rolland, perhaps we can still find and confront them both."

"Now I have even more reason to track him down," Godfrey said. "I promise, I won't fail you again."

Arnulf was still bubbling with elation by the time he found Canon Rolland.

"I've been a fool!" he told Rolland. "I've been looking for a cleric. Of course Astrolabe wouldn't travel as himself. But we were right that he took refuge with the merchant and his family. He was their guard all the time. I actually spoke to him and never guessed it. I thought you said he looked like his father."

"So he does," Rolland insisted. "I don't know how he tricked you."

"I wasn't expecting a man in armor." Arnulf chewed at a nail. "I still wouldn't have known him if someone hadn't said his name. He was with that John, the Englishman, and another soldier. At least I think he was a soldier. Maybe he was Heloise in disguise."

"Oh, surely not!" Rolland exclaimed.

Arnulf squinted to make out the canon's face in the dim lamplight. It was hard to be sure if the man was serious. He seemed to have missed any lectures that involved the use of irony in rhetoric. No wonder Abelard had found him such easy prey.

"Do we have him arrested now?" Rolland asked. "We should go at once to the bishop of Tours and tell him we found the murderer."

"Oh, how I wish we could!" Arnulf groaned. "But we don't dare yet. Now that we're sure he's here, we need to gather the men who captured the Eonites so that they can swear he is the same one. Even then, I'm worried that he'll be able to talk his way out of it. The man has powerful friends."

Rolland gave an exasperated snort. "You didn't seem concerned about this when we were chasing him!"

"I know," Arnulf said. "But I've been making inquiries the past few days, generally, you understand. There are many who hate Abelard's memory as we do. But when I mention the son, they all look blank."

"Have you told them that he is a worse heretic than his father, and a murderer as well?" Rolland asked.

"I suggested it to Geoffrey, Abbot Bernard's secretary," Arnulf said. "I know he has no love for Abelard. He told me it was nonsense. Astrolabe was a nonentity, not worth bothering with."

"Geoffrey is very much involved with the heresy of Bishop Gilbert," Rolland observed. "Canon Peter and he are always in some corner, discussing it. Perhaps he can only focus on one thing at a time."

"As if that bookish heresy is half the threat that these Eonists are," Arnulf sniffed. "Arguing about the essence of the Holy Spirit when most people believe it's a dove that whispers in virgins' ears to get them pregnant."

"Arnulf!" Rolland was shocked. "I think you've been out of your monastery too long. Are you sure your abbot gave you leave to be away for so many weeks?"

"Of course," Arnulf answered. "He understands the importance of my mission."

"Which monastery are you from again?" Rolland asked. "Marmoutier, wasn't it?"

"A dependent priory," Arnulf answered hastily. "Near Rennes. That's how I became involved with all of this. It was practically at our doorstep and no one local would do anything about it. I was sent to make sure justice wasn't ignored."

"Ah, yes." Rolland thought a moment. "Well, we can devote all our energy to your problem. The doctrinal errors of Bishop Gilbert are not our concern. I have listened to the masters of Paris discuss him, and I've no doubt that he will be made to correct his mistakes. The council will be sure that they are not allowed to spread."

"It's not easy to keep such things from propagating," Arnulf mused. "It's like pouring poison into a river. All who drink from it, all the way to the sea, will be tainted, even if it is too diluted to kill them."

"Like rumor," Rolland said slowly.

He stared with his round eyes off into the distance. Arnulf could tell he was thinking deeply, as the only thing in his scope of vision was a stone wall.

After what seemed to Arnulf an interminable time, Rolland focused on him again.

"I think we've been fighting with the wrong weapons," he said.

"What do you want us to use, siege engines?" Arnulf was not in the mood to humor the canon.

"Nothing so direct," Rolland told him. "Look, we are agreed that it would be entirely too easy for Abelard's son to slip out of the noose. If we bring him before the council, his friends will speak for him. He'll deny he believed in Eon."

"Most likely," Arnulf said. "That's why we need to find the witnesses."

"No." Rolland smiled. His teeth gleamed wetly in the lamplight. "We need to see to it that by the time Astrolabe is brought to trial, everyone already believes him to be guilty."

"And how do we do that?"

The smile grew broader. "We pour some poison into the stream."

Catherine insisted on being allowed up the next morning. She had anticipated an argument from someone and was vaguely disappointed when no one protested.

"Good. We can finally get the bed put away," was Annora's only comment.

"True, it has been an obstacle," Catherine agreed. "It's difficult for all of us to dress and prepare our hair even with the beds folded."

Annora wasn't paying attention. Her maid was braiding her long blond hair in an intricate pattern. She had been cautioned not to move during the process. Catherine took advantage of this to talk with her.

"How is your cousin?" Catherine asked. "Has he recovered from the attack?"

"I wouldn't know," Annora said, staring straight ahead. "I told you we don't speak to that side of the family. I'm sorry that the demon didn't get him. It would have saved a lot of trouble. I'm sure he intends to claim Saint Gwenoc's cave again. It won't do any good, though. I'll fight him right up to Rome if I must."

"Who was Saint Gwenoc?" Catherine asked.

"An ancestor of ours," Annora said proudly. "He was a very holy hermit ages and ages ago. He performed miracles. They say he had a tame bear that would sleep at the entrance to his cave to protect him from the night spirits and keep him warm in the winter."

"And this land you're fighting over was his hermitage?" Catherine asked.

Annora nodded, then winced as the maid yanked the braid tight.

"There's a little chapel there still, where the bear slept, but it's in ruins," she said. "We have no priest to maintain it, but I'm hoping that Countess Sybil will donate the funds to support one."

"And what does Gui want to do with it?"

"He says that he'll give it to the white monks for a priory, but I don't believe him," Annora said. "More likely he'll use it as Henri of Tréguier did, as a place to keep his mistresses."

"I must admit that he didn't strike me as a spiritual person," Catherine said. "But in these uncertain times many people are thinking of the fate of their souls. He might well be sincere."

"Not Gui!" Annora insisted. "If anything, he's hoping to collect the revenues from the pilgrims who will come."

"I doubt the monks would be such bad bargainers as to give up revenues to him," Catherine said. "But why would there be pilgrims?"

"Because there are still miracles, of course," Annora said. "There's a spring inside the cave. The water is known to cure the choking sickness that babies get."

"It does?" Catherine's voice shook.

"So they say." Annora wiggled impatiently on her stool. "My father let the local people get some whenever they wished, but he didn't want strangers wandering over our land. So he discouraged stories about it."

"But if it could save a child's life," Catherine protested. "Then what would a little inconvenience matter? I lost a baby to the winter fever. I would have gone anywhere to save her."

The maid finished the long braid and looped it up over Annora's shoulder.

"My Alexander was taken by the coughing sickness," she said. "I vowed to walk barefoot to Rome if only God would spare him. But he died anyway. Will that do, my lady?"

She held up a mirror with an unsteady hand. Over Annora's head Catherine met the maid's eyes. She never spoke to the woman or saw her after the council, but Catherine always remembered her as a sister.

Annora took the mirror from the maid and held it steady. "It's fine, thank you. You may go now. The water doesn't always work, you know," she added to Catherine. "That's another reason my father wouldn't have it exploited."

Catherine felt again her helplessness during the illness of baby Heloisa, having to watch her burning with fever, coughing and gasping for air until she finally fell silent. Nothing in Catherine's life had ever hurt so much.

Fiercely, she forced the image from her mind and concentrated on the problem before her.

"Annora," she asked, "if you were to die without children, who would get your property?"

"Well, the castellany is held from the duke of Normandy and the bishop of Rouen so they might give it to one of their men." Annora was undisturbed by the question. "But Gwenoc's cave belongs to the family and there aren't many of us left, just Gui and some other cousin who's been in a monastery for years. So I suppose that it would come to Gui. Of course I could give it to the church now." She smiled at the thought. "That would really infuriate him."

"I see," said Catherine.

Annora looked up at her.

"You don't think Gui had anything to do with Cecile's death, do you?" she asked. "That is nonsense, I assure you. After all, he was the one attacked by the demon."

"What if it weren't a demon?" Catherine suggested. "What if Gui were on his way to strike at you and was stopped through divine or perhaps human aid?"

Annora stood up proudly, suddenly annoyed. "You overstep yourself, Catherine. Whoever killed Cecile, it was not a member of the family. Gui may be dissolute, but my cousin is not a murderer and it is not your place to imply that he is."

Chin high and braids swinging, Annora swept from the room.

Catherine finished combing out her own tangled black curls, thankful that as a married woman, she could cover the result with a long scarf. She sighed. She should have expected Annora's reaction.

"I ought to have kept my speculations to myself," she sighed. "Mother would be so ashamed of me. No one wants to hear evil of their family, even if they say it often enough themselves, and they certainly don't want to hear it from someone who is beneath their station."

There was a sound at the doorway. Catherine turned and saw a woman peering in at her. She looked around the room to see whom Catherine was talking to, then retreated when she realized Catherine was alone.

Catherine decided it was time to go find Astrolabe before someone else came in and discovered her having a conversation with herself. The other women were already starting to avoid her, having marked her predisposition for accidents. Only Margaret's exalted status and the patronage of Countess Sybil kept them from suggesting that she sleep elsewhere.

Although the air was brisk, it felt good to be out again. Catherine wrapped her fur-lined cloak warmly about her. The wind blew it open again. In her haste to be gone, she had forgotten to bring something to pin it with. As she pulled it tighter, something thumped in her sleeve.

Carefully, she untied it and the brooch fell into her hand. She turned it over. The gold was rich and soft, the topazes carefully matched. The pin was bent and the catch torn. Edgar could have repaired it easily. She examined it more carefully. The materials were good but the workmanship mediocre. She should have asked Annora if it were Gui's. That was twice she had forgotten. Perhaps the events of the past few days had affected her more than she had thought. This time she must find out if it belonged to Gui. If it didn't, then it was the only real clue they had to his assailant. She carefully tied it back in the sleeve.

She finally found Astrolabe among the crowd in the parvis in front of the cathedral. He had found a spot out of the wind and was sitting on the ground, his sword laid across his knees in a manner that implied it could be used at any minute. Catherine sank down next to him gratefully.

Astrolabe was delighted to see her. "We were worried about you," he told her. "You must think you're Saint Margaret, chasing demons all on your own."

"It wasn't a very big demon," Catherine assured him.

"Well, I've been busy while you were recovering." Astrolabe handed her a piece of cheese from the recesses of his cloak. "Settle back and hear the news."

"I want you to tell me everything you've found out," she said, taking the cheese. "I feel as if I've been gone for a month."

She nibbled on it as he told of his interview with Gui and John's discovery of the name of the canon of Paris who had been following them.

"Rolland?" She shook her head. "I don't think I ever heard his name. I wonder if Edgar knew him. He was Abelard's student long before I met him. I can't imagine why he's involved in all this. Certainly not to hurt you. Why would he care?"

"It really doesn't matter," Astrolabe said wearily. "He is involved. But I'm sure someone is directing him."

"The unknown monk?" Catherine asked, licking cheese from her fingers.

"Perhaps. We won't know until we find him." Astrolabe stood. He gave Catherine his hand to help her rise. "We had another incident last night." He explained about the slip with his name. "We aren't sure that the monk who overheard was the one who has been following me, but we must assume he is. Godfrey has offered to watch Rolland until the two make contact."

"Ah, that explains why Gwenael was scrubbing the convent kitchen floor with such angry energy this morning," Catherine said. "I looked in on her and she was muttering about having to earn her keep since no one had time for her."

"Godfrey should have explained that he was helping in the defense of her dear master Eon," Astrolabe said. "But Godfrey doesn't like her devotion to him."

"Nor do I," Catherine said. "No matter how innocuous you feel this Eon is, if he can inspire such heretical passion in his people, then he's dangerous."

"Perhaps, but I can't see him as a threat to Christendom," Astrolabe said as they headed toward the cathedral. "I suppose I have a weakness for those persecuted for their beliefs."

He gave Catherine a wry grin. She took his arm.

"Well, I have a weakness for people who are persecuted for no reason at all," she said. "You mustn't worry. No matter what your enemies say, we know you're innocent. The accusations of these little men will have no effect."

"I'm not really that worried for myself," Astrolabe told her. "It's poor Cecile. I don't want her death to be ignored."

"Of course not," Catherine said. "We won't forget her. I promise."

"What about this sacred cave that Gui and Annora are fighting over?" Astrolabe asked after a pause.

They had to maneuver around a group of four lepers, sounding their clappers and calling loudly for alms before Catherine could answer.

"I'd never heard of it, or the saint, before," she said, looking back at the little cluster of the unclean. There was something odd about them.

"Do you think it's important?" Astrolabe persisted. He turned to see what so intrigued her. The lepers were moving away from them now.

"I don't know," Catherine answered. "Annora says that if she dies, the cave will come to Gui. Could he have killed Cecile to clear the way for himself?"

"If I wanted to inherit property, I'd start by doing away with the ones not in religious life," Astrolabe said. "He wouldn't have had to worry about Cecile leaving descendents."

"That's true." Catherine stopped again to examine some pilgrim badges being sold by a man who carried them on a strip of felt tied to a pole.

"You can wear it next to your shell of Saint James," the man said. "Even the hardest rogue might think twice before stealing from one who is protected by Saint Remigius and the apostle James."

Catherine shook her head. She wore her Compostelle proudly, for the journey to the shrine of Saint James had been a true pilgrimage. It would be shameful to pretend she was in Reims for the same reason.

The badges reminded her of the brooch. When they reached the pie stand on the other side of the parvis, she took it out while Astrolabe was getting them some fish in pastry. When he returned, she showed it to him.

"Could you take it to Gui and see if he recognizes it?" she asked.

"You should have shown this to someone before," Astrolabe said. "It would have put an end to the stories about demons in the convent."

"I know," Catherine agreed. "I don't seem to be thinking very clearly lately."

Astrolabe took the brooch from her and put it in the pouch around his neck. He tucked the pouch back inside his *chainse* and tied the neck strings so that the pouch couldn't be seen.

"You have too much to worry over," he said. "My mother owes you a great deal, as do I, for making this journey on my behalf."

Catherine shook her head. "I only wish I were being more useful. There must be something more I can do to help."

Catherine chewed on her fish pasty, occasionally stopping to take the fine bones out of her mouth. It was nearly Tierce. She wondered if the council would adjourn soon to allow the delegates to take some food and rest before beginning again in the afternoon. Some of the bishops and abbots were elderly, like Gilbert of Poitiers, and others weren't in good health. She had heard that one of the two English bishops who had come had fallen ill on the first day. Between the rigors of travel and the draftiness of the cathedral, she imagined that more would succumb before the end of the council.

"Margaret must be wishing now that she were less important," Catherine said. "She could be with us filling our stomachs instead of listening to a roll of church officials being anathematized."

"I've never noticed that Margaret felt herself to be of particular importance," Astrolabe observed. "Edgar seems to have gotten all the haughtiness in the family."

"You've never met his father and brothers," Catherine said. "And pray you never do. Yes, Margaret is not at all proud. That's why, when we've settled your problems, I must find a way to keep her with us. She needs to be with people who love her. She had so little affection when she lived in Scotland."

Astrolabe took his handkerchief from his sleeve and wiped Catherine's mouth.

"I would think that with Edgar, Solomon and your children, you would have enough family to worry about." He smiled. "Instead you took Margaret in. And, while I know you came to Reims because my mother asked it, you have already risked far too much for my sake. You shame me, Catherine."

Catherine shrugged and looked away.

"There seems to be some commotion at the cathedral door," she said. "What could it be?"

Three men had just ridden up. Two of them dismounted and placed a block for the third to climb down more slowly from the saddle. Then one of the men took a long staff from a sling at the side of his horse. Catherine thought at first that it was a spear, but then she realized that it was a bishop's crosier.

"How strange," she said. "Who could that be arriving so late?"

The bishop took a moment to let his men arrange his robes. Then he signaled them to open the door.

"He'll never get through the crowd," Astrolabe said.

But as he approached, the people around the doorway stepped aside. Many bowed to him. Followed by his clerks, the bishop entered the cathedral.

"Now I really hope they recess soon," Catherine said. "I must know what that was all about."

There was no sign of people starting to leave. Catherine looked into her pasty and saw a fish eye staring back.

"Look, there's John," Astrolabe said. "Maybe he can tell us."

John was running toward them from the same direction in which the three riders had come. In his haste he bumped into people going the other way. Catherine and Astrolabe could see his excitement. Even a particularly irate man who refused to be mollified for his spilt beer couldn't keep the grin from John's face.

"He's here!" John shouted as soon as he was close enough. "He's made it after all. You won't believe the story. And he promised to introduce me to the archbishop. Thank God and all the angels, I may get a place at last."

# Thirteen

The cathedral. Monday, 11 kalends April (March 22), 1148.
Feast of Saint Lia, one of the widows who mortified her flesh
for the sake of God and Saint Jerome.

*Ecclesia Dei vobis commissa est, et dicimini pastores, cum
sitis raptores. Et paucos habemus, hue! pastores; multos
autem exommunicatores. Et utinam sufficeret vobis lana et
lac! sititis enim sanguinem.*

The church of God was entrusted to you,
and you are called shepherds, although you are really
predators. And we have, alas, few shepherds; but many
excommunicators. Oh would that it be enough for you to
have wool and milk rather than thirsting for blood!

Bernard of Clairvaux, sermon preached at the Council
of Reims

*M*argaret felt the ripple of surprise run through the cathedral before she saw the man who caused it. First there was a rustling at the door, just at the most solemn part of the ceremony. The pope looked up, annoyed, and signaled for someone to attend to the disturbance. But it didn't lessen. Instead the noise grew and became gasps of amazement and then cheers. Eugenius opened his mouth to order silence. Then he saw the man approaching. He put down the silver cone with which he had been about to extinguish the candle before him, the action symbolic of the darkness into which the recalcitrant bishops were about to fall. Instead he stretched out his arms in greeting.

"My son!" he cried.

The bishop knelt before him, his head bowed and his hands held out, clasped together in a gesture of supplication.

"My lord pope," he said. "I come at your command and beg forgiveness for my tardiness."

"Rise, my lord archbishop." Eugenius bent to help him. "Your presence is welcome, all the more because we know that you have defied your earthly lord to be here."

Margaret leaned over the chair and whispered to Mahaut.

"Who is he?"

"Theobald," the countess answered, her voice rich with curiosity and surprise. "The archbishop of Canterbury. I'd give half my jewel case to know how he managed to evade the soldiers Stephen sent to keep him from leaving the country."

Margaret was surprised at the amusement in the countess's face. After all, King Stephen was her brother-in-law.

Although everyone was burning to know the circumstances

of the archbishop's last-moment arrival, the ceremony continued. There were still many who had willfully disobeyed the summons of the pope. The candles were lit and extinguished. Bishops and abbots all over Christendom were cast out, forbidden to say Mass or give any of the other sacraments. Margaret had lived in a land under anathema; she didn't want to do it again. She was glad that the bishop of Paris had not ignored the summons.

But soon she wished again that she could be somewhere else. The excitement over, it was time for the pleas and debates to begin once more. Margaret forced down a yawn. She stood on tiptoe, trying to see what had happened to the archbishop. After a few moments, she found him among the others to the right of the altar. Someone had provided him with a chair. His clerks were standing behind him. Theobald looked amazingly fresh for one who had rushed from London to Reims, presumably pursued by soldiers. However, the same could not be said of his clerks. Their robes were stained, the material limp with many days of wear. She couldn't make out the faces, but their stance indicated that the two men were much more tired than she.

The archbishop must have realized this, too. After a few moments, he dismissed them. Margaret felt a rush of envy as she watched the clerks leave.

The Latin of the debates was far beyond her. This left Margaret nothing to do but worry.

Countess Mahaut spent much of their time together regaling Margaret with stories of her childhood home. She was so certain that Margaret was as excited as she that she didn't appear to notice that the girl's enthusiasm was at best polite. Margaret hated herself for the cowardice that prevented her from protesting against this upheaval in her life. Carinthia loomed in her nightmares like the gateway to Hell.

As she waited for the proceedings to end, she imagined herself standing proudly, vowing that she would marry no man except by her own choice. In her daydream, everyone bowed to her decision, awed by the nobility of her presence.

The problem was that even in this imaginary scene,

Solomon insisted on standing in the doorway, half hidden by the curtain, watching her with that mocking yet tender smile of his.

Margaret blinked back tears and tried to force her mind back to the endless wrangling of the lords of the church. Some dreams were too impossible even for fantasy.

It was some time before they could get any sense out of John. Finally Astrolabe sat him down at a table by the beer stand, filled a bowl and waited until he had drained it.

"Now, what has happened?" he asked. "Who is here?"

John took a deep breath and grinned at them all.

"My friend, Thomas, has arrived from Canterbury with Archbishop Theobald," he said. "I ran into him this morning as they were preparing the archbishop to present himself before the council."

"But how?" Catherine asked. "I thought King Stephen had placed guards all around the archbishop's palace."

"I don't know the whole story," John said. "Thomas and I only had a few moments. From what he said, it sounds as though Theobald disguised himself and sneaked out of Canterbury with only Thomas and one other cleric. Nobody guessed that he would leave without his retinue."

"That seems incredibly dense, even for the English," Catherine said.

"The guards were probably Flemish," John commented.

"Ah, well, that explains it," Catherine laughed.

"Wait!" John said, standing and pointing across the square. "Here he is. You can have him tell the story."

The man approaching them was tall and light complexioned, with indeterminate brown hair. He greeted John with a hug and a broad smile. John brought him to the others.

"This is my friend, Thomas of London," he said to them.

Thomas bowed. Catherine rose to be introduced.

"You remember Edgar of Wedderlie, don't you?" John asked his friend. "This is his wife."

"I'm glad to know it," Thomas said. He bowed again. "I remember your husband well. He and I often went with Master Abelard to dine and discuss philosophy. I'm sorry not to see him. Has he gone on the king's expedition?"

Catherine shook her head. "Only on one for the family," she explained.

Thomas smiled with a polite lack of interest and turned to Astrolabe. "Have we met? You seem familiar, but . . ."

"Don't worry, you don't know me," Astrolabe smiled. "It's my father you see in my face."

Thomas squinted at him. "Saint Brice's babbling bastard!" he exclaimed. "You can't be Abelard's son!"

"My mother assures me that I am." Astrolabe shrugged. He looked around. They were a good distance from anyone else. "But please, my name here is Peter, and I'd rather you didn't mention my presence here to anyone else."

"If you wish." Thomas looked puzzled. "I am curious as to what you are doing here in that outfit. I thought you were in minor orders."

"We'll tell you all about it, Thomas," John said, "later. Peter has good reason for his appearance. But first you must tell us how you got here."

Thomas took a seat next to them and got out his bowl.

"It was exciting," he said, "and nothing I'd care to do again. The wrath of kings reaches far. We managed to elude the guard in Canterbury and raced for the coast, certain that Stephen's army was right behind us. When we got there, we learned that all the ports had been blocked. I was sure we'd have to return. But Lord Theobald was so determined that I feared he might try to swim to France. We almost did."

He took a drink.

"The archbishop finally rented a fishing boat, crude and leaky," he continued. "There was no shelter on it and barely room for us and the crew. I vow I never prayed so fervently in my life as I did during that voyage."

"How awful!" Catherine exclaimed. "And how brave!"

"Catherine isn't fond of boats," Astrolabe explained. "She'd prefer martyrdom to crossing the sea again."

Thomas grinned. "At the moment, I'm inclined to agree, although at the time I was eager enough to jump into the boat rather than face the soldiers."

He leaned back against the wooden wall of the beer stand.

"Now, tell me your story."

With many digressions and corrections, they did.

As he listened, the clerk's face grew serious. He looked from one to the other of them, as if trying to decide how much of the theories and speculations to believe.

"A demon?" he asked.

"Well, probably not," Catherine said. "We're going to find out who owns the brooch I found. I expect him to be human."

Thomas shook his head, as if to clear it. "I suppose that will help," he said. "There seem to be a number of things going on here, but I don't see how they all connect with each other."

There was a collective sigh.

"We don't either," Astrolabe admitted. "These men seem to be waiting until the heretic Eon is brought before the council. We think they mean to denounce me when I speak for him."

"You intend to defend this Eon?" Thomas asked in astonishment.

"Not his beliefs," Astrolabe said. "They are ludicrous. But the man himself is harmless. I'd hate to see him burn. It's my duty to speak on his behalf whatever the risk."

"And who is this canon from Paris?" Thomas asked. "I don't remember any Rolland among the students in our day."

"He's Breton," John said. "A big man, blond, with bulging eyes. In our student days, he couldn't tell *qua* from *quae* from *quicuid*."

"A harsh thing to say of any man," Thomas said. "No, he's not familiar. Nor do I see where he fits in to your problem."

"The murdered woman, Cecile, was in a convent in Brittany," Catherine said. "And it was her cousin who was attacked the other night."

"That's rather a reach, suspecting him because he's also Breton, unless you can prove it was the canon who attacked the cousin."

That was a new thought.

"Annora said the demon shape was very large," Catherine said. "It might have been he. Perhaps one of us could find out if Rolland is missing a brooch."

"It would be a place to start." Astrolabe wasn't enthusiastic. "But we have no evidence that Rolland was in Brittany last winter or ever knew Cecile."

Gloom settled on the group.

Thomas cleared his throat. "I know that your situation is serious, but I'm also interested in finding out what is happening concerning the debate on the work of Master . . . that is, Bishop Gilbert."

"Now that is a fascinating story!" John began. "It seems the trouble was started by two of his own archdeacons."

Catherine joined in the conversation, although she felt guilty about ignoring Astrolabe's worries, even for a moment. The trial of Gilbert was to her the most important part of the council. Was he really mistaken in his theology, or was he the victim of envy? John believed the latter.

"His work is so dense that it's easy for an untutored mind to misinterpret it," he insisted. "But there's nothing heretical in it. I don't believe the matter would have come this far if Bernard of Clairvaux hadn't been brought into the debate."

"But no one would consider Abbot Bernard a scholar," Thomas said. "He doesn't pretend to be one."

"He is suspicious of the use of philosophy to explain doctrine," Catherine said. "And he is easily influenced by the opinions of his friends. He won't be the one to debate Bishop Gilbert, but he will be the one organizing the trial. Wait and see."

Astrolabe tried to pay attention for the sake of manners, but he didn't understand the arguments. The name of the abbot of Clairvaux brought back bitter memories of the condemnation of his father's work. Astrolabe believed that the trial Bernard chaired at Sens had hastened Abelard's death. Bishop Gilbert was an old man already. Could he endure the humiliation of public rebuke? Would they take away his see? He feared that, like Abelard, Gilbert would come to the court already condemned.

He wondered if the same thing was about to happen to him. His plea on behalf of Eon could well lead to his own condemnation. He had considered the possibility before coming to Reims but hadn't really believed it. He was beginning to understand now.

As the others talked, Astrolabe lost the thread. He found himself wondering where Godfrey was and if he'd discovered the name of the monk who had traveled with Rolland.

The conversation was becoming heated and some German clerics passing by had stopped to join in. Catherine was having a wonderful time. Astrolabe noted her eyes shining in a way he hadn't seen in many years. The language had now switched to Latin to accommodate both the foreign clerics and the difficulty of the subject. Catherine was leaning across the table tapping on it with a finger to make her point. A few of the men had looked askance at her when they entered the talk, but all had soon been swept away by their mutual interest.

A spasm of pain crossed Catherine's face. She bent in her seat. Astrolabe was by her side at once.

"It's nothing," she whispered to him. "A false labor, I think. But I'd be grateful if you'd take me back to Saint-Pierre."

They made their apologies to John and Thomas, but it wasn't necessary. Catherine's place was taken at once and the discussion went on without a break.

Catherine walked slowly at first, leaning on Astrolabe, but she soon straightened.

"There," she smiled at him. "I'm better now. I think it was the excitement. I forget that I'm an old married woman, no longer a scholar."

"Well, I didn't notice anyone of those men treating you as anything but an equal," Astrolabe soothed her. "You silenced that one across the table quite effectively."

"Yes, I did, didn't I?" she sighed in contentment. "Now, you can leave me at the gate. I'll see if Margaret has returned. Thank you for allowing me a few moments of dissipation. Now I shall give my constant attention to our real mission here."

"I'm going to find out if Godfrey has learned anything," Astrolabe said. "Are you sure you're recovered?"

"Completely," she said. "I expect a full report from you tomorrow."

She made her way slowly up the stairs to the sleeping room. Halfway up, she stopped to catch her breath. The cramp that had stopped her intellectual holiday was returning.

"Don't you dare try to appear now!" she ordered the baby. "You need another four months yet. Your father promised he'd be here for your birth. I won't disappoint him."

"Catherine?"

Annora was standing at the top of the stairs. "Are you ill?"

"No," Catherine replied frostily. "I'm quite well, thank you."

"Oh, good." Annora didn't move as Catherine continued up the steps. "Um, I must beg your forgiveness for my outburst this morning. I know that it is your job to find the one who killed my sister. You can't ignore any possibility."

She moved aside to let Catherine enter the room. Too tired to set up one of the beds, Catherine collapsed on the pile of mattresses in the corner.

"You aren't well!" Annora rushed over to her. "Shall I call the midwife?"

Catherine shook her head. "I know what to do. If you could just help me get these pillows under my feet, I'll rest awhile and wait for Margaret."

"Of course." Annora got all the pillows she could find and started stuffing them under Catherine's feet.

"Enough, enough!" Catherine laughed. "Now there is no need for me to forgive you. You were right. It's not my place to criticize your family. At least not to your face."

"I gave you reason to think I would welcome Gui as a suspect." Annora sat down on the leftover pillows. "He is greedy and debauched. I wouldn't be surprised if he knew Henri of Tréguier and had visited him in his brothel. But he wouldn't have ever hurt Cecile. I'm sure of it."

"Astrolabe says he was very insistent that he would take the saint's cave back from you and Cecile," Catherine objected.

"Exactly," Annora answered. "You see, he doesn't even know what happened to her. He means to get it by bribing the judges again, not through violence. You can't kill to get something holy."

An image flashed in Catherine's mind of the soldiers of King Louis slaughtering Saracens to reach the Holy Sepulcher. She shook it away. That was completely different. The infidel wanted to desecrate the sacred sites. Annora and Gui would both revere their saint's shrine.

But then, she thought, what if there were another person trying to lay claim to Saint Gwenoc's cave? Who would get it if Gui died without heirs? If someone else wanted it, that would explain why he was attacked. She looked at Annora. If that were so, then she was in terrible danger. Perhaps she should be warned.

Annora sat next to her, looking repentant and concerned. Her eyes were a grey-green in the afternoon light, almost the color of the ocean. She gave Catherine a tired smile.

Catherine made her decision. She couldn't make life harder for the poor thing. Annora had lost her parents and now her only sister. She was far from home and dependent on the benevolence of Countess Sybil to protect her. Any day now she might be asked to wed a stranger. Why alarm her on a rather far-fetched theory? They would just have to keep her under careful guard. Perhaps a word with the countess would help narrow down suspects as well as increase the protection of her ward. Sybil would know who was in line after Gui.

Catherine knew she was grasping at this because she wanted Cecile's death to have nothing to do with her association with the Eonites. If attention could be diverted to the attack on Gui, then it would help to ease the danger of Astrolabe being brought into the matter.

She wished she could have another look at the wounds Gui had received. His face had been badly scratched, she assumed by the laurel bush. Why had his assailant dragged him into the bush at all? To finish him off away from intrusion? If so, then why was Gui still alive?

There was a piece missing. It annoyed her no end. The brief

excursion back into the world of logic and syllogisms had left her with the feeling that everything could be understood if only one arranged the facts in the proper order and formed the inevitable conclusions. Abelard had believed that even the mind of God could be approached in this way. Why couldn't she figure out a much lesser human design?

As the other women came back to the room, retrieved articles or changed their *bliauts*, not one of them suspected that the woman lying on the floor with her feet propped up so high that her skirts had slipped above her knees was engaged in serious philosophical rumination.

Godfrey had found Canon Rolland with ease. First he had asked for the contingent from Paris. When he found where they were staying, he simply waited until the man appeared. He recognized him immediately from the encounter on the road.

There was no trouble in following Rolland. The man was big enough to be seen even if there were others in between. The streets were too busy for him to notice anyone keeping pace with him at a safe distance.

But Rolland never even looked back. He apparently had a number of errands to perform. Godfrey trailed him first to a feltmakers, then a dyers. The canon stopped for a moment to talk with an egg peddler but bought nothing. Next he went to the draper, then a candlemaker. What was he doing, Godfrey wondered. Weren't there servants for this sort of job?

When Rolland finally entered a tavern, Godfrey was grateful to go in after him. This must be where he would meet the elusive monk.

But Rolland only ordered a cup of pinot, the sour wine that peasants drank. He stood awhile, chatting with the tavern keeper, finished his drink and went on.

Godfrey trailed along, becoming increasingly puzzled. Could Rolland know he was being followed? Was he amusing himself at Godfrey's expense? With increasing annoyance, Godfrey plodded on.

Still Rolland continued his peregrinations. He went past the cathedral and out the city gates at the Porte Bazée and down the road toward the abbey of Saint-Rémi. It was harder now to follow inconspicuously. The houses were farther apart. Fewer people were on the road. There were vineyards and fields of sprouting grain. Godfrey dropped farther back, still keeping the blond head in view.

Suddenly, the head vanished. Godfrey started running, then stopped short. He knew that trick. If Rolland had noticed that he had a shadow, then nothing would be simpler than to step into an alcove or behind some bushes and wait, either for the follower to go by or, more likely, to pounce on him.

With effort, Godfrey forced himself back to a stroll. As he reached the spot where Rolland had disappeared, his body tensed and his right hand went to his knife. He made a quick turn, ready to fend off attack.

A narrow path led toward a monastery not far away. Godfrey was just in time to see Rolland go by the gate and into a garden outside the walls.

More carefully this time, Godfrey went down the path. The garden was enclosed by a woven withy fence. There was no place from which to observe without being spotted. Godfrey decided to walk by as if heading down to the river. As he passed, he saw Rolland go up to a man in monk's robes who was sitting on a fallen tree trunk. The man rose, as if he had been waiting. Godfrey cursed the hood the monk wore. It was impossible to make out his face.

Once out of sight of the monastery, Godfrey doubled back, hoping to catch Rolland on his return trip. But the bells tolled for Sext and None and still Rolland didn't appear. As the day faded, Godfrey decided that Rolland was either staying the night with the monks or had gone back by another route.

When he reached the Porte Bazée, he was surprised to find guards with crossbows blocking his way.

"Has something happened?" he asked. "No, I don't need to pay the toll again. Here's the marker the guards gave me when I left. I've only been gone the afternoon. What's going on?"

"Word is that the heretics are planning to riot," the gatekeeper told him. "They mean to free that Breton and burn the cathedral."

"Sounds serious," Godfrey said. "Do you need another sword? I can ask my lady Sybil if she will release me to help you."

The man lowered the weapon. "Nah, we have enough, with the pope's guards. Your lady may well want you on hand to protect her."

"Yes, probably," Godfrey answered. "Good luck to you."

The gatekeeper grunted and waved him through.

On his way to meet Astrolabe, Godfrey noticed that there were more men in chain mail in the streets and they were in groups so that they could watch each other's backs. He knew the formation. He'd used it often enough. As he passed through, he overheard more about the heretics threatening the city.

"The real leader isn't the one in prison," a woman told him while they both waited for a procession of German bishops to go by. "It's some crafty fellow who's been secretly corrupting good Christians for years. They say he goes from town to town, establishing cabals of these evil ones. When he gives the word, they'll all rise up and murder us in our beds."

"Where did you learn this?" Godfrey asked.

"In the market," the woman said. "Everyone is talking about it. My husband has gone to the ironmonger for a bar to put across our door."

The procession eased enough for them to cross and Godfrey lost sight of the woman.

She was right in that the imminent invasion of the heretics was the only topic in the town. Godfrey heard a dozen versions, each one more terrifying, before he arrived at the tavern. Inside, the panic was palpable.

From the far side of the room, Astrolabe waved at him. He was also in full mail, with a wool hood in place of his helmet. Godfrey had to push several men aside to reach him.

"I don't understand it," he said, taking a seat next to his friend. "I left the city not four hours ago. I return to find that the devil himself is expected to make an appearance tonight and fight hand to hand with Pope Eugenius on the altar of Notre-Dame."

"I hadn't heard that one," Astrolabe said. "All I know is that someone has spread the word that Eon's followers are going to try to release him. Do you think Gwenael has been contacted by others who escaped? I thought she was the only one from Brittany here, except those already imprisoned."

"So did I." Godfrey watched the way the men were drinking, beer and wine tossed down with hardly a breath between bowls. "If there were any such plot, I hope the leaders have changed their minds. Reims is forewarned now."

"Yes, any attempt to free Eon would end in slaughter," Astrolabe agreed. "But you should know from talking with Gwenael that these people aren't sensible. For all we know, they may be courting martyrdom. Or they may be expecting a miracle."

"But who are they?" Godfrey said in exasperation. "Where are they?"

"No one seems to know." Astrolabe shivered. "Some even say that they're invisible."

Godfrey patted the empty place next to him, just in case.

"Are they heretics or spirits?" he asked.

Astrolabe sighed. He gave Godfrey all that remained in the pitcher. "Enjoy it. We haven't a hope of getting more today," he commented. "I have no more reliable information than you do. I wonder if anyone has gone to the pope about this."

"I'd bet not," Godfrey said after considering. "Samson Mauvoisin wouldn't want the other bishops to think he couldn't control his city, especially so soon after the rebellion by the commune. As archbishop, it's his job to maintain order in Reims."

"You can't destroy rumor with a sword," Astrolabe said. "The pope is sure to learn of this soon, if he hasn't already."

Godfrey shifted uncomfortably on the bench.

"I wish I could say I'd solved the mystery," he said. "Rolland did indeed meet with a monk, but I couldn't get close enough to see him. Look, I think I should find Gwenael. If there really is some sort of plot, she'll know of it. If I can't talk her out of joining the other heretics, perhaps I can lock her up until the worst is over."

"She won't thank you," Astrolabe warned.

"Believe me, I don't expect thanks from her, ever."

Godfrey got up and shoved his way back out into the night.

"Are you sure you're well enough to come down for dinner?" Margaret asked Catherine.

"Completely," Catherine said. "I overexcited myself a bit, that's all. Just don't let me have any parsnips. I love them, but I won't sleep tonight if I eat one. Anyway, how could I stay up here with all this going on?"

The room was buzzing with gossip as usual, but tonight it held an edge of fear.

"I knew something like this would happen," someone said. "All the fighting men gone, what better time to try to take over?"

"That's what Baldwin of Hainaut did to Flanders," Annora agreed. "He's probably in league with these demons."

"Flanders is Baldwin's by right," another woman said. "He's my cousin's brother-in-law, and I know the facts of the case. He was only taking back what should have been his in the first place."

"Well, I say only a coward would wait until a lord had left for the Holy Land before invading his territory," Annora continued. "Such a man wouldn't balk at using heretics to get what he wanted. I notice that Baldwin isn't here to present his case before the council as my lady countess is."

"That's enough!" came a voice from the other side of the room. "Such dissension shows that the devil needs no help to work among us."

The room was instantly silent. Countess Mahaut had entered, unnoticed by the bickering women. Her attendants went to her and knelt for pardon.

"We have listened to idle rumor," the eldest told her, "and given way to fear. That is not behavior worthy of our stations."

"Indeed it isn't," Mahaut said. "I came up here to reassure all of you. I have spoken to Count Thibault, Countess Sybil and many of the lords of the church. None of them believe that there is a band of heretics preparing to overrun the city. But to be certain, I understand this Eon has been moved to a more secure prison in Bishop Samson's palace. Our guards are all on alert. Now, it is our duty to behave with dignity, not act like common peasant women gossiping at the well."

The women all seemed abashed by the countess's scolding. They finished their dressing almost in silence and filed out under her reproachful eye. Margaret came last with Catherine. As they reached the doorway, Mahaut stopped them.

"I have heard one bit of rumor that I find very upsetting," she said in a low tone. "One of my brother's deacons told him that some people have given a name to the one who is thought to be the leader of these heretics."

She looked around to be sure all the other women had left.

"The name they give him," her voice sank even more, "is Astrolabe."

# Fourteen

Reims. Tuesday, 10 kalends April (March 23), 1148. Third day
of the council. Feast of Saint Victorian, proconsul of Carthage,
martyred with many others by the Arian heretics. Also thought
by some to be the day on which God created Adam.

*Fama, malum qua non aliud velocius ullum . . .*
*Monstrum horrendum, ingens, cui, quot sunt corpore plumae*
*Tot vigiles oculi subter (mirabile dictu)*
*Tot languae, totidem ora sonant, tot subrigit auria.*

Rumor, the swiftest of all evils . . .
A vast hideous monster. For every feather in her body
There are as many watchful eyes below and, wondrous to
tell, as many tongues, as many mouths sounding,
as many pricked up ears

Virgil, *Aeneid*

*W*e knew this would happen eventually," Astrolabe said. "I'm almost glad they've finally made their move."

They were sitting in an apple orchard near the church of Saint-Hilarius up against the north wall of the city. Astrolabe was hunkered down as if to make himself invisible. His voice was hollow with shock, his face pale beneath the greying beard.

"I never expected them to stoop to this kind of anonymous slander," John said miserably. "I went to bed last night sure that the world was going reasonably well for a change. When I woke up the air was full of wild fantasies about Astrolabe leading an army of heretics, monsters, demons and Saracens to conquer Reims."

"I hadn't heard about the monsters," Godfrey added. "Everything else, though. I did try to find out where the tales began, but it was like trying to find the beginning of a circle. Everyone heard it from someone else."

"And now everyone believes it to be true," Catherine sighed.

"But why, Astrolabe . . . Peter, that is," John stumbled. "Who are these men who hate you so much? A canon of Paris? A nondescript monk? Why would anyone go to such lengths to hurt you?"

"I've been trying to figure that out since this whole nightmare began." Astrolabe sounded as if speaking from within a tomb. "It seems incredible that their only reason is resentment of my father."

The look he gave them smote Catherine's heart.

"Could someone else be trying to ruin your reputation simply to keep you from defending Eon?" she asked.

"It's possible," John considered. "But why bother? Unless the poor man recants, he's sure to be condemned. All, um, Peter here planned was to plead for clemency. What harm could that do to anyone?"

"What if the person who killed Cecile thought that I could identify him?" Astrolabe suggested. "Blackening my name would be a good way to cast doubt on any accusation I might make during Eon's trial. And it would make it easy for others to believe that I am the one who killed her."

"Yes," Godfrey said. "This rumor will make any attempt to defend Eon even more suspect. But it seems an overly exaggerated means to silence you."

Catherine had a thought. "Could Eon have witnessed Cecile's murder?"

"Perhaps," Astrolabe said. "But his mind is so addled that he might not have understood what he saw. He couldn't testify in any case. No one would believe him."

"But if the murderer thought he had told you first, then he would have good reason to fear you." Catherine tried to make this fit. "Killing you would only cause more attention to be paid, unless they could make it appear an accident. Really, discrediting you might have seemed the safest plan."

John nodded. "I like it. That makes sense. But is it the correct answer?"

"My dear friends," Astrolabe interrupted. "Don't you understand? It doesn't matter, at least not for my sake. The thing I feared most has happened. My name has been linked with this scandal. Even if I'm completely cleared of any wrongdoing, the world will only remember the lie. My mother will be tainted by it, too."

No one answered. They knew that he was right.

Finally, Catherine rallied. "Would you be defeated by that lie? Are you going to allow Cecile's death to be unavenged? Mother Heloise would be more ashamed if you turned your back on that duty than by any libel."

"I will see the one who killed her punished, if I spend the rest of my life in hunting him down," Astrolabe said passionately. "But what chance do I have now to convince anyone that I didn't do it? After today, the people of Reims will credit me with any evil."

"The local citizens, perhaps," John said. "But we have here in the city the very men who are most likely to listen to you without prejudice. If you fear to be condemned as your father's son, the same heritage will incline many of the council in your favor. There are many, like me, who feel Abelard's work was unjustly condemned. I can speak to men I know from my student days. They can pass the word along. If you have to face the council, we'll be prepared."

"And as for Cecile," Catherine added, "there are many now who will tell her story: Annora and Countess Sybil, Abbot Moses, whose abbey Henri appropriated. Abbess Marie will testify as to the abduction of the nuns from Saint-Georges."

"That will only tell the world the humiliation she suffered," Astrolabe said. "It won't bring her murderer to justice. Think how easy it would be to blame everything on Eon, if not on me. No one will care to find the truth."

Catherine heard the catch in his voice. She had wanted for some time to ask Astrolabe how close he had been to Cecile, but she couldn't intrude on his pain any more than she had already.

"Perhaps someone at the council will show us a way to do that, too," she said.

"The only problem we have is keeping you alive until then," Godfrey added.

"Godfrey!" Catherine exclaimed.

"No, Catherine," Astrolabe said, "he's right. It may not be the only problem, but for me it is the essential one. But if I have to remain in hiding, I'll no longer be able to help with the search for the real culprit."

"Thomas will aid us," John said. "With his duties, he can't take the time to wander about questioning people, but I'm sure he'll take Peter in with him and see that he's protected. For once, we English are heroes here in Reims. No one will think to ask about an extra member of their party."

"I don't speak English," Astrolabe reminded him.

"Neither does Thomas," John said. "That honor is reserved for defeated people like Edgar and me. Just practice a Norman accent."

"Catherine." Astrolabe turned to her abruptly. "What are you worrying about?"

"Everything, of course," she answered. "What do you mean?"

"You're chewing the end of your braid," he said. "That has always indicated deep perturbation."

Catherine dropped the braid. "Sorry. It may be nothing, but ever since we arrived here, I've had the feeling that I was missing something important. It just won't come to me. For instance, the person who wants to harm you doesn't seem to know what you look like. If he saw you with Cecile, then he should know your face."

"Many friends haven't recognized me in mail and bearded," Astrolabe reminded her.

"But you had the beard when you lived in Eon's camp," Catherine said. "Anyone who saw you with the heretics would know you. Didn't Gwenael? *Avoi*, we already know that Canon Rolland is searching for you. What we don't know is why and who has sent him. If it's this mysterious monk, then he must have seen Astrolabe in Brittany at some point to connect him with Eon in the first place."

"You think they were both sent by someone else?" John asked.

Catherine sighed. "I don't know. It all seems a muddle to me. I just wondered if this hideous defamation was intended to get Astrolabe to reveal himself, if only to defend his honor."

"If so, the plan miscarried. Instead, I've become a mole, traveling under the ground." Astrolabe sighed, too. "There's so much more to be done. I didn't have a chance to ask Gui about the brooch Catherine found. I still have it here."

He took it from the leather pouch and handed it back to Catherine. Godfrey looked at it, glittering in the sunlight.

"Do you think Gui would speak to me?" he asked suddenly. "I'm just a guard, harmless in his eyes."

"He thought I was a guard," Astrolabe said. "And even in a haze of the potions he had been given for the pain, he wasn't about to answer my questions."

"Well, I know he won't tell me anything," Catherine said. "He knows that I'm a friend of Annora's. You could try." She handed Godfrey the brooch.

"He probably wouldn't talk to Godfrey," Astrolabe said. "Gui seems highly suspicious of everyone."

"Well, I can at least find out if he's still in the Temple infirmary in case we find someone he will confess to." Godfrey got up and put the brooch in the bag that hung at his belt. "I don't like doing nothing."

Astrolabe smiled. "Thank you, my friend. You've already done far more than your duties would require."

Godfrey laughed. "It depends on what kind of duty you mean. I owe much more to a comrade-in-arms than I would to a master."

He picked up his helmet, put it back on and left. Astrolabe was too stunned by the compliment to reply.

John got up, too. "I'll go to the cathedral," he said. "Thomas will get me in to watch the proceedings. I'll speak to as many of Abelard's old students as I can find. After they adjourn for the day, meet us at the house where the archbishop of Canterbury is staying. Will you be all right until then?"

"I'll take care of him," Catherine said. "After all, the guard, Peter, is supposed to be protecting me."

In a chapel of the church of Saint-Symphorian, Rolland stood next to Arnulf and lit a candle of thanks.

"That went even better than I expected," he said.

Arnulf grunted. "Spreading false tales is sinful," he said, "and ill bred. You should have cleared this plan with me before you did such a thing."

"Oh, really?" Rolland looked down on the monk's ragged tonsure. "To protect the Truth, I would do much worse. Anyway, I only needed to plant the tale. It grew on its own. I never would have added Saracens to an army of heretics. They're much too far away."

"You didn't say that the Eonists could turn themselves invisible?" Arnulf asked.

"Of course not," Rolland sneered. "If they could, they never would have been caught."

"Oh, yes, I hadn't thought of that," Arnulf admitted.

Rolland smiled. "Neither has anyone else. That's the wonderful thing about such stories. No one questions the logic. If your neighbor heard it from a friend, who heard it from the blacksmith, who had it from a man who knew, then of course it's true."

For the first time, Arnulf looked at the canon with something approaching admiration.

"This will certainly make it difficult for Astrolabe to protect Eon," he said. "He may barely escape the flames himself. Even if he gives a profession of faith, he's sure to be sentenced to a long penance. It seems we've won."

Rolland set another candle on the altar. "That is why I'm giving thanks."

Margaret presented herself to Countess Mahaut for inspection.

"Lovely, my dear," the countess told her. "The gold fillet I gave you is beautiful against the flame of your hair."

"Thank you, my lady," Margaret said softly.

Mahaut examined her more closely. "Is something the matter? You seem melancholic today."

"It's only that I'm worried about Astrolabe," Margaret said. "All those things they're saying in the streets."

"Margaret," Mahaut spoke sharply, "where were you to hear street gossip?"

"One of the scrubbing women told me." Margaret didn't name Gwenael, who had come to her in great agitation when she couldn't find Catherine. "Do you know what people are accusing him of?"

"I do," Mahaut admitted. "This will grieve my dear Heloise more than I can say. But this is still lowborn nattering. No one of any refinement will give credence to such a parcel of nonsense."

Margaret was slightly reassured. "So you don't think that anyone will try to punish him along with the Eonites?"

"Of course not," Mahaut said firmly. "At least," she added, "not on account of this wild rumor."

"Catherine has gone to see what she can do to help," Margaret said hopefully. "I thought that I might stay behind today. I'm too concerned to concentrate on the proceedings. And I want to help, too."

Mahaut patted her cheek fondly. "That's very fine of you, *ma doux,* but what could you possibly do? And you can't want to miss the council today. They're going to decide once and for all if Raoul and Elenora can have a divorce. The discussion will be much more interesting than the wranglings of the past two days."

She nodded to the count's cousin, Elenora, a gentlewoman in her mid-forties, who looked as if she'd just as soon be somewhere else.

"My dear Mahaut," Elenora said, "why expose the poor girl to all these sordid matters, especially when she's about to be married herself?"

Margaret looked at her with alarm.

Mahaut thought a moment. "You have a good point," she said. "But of course Raoul's behavior is very much the exception, Margaret. My cousin in Carinthia would never treat you so shamefully. Still, Elenora is right. There's no need to expose you to the ugly side of marriage."

"You'll discover it soon enough yourself," Elenora said in Margaret's ear as they filed out.

"You may stay in the garden with the nuns until Catherine returns," the countess told Margaret. "Remember, a true noblewoman does not pass her time in idle talk, especially with servants. Do you have some sewing with you?"

"Yes, my lady." Margaret showed her the small embroidery hoop and threads.

"That's a good girl," Mahaut said fondly. "Come, Elenora. It will soon be over."

The women left. From the window, Margaret saw them meet with Count Thibault's party. She regretted missing the divorce pronouncement. Even though the matter had been decided beforehand, there was always the chance that Abbot

Bernard would insist that the marriage bond be honored. It was well known that he opposed Raoul's open adultery. He had tried many times to reconcile the count to his lawful wife, but to no effect.

But another day of standing from Tierce to Vespers in that drafty cathedral would have driven her mad, if not brought about an ague. There were too many people. The glitter of the jeweled miters and rings hurt her eyes. The constant murmur of voices grated on her nerves.

Margaret wanted to go home.

The nuns of Saint-Pierre never guessed the rebellion in her heart as they passed the young woman sitting patiently in the garden, working on a bright piece of embroidery. They ignored her, each busy with her own affairs.

Margaret bent her head. Tears dropped on the cloth, shone in the sunlight and then vanished into the pattern. She knew she had to work up the courage to tell the countess that she wouldn't go to Carinthia, but whenever she was with Mahaut, resolve failed. Catherine would have to help her. Catherine would make everything all right.

The despair she felt was really because she knew in her heart that she must eventually marry some man or become a bride of Christ. Either way, she would lose the one person she wanted most. She had told herself a thousand times that there was no point in hoping, but she would have been happy to stay with Catherine and Edgar forever as long as Solomon was part of the family.

The cloth in the embroidery frame was becoming so damp that the color in the thread was beginning to run.

Gwenael interrupted her morose reverie by arriving with a basket of damp linen. The Breton woman had been sent to lay out tablecloths in the sun to dry. The laundress had not meant for her to do it in the nuns' garden, but that didn't concern Gwenael.

Margaret wiped her eyes quickly as Gwenael approached. She managed a smile of greeting.

Gwenael didn't bother with polite phrases.

"Is master Astrolabe still free?" she asked.

"I think so," Margaret answered.

"Thank God! Do you know where they've taken my master Eon?" she continued. "I heard they have him so weighed down with chains that he can't lift his head. Those *euzhus* men will be punished in Hell, I can tell you. Satan will hang weights on them, sure enough, right from their . . . oh . . . excuse me, Lady Margaret."

She covered her mouth with her hand.

"It's all right," Margaret said. "You are very upset. I can't tell you any more than when we last spoke. Someone said Eon is in the bishop's palace. I don't know if it's true."

"Master Astrolabe will save him no matter what they do," Gwenael said with confidence. "I didn't know he had an army waiting for the right moment. I wish he'd told me. I wouldn't have worried so."

"An army?" Margaret said. "Gwenael, I thought you understood. There is no army. That's just some story that's going through town."

"No!" Gwenael stepped on the linen she was laying out, leaving a muddy print. "Of course it's true. Why else would he have come all this way if not to free my Lord? I suspected from the moment I saw him in the square that he was really one of us after all."

"Oh, Gwenael!" Margaret didn't know how to respond to this. She wished Catherine were there. "These rumors about Astrolabe, they're slander, started by his enemies. You can't credit them at all."

Gwenael's face flushed with anger. "You're the one who's lying!" she said through clenched teeth. "He believes in Master Eon as much as I do, in his own way. He says not only to keep suspicion from falling on him. But I know he'll free us all. How can you doubt it? I thought you were his friend."

"I am," Margaret protested. "That's why I know these stories are all moonshine. You must trust me in this!"

"Why?" Gwenael retorted. "Your kind never spoke truth before. Only my master, my lord Eon, gave us honesty. And now you deny what Astrolabe really is. Are you like the Jews, handing him over to be crucified? Don't you dare betray him! If you do, may God strike you down!"

"Girl! What are you doing in here?"

Margaret pulled her gaze from Gwenael's furious face, only a few inches from hers, to see the laundress and one of the potboys running across the garden toward them. The laundress reached out for Gwenael as soon as she was within range.

"How dare you come in here and bother the lady!" she shouted, whacking Gwenael on the side of her face with the washing paddle. "It's a good beating for you and then out in the streets!"

"Oh, no!" Margaret stood, trying to get between the laundress and her target. "Please don't hit her! It was just . . . We were only . . ."

She looked at Gwenael, whose anger was now overlaid with fear.

"My lady," the laundress said, trying to regain some composure, "you are too kind. We took this one in for charity's sake and I've regretted it ever since. She's sullen and lazy. I'll not have her beat, if you don't wish it, but there are many more poor souls who would be grateful for her place by the fire and bread every day and give good return for it."

Margaret licked her lips, trying to think. From nowhere, she suddenly had a vision of Edgar's fishwife face.

"I have said that I don't wish her harmed," she told the laundress. "Nor do I wish her turned out. I forgive her for her insolence. I shall pray that she learn the proper appreciation for your generosity and that you learn patience. That is all."

She waved to dismiss them.

For a moment, no one moved. Margaret wondered what she would do if they refused to obey her. Then the laundress collected herself and bowed. She turned to the potboy, who was clearly enjoying the scene.

"You, Odo, pick up the linen!" she ordered. "Since you have nothing better to do, you can lay it out to dry in the kitchen garden."

She took Gwenael by the arm and led her away. Margaret thought about following to be sure the laundress didn't continue the punishment out of sight. She decided that it would ruin her illusion of authority.

She rolled up her embroidery and returned to Catherine's room. Sitting in a corner, she wrapped a blanket around her shoulders. Gwenael's anger had chilled her to the bone.

Perhaps the woman should be turned over to the bishop to be jailed with the other followers of Eon. It was obvious that her misplaced devotion had not ebbed. Instead, Astrolabe had become confused in her mind with the heretics. Margaret suddenly thought of what Gwenael might say if questioned. Would her interrogators realize that she was as deluded as Eon? Or would they believe that her attachment to Astrolabe must have a basis in the fact that he was also a heretic?

"Oh, dear," Margaret said. "I wish I had stayed at the convent."

It was only a few moments later when another maid poked her head in the doorway. Hastily, Margaret dropped the blanket and picked up the sewing.

"Yes," she said, "who are you looking for?"

"You, my lady," the girl said. "One of Countess Sybil's guards is at the gate with a message for you."

"Tell him I'll be right down."

Could it be Astrolabe? Margaret grabbed her cloak and street shoes. She was at the gate only an instant behind the maid.

"Godfrey!" she said in surprise. "Is something wrong?"

"No, no," he said. "Everyone was fine when I left them not an hour ago. I came to ask a favor of you."

His eyes moved to indicate the maid still standing behind her.

"You may go," Margaret told her. "This message is private."

The maid blushed. "I'm not to leave you alone, my lady."

"I'm not alone," Margaret said. "Godfrey is with me. It is his job to see that I come to no harm."

"Yes, my lady." The maid left, frowning.

"Tell me quickly," Margaret said. "She's only gone to ask what to do next. The portress will send her back immediately."

"I need someone important enough to make Lord Gui tell us about what happened when he was attacked," Godfrey said all in a rush. "He knows Catherine is friends with Annora. He'll say nothing to Astrolabe, so he won't to me, either. I think you could win his trust. Will you come with me to the Temple?"

"Of course." Margaret tried not to show how thrilled she was by the commission. "I'm ready. We should go at once."

He helped her with her cloak and knelt to fit the wooden sabots over her shoes. When the maid returned, she found the room empty.

Catherine dozed on Astrolabe's shoulder. He leaned against the stone wall softened by winter moss. The apple trees around them were budding. Birds pecked in the bark for grubs. A baby rabbit hopped through the new grass, its ears barely visible through the green. Astrolabe watched it all wistfully. Spring had no interest in heresy.

He sat contentedly in the sunshine until Catherine stirred.

"I'm sorry," she yawned. "How rude of me to fall asleep."

"You didn't snore," Astrolabe teased. "Much."

She looked into this face. "You're better?"

"For the moment."

"It must have been Rolland, you know," she said after a pause, "who started the rumors."

"Yes," he said. "I guessed it when Godfrey described his stops in the town yesterday. How better to incite a scandal than to drop a word here and there at a few shops, tell a story in the tavern. What I don't understand is why he hates me so much. Even if he's working for someone else, there seems to be a personal malice in him. What does he have to gain from my humiliation? He doesn't know me."

"His own glory, perhaps?" Catherine suggested. "Could he be trying to make himself more important so that he'll be promoted in the church?"

"It seems outlandish. He'd either need to be from a good family or have great ability in administering the finances of the bishopric to move up very far," Astrolabe said. "I would guess Rolland is lacking on both counts. Even if he were the one to capture me, that wouldn't give him credit for long."

"Do you think his resentment of your father runs that deep, then?"

Astrolabe spotted the mother rabbit crisscrossing the orchard, perhaps in hunt of the adventurous bunny he had seen earlier.

"I don't know," he said. "You would be better able to judge than I."

"Edgar and I know many people who were students of Abelard," Catherine said. "Some disagree with points in his theology, but no one ever claimed to dislike him. At least not at my table."

"I can name many who feel that even now, six years after his death, my father's philosophy is still corrupting scholars," Astrolabe commented. "Abbot Bernard's secretary, Geoffrey, is one of them. Bishop Gilbert is another. It's strange that they are opposing each other now."

Catherine wasn't about to be diverted again, even by something so seductive as Gilbert's controversial commentary on Boethius.

"But what about Rolland?" she asked. "I think we should get John to confront him. We need to know who's directing his actions."

"We could try. John would probably enjoy that," Astrolabe said. "It seems to me that we'll know the answer soon enough, though. I'm sure the intent is to see that Eon and I are condemned together."

"I'm not." Catherine rolled onto her hands and knees, preparatory to trying to stand. "I can't help but feel that there's something more going on. I don't mean to belittle your problems, but I think someone is using you as a decoy."

"Then it must be maddening to them that I can't be found." Astrolabe gave her his hands. "There's mud on your *bliaut*."

"I can brush it clean when it dries." Catherine spoke from long experience. She wiped her hands on a clear space of the cloth. "Astrolabe, look over by the dung heap at the far side of the trees. See?"

"Lepers," he said. "They shouldn't be out without a keeper."

"I know. I saw them yesterday in the square." Catherine shaded her eyes to look at the four people. "They have the bandages and clappers, but they don't move like lepers."

"Perhaps the disease hasn't progressed very far," Astrolabe said.

"Mmm." Catherine was unconvinced.

"Catherine, no one would pretend to be a leper," Astrolabe continued. "In any case, they have nothing to do with us, thank the saints."

"No, I suppose not." Catherine went on staring at them. "But it is curious."

"My dear friend," Astrolabe said. "In your mind, everything is curious. I understand now why my mother didn't grieve overly when you decided against taking vows at the Paraclete. You'd have found conspiracies in the hymnals, I swear."

Margaret was trying hard not to chatter. She was normally such a quiet person that she had a horror of words pouring forth unconsidered. But she was so excited to be asked to be a part of things that it was difficult not to gush.

"How will you introduce me?" she asked. "I don't look like a great lady, although Eleanor was queen at my age. What is my reason for coming to see Gui? Should I just inquire about his injuries? How do I know about them? I suppose I shouldn't admit that I know Annora. Should I ask about the demon? It's not really polite to insinuate that someone is of interest to Satan, I think. Unless of course, one is a holy hermit. I understand demons consider hermits a challenge and bother them all the time. What do you think?"

She stopped talking so suddenly that Godfrey wasn't prepared to respond. He hadn't been paying close attention.

"Think, my lady?" He guided her past a crowd that had gathered to head off a goat that had escaped from its pen. From the cries, it didn't want to return and was biting anyone who tried to curb its freedom.

"Think I should do?" Margaret prompted.

Godfrey scratched his head. "Well, I thought we'd just go in, show him the brooch, ask if he recognizes it and go."

"Just that?" she asked. "Won't he think it peculiar that two strangers should visit him to ask about a piece of jewelry? Don't you feel we should have some story to tell him?"

"To tell the truth," Godfrey said, "I hadn't got that far. I thought women like the countesses went to see the sick as an act of charity. You know, give them bread and say a prayer for them, that sort of thing."

"Oh, well, sometimes, I suppose." Margaret tried to remember. "My mother would distribute alms at our family monastery, but that was all my father would allow. On feast days in Paris many of the nobles send bread and wine to the poor, but I never heard of someone just wandering into a sickroom and offering to pray."

"You could say it's the custom in Scotland, where you come from," Godfrey said hopefully. "Who could challenge you?"

Margaret didn't want to disappoint him but, "For one thing, we didn't bring any wine or medicine to give him. One can't give alms empty-handed."

Godfrey wouldn't be dissuaded. "I know you can think of something. We can't let Astrolabe down."

"No, of course we can't," Margaret said. "Just give me a few minutes to think."

"How many do you need?" Godfrey asked. "Because we're here. The Temple is that building in front of us."

# *Fifteen*

The infirmary of the consistory of the Knights of the Temple of Solomon, Reims. A few moments later.

*Audivi etiam, quod super damnatione Petri Abaelardi Diligentia vestra desideret plenius nosse similiter vertatem, cujus libellos piæ memoriae dominus Innocentius papa secundus in urbe Roma, et in ecclesia beati Petri incendio celebri concremavit, apostolica auctoritate haereticum illum denuntians.*

I have heard that Your Assiduousness wished to know the more complete truth about the condemnation of Peter Abelard whose books were incinerated in the church of St. Peter in Rome by Pope Innocent II of blessed memory, who declared him to be heretical by apostolic authority.

Geoffrey of Auxerre,
letter concerning the trial of Gilbert, bishop of Poitiers

*T*he atmosphere of the courtyard of the Temple was both military and masculine. There was a pronounced odor of horses, unwashed clothes, damp leather and sour wine. Godfrey stopped as they passed through the gateway. The porter had asked no questions after Margaret had given her name as the granddaughter of Count Thibault. For what the ruler of Champagne had given the knights, he thought, the girl could hang tapestries in the stables if she liked.

To Godfrey, the scene was normal, men practicing swordsmanship, mending harness, grooming their horses, spitting. Suddenly he saw it through the eyes of a girl who had recently lived in a convent.

"Forgive me, my lady," he spoke in panic. "I didn't think. Perhaps we should leave. This isn't the proper place for you."

"Why not?" Margaret looked around. "That man holds his sword as if he were trying to stick a pig. He keeps letting his shield droop. I hope he doesn't ever have to fight for his life."

They passed a group of men throwing dice.

"They'd better not let the marshal catch them," Margaret whispered. "Games of chance are forbidden to the knights. I know that game. I used to have a set made of bone that my brother Robert made for me. There was a trick to throwing them so that I could win whenever I wanted."

"My lady Margaret!" Godfrey was shocked.

"Oh, I never played for money," she assured him. "Just for fun. And I always confessed to the priest and did my penance. What's wrong?"

"Nothing," he gulped. "I wasn't aware that you were so familiar with such things."

"I was born in Scotland," Margaret said. "With five older brothers, legitimate ones, that is. I don't know how many others. I learned to count from the spots on the dice. Now, I've thought of a way to approach Gui, but you'll need to give me the brooch and wait by the door so he doesn't think you're listening."

"Yes, of course . . . my lady." None of the last few minutes had been part of the scene Godfrey had imagined when he asked Margaret's help. He felt an intense need for strong wine and a place to sit.

The infirmarian greeted them with deference. Someone had run ahead to tell him who had arrived.

"Lord Gui is much better today," the monk told Margaret. "His wounds were not severe, mostly cuts. His weakness, I suspect, is from some noxious substance inhaled when he grappled with the demon. Or," he added, "he was just scared out of his wits."

"As anyone would be." Margaret nodded gravely. "I'll not tire him."

Gui was lying with his back to her. She guessed he was only feigning sleep. His body was tense under the thin blanket. She sat on a stool next to the bed and took out her sewing.

After a few moments, Gui stirred. He rolled over and opened his eyes. Margaret smiled.

"Who the hell are you?" he asked.

"Margaret of Wedderlie," she answered. "I saw you at dinner the other night. You may not remember. I was sitting across the room from you, near my grandfather, Count Thibault."

Gui's eyes opened wider. "Saint Martin's sacred horse-shit!" he exclaimed. "I mean, that is . . . You honor me, my lady. I beg your pardon for being in this state."

"You can hardly help being injured," Margaret said. "That's why I'm here."

"You are far too kind," Gui said, still obviously puzzled.

"I understood that your attacker had left deep cuts on your face," she said. "But perhaps that was an exaggeration?"

She looked closely at his face. Most of the bandages had already been removed. From what she could see, the cuts were not serious. They were light, as if from cat claws. Something had raked down both sides of his face.

"They were not as bad as first appeared," Gui said. He was beginning to regain his poise. "I should have no permanent scars, thank the Virgin."

"I'm glad to know it," Margaret said. "Then you need not fear this."

She turned her face so that the sun shone on the ragged red line running from her left eyebrow to her chin. Gui let out a soft cry and reached out to touch her. He quickly drew his hand back.

"I understand, my lady," he said less roughly. "It was kind of you to offer consolation. Did you also run afoul of a demon?"

"Several," she said.

She bent her head, letting the braid fall back over the scar.

"But they were in the form of men," she said softly. "I don't remember much of what happened. Only that I nearly died. The love and prayers of my family saved me. I understood that you had no family here to pray for your recovery. I thought I might take their place."

Gui covered his face with his hand.

"My lady, you must be a saint," he whispered. He seemed to be having trouble speaking. "I am not worthy of your great kindness. Believe me, I am a sinner. But you give me hope for redemption. I wish my wounds were more severe so that I might have the joy of having you visit me again."

Now Margaret was taken aback. "Oh, you mustn't ever wish such a thing! I rejoice that you were not as badly injured as was reported to me."

"I confess that my spirit was worse hurt than my body," Gui said, staring up at her. "But your presence is like cool water on the desert of my soul."

Margaret didn't know how to respond. This was court talk, the sort that poets sang to great ladies or clerics wrote to their patrons. No one had ever addressed it to her before.

"I'm sure that a priest would be able to give you more comfort than I," she said. His gaze was making her ill at ease. "Shall I call one?"

"Priests!" he spat the word. "There's no comfort there, nor truth. They are full of worldliness and flesh. They don't guide us to God, but block the way. How can we follow those whom we can't respect?"

If he expected Margaret to be shocked, he was doomed to disappointment. She had heard it all before. What surprised her was that Gui had thought about such things at all. From Catherine's description, he thought of little more than his own property and advancement.

While trying to think of a suitable reply, Margaret absently began fumbling with her sewing bag. Still looking at Gui, she let the bag turn over. As she had hoped, the brooch fell out.

"Oh, yes," she said as if she had just recalled it. She picked up the brooch and held it out to him. "This was found in the grass near where you fell. I thought you might want it back."

Gui looked at it. His face hardened.

"Is this some sort of ploy to mock me?" he demanded, grabbing Margaret's arm so that she dropped the brooch onto the bed.

"I . . . I don't know what you mean!" Margaret tried to pull free. "It seems old. I only thought it might be something you treasure."

Tears formed at the corner of her eyes. Her lips trembled.

Gui let go.

"I seem to be fated to ask your forgiveness," he muttered. "You couldn't know. This is something I treasure, but it's not mine. It belonged to my grandmother, whom I loved more than my own mother. But, along with many other things, when she died, it went to my cousin, Cecile. She entered a convent some time ago, and before she left, I asked if I might have it. She refused. If you found it in the garden, then I suppose it was dropped by my other cousin, Annora. She was always careless with such things. The only importance it has for her is that I wanted it."

Margaret let her heart make a decision. Reason told her it was a mistake, but there was something pathetic about this man.

"If she lost it, then to her it's gone." Margaret got up. "I give it back to you. May having it comfort you as you recover. Now I must go. I'm glad that my prayers were unnecessary and hope you will soon be completely healed."

Gui sat up in bed, calling after her.

"My lady, I beg you, never leave me out of your prayers!"

Godfrey got Margaret back to the convent as quickly as possible. Neither of them spoke on the walk. Margaret was dazed by Gui's reaction to her, Godfrey horrified by what Catherine and Astrolabe would say when they found out what had happened.

Before she went in, Margaret broke the silence.

"I don't think Gui's killed anyone," she told Godfrey. "But neither was he attacked. He made the scratches on himself. Be sure to tell Catherine."

The bells were ringing for Vespers. Godfrey hoped that Astrolabe was no longer in the apple orchard. Then he could wait another day before having to confess his expedition with Margaret. However, when he got there he found both Astrolabe and Catherine waiting. They were warming themselves with hot meat pasties, bought from a street peddler.

Catherine handed one to Godfrey, whispering, "I think they're made from rabbit, but don't tell Astrolabe. He's been watching bunnies all day."

Godfrey wondered if the spring air had addled Catherine's mind, but he took the pasty. Before he bit into it, he told them what he had done that afternoon. Halfway through, Catherine clenched her fist, crumbling crust and sauce down her sleeve. Godfrey finished quickly, adding, "And Lady Margaret is safely back at Saint-Pierre now."

"Christ's teeth, Godfrey, what were you thinking, taking her there!" Astrolabe exclaimed. "What if word gets back to Count Thibault?"

"Godfrey was only trying to help you," Catherine said gently. "I wouldn't have permitted it had I known in advance, but really, there's no harm in going to the Temple. After all, those men take a vow of chastity."

Both men looked skeptical about that.

"I never let her out of my sight," Godfrey insisted. "And Gui gave her information he wouldn't have told us."

He went on to relate the history of the brooch, along with Margaret's conclusion about the attack.

"But how could Gui have feigned such a thing?" Catherine protested. "Annora and I were there."

"You said you had your back to the door," Astrolabe reminded her.

"But Annora was watching. She saw a black form rise from the ground and envelop him."

"She could have been mistaken," Godfrey said. "It was dark. He may have simply swirled a cloak around himself and then crawled off. Anyway, Lady Margaret was very sure. I'm inclined to believe her."

"I always believe Margaret," Catherine sighed. "She wouldn't have told you if she hadn't been certain. But why would he do such a thing? And he told her the brooch was Annora's? Then I suppose we should take it to her and find out if she was wearing it that night. I should have shown it to her right after I found it, but in the confusion and my exhaustion, I forgot."

Godfrey shifted uncomfortably.

"Well, about that . . ." He finished his story.

Catherine stared at him, blinked a few times and then shook her head to clear it.

"I need to talk with Margaret at once," she said. "She may be ill. This is not the action of my sensible sister-in-law."

She got up to go. "But I shouldn't leave you alone," she said to Astrolabe.

"It's late enough for me to go find John and Thomas," he said. "Godfrey, why don't you escort Catherine home?"

"Oh, no," Catherine said. "We'll both see you into John's keeping. Only then will I go home. I've had enough shock for one day. I don't want to learn tomorrow morning that you've been caught roaming the streets and thrown into a cell with Eon."

Arnulf was making his bowl of beer last as long as possible. It was shameful how lacking in charity tavern keepers were. Everyone knew monks had no money, yet they still expected him to pay.

He had been sitting there most of the day in the hope that Astrolabe would return. But the man must have realized that he was no longer safe. All it needed now was for one person to point him out. The town was so on edge that it was likely he wouldn't survive his capture. Arnulf hoped to be that person.

But what he wanted most was to fulfill his commission. Once that was over, he could get out of these rough robes and wear silk for the rest of his life. Soon, he reminded himself, very soon.

Arnulf looked at the dregs in his beer bowl. He'd make sure he never ran low on drink, either, if he had to build his own tavern to do it.

Around him the talk concentrated on what would happen the next afternoon, when the heretic Eon was brought before the pope. Arnulf smiled and swallowed the dregs. Despite the absence at the moment of his major scapegoat, the plan was proceeding beautifully.

Thomas had brought Astrolabe fresh clothes.

"I spent most of the morning getting myself some new garments," he said. "I arrived in that cursed boat with nothing. Thank goodness Reims has so many clothiers. Good material, too. There are enough for you to borrow. You can't go to the council in that."

Astrolabe reluctantly agreed. He had grown comfortable in his leather *braies*, wool tunic and mail. But they were badly stained.

"Aromatic, too," Thomas said. "I have some scent you can use if we can't get you into a bathhouse tonight."

John laughed. "Thomas, you always appreciated the best.

Wasn't your father a merchant? They always have better taste than the people they serve."

Thomas's eyes narrowed. "My father did engage in trade. He was also sheriff of London for a time."

"Of course," John said hastily. "Edgar's become a merchant, did you know that? His father-in-law was one. Born in Rouen, as a matter of fact. Perhaps he knew your father?"

"I have no idea," Thomas said coldly. "Now, to the matter at hand. John has explained your problems, Peter. And from the talk in the street, they are giving you horns and the tail of a goat as of this afternoon. I agree that your best chance to remain unharmed is to come with us tomorrow to speak with those who might be inclined to help you."

"I'm very grateful," Astrolabe said as he selected one of the plainer *chainses* and tunics. All were well made. Reims was becoming famous for its cloth and, despite his reluctance to admit to his background, Thomas had an expert's eye. "Do you think there will be enough of our friends who will speak up to counter these insane charges?"

"Oh, yes." Thomas seemed unconcerned. "There is already some feeling that Bishop Gilbert is being unfairly harassed, and it's causing people to remember Abelard's trials. Some will support you now because they didn't have the courage to stand up for him then."

"But we mustn't be too confident," John warned. "Many of the bishops have had to deal with heretics in their own lands. They're predisposed to be severe with people like Eon who disrupt order in the villages. I don't know which way the pope will go. Eugenius respected Abelard, but he is in exile from Rome because of the heretic Arnold. He might see Eon as a similar threat."

"I know," Astrolabe sighed. "Arnold was also a friend of my father. Eugenius knows that."

"You chose to come here rather than run," John reminded him. "You must have known there was danger."

"I came because I thought that there was a chance of discovering who killed my . . . friend, Cecile," Astrolabe said. "I wanted to be sure that, if Eon were punished, then Henri of

Tréguier would be, too. Both of them committed sacrilege, but Henri did it on a much grander scale. Eon took food and clothes from hermits and parishes because he and his people needed them. Henri has desecrated a monastery and violated nuns. Yet he still wallows in his sins. I thought that he would be brought to justice if I could lay this murder on one of his followers."

He paused. "To be honest, I didn't really understand how great the danger might be. And now I'm no longer sure that Henri had anything to do with Cecile's death, for all his other crimes. There's been no sign of him in Reims."

"He might be the one who set this phantom monk on you," Thomas said. "And if you bring Henri into the matter, we might get the support of Engebaud of Tours. He wanted Eon caught, but he is furious about Henri's actions as well. He doesn't care about you particularly, I believe. What he wants most is the submission of the bishop of Dol. If you can help Engebaud prove that all these irregularities happened because Dol has allowed anarchy, then he'll take your side without question."

"I always said that Eon wouldn't have lasted so long or gathered so many people to him if the bishop of Dol hadn't ignored the problem," Astrolabe said again. "I can tell Archbishop Engebaud that much in all honesty."

"Very well." Thomas carefully folded the clothes that Astrolabe had chosen and gave them to him. "I must attend my archbishop for now. I've told my servant that you will be sharing the room. He'll bring both of you something to eat."

"And drink?" John asked with a grin.

Thomas grinned back. "Of course, old friend. Where you are concerned that goes without saying."

When Godfrey brought Astrolabe to the house where the English were staying, he hadn't expected to be offered a bed with the clerks of Canterbury, and he was right. Not even Astrolabe had bothered to ask where he was staying.

He left Catherine at the convent gate and went to see if he could find shelter with Countess Sybil's men, even though he wasn't officially one of them. It might be only a place on the floor, but at least he could sleep rather than keeping one eye open all night to guard his possessions the way he would if he went to an inn. Lacking that, there were always the churches.

What he really wanted was to get Gwenael in a nice dark corner. Perhaps some physical proof of his interest would finally convince her to renounce Eon. He went by the kitchens at Saint-Pierre, just in case she were free.

The laundress growled when he asked for her.

"That one's a troublemaker," she said. "Thinks she's better than the rest of us. Hmmph! She can't even scrub a floor properly. Of course, the only thing she's likely any good at is what you no doubt want her for. Well, it makes no matter to me. I put her to work out by the midden, cleaning fish. That should make her appealing. You can have her when she's done."

With a nasty laugh, she shut the door in his face.

Godfrey went around to the back. He found a basket of cleaned fish and a pile of offal on some sacking, but Gwenael had gone.

"Thomas and I are going out with some of the other Englishmen," John told Astrolabe. "He has suggested that we leave you at the bathhouse and pick you up on our way back. Do you mind?"

"Mind? I haven't had a bath since Paris," Astrolabe said. "You can leave me there for days if you like."

"Sorry, we have to be back by Compline," John said. "Think you can scrape off all the grime by then?"

"I'll make a start on it."

The bathhouse was busy but not overly crowded. Astrolabe spent the last of the silver coins of Troyes that his mother had given him and got a tub to himself curtained off from the world. The water was steaming. He climbed in and leaned back in ecstasy. Soon he would dredge up the energy to soap himself, maybe even find a barber. He rubbed his beard. It was time to get rid of it. He couldn't spend his life fearing to show his father in his face. He wasn't ashamed of being Abelard's son. It was far too easy to hide behind the growth and become someone else. Perhaps that was why clerics were supposed to stay clean shaven. And why hermits weren't.

Tomorrow he would come before the leaders of the Church. For that, he should appear as himself, whatever the cost.

That was the highest level of theological speculation that he aspired to. It was too much for tonight. Now all he wanted was to lean back and let the warmth penetrate his skin. Until this moment he hadn't realized how chilled he was, body and soul. Astrolabe closed his eyes and let himself drift.

"We don't need to mention this to Annora, do we?" Margaret said in a small voice. "I know I shouldn't have given away her property, but Gui was so miserable."

Catherine thought he couldn't have looked any more pathetic than Margaret did now. There had been no point in scolding her; she had punished herself quite adequately.

"But I don't understand." She took both Margaret's hands and looked into her eyes, searching for sense. "If you were already sure that he faked the attack, why did you believe him about the brooch?"

"I don't know," Margaret admitted. "I just did. It was the way he looked at it. The way his face softened when he spoke of his grandmother. I never met either of mine. I don't know! I'm sorry, Catherine."

He face was flushed, the scar a jagged furrow in her face. Catherine wondered if it would ever fade completely. It had been more than two years since the attack.

"It's only that I was worried about your safety," she said. "Gui has admitted that he hates Annora and her family. He could have arranged to be in the party that captured the Eonites. He could have killed Cecile. You mustn't feel pity for someone who might be a murderer."

"But I do, Catherine," Margaret said, puzzled. "I know he was lying about something to me, but it's not what we expected. I wonder if he even knew he was lying."

"Margaret?" Catherine stared at Margaret's eyes in shock. While she had been speaking, the color had changed from warm brown to an almost icy blue.

"What is it, Catherine?" Margaret smiled. The color was back to normal.

"Nothing." Catherine rubbed her eyes. "It must be the fumes from the brazier. This room is very close."

Margaret was instantly solicitous. "You shouldn't have stayed out in the wind all day," she said. "You need some spiced wine and a thick soup. I'll see you down to the hall before I go to dine with Grandfather. Then, when I get back, I'll rub your feet with rosemary oil. That will warm you. And tomorrow I'll confess everything to Annora if you want me to."

"Thank you, *ma doux*." Catherine hugged her. "You're a good sister to me. And, no, perhaps we won't say anything to Annora for now. If the brooch is hers, then she must have dropped it in the garden that evening. In that case, it won't help us learn more about who killed Cecile. If you are quite sure that Gui faked the attack, then we have to figure out why he contrived such an elaborate ruse. I don't suppose you have a feeling about that, do you?"

"Sorry," Margaret said, "but I think it has more to do with Annora than anything else. Gui doesn't seem interested in Astrolabe at all."

While the promised spiced wine and soup helped Catherine's body, she was out of sorts all evening. She knew that all of these elaborate dinners were important. This was where the real business of the council was conducted. Now that their marriage had been declared canonical, Raoul of Vermandois and Petronilla were celebrating the betrothal of their children to Sybil's. Sybil would now expect military help from Raoul, and he would count on her to smooth the path for any relations with Sybil's nephew, Henry, especially if he eventually became the next king of England.

The nets spread far. In return for withdrawing his objections to Raoul and Petronilla's marriage, Count Thibault knew that they would support the next nephew of his who needed a bishopric. Or Sybil might be asked to give property to one of the count's favorite monastic houses. It was how the world worked.

Catherine had no objection to that. It was a good system that bound families to each other and helped prevent warfare. But she wished it didn't involve long, elaborate dinners, at least not ones she had to attend. Her only hope was that the entertainment would be lively. If not, she'd commit the social blunder of falling asleep right in her trencher bread.

Or soaking the bread with tears. Sitting at the table, surrounded by loud strangers, she longed horribly for her own home, for the warmth of Edgar beside her and the noise of the children.

She looked around for Annora, the only person at the dinner whom she knew at all. She wasn't there. When the page came by to refill her wine cup, she asked if he knew where she was.

"Not well, I think," the boy said. "She didn't come down. Someone else was asking earlier, and the countess said she was resting in her room."

"Thank you," Catherine said.

She ate some more of the potage, feeling terribly out of place. The page must be mistaken. Annora wasn't in her room. It was the same as Catherine's.

So where was she?

Margaret was having a better time than Catherine. The dinner at her grandfather's was much more informal. No one had said anything this evening about how much she would like Carinthia. All attention was going to Elenora, who had stood before the prelates and nobility of Christendom that afternoon and announced that she really didn't want to be reconciled to a husband who had abandoned her for a woman less than half his age.

"You were very dignified," Mahaut told her for the tenth time. "Everyone in the room felt sympathy for you."

Elenora, sitting between Mahaut and Margaret, thanked her.

"But I didn't want their sympathy, Aunt," she said. "I wanted their respect. And I wanted them to at least set Raoul a penance for his treatment of me."

Her voice had risen slightly. She signaled for another serving of turnips.

"Now Elenora," Thibault said from his wife's other side. "You know how long it took to make even this arrangement. Believe me, the lands, tithes and tolls that Raoul and Petronilla have turned over to you will make you one of the richest women in Champagne. You'll be able to travel from Arras to Aquitaine and be lodged every night by someone who owes you fealty. What more could you want?"

"Honor, Uncle," Elenora said so softly that only Margaret heard. "And perhaps a little love."

The conversation continued on without them. Next to Thibault was his friend, the abbot of Clairvaux. How he had been convinced to keep silent about the divorce was something Margaret would have given a great deal to know.

She leaned back on her stool to see him better. Bernard was a thin man, of middle height. He didn't appear very imposing. But Margaret had seen him preach. There was a passion in him that could only be divinely inspired. She wasn't sure how she felt about him, though. It was his words that had sent the armies to the Holy Land and, indirectly, caused the murder of Jews. But he had dropped everything and rushed to stop the persecution. On the other hand, he had been the chief persecutor of Abelard. Was he a saint, as some said, or only a man too easily guided by his friends? She had heard that he was gathering a faction together to assure the condemnation of Bishop Gilbert of Poitiers. But that struggle had nothing to do with her. What Margaret feared was that this terribly powerful man would speak out against Astrolabe.

The abbot turned and caught her staring at him. Margaret gasped and nearly fell from the stool. She managed to steady herself, looking back up to see if he had turned away. Obviously amused by her awe, the saintly abbot of Clairvaux smiled and winked at her.

Margaret kept her eyes on her food for the rest of the meal.

The bishop of Paris had lodging rights at a very fine house just outside the walls of Reims. Along with the rest of the party, Rolland had been given excellent hospitality, perhaps a bit too much for the Lenten season. His stomach was rumbling alarmingly. It was with great effort that he managed to suppress a mighty belch during the after-dinner prayer.

As the canons filed from the hall, the doorkeeper stopped him.

"There was a messenger here for you," he said. "I told him you were eating and I'd give you the message when you'd finished. He said that was fine, but he wasn't going to wait until then. He'd only been given a penny for the task."

"Did he say who had sent him?" Rolland asked.

"No." The doorkeeper rubbed his palm suggestively.

Rolland grunted and put a penny in his hand.

"Did he leave the message?" he asked.

"He did." The doorkeeper tucked the penny in a pouch at his belt. "It's 'the toll hut by the river; come as soon as possible.' Found a friend in Reims, did you?"

He chuckled. "Better hurry. They check for empty beds in the dorter after Compline."

Rolland didn't bother correcting the man's misapprehension. It must be important news to send a messenger so late. He signaled to one of the other canons that he was going outside, holding his stomach and grimacing in explanation.

The cool evening air energized him. He took a deep breath and released all the gas that had been tormenting him. The sound shattered the still night. From the courtyard next door a dog began to bark, soon joined by all the others in the neighborhood.

Rolland smiled. In all respects, he was a satisfied man. Abelard's son was soon going to receive the punishment he deserved. An old wound could now begin to heal.

It was a dark walk to the river. The road had a line of houses and sheds along it and then nothing but fields beyond. There was no sound from any of the buildings; everyone was either asleep or in the taverns. Rolland walked with the confidence of someone protected by clerical garb and a strong right arm. He could hear the river not far away. The toll hut must be nearby.

There it was, a crude wooden construction, one room with a window that could be opened to make a table for collecting the money from travelers and tradesmen arriving by water. Now the board was up and barred. But the door wasn't locked. There was nothing inside to steal. Takings were brought into town each night to be counted and assigned.

Rolland thought it was an odd place to meet. But in the battle against evil one had to do some unusual things.

He pushed open the door. The hinges were rusty in the moist air and gave a high-pitched squeal. Rolland stepped in. Something caught at his ankles, and he fell full length on the dirt floor.

"Saint Alban's bloody scourge!" he cried. "What the hell was that?"

It was the last thing he ever said.

# *Sixteen*

The convent of Saint-Pierre-les-Nonnains. Wednesday, 9
kalends April (March 24), 1148. Feast of thirty-six people
martyred in Palestine during the time of Julian the Apostate.
They're not prayed to very much
because no one knows their names.

*Hirena: Non perducent.*
*Sisnius: Quis prohibere poterit?*
*Hirena: Qui mundum sui providentia regit . . .*
*Sisnius: Ne terreamini, milites,*
*fallacibus huius blasphemae praesagiis.*
*Milites: Non terremur, sed tuis praeceptis parere nitimur*

Irene: They will not take me.
Sisnius: What could stop them?
Irene: The divine providence that rules the world! . . .
Sisnius: Soldiers, don't be fearful
of this heretical woman's false prophecies!
Soldiers: We aren't afraid but strive
to complete your commands!

Hroswitha of Gandersheim
*Dulcitia*

*L*ady Catherine, wake up at once!" Gwenael was shaking her.

Catherine tried to open her eyes. Around the room there were moans and sharp commands for quiet.

"Gwenael?" she asked, staring at her blearily. "How did you get in here?"

"It doesn't matter," the woman said. "You've got to come with me right now!"

"But it's not dawn yet." Catherine tried to roll over, but Gwenael gripped her shoulder tightly and shook her again.

"Get that woman out or I'll send for the guard!" someone ordered from under a blanket.

"Please!" Gwenael's voice was shrill with fear.

With a groan, Catherine swung her feet to the floor, sorry for once that she had been sleeping on the outside. She felt around for her shoes.

"I have them." Gwenael took her by the hand and dragged her out to the landing. "And your *bliaut*."

Catherine took her shoes. "My hose!" she complained. "And my belt. I'll trip."

"Here, take this." The woman untied the rope from her own waist and gave it to Catherine. "Though I can't see that you need it, the way your belly is swollen."

Catherine pulled the *bliaut* over her head and gathered the material up over the rope, tying it above the offending stomach.

"Very well," she said. "I'm dressed; I'm almost awake. What is so important that you must rouse me and aggravate a roomful of women? Has someone died?"

"Not yet." Gwenael's eyes moved left to right and back

again, as if trying to see behind her own back. "But I might be dead unless you can hide me."

"What do you mean?" Catherine asked. "What have you been doing?"

Gwenael lifted her chin proudly, but she remembered to keep her voice low.

"I grew tired of waiting for Master Astrolabe to free Lord Eon," she said. "So I went to the palace of the bishop to do it myself."

Catherine's jaw dropped. She looked around the narrow landing, lit by a small oil lamp. There was nothing to sit on. She leaned against the wall. Some news shouldn't be given to sleepy people when they are standing.

"However did you propose to do that?" she asked.

"A woman can always get into a place where there are men sleeping alone"—Gwenael shrugged—"or having to watch through the night."

Catherine accepted this. "But how did you mean to get Eon out?"

Gwenael sagged. "That's where I didn't think it out carefully. I supposed I could steal some keys and open his cell."

"What happened instead?" The fact that Gwenael was here with her instead of in chains meant that she had succeeded in part.

"The guards were smarter than I expected," Gwenael said. "Or better provided for than most. They guessed what I was doing."

"And so you left." Catherine yawned. "Well, it was very stupid of you, but it doesn't sound as if you're in any danger. Why don't you go back to bed?"

"I can't." Gwenael swallowed, looking so guilty that Catherine was finally alarmed. "They're outside the convent now. Oh, please forgive me, my lady! I was afraid and a coward. I don't want to burn."

"If you renounce this insane heresy, you won't," Catherine said sharply. "Simply keeping your mouth shut would save you, for that matter. Now, what did you promise them?"

It probably wasn't wise to be so curt with her, Catherine reflected. But she was cold and tired, and the baby was sitting directly on her bladder. Forbearance was more than could be expected.

Gwenael immediately became defensive.

"Nothing," she said. "I only mentioned that I knew where they could find this Astrolabe everyone was talking about. They didn't believe me at first, but I told them I'd seen him myself."

Catherine grabbed Gwenael by the shoulders and shook her hard.

"How could you betray him?" she spoke through clenched teeth. "After all he's done to help you and save your Eon."

"I didn't t-t-tell them," Gwenael managed to get out. "I just said I knew so that they would let me go. But they wouldn't take my word. They insisted that I stay with them until he was found. I didn't expect that. So they came here with me."

"You brought guards here, to the convent?" Catherine rubbed her forehead. "What did you tell them, that he was masquerading as a nun?"

"I said that a woman staying here was a friend of his and knew where he was." Gwenael spoke so quickly and her voice was so low that Catherine thought at first that she had misunderstood.

"I see," she said finally. "And so you brought them to me. And now what do you expect? Am I to hand myself over to be questioned?"

"Oh, no!" Gwenael was horrified. "You've been kind to me. I would never want that. It was just the first thing I thought of. You know important people. You're clever. You'll know what to do."

"Oh, Gwenael!" Catherine threw her head back so that it thumped on the wall. "It may surprise you, but I can't think of a thing."

Gwenael took her hand again and started pulling her toward the stairs.

"You must come," she said. "The men say that if I don't return soon, they'll come in and get me."

That woke Catherine.

"That's nonsense!" she said, even as she started down. "Men entering a convent in the middle of the night? Have they no fear for their souls? Have they no fear of the abbess?"

As they left the guesthouse, Catherine noted that the portress had already called the lay brothers to defend the entry to the convent. She hoped this could be settled before someone woke Abbess Odile. Once she was involved, there would be hell to pay.

The portress glared at them as they entered. "I should have known this one would be the cause of such a disturbance," she said, pointing at Gwenael. "I know all about you, girl. You've disrupted both the laundry and the kitchen. I should turn you over to these men right now."

Gwenael tried to hide behind Catherine. In the room were four men, all fully armed and angry. The portress had given them a tongue-lashing that made it clear that anyone who woke her up for no good reason was in serious trouble and that they weren't too big for her to take a birch switch to them.

Catherine put a hand up to smooth her hair and realized that she had not brought anything to cover her head. It made her feel undressed. Silently, she cursed Gwenael in terms that would have shocked even Edgar.

"Are you the woman who's protecting the heretic Astrolabe?" the captain asked her roughly.

"My name is Catherine," she answered. "I am of Paris but I am here by the kindness of the Lady Sybil, countess of Flanders."

The men were not impressed.

"Your servant girl said you know where this heretic leader is," the man said. "You are risking your immortal soul if you lie to us."

Catherine raised her eyebrows. The guard had no suspicion of what he had just let loose.

Catherine smiled. It wasn't a friendly sign.

"You break into a house of women religious after Compline and you dare warn me about my soul?" she asked in an almost conversational tone. "I believe you are at a disadvantage. Your souls are in peril at this very moment, as are your places at the palace. The archbishop will not be amused to find you've left your posts on such an errand."

"Never mind that," the guard began.

"As for this Astrolabe person," she said. "I have heard the tales circulating for the past day or so. Who hasn't? I find them hardly plausible. An army of demons? Such fantasies are for children or credulous peasants on a winter night. And what sort of person is named Astrolabe? A demon king, perhaps? They say he'll unleash the forces of Hell against us. Really? In Reims, with the pope in residence along with cardinals, archbishops, bishops, abbots, archdeacons, deacons, canons, priests and monks? You can't believe such nonsense!"

"That's as may be," the guard made a brave attempt to reclaim control. "But what about what this woman told us?"

Catherine moved away so that Gwenael was clearly visible to all. The portress made a snort of disgust.

"Lowborn *jael*," she muttered. "Never should have let her in the kitchens."

"Gwenael was taken in and given some work as an act of charity," Catherine explained. "She has lost her home and family. We have done our best, but I fear that her trials have affected her mind. Did she tell you why she tried to get into the archbishop's prison?"

The guard shifted from one foot to another. From behind him, one of the men said, "We just thought she wanted a bit, you know, in return for some food."

"Stuff it!" the captain shouted. "She was trying to seduce one of us into giving her the keys to the cell where the Breton heretic is kept. As if we didn't know that one. She talks like they do. I figure she's one of them. She's free only because she said she'd turn the leader in."

"It's possible that she's one of the Eonites," Catherine answered. She was thinking as quickly as she ever had in her life. "But if she is, then she would believe that a demonic force was coming to rescue him. Why risk her freedom with such an obvious scheme when help was on the way?"

"Right," the portress said before the captain could respond. "I told you, she's just a poor addled slut. And she's made fools of the lot of you. Now go back to your posts before the Night Office begins or I'll have the abbess down here to report your names to Archbishop Samson."

She shooed them toward the door and, in some confusion, they let her. The captain turned and gave Catherine one parting shot.

"We know you now," he warned. "If we find you've lied to us, not even that brat you carry will save you. You'll go to the pyre the day it's born."

"OUT!" the portress said. The guards had barely crossed the threshold when she gestured for the lay brothers to shut and bar the door.

"As for you"—she swung about to face the cowering Gwenael—"if it were my say, you'd be out on the streets this moment. Look what trouble you've put Lady Catherine to. Shame!"

Catherine heartily agreed. The man's last words had shaken her more than she dared show. However, she had taken Gwenael in and now the woman was her responsibility.

"Thank you," she told the portress. "It is you who have been put to trouble and I am most deeply sorry. I'll see that Gwenael is properly chastised for her behavior."

"I'd suggest a few months on bread and water," the portress answered. "And the same time spent on her knees, scrubbing and praying."

"A distinct possibility," Catherine promised. "Now, Gwenael, I want you to go to your own bed and not leave it until I send someone for you. Do you understand me?"

Gwenael nodded. "Yes, my lady. Thank you, my lady. I'm sorry, my lady."

She dropped to her knees, taking Catherine's hand and kissing it. "They would have killed me, I know, but for you, my lady. I knew you would save me."

"Next time you might try putting your faith in Our Lord." Catherine drew her hand away. "Of course, if you had in the first place, this wouldn't have happened. Now, please, Gwenael. I want to go back to sleep."

Having finally got the woman off, Catherine made a stop

at the latrine and then wearily made her way back up the stairs. She was too tired even to be furious. That could wait until morning. All she could think of now was the warmth of the bed.

But there was a hollowness inside her. She had felt pity for Gwenael. Now all she felt was terror at what the woman's foolish act might have brought upon them all.

It wasn't until she returned to bed that she realized only Margaret was in it. Annora had never returned.

"Good Lord!" Thomas exclaimed. "I think I'm seeing a ghost."

"You see why I liked the beard," Astrolabe said. "Maybe I shouldn't have had it shaved. Now there will be men at the council sure that my father is haunting them."

"It will do them good," John said. "There are some who should examine their consciences on that score. No, you did the right thing. You came here to face your enemies openly. You might as well show that face to the council."

He cocked his head, studying Astrolabe's naked countenance. "You're leaner than you used to be. Harder. I noticed that you didn't have the tonsure shaved as well."

"It didn't feel right, somehow," he answered. "To hide behind minor orders. I'm tired of hiding. It didn't help avoid the scandal. Perhaps I've made things worse by coming to Reims in disguise."

"If you hadn't, you might not have got here at all," John said. "Rolland and his friend may well have meant to kill you before you could defend your name."

"Anyway," Thomas laughed, "if I had to suffer the indignity of wearing rough, salt-soaked fisherman's clothes to make my way here, it assuages my spirit to know that you had a like experience."

Astrolabe laughed with him but secretly felt that he was going to miss being Peter. The cleric's robes felt far too light after the mail.

"Very well," he said. "My most important objective is to report Cecile's death officially. I need to go to the archbishop of

Tours and tell him everything. He should know that one of his men may also be in the pay of Henri of Tréguier."

"And if you are denounced by this Canon Rolland?" Thomas asked.

"I can defend myself. Unlike when I first arrived," Astrolabe said, "I have friends who will stand by me."

"More than you realize," John told him. "From what we learned last night, Rolland's plan of setting the populace against you has only infuriated the council members. Archbishop Samson is particularly displeased. It's only a few weeks since the commune was put down. He wants no excuse for the townspeople to revolt again."

"Then it seems that the worst has already happened," Astrolabe sighed in relief. "And we've survived. Although my name may become a threat to the children of Reims for many generations. 'Eat your porridge or the Astrolabe will get you!' It's a legacy I can endure."

"So we try to reach Archbishop Engebaud before he leaves for the council," John said. "Then, if you still feel obligated to defend Eon, you can appear there this afternoon when he's due for trial. If the archbishop is willing to trade for your testimony against the bishop of Dol, you may even be able to get the poor fool released to the custody of a monastery."

Astrolabe stretched his arms over his head, almost feeling the weight lift.

"Then I can take Catherine safely back to my mother," he said, "and get on with my life. After all the insistence that she come to be able to overhear Latin conversations unnoticed, she really hasn't had any cause to do so. I've stolen her from her family for nothing."

"I'm sure she's been of use to Countess Sybil," John mentioned. "And she may yet be asked to participate in the debate concerning Bishop Gilbert."

Astrolabe stared at him.

"Joke!" John said. "Although I'm sure she could give a good account of herself. I just had an image of her going nose to nose with the Lombard. It would be more than many of the elderly members of the council could survive."

The thought of this put them all in a good humor. They descended the steps to the hall, ready for bread, cheese and beer to break their fast and fortify them for the day.

Instead they found chaos. No one had put out the food. The tables weren't even set up. Servants appeared carrying bags of altar linen and the instruments of the Mass. The other English clerk came running down from the bishop's chambers with a chalice tucked under his arm.

"What's happening?" Thomas demanded.

"They found a body by the river," the man told them. "Someone identified him as the man who had warned him about the heretic army. Now everyone is in a panic. They say the Astrolabe has come. Do you have any idea what that means? Why should anyone be afraid of an astrolabe?"

Astrolabe reached back and pulled his cowl over his head. It seemed he had decided to resume his own identity too soon.

"Godfrey!" Catherine called down from the window. "We've been told not to leave the convent until things have calmed down. I have to send a message to John. Meet me in the entry."

Godfrey cupped his hands over his mouth to be heard above the noise in the street.

"At once, my lady!"

A few passersby looked up to see whom he was yelling at, but most continued on, either heading toward the bishop's palace next to the cathedral to be in on whatever was going to happen, or running as quickly as they could to take cover from it.

"Never take refuge in a convent," Catherine greeted him a few moments later. "It's far too easy to find yourself trapped inside for your own good."

"It sounds like Heaven to me," Godfrey answered. He realized what he had just said. "Begging your pardon."

Catherine was pale and drawn that morning. She hadn't slept again after the incident with Gwenael, and the news they had awakened to had set her in a frenzy of worry. If she hadn't seen Godfrey in the street, she might have made a rope ladder and let herself down from the guest house window.

His words made Catherine blink. Then she laughed. The guard relaxed.

"We all have different images of Heaven," she said. "Mine is to be home with my husband and children, not cooped up with a dozen women, all of whom want to be out as much as I do. *Avoi*, I need you to find John. Do you know anything about this murder last night?"

"Me? No," he said quickly. "I spent the night camped out by Saint-Hilarius. I learned of it this morning. They say the dead man is a canon of Paris. Rolland, I'm sure."

"That's what Lady Sybil's men told us," Catherine said. "Do they know how he died?"

He shook his head. "No. There are a thousand speculations. Many are sure he ran afoul of the demon lord because he tried to warn people of his plans to conquer the city. The methods they suggest could only have been accomplished by demonic energy. But I seriously doubt that the body was found with all his organs having been pulled out through his mouth."

"What do they mean, 'conquer the city'? I thought the story was that the demon was merely going to free Eon," Catherine said.

"That was yesterday," Godfrey said. "By tomorrow his army will have already overrun Spain and Provence and be at our gates demanding a tribute of gold and virgins."

"No doubt," Catherine said. "Godfrey, I need to know how Rolland really died. Was he drowned, strangled, run through, poisoned, hanged, stabbed through the heart or hit over the head?"

Godfrey took a step back. "Is there one method you'd prefer?" he asked.

"I have a suspicion," she said. "Of course, I knew someone once who took pride in inventing appropriate ways to dispatch each of her victims, but most people have a favorite and stick to it."

"You've had much experience in this?" Godfrey stepped back again.

"More than I care to," Catherine said absently. "Of course,

he might not have been murdered at all. He could have fallen or had a fit. But we wouldn't be that lucky."

"I'll find out for you," Godfrey promised. "Is there anything else?"

"Yes, but first I have to tell you what Gwenael has done." Catherine did.

"So don't try to see her today," she concluded. "She's in the nuns' chapel, cleaning the floor. Someone will be watching her constantly."

"Stupid, stupid woman!" Godfrey looked around for something to put his fist through. "I knew something was wrong when I couldn't find her last night. She's as mad as that heretic lord of hers. Give her up to the bishop."

"You don't know how much I'd like to," Catherine sighed. "I have no idea how to pierce her faith in Eon. She needs someone far more skilled than I am. But I'm sure that, even in her madness, she might be able to help Astrolabe. And we can't risk what she might say if she were questioned now without one of us nearby."

"She's convinced that Astrolabe is going to free Eon," Godfrey admitted. "It would be hard to explain that her belief has no substance."

"Now, if you'll try to discover all the particulars of Rolland's death," Catherine continued, "that will help me. After that, find John. Ask him please to come here as soon as he is free. I'm hoping that the tumult in the streets will die down soon. If it does, then I'll do my best to be at the cathedral this afternoon when Eon is brought in."

"But surely it was Rolland who intended to denounce Astrolabe," Godfrey said. "So now there's no danger."

"Perhaps that was Rolland's intention," Catherine answered. "Someone else was certainly willing to let him be the visible target. That was very wise. But now that he's dead, the threat to Astrolabe is even worse. Aren't they saying in the street that he killed the canon?"

"Yes, but you haven't listened closely," Godfrey said. "No one thinks he's a man anymore, but some sort of demon king.

There are even those who now are certain that Rolland was really his messenger and struck down by God."

"No tale would be too incredible," Catherine said, "for those already infected with panic. But those who have the job of investigating the death are not going to listen to the streets. They will look for a human hand. That's why I need to know how it happened."

She rubbed her temples with both hands. "I can almost see it," she complained. "Eon, Cecile, Annora, Gui, Rolland, that unknown monk, even Gwenael. Somehow they all fit together. Astrolabe has been caught up in a tangle worse than Margaret's thread box. We must work harder or he may be the only one who can't escape."

"I'll do as you ask, my lady," Godfrey said. "I promise to return before Nones with Master John if I have to drag him from under the nose of the pope himself."

"Thank you. Also," Catherine called after him, "find out where the body is now. Examine it if you can."

Godfrey gave her an incredulous stare and then vanished into the crowd.

Catherine went back upstairs to find the windows wide open. The women were leaning out of them, trying to see everything that was happening. The convent overlooked a square only a short walk from the cathedral and across from the church of Saint-Etienne. They could see the people heading toward the bishop's palace next to the cathedral, and hear the shouts.

"I'm not going to wait here any longer," one woman announced. "I'm not cloistered. No one has the right to keep me here. I don't see Countess Sybil hiding. She left this morning to consult with the Flemish bishops."

"Aren't you afraid of the mob?" another woman asked.

"I'm calling for my horse and a guard," the first one said. She took riding boots and gloves from her box. "I may not be able to go hawking, but at least I can ride outside the city. Anyone who tries to stop me will regret it."

"I'll come with you," someone said from the window. "The commotion seems to be moving west to the cathedral. My lady doesn't need me today, and I can't bear this noise and enforced seclusion."

Once the suggestion had been made, others admitted that they also needed a day in the countryside. Catherine and Margaret watched them in amazement.

"Don't they understand what's happening out there?" Margaret whispered.

"I don't think they care," Catherine whispered back. "This isn't their city. They aren't credulous enough to fear a demon army. Why shouldn't they go riding? It will harm no one."

*And*, she thought, *it will make it easier for me to slip out later.*

As the room slowly cleared, Catherine noticed a bedraggled figure come out from behind the curtain in the corner.

"Annora!" she cried. "When did you return? Where have you been? I've been worried about you. The countess's servants said you were ill."

"How silly of them," Annora said. "The countess knew where I was."

"What happened to your clothes?" Margaret asked.

"I went out to dine at the table of Archbishop Hugh of Rouen," Annora said. "I hold part of my castellany from him. He is staying outside the city gates, and by the time the dinner ended, it was too late for me to return."

Catherine raised her eyebrows but said nothing. Margaret was not so circumspect.

"Was there no bed at the archbishop's?" she asked. "You have grass stains on the back of your *bliaut*."

Annora checked her skirts and saw that Margaret was right.

"I have no idea how that happened," she said. "I slept very badly at the archbishop's and then had to force my way through the rabble in the streets to get back. Isn't it today that Eon is to appear before the council? I want to be there to speak for Cecile, but I must have some rest and a wash first."

She said this as if accusing Catherine and Margaret of keeping her from both.

"We were just leaving." Catherine nudged Margaret. "A walk in the garden, don't you think, Margaret? Until Godfrey returns?"

"Oh, yes." Margaret got up at once. "I would love to walk in the garden. Of course most of the plants are still sleeping, but one can imagine the flowers."

"That will be a fine mental exercise," Catherine said, trying not to laugh.

Annora paid no attention. She was obviously exhausted. She removed her belt, shoes and *bliaut* and crawled into the bed in her *chainse*.

"We'll be going, then," Catherine said.

Annora pulled the blanket over her head.

"I hope Countess Sybil never finds out where she really was last night," Catherine commented as they reached the garden.

"Why? Where was she?" Margaret asked.

"I have no idea," Catherine answered. "But it wasn't dining with the archbishop of Rouen."

"Even to me the story sounded thin," Margaret said. "But I can't think of any other place she could have gone. Who else does she know?"

Catherine kicked at the earth in frustration. "Just when I thought all the pieces were fitting, she has to jumble them again. I hope Godfrey was able to get the information I wanted."

"Will that make everything clear?" Margaret asked.

"Probably not," Catherine said. "Unless it turns out that Rolland did indeed have his entrails pulled out through his mouth. Then we can confidently blame a demon."

They walked in silence for a while, each occupied with thoughts that had nothing to do with immediate problems.

"I forgot to tell Sister Melisande about that rash Edana had on her bottom," Catherine said.

"She noticed," Margaret told her. "She had a salve that worked very well."

"Oh, good," Catherine said without enthusiasm. She thought she should have been the one to take care of her daughter's rash.

They started another circle of the garden.

"I haven't spoken to Countess Mahaut yet," Margaret blurted. "Won't you please do it for me? I can't go to

Carinthia. She doesn't want to wait until Edgar returns but to send me as soon as she can have my clothes ready. Grandfather said he'd provide the dowry so Edgar needn't worry. It's all happening so quickly! I don't know how to stop it."

"Margaret, you must speak out," Catherine said. "I can protest, if you like, but yours is the only voice they'll listen to."

"I can't!" Margaret said in despair. "Every time I try, Countess Mahaut says something about how lovely the country is and how much I'll enjoy it. Or Bishop Henry asks me to say something in German. Catherine, I can't even remember the name of the man they want me to marry. They only mentioned it once. The rest has been about what a wonderful alliance it will be."

She gulped and wiped her eyes with her sleeve. "I know that Astrolabe's fate is much more important than mine. I try not to bother you with this, but I need you, Catherine. I'm so afraid."

"Oh, my poor sister!" Catherine took Margaret in her arms and let her cry. "You are just as important as Astrolabe and much more dear to me. I won't let you go. We'll find a way through this, I promise."

But Catherine wished heartily that Edgar were with her. This was one dilemma too many for her to cope with.

Margaret was still sniffling when the portress came to tell them that Godfrey had returned with a priest.

"That must be John," Catherine said. "At last we've brought someone to the door that she approves of."

They hurried to greet them.

"Is our friend Peter safe?" Catherine asked first.

"Under the protection of Archbishop Theobald," John said. "And," he added with pride, "I think I may soon be as well."

"John, that's wonderful!" Catherine said. "It will be a great thing for you. I know you'll serve him well. Now, about the body."

"Catherine, you would never survive the ceremony at court," John said. "You never bother with the polite preludes to important discussion."

"No, I don't," Catherine said. "This week has taught me

that. I don't have time for manners. Godfrey, did you see Rolland's corpse?"

Godfrey winced. "I did. It wasn't well guarded. Do you want to tell me how he died? You said you had a guess."

"His throat was cut," Catherine said. "From behind, likely, unless he was unconscious."

"You have it," Godfrey said. "How did you know?"

"That was how Cecile died." Catherine rubbed her hands together as if trying to remove a spot of grime. "People tend to stick with what works, even in murder. Now why would the person who killed Cecile want to get rid of Rolland, too?"

# Seventeen

The same day, a little later.

*Juventute equidam exigente, quondam nobilem mulierem
mihi concubinam adamavi, & peccato instigante Moyse
predicti lici Abbate inde a me ejecto, predictam concubinam
peccatis exigentibus intrusive posui. . . . Refellatur itaque, . . .
omnis calumnia & Monialum Redonensium questio falsa
omnino supplodatur.*

In the passion of my youth, I fell in love with a certain
noblewoman and made her my concubine. Instigated by my
sin, I evicted Moses, abbot of the aforesaid place, and
installed my concubine to satisfy the desires of my sin. . . .
Therefore, let every rumor and false doubt about the nuns of
Rennes be stamped out.

Henri of Tréguier, count of Penthievre, letter to Pope
Alexander III, written when Henri was in his eighties and
concerned about finally making amends

$\mathcal{T}$he streets had been cleared by the archbishop's guards. Archbishop Samson was not going to let his fellow prelates think that he couldn't control his own town. He had accomplished this control in two stages. First, with the aid of Raoul of Vermandois and his men, soldiers on horseback herded the citizens back into their homes. Then the archbishop announced that he was opening his granary north of the city. Every resident of Reims was to receive one *sestier* of barley as a gift in gratitude for their tolerance of the inconveniences the council had caused.

The town emptied almost at once. Heretics and demons were ephemeral terrors. Famine was real.

At the houses where the attendees were staying, servants began putting the hastily packed valuables out again. The council resumed.

Thomas dressed hurriedly but with great care, making sure that his gauffered sleeves hung just so and that there were no smudges on his soft leather shoes. John and Astrolabe watched in amusement.

"You'd be right at home in a king's court," John told him. "I know many noblemen who don't dress as well as you."

"I need to make a good impression," Thomas said amiably. "I don't want to dishonor my master."

"Well, since you're doing it on my behalf, I shouldn't mock you for it," John answered.

Thomas turned around, his sleeves making an elegant swirl.

"On your behalf? I don't understand," he said.

"You were going to introduce me to the archbishop, weren't you?"

John's voice ended on a nervous high note. Astrolabe looked from one to the other, wondering if he should leave. Thomas gave John an embarrassed glance and then spent a moment earnestly examining a loose thread on his belt loop before he spoke.

"John, you are welcome to a bed here," he explained, "and I will do whatever I can to help Astrolabe defeat these slanderers, but I can't put you forward for a position in Theobald's household. I thought you understood that."

John sat up straight, his hands clenched at his sides. "I had assumed, because of our friendship . . ." His voice trailed off.

Thomas sighed. "I have many friends, John, who want something from the archbishop. Part of my duty is to protect him from office seekers. More important, it wouldn't do any good even if I did present you to him. He won't take anyone without a recommendation from someone of high rank. I just run his errands and write his letters."

John's stricken expression told Thomas how much he had counted on this.

"I'm truly sorry," he said. "I thought you knew what my position was."

"No." John shook himself. "I should have realized. It was stupid of me. I beg your pardon for putting you in such an uncomfortable situation."

Thomas took a step toward him, hand out.

"I wish you luck, John," he said. "And if you do find a way to join us at Canterbury, there's no one who will welcome you more heartily than I."

John took his hand and tried to smile.

"Now, I must hurry." Thomas nodded to Astrolabe, glad to change the subject. "I will ask what's being done about this murdered canon of Paris. Since he died here, it may be the jurisdiction of Samson Mauvoisin, but the bishop of Paris may feel he has a say, and then there are the local lords. Do you know who has the high justice for Reims?"

"It might be Count Thibault," Astrolabe answered.

"Perhaps you should go to him," Thomas suggested. "Hugh of Rouen should be consulted, too, since you say the woman who died in Brittany held land of him. They are both reasonable men. I feel certain we can clear you of all suspicion in both cases."

"Thank you," Astrolabe said, aware that he was being dismissed. "John, we should be going, don't you think?"

"What?" John came out of his trance. "Oh, yes, of course. We have much to do now that the populace has stopped crying for your blood."

Astrolabe stood. Taking John by the arm, he headed for the door. "And I'd like to get my work done before they start up again. My thanks to you, Thomas of London, for your hospitality."

John managed to get as far as the street with no loss of dignity. But as soon as they were out of view of the windows, he collapsed against Astrolabe, tears flowing.

"I was so sure," he gulped. "I thought he . . ."

With an effort, he stood on his own. He rubbed his eyes angrily, forcing the tears to stop.

"It doesn't matter what I thought," he said. "I was wrong. Oh, Astrolabe, Thomas was my best chance. Now I have no idea how I'm going to earn my bread."

Astrolabe took him by the shoulders, pulling him up straight.

"That makes two of us." He grinned. "Of course, in my case, the question may soon be resolved. Unless I'm cleared in Rolland's death, my need for food will be abruptly terminated."

Samson Mauvoisin, archbishop of Reims, was becoming increasingly annoyed by the disturbances to the council. It was Pope Eugenius who had fixed the place for the meeting. Reims was one of the oldest bishoprics in France. The cathedral had been built in the time of the Carolingian emperors and was the site of the anointing of the kings. It was only appropriate that the church convene here. It was almost a tradition.

But Eugenius might have chosen a better time.

The burghers were still smarting from the breakup of their commune the previous autumn. They were threatening to move the expanding cloth-making industry to a friendlier city. Food was dear. The news from the Holy Land was uniformly bad. And now some canon from Paris had tried to incite a riot and then been murdered. The last was the only good news Samson had received in weeks.

But the bishop of Paris was agitating for the capture of the killer. The countess of Flanders had sent word that the interests of one of her wards was involved, God knew how. The archbishop of Tours insisted that the matter was somehow tied up with this heretic now languishing in Samson's prison. He also hinted darkly that Bishop Olivier of Dol was ultimately responsible since the canon was Breton and, no doubt, in the bishop's pay.

Samson had no interest in the state of affairs in Brittany. Therefore he was extremely irritated to have it left at his doorstep. The only thing he was curious about was why the name of this phantom demon king was Astrolabe. He wondered if the people knew that it was a computational device for measuring the height of the sun and stars in the sky. Useful for astrologers and physicians, but hardly demonic. However had the street gossips got hold of the word?

Nevertheless, it was up to him to see that the issue of the canon's death was resolved.

"Ermon," he called his servant. "Have messages sent to the archbishops of Tours and Rouen, the bishop of Paris, Countess Sybil of Flanders and, for good measure, Count Thibault. Ask if they will join me this evening. No doubt this canon was set upon by thieves and killed for his purse. What could he expect, alone outside the gates at night? Nevertheless, I shall have to hold an inquiry, and I want all of those people here so that they can't say later that I impeded justice."

"Yes, my lord." Ermon bowed.

"Ermon?"

"Yes, my lord."

"Just send the invitations. The rest of my speech you will forget."

"Of course, my lord."

*   *   *

Catherine met John and Astrolabe at the entry to the convent. Margaret was with her, having begged off spending another day at the council.

"Godfrey said you needed us," Astrolabe began. "You've heard about Rolland, then?"

"I have," Catherine said, staring at him, "but not about your metamorphosis!"

She reached up and felt his smooth chin. "I don't know, I was getting rather fond of the beard."

"Sorry," Astrolabe said. "I thought it best to remind people of my clerical status, just in case I'm arrested."

"Do you think it will come to that?" Catherine asked, alarmed. She turned to John.

"It's possible," he admitted. "Archbishop Samson has now become involved, and he isn't going to let the murder of one of the men attending the council go unpunished, even if Rolland wasn't very important."

"I'm sure that whoever killed Cecile also murdered Rolland," Catherine announced. "The method was the same. So now we can be certain that the person we seek is in Reims. We have to find the monk Rolland was traveling with. If he didn't commit the murder, I suspect he knows who did."

"We saw his face, but too briefly," Astrolabe said. "I've been looking at every monk I pass, but the fact is, I'm not sure I'd know him. He had one of those faces that you see and forget."

"I know," Catherine agreed. "Rolland was the one we all remembered."

"Perhaps that's what he was there for," Margaret suggested.

They looked at her.

"Well, it was only a thought," she said nervously.

"A good one," Astrolabe told her. Margaret gave him a shy smile of thanks.

"But it doesn't help us, I'm afraid," Catherine said. "Now, let's go somewhere to sit and discuss what to do next."

"Do you have enough money for a flask of good wine?" Astrolabe asked.

"I'm sure I do," Catherine said. "Why? We can't be celebrating anything."

"Just the opposite," Astrolabe said. "John has had a nasty shock this morning. He needs something more potent than beer."

The two men explained what had happened with Thomas on the way to the wine merchant. After learning the story, Catherine had no qualms about buying four *pintez* of wine, enough to fill a good-size jug. She understood Thomas's difficulty, but it was still cruel of him to destroy John's hopes like that.

She did think that the wine should be padded with solid food, so they stopped at a baker's where they were charged an outrageous amount for bread.

"Didn't you hear that the archbishop is giving away barley?" she asked the baker.

"Fine, if you want to cook it yourself." The man made to take the bread back. Catherine held tight to it.

"This is good bread from wheat and rye flour," he went on. "I've been selling over a hundred loaves a day, just to the German bishops. I'm almost at the bottom of my stores. This will have to keep me until I can get more, maybe not until the next harvest."

Still grumbling, Catherine paid.

At last they found a quiet spot, again by the church of Saint-Hilarius. The orchard ended in a graveyard next to the church. Catherine thought of Rolland and wondered if anyone would pay to have him properly interred. She didn't think it likely that his body would be sent back to Paris.

Astrolabe fetched water from a nearby well. Catherine had bought a pair of clay cups at a stall by the wine shop. They had been crudely stamped with the papal insignia and the dove of Reims. Souvenirs of the council. She and Margaret shared one, diluting the wine. John and Astrolabe took turns with the other. Catherine didn't notice much water being added to their cup, but she said nothing.

"Do you think that now that Rolland's dead, the people will still believe the stories he told about Astrolabe?" Margaret asked.

"Some might." Astrolabe shrugged. "They could well imagine that he was killed because of his warnings. But now that they've seen Raoul's soldiers again, they may believe that his men can fend off any band of heretics, even one aided by the devil."

"According to Gwenael, Raoul's soldiers are the ones the devil favors," Margaret said.

"Margaret, you mustn't let Gwenael's rantings confuse you," Catherine said. "She's had a hard life."

That sounded a feeble excuse, especially to Margaret, whose life had already been tragic.

"But why does she hate them all so much?" she asked. "I'm sure there were lords who hurt her, but she seems angry with almost everyone."

Catherine started to form an explanation when she was interrupted.

"I think," John said from the depths of the wine, "the saddest thing about Gwenael is that no one but Eon ever treated her as if she were worthy of love. Of course she believes him to be Christ. Only God loves everyone."

Margaret thought that over.

"Thank you, John," she said. "Now I understand."

Gwenael was at that moment trying to find a way out of Saint-Pierre-les-Nonnains. The servants were keeping a close watch on her, although no one had yet suggested that she was a prisoner. She knew they would have been glad to see the back of her but had to follow Catherine's orders, supported by those of the abbess. Although they'd been forbidden to abuse her, the people in the laundry and kitchen were unaccountably clumsy when they were near her. Hot drippings spilled; crockery landed on her fingers; her feet were constantly trod on. Gwenael knew they were waiting for her to snap, to lash out at them so that they could hit her and claim they were just defending themselves.

Gwenael hated them, every one.

When Eon came into his kingdom, then they would be punished, she reminded herself. She passed the time inventing torments for them in Hell. On that glorious day she would be among the chosen, despite her sins, for true believers are always forgiven. That's why she had to go on believing as hard as she could, no matter what anyone said. They would see. Gwenael knew the truth. Judgment was at hand.

And it wasn't going to find her scrubbing out chamber pots.

When the bells rang Sext, the cook, who had a hidden pity for the Breton woman, went to bring her a bowl of soup.

She found chamber pots stacked one inside the other against the wall up to the open window. Gwenael was long gone.

"There are those lepers again," Catherine said. "See, sitting on the stones in the graveyard."

"I'm surprised no one has driven them from town," Astrolabe commented. "You'd think the guards would have been called as soon as someone noticed that they didn't have anyone watching them."

"I told you there was something strange about them," Catherine insisted. "Look."

The four had been resting on the stones, but now they were standing, each with arms raised in prayer. Their hoods were thrown back and, even at a distance, it was clear that there were no marks of leprosy on their faces. Two women and two men, all thin and pale enough but not disfigured at all.

"What does it mean?" Margaret asked.

"I have no idea," Catherine said, getting up, "but I want to find out."

"Catherine!" The other three all spoke at once. Astrolabe caught her arm.

"You can't go over there!" he said. "Their deformities may be hidden beneath their robes. You can't risk it."

"I'm sure they're using the lepers' robes as a disguise," Catherine insisted.

"Sure enough to imperil your life and that of your child?" Astrolabe had not let go of her.

Catherine stopped resisting.

"Very well," she said grudgingly. "But only because they may have some other horrible disease that doesn't show itself so blatantly. I know they aren't lepers."

At this moment, one of the women glanced in their direction. She said something to the others, pointing toward the group in the orchard. All immediately put their hoods back on so that they hung far over their faces. They hurried away in the other direction, behind the church and along the wall toward the temple of the Knights of Solomon.

"Did you see that?" Catherine pointed. "I tell you, those people are up to no good!"

The people in lepers' clothing stopped when they reached the street running under the city walls. The youngest was panting in fear.

"They were too far away to see us clearly," the older woman told her, "but we may need to change our disguise. That woman was obviously too interested in us."

"We should never have left the forest," the man complained. "It's too dangerous, with all this talk of heretics. Do you want to be asked to make a profession of faith?"

The woman made a grunt of irritation. "No one is going to bother with that unless you insist on preaching in the churchyards. We had to come. Did you want to survive on acorn bread?"

"Do you still think your cousin will help us?" the younger woman asked the elder.

"Yes, Susanna, I'm sure of it," she said firmly. "He has already decided to join us. He'll find the courage soon to renounce his old life. I know he won't disappoint me."

"How much longer?" one of the men asked. The other man was silent. "I worry that some of the other Eonites will find me out. They won't understand that I've converted."

"It won't be long," the woman answered, but there was a note of uncertainty. "My cousin told me he only needs to finish something here. Then we'll have enough to last the summer."

"And to go south?" the man persisted.

"Yes, if you're sure that's what you want," she answered. "I think he may even come with us. Then you have renounced your false prophet?"

"Completely," the man said. "I have found the true faith."

He put his arm around Susanna, who nodded.

"We're tired of being on our own, and having to hide what we are," she said. "We want to be where there is a community, with a priest and other good people."

The older woman sighed. She brushed back a loose strand of greying blond hair and adjusted her hood. "We renounced earthly goods and pleasures and I don't regret it. But you're right. It's difficult to follow the path with no guidance but our own prayers. I agree. As soon as my cousin gives us the funds, we will start for Provence."

"Until then, we should get rid of these clappers and bandages," the man said. "I fear that woman will report us if we keep up this pretence any longer."

A few moments later a rag picker found a pile of linen by the side of the road. She leapt at them joyfully, until she saw the wooden clappers beside them. Then she backed away, crossing herself over and over. No cloth was fine enough to risk the touch of a leper.


Count Thibault was becoming concerned about his granddaughter. He had been pleased when Mahaut had suggested this alliance in Carinthia. So far, all the brides had come west. It was time to send someone to remind the Carinthians of their connection to France. Thibault wanted to know that Margaret was settled well before he died. He felt he owed it to her. She was a sweet child, with the same face as the love of his youth, her grandmother. Margaret should have been overjoyed, but he'd been watching her. When she thought no one was looking, her face would change as if she'd slipped off a mask. He saw then a sadness that wounded his heart.

"Are you certain that Margaret wants to go?" he asked his wife as they prepared to attend the archbishop's meeting.

"Of course," Mahaut answered. "We have her wardrobe almost planned."

"But it's so far away," Thibault said.

Mahaut gave him an incredulous stare. "I know. I've made the journey."

"She's not as strong as you, my dear," Thibault said. "Perhaps we should wait until her brother returns. He could be her escort."

"My dear husband." Mahaut patted his cheek. She was the only person in the world who could get away with it. "All this fuss about Elenora's divorce has upset you. Margaret is a dutiful girl and bright. She'll learn the customs quickly and be a great asset to both our families. And if she wants to see her brother, we'll commission him to buy amber for us. He can visit her on the way. It will save on the tolls, too."

All of these statements were sensible, and he knew there were good reasons for the marriage. Thibault knew it was the right thing to do. He just wished he could feel that Margaret was happier about it.

"Do you know why Samson Mauvoisin has asked us to see him?" Mahaut asked, breaking into his reverie.

"Perhaps he wants to explain the goings-on among the townspeople," Thibault suggested. "No matter what we think of Raoul, it's good that he was prepared for trouble. Samson didn't have the men to put down a serious rebellion."

"To be honest," Mahaut said, "if I have to sit through another day of this council, I may revolt as well. I've done my duty by Elenora. If this goes on much longer, I believe we shall return home. Will that be acceptable?"

"Oh, yes," Thibault said. "I only wish I could join you. But you know I'm expected to remain until the last candle is extinguished."


"My lord Archbishop." Ermon was at the door. He coughed apologetically. Samson had taken a few moments to rest between the sessions of the council and he hated to be interrupted. "There is a man who insists upon seeing you. He won't be put off."

"Ermon, unless he has a knife at your throat, you can get him to wait." Samson didn't open his eyes.

"Yes, my lord," Ermon answered. "He did say it was about

the murder last night. He's in a great state of agitation, but I believe that he really does know something. I thought that you might want to see him before tonight."

Samson swung his feet to the floor. "Very well, tell him I will see him as soon as I finish dressing. Have Godric come up at once to help me."

He descended a short time later in full regalia, with every intention of crushing the temerity of this person who had interrupted his nap.

He saw a nondescript monk, with narrow eyes and a feeble chin. Before Samson had reached the bottom of the stairs, the monk threw himself on the floor in front of him.

"My lord!" he cried. "I beg your indulgence, your generosity, your pity! My dear friend Rolland has been brutally slaughtered by the godless fiend we have been pursuing. You must capture him before he kills me as well."

Samson's eyebrows rose. "I must? And who are you to make such a demand?"

If it were possible to go lower than the floor, the monk would have done so.

"Forgive me, your Graciousness!" he cringed. "My name is Arnulf. I was among those who apprehended the heretic Eon, that is, I was there when he was brought into Nantes. One of Eon's most dangerous followers escaped on the road, but only after killing a wellborn lady who had been the prisoner of these heretics. I was sent to find him so that he could be made to pay for his crimes."

"You?" Samson asked. "Why not a troop of knights?"

"It was a . . . delicate situation," Arnulf stammered.

"Very well," Samson relented. "Get up and tell me the tale, man. I can't understand you when you're talking into the carpet."

Arnulf scrambled to his feet, but he then bowed so low that the effect was almost the same as before.

"We had heard a rumor that Eon was being protected by certain lords of the region who are deeply into the foul pits of sin and error," Arnulf began.

Samson sighed but didn't interrupt.

"One of Eon's family went to try to convince him to renounce his evil." Arnulf warmed to the story. "Through the
work of minions of the devil, Eon offered this good man a
great feast, with every delicacy known, served on platters of
gold. Mindful of his soul, the man refused but his servant ate.
As they were leaving, the servant was plucked up by a giant
eagle and never seen again."

"Really." Samson yawned. His dreams were better than
this tale.

"But while he was there," Arnulf continued hastily, "the
knight saw a man he knew, from the village of Le Pallet."

"Isn't that the place where Peter Abelard was born?"

"Yes, your Astuteness." Arnulf bowed even lower. "This
man consorting with the heretics was Abelard's son. Of
course the lord was shocked. But we know that the sins of the
father are often repeated in the son. The visitor also made the
acquaintance there of one of the more venal of these heretics.
For a few coins, this person agreed to signal the archbishop's
soldiers to attack when they would be least able to mount a
defense.

"Thus"—he spoke more quickly; Samson was showing
signs of impatience—"Abelard's son was caught by surprise.
In order to protect his identity, he then killed the lady Cecile,
a poor prisoner of these brutes, and ran for his life. My lord
begged me to find the murderous villain. I tracked him to Paris
where Canon Rolland bravely offered to help me. Together we
ascertained that he would be at the council in order to rescue
his miserable master Eon. Last night I was to have met with
Rolland to arrange the final trap. But he never appeared.

"This morning I learned of his death. I have come to place
the matter before you and plead with your Wisdom to see that
this vile murderer is brought to justice."

"I see." Samson nodded. "A serious charge. Also many la-
cunae in the telling. I shall have my soldiers locate this heretical son of a heretic and bring him in."

"Thank you, thank you, your Generosity!" Arnulf exulted. He
finally dared to look up. "I know that you won't let his friends or

his slippery dialectic keep you from seeing the truth. Your Perceptiveness will realize at once that Astrolabe is guilty."

"Astrolabe!" The archbishop smiled. "The 'demon king'! Now I see. Thank you, Brother Arnulf. I shall expect you this evening immediately after Vespers to repeat your accusation before witnesses."

"Of course, my lord." Arnulf backed away until he hit the door as it opened.

Ermon entered. Arnulf barely avoided knocking him over as he made his exit.

"Was I mistaken in waking you, my lord?" Ermon asked.

"No, you did well," the archbishop answered. "Now I need you to find some information before the meeting tonight. Also, send the captain of my guards in. I have a commission for him."

The town was back to normal by the time Catherine and Margaret returned to the convent. From the smell, people were making barley soup and brewing barley beer. If anyone expected an invasion, there was no sign of it.

"It's amazing how a little food can restore sanity," Catherine said, looking from the window.

"It didn't always work with my brothers," Margaret replied. "They seemed to think a good meal was a prelude to battle."

"Well, I'm glad it was successful in this case." Catherine went to her packing box to see if she had anything clean enough to wear that night.

"I haven't been invited to any banquets," she said, "I'm glad to say. Has your grandfather told you to dine with them?"

"I haven't had a message today," Margaret answered. "Could we go eat at a tavern?"

"Unaccompanied? Of course not!"

"Then I suppose we should see what the cook here has prepared for guests." Margaret wasn't impressed with the convent kitchens.

They rested until Vespers ended, then went down to the dining hall. There they found Godfrey waiting for them.

"Countess Sybil told me to bring you as soon as you came down," he said.

"What? Where?" Catherine asked. "I'm not dressed for dining with company."

"Dining? You're going to the archbishop's palace," Godfrey said. "The countess received a summons this afternoon. Samson is holding an inquiry into the death of Canon Rolland."

"I'm glad he's taking an interest," Catherine said, "but why do we have to be there?"

"Because his men have just brought in the murderer," Godfrey told them. "He was accused this afternoon and is now in custody. I saw the soldiers taking him in."

"That was quick work," Margaret said. "I'm so relieved that it's over."

"Margaret," Catherine said, "I don't think that's what Godfrey means, do you, Godfrey?"

"No, my lady." Godfrey's mouth was tight with anger. "They've imprisoned Astrolabe in the bishop's dungeon."

# Eighteen

Outside the bishop's palace. That evening.

*Noverit prudentia vestra me venisse Remis ad apostolicum, et comitissa Flandrensis me duxit illuc pro negotio suo, ibique et de ejus et de meo tractamus negotio.*

It is known to your Prudence that I have come to Reims to the pope, and the countess of Flanders took me there on her business and there we managed both her business and mine.

Raoul of Vermandois, letter to Suger,
abbot of Saint-Denis in Reims, 1148

*C*atherine, I'm terrified." Margaret looked up at the three-story building shadowed by the bulk of the ancient cathedral.

"Margaret, darling, nothing will happen to you," Catherine said. "We've feared all along that Astrolabe might be taken before we could find the real culprit, but I know we can prove that it's all a horrible mistake."

"What if I say something wrong?" Margaret worried. "Words are such slippery things. I won't have to answer in Latin, will I?"

"I'm sure not." Catherine took her hand. "You might not be asked anything at all."

There was a light on the second floor. Someone was burning a fortune in candles.

"Catherine! Wait!"

They looked up the road and saw John running toward them. He stopped at the gate, bending over to catch his breath.

"I just found out what happened," he said. "I had gone out for a pitcher, and when I returned, Astrolabe was gone. Thomas said that the archbishop wanted to question him. I must be at the meeting to speak for him. Let me come in with you, please. I won't be admitted otherwise."

"Of course, John," Catherine said. "But are you sure you want to do this? People are not usually comfortable hiring a clerk with heretical connections."

"It doesn't matter. Astrolabe is my friend," John answered.

Together, they entered the bishop's palace.

\* \* \*

Engebaud, archbishop of Tours, was puzzled by Samson's invitation. What could the death of a canon of Paris have to do with him? Perhaps he had been asked to help make a judgment. He was honored that his judicial wisdom was so well known, but it had been a long day and his bed was much more alluring than any accolade would be.

He was surprised to see Hugh of Rouen there as well, and not entirely pleased. Since their sees were next to each other, they had had many occasions to argue about areas where the boundaries appeared to overlap.

"Good evening, my lord," he greeted Hugh.

"And to you, my lord." Hugh gave him a wintry smile.

Engebaud looked around the room. He had expected Count Thibault to be present; he had the right of high justice. If it were a matter of hanging, then no ecclesiastical court could pronounce judgment. Of course Countess Mahaut would join him. But why was Sybil of Anjou in the room? And who were those other women? Her attendants? This was altogether peculiar.

Archbishop Samson greeted him with proper respect, which soothed him somewhat.

"My dear lord Archbishop," he bowed. "I am honored that you are able to join us."

"I am always at your service." Engebaud bowed in return. "Although I confess I am perplexed as to the form that service is to take."

Samson smiled at him. "I believe you'll discover that it is I who may be able to serve you. Please be seated. Would you care for wine?"

Engebaud took the offered cup, noting that the silver was plate.

When they were settled, Countess Sybil stood to address the group.

"Most of you know that I came to this council in the hope of receiving aid in my struggle against the invader of my land, Baldwin of Hainaut. However, I also accepted a commission from my friend, Heloise, abbess of the Paraclete."

Mahaut leaned forward. "Heloise? She told me nothing of this."

Sybil pressed her lips together, then continued in a polite tone.

"She might not have entrusted me with the information if it had not involved my ward, Annora of Beaumont." Sybil indicated Annora, standing with Catherine and Margaret across the room.

Mahaut was appeased for the moment. Catherine knew that it hurt her to know that Heloise had gone to Sybil and not her.

"Archbishop Samson is faced with a serious crime, that of murder, committed on a member of the household of the bishop of Paris while he was attending the council here in Reims," Sybil continued. "I have come to believe that this murder is directly connected with that of Cecile, a nun of Saint-Georges-de-Rennes and sister to Annora."

Engebaud was still confused. Sybil took pity on him.

"You may recall the capture of the heretic Eon and his followers?" she asked him.

"Of course," Engebaud said. He was looking forward to the trial the next day. *That* would put an end to the pretensions of Olivier of Dol.

"Cecile was the woman who died as a result," Sybil said.

"Not by one of my men!" Engebaud exclaimed. "They were under strict orders not to harm the heretics unless they were themselves attacked. That woman was killed by one of Eon's people! I have witnesses!"

"You do?" Catherine blurted. "Then you knew of her murder?"

All eyes turned to her. She clapped her hand over her mouth. "I most humbly beg your forgiveness," she said.

"And who are you?" Engebaud asked frostily.

"No one, my lord," Catherine answered, cheeks flaming. "My name is Catherine."

"Lady Catherine was also sent as a representative of the Paraclete," Sybil said.

Archbishop Engebaud was becoming annoyed. He turned to Archbishop Hugh for support.

"I don't understand what business any of this is with Heloise," he complained. "If the woman who died was Norman and subject to you, then it seems that is something we should handle privately. I understand we now have the man who did it."

"I'm sorry, Engebaud," Hugh said. "I know no more than you. Until this moment, I was unaware that Cecile of Beaumont had died. I shall arrange a Mass for her. I agree that if the culprit has been captured, it only remains to sentence him. Heloise has no jurisdiction in the case."

"It is very much her concern, however," Sybil continued. "The man accused of both these crimes is her son."

"What! Margaret, did you know about this?" Countess Mahaut asked.

"Yes, my lady." Margaret held herself stiffly, as if expecting a blow. "But he didn't do it. We know he didn't!"

"Of course not," Mahaut said firmly. "I know him well. The very idea is ludicrous. If that is what we have been called here for, then we've wasted our time."

Archbishop Samson intervened.

"The information I have indicates otherwise," he said. "I have questioned Astrolabe, and he admits to being with the Eonites, although he denies he is one of them. He also admits to knowing that Canon Rolland instigated the stories about him that nearly led to riot and cost me a thousand *sestiers* of barley. He was known to be in a position to murder the nun Cecile. He refuses to state his whereabouts last night when the canon was killed. In this situation, I feel that something more is needed besides a belief that he is not the sort of person to commit murder."

"My lord." John stepped forward. "My friend is being unnecessarily prudent in refusing to bring others into his trouble. I was with Astrolabe last night, as was Thomas, a clerk of the archbishop of Canterbury. He couldn't have killed Canon Rolland."

"Oh, John, thank you," Catherine breathed.

Samson stared at him.

"And you are?"

"John, of Sarum in England, and lately clerk to Abbot Peter of Celle," John said. "I've known Astrolabe for many years. He stayed with me last night at the residence of the archbishop of Canterbury."

"So you never left his side all evening?" Samson asked.

"No . . . well, we left him at the bathhouse for a couple of hours," John admitted. "But the people there will confirm that."

"Actually, he mentioned the bathhouse. I've already had the attendants questioned," Samson said. "It seems they left him in his tub and didn't go back until he called for a barber much later. He could have sneaked out and returned with no one the wiser. You must admit that if one were to slit a man's throat, a bathhouse would be the perfect place to wash away any evidence of the deed."

"But that's ridiculous," John sputtered.

"Unfortunately, it isn't," Samson told him. "Now I presume you all understand why I asked you to help me adjudicate this matter. I propose to bring both Astrolabe and his accuser in. You may listen to both their stories. If any of you have more information, either in support or refutation, then I hope you'll add it. I admit that if I had known the man's parentage, I might not have had him arrested immediately. However, upon questioning him, I did not find that his answers convinced me of his innocence and I am not inclined to release him without further proof."

"Then bring both men before us now!" Thibault ordered. "But I warn you, Samson, I'm not going back to Abbess Heloise and tell her that I left her son in chains in your prison."

"I assure you, my lord count, that in any event he won't be long in my prison."

Samson nodded to the guard at the door. A moment later Astrolabe was brought in by the guards. Just behind them was a monk. Although he tried to keep his face hidden, Catherine recognized him at once.

"You were with Rolland!" She pointed accusingly at him. "I know you!"

He glared back at her. "And you're the woman who told us you knew nothing about the heretic we were seeking. I knew you were in league with him. You consort with Jews as well. I know. Your aberrant life has been noted.

"My lords, my ladies." Arnulf turned to the rest of the assembly. "This woman has shown herself to be a liar and a protector of heretics and infidels. Her house in Paris is infamous. Nothing she says can be trusted."

"How dare you!" Catherine started toward him.

Countess Sybil waved her back with a warning gesture.

"Have they harmed you?" she asked Astrolabe. "Your cheek is bruised."

He shook his head. "I tripped on the steps. I'm not accustomed to walking in chains."

Catherine suppressed a cry. She was more angry with herself than the monk or the archbishop. She should have done something to stop this man before he could bring Astrolabe to such a state. They shouldn't have been so afraid but gone at once to the archbishops and told them everything. Heloise had counted on her to protect her son. She had been useless.

Archbishop Samson gestured for the two men to stand in the center of the room, facing the prelates and nobles.

"This is Arnulf, a monk of Brittany," he told them. "He has come to me with a story of heresy, deception and murder. I shall have him repeat it for all of you. Of course you, my lord archbishops, my lord count, my lady countesses, are welcome to ask anything you wish in order to get to the meat of the matter. The rest of you"—he stared pointedly at Catherine and John—"will speak only when addressed, or I will send you out. Do you understand?"

They nodded.

Arnulf began his tale. He told it well, dwelling on his certainty that Cecile had been a prisoner of the heretics, ignoring the horror she had fled at the hands of Henri of Tréguier. He reminded them that Astrolabe had not denied that he had spent a winter in Eon's camp and been captured there.

"And when he escaped from Archbishop Engebaud's men,

did he come to Tours and throw himself on the mercy of the church?" Arnulf asked. "No, he fled to Paris. And again, his first contact was not a cleric, who might have given him spiritual guidance and brought him back to the faith. No! Astrolabe, who will tell you he is a good orthodox Christian, summoned a Jew to give him aid. This I saw with my own eyes!"

"He said someone was following us," Astrolabe muttered. "I should have listened."

"There!" Arnulf said triumphantly. "He condemns himself! And then where did you go? To the bishop of Paris? Of course not. Instead you sought refuge with a merchant, a foreigner known to be friendly with any number of undesirables. And when they should have turned him over at once, he convinced them instead to smuggle him out of Paris, to Champagne and the protection of his doting mother. Do you deny this?"

He rounded on Astrolabe.

"No, but—" Astrolabe began.

Arnulf cut him off.

"Exactly," he said. "Are these the actions of an innocent man? Whatever his family, whomever his friends, I tell you Astrolabe of Le Pallet is a heretic and a murderer who must not be allowed to remain free."

Catherine waited for an angry outburst from Countess Sybil or Count Thibault. Instead, there was silence. Arnulf wiped his face with a cloth and gave a satisfied smile.

"Very serious accusations," Count Thibault said at last.

"B—" Catherine opened her mouth. Margaret kicked her before she could get a sound out.

"What can you say in your own defense?" he asked Astrolabe.

Astrolabe spread his manacled hands in uncertainty.

"I cannot deny the facts, only the interpretation Brother Arnulf has put on them," he said. "I have killed no one. I am a good Christian, as much as I am able. My behavior may have seemed cowardly. I suppose it was," he sighed. "I couldn't let Cecile's death be ignored, but I wanted to protect my mother from just the shame that has come upon me here. She has had enough grief in her life."

"Brought it on herself," someone muttered. Catherine thought it might have been Hugh of Rouen.

Astrolabe's strong chin lifted. "I am proud of both my parents," he said, "and only wish I were a more worthy reflection of their learning."

"Yes, of course," Samson waved that off.

Samson faced the others. "You see my dilemma," he said. "He has declared his innocence and yet not provided me with proof of it or with an alternate suspect."

Catherine could bear it no longer.

"Please, my lord," she said. "I will swear on the bones of Saint Remigius, on the Holy Cross itself, that Astrolabe is innocent."

"As will I," John said.

"Me, too," Margaret added, with a nervous glance at Count Thibault.

Samson glared at them. "I will excuse your outburst this once. Your offer of compurgation is noted. However, I believe we all would prefer to have the truth rather than simply the belief of his friends. Count Thibault, what do you say?"

"I believe Astrolabe's story implicitly," the count stated. "Brother Arnulf may have acted in good faith, but his conclusions must be incorrect."

However, there was an edge of doubt in his voice. Catherine gripped Margaret's hand in fear.

Archbishop Engebaud stood to address them. "I don't want to believe that this man, of good birth and education, could be led into heresy and violence. But I agree that we have not been given an alternative to his guilt. If the deaths of this woman and the canon are connected, who else would have had a reason to kill them both? Who else was even present in both places?"

Catherine bit her lip. This was what she should have discovered.

"I agree," Archbishop Hugh said. "I was in Brittany only a year ago, and I'm acutely aware of how heresy and violence have been allowed to flourish, even among the nobility. His family connections do not guarantee that this man is innocent."

"Then you'll support my plea for the excommunication of Olivier of Dol?" Engebaud asked eagerly. "It is his fault that these heresies have spread so far."

"Yes," Hugh answered. "It's clear that he has not been a good shepherd and should be deposed if he will not submit."

"Thank you!" Engebaud said. He seemed to have forgotten the matter at hand in his joy at acquiring an ally.

Sybil brought him back to the present.

"I have taken Astrolabe into my household and under my protection," she said. "Since we are not agreed on his guilt, I insist that he be released to me. I, for one, would like to see more proof on both sides."

"You'll guarantee that he won't flee?" Samson asked.

"The woman murdered was the sister of my ward," Sybil said. "I promised their father I would watch over them. Finding the one who killed Cecile is of the utmost importance to me. I don't believe it is Astrolabe. Therefore, I shall make my pledge for his compliance in your final decision. If he absconds, I will make restitution from my own purse."

"Oh, my lady!" Astrolabe said.

"Are we agreed?" Samson asked the others.

They all nodded.

"This must be resolved soon," Samson continued. "I have far too many obligations to allow this to take up much more of my time. I shall give Brother Arnulf and Astrolabe until Saturday morning to collect more substantial proof. Then, after consulting with the rest of you, I will decide the truth as best I can. Remove his chains."

Arnulf strangled a protest. Regaining his poise, he bowed to all and left.

Astrolabe was taken away to have the shackles struck off. Catherine hoped they would be gentle about it.

The archbishop thanked his guests for coming and offered them more wine and some sugared almonds. The dish was pointedly not passed to Catherine's corner.

"Didn't I tell you it would be all right?" she said to Margaret, when they were back down in the street.

"Are you sure?" Margaret answered. "It didn't sound settled to me. I thought my grandfather would say the charges were nonsense and tell everyone to go home."

Catherine had actually been hoping much the same.

"I suppose he couldn't," she said. "He can't appear to be inequitable before the other lords and the archbishops."

"That wouldn't have bothered me," Margaret said firmly.

Compline was long past and the street was deserted. Outside the gate they saw one forlorn soldier keeping watch. As they came out, he ran toward them.

"Godfrey!" Catherine said. "We have another chance. They're letting him go, for now."

"For now?"

"We have more time, at least, to find the real murderer," she said. "That's something."

A moment later John came out. Astrolabe was with him.

"Are you all right?" Margaret asked him. "Oh, dear, that was a stupid question, wasn't it? I can see you aren't."

Astrolabe gave her a smile and a hug.

"I can tell you, I'm much better than I was a few moments ago," he said. "Chains!" He shuddered.

"Many noblemen, kings, even apostles have been unjustly fettered," Catherine told him. "We even have a feast for Saint Peter in chains, right?"

Astrolabe looked at her a moment and then burst out laughing. The sound echoed down the dark street. He laughed so hard that he couldn't catch his breath, and John had to pound his back.

"Hysterical," he told the others. "After a day like this, I don't blame him."

"No," Astrolabe was still chuckling. "It was just so idiotic, the image of me as Saint Peter. Catherine, do you see the whole world as an analogy?"

"I was only trying . . ." Catherine began.

"Never mind," Astrolabe said. "I understand. Thank you. Thank you all for offering to stand for me. I don't think I had truly understood how damaging the facts were. If you hadn't been there, I might have been convicted tonight."

"Instead, you'll have to endure my snoring again," John said.

"That would be music," Astrolabe said. "But I can't take your hospitality. Countess Sybil spoke to me before she left. I'm to stay in the guardhouse by the convent. I believe this time I'm the one to be guarded. She's pledged me to appear in two days. She can't take the chance that I'll run off."

"Ah, then *I'll* have to listen to you snore," Godfrey said happily. "Have you ever thought about the noise a nose like yours can make?"

They all started at the sound of a shutter being thrown open.

"You down there!" a man shouted. "Take it somewhere else! I'm trying to sleep!"

"A good idea," John whispered. "I'll be at the convent at first light tomorrow. I know we can solve this. I wouldn't be surprised if that Arnulf wasn't the one who killed Rolland. He's the sort who would plan how to cover up a crime before he committed it."

"If only we could find a motive," Catherine sighed. "I'd cheerfully see him taken to the gallows. Or sent on a long and dangerous pilgrimage," she added hastily.

They set off for Saint-Pierre, parting from John at the corner.

"Do you want me to go with you?" Godfrey asked him. "There's no one out at this hour but cutthroats and drunks."

"I'll run," John said. "I've had years of practice racing the cutpurses home from the tavern. Don't worry. It's not far."

By the time they got back to the convent all was dark except for one small oil lamp left to guide their way up the stairs. Godfrey and Astrolabe saw the women past the guard at the gate before going to sleep with the other guards.

"I'm so weary I don't think I can even get my shoes off," Catherine moaned as they went up the stairs.

"I'll help you," Margaret said. "I hope Annora is still up. Then we won't be the only ones disturbing everyone."

"Goodness, I had forgotten all about her." Catherine stopped at the middle step to rest. "She was so quiet during the questioning. I hope the evening didn't upset her too much."

When they entered the room, the light showed all the other

women asleep in their beds. Margaret shone it into the corner where their bed was to see if Annora was awake.

Once again, Annora's place was empty.

"We assumed she was with you," one of the women told Catherine the next morning.

"She probably stayed in the countess's room," another yawned, "rather than disturb the rest of us."

Catherine let the rebuke pass. Where had Annora gone? The first thing that occurred to her was that the woman had a lover. But it didn't seem like Annora to do something that would certainly infuriate Countess Sybil. So far, none of the women had reported her absence, but if this went on, Catherine was inclined to tell the countess herself.

In the meantime, she had to face another day.

"Only four days past the equinox." Catherine tried to make her tired body stand. "I feel like it's a midsummer dawn. I'm sure I just went to sleep."

"Perhaps you should stay in today." Margaret's face was creased with worry.

"With all we have to do?" Catherine said. "Nonsense! I'm fine. I was just grumbling."

"What do we have to do?" Margaret asked.

"Find Annora, first." Catherine sat on the edge of the bed and let Margaret help with her hose and shoes. "Then I want to find out as much as we can about this Canon Rolland."

"The man who was murdered?" one of the women asked.

Catherine cursed herself for speaking thoughtlessly. "I was just curious about how it happened," she said. "They say he was found in the toll booth by the river. What would he have been doing there?"

"What do you think?" the woman said with a smirk.

Everyone laughed. "The lower clergy are always too poor to pay for a proper whore in a brothel. They take it whenever they can get it."

"The *jael* probably was working with a gang," the woman finished. "She lured him to the hut and her confederates dispatched him." She ran her finger across her throat. "I'm just surprised they didn't dump the body in the river."

"Likely it was too heavy," someone else suggested. "My brother says he ate enough for four the night he died."

"How does he know that?" Catherine asked.

"Felix is a subdeacon of Paris," she said. "He was at the dinner with all the others from the chapter."

"Do you think he'd talk to me about it?" Catherine asked.

"Why? Do you want the menu?"

"It's important that I find out all I can about what Rolland did that night," Catherine persisted. "The countess will confirm that my interest is not idle, if you ask her."

"It's nothing to me," the woman said. "Felix will be at the cathedral this afternoon. Remind me and I'll introduce him to you."

"That was stupid of me to speak in their hearing," Catherine said to Margaret as they hurried to meet the men. "I must watch my tongue."

"But the slip gave you information," Margaret consoled her. "Although I can't think it matters where Rolland ate or what."

"Anything he did might be important," Catherine said. "I also want to know more about this Arnulf. At least now we have a name to put to him."

"I had thought that the archbishop of Tours knew him," Margaret said. "But he didn't seem to last night."

"Yes, that's odd. I could have sworn that when we met them on the road, he said that he and Rolland were working under Archbishop Engebaud's orders."

They found John, Astrolabe and Godfrey waiting for them.

"I meant to tell you last night," Godfrey began as soon as they were away from eavesdroppers, "but I didn't want to give you further cause for worry when there was nothing to be done so late. Gwenael has run away. I searched for her yesterday afternoon but had no luck."

"I'm sorry for that," Astrolabe said. "But it might mean that she finally realized there was no use in trying to free Eon. I hope she finds her way back home."

"Annora seems to be missing as well," Catherine said. "At least she didn't sleep with us last night. The countess may know where she is, but I'm afraid to ask her, in case she doesn't. Annora would never forgive me."

"It is strange that she would do something so foolish," Godfrey said. "I wonder if her absence might have something to do with the people who came for Lord Gui."

"He's no longer in the infirmary?" Catherine asked in consternation. She still had questions for him, based on Margaret's conclusions. "How do you know?"

"That was one of the places I checked when I was looking for Gwenael," Godfrey told her. "They told me that some of Gui's relatives had arrived and that he left with them. Apparently he felt much better. I tried to discover more, but apparently they were so glad to be rid of him that no one asked any questions. They were all sure that he was glad to see his family and went willingly. Could Annora have been among them?"

"It doesn't seem likely," Catherine said, "knowing how they feel about each other. Annora didn't even greet him when they were at the same dinner last Friday."

"I think the time has come to inform the countess," Astrolabe said. "She may know where Annora is. There's no point in being anxious about her if she's safe with Lady Sybil."

"I'll go back and ask," Margaret offered. "Will you wait for me?"

"At the beer stand," Astrolabe said. "We won't move until you return."

"And perhaps not for some time after," said Catherine.

Margaret hurried back to the convent. It was still early; the nuns had hardly begun chanting Prime. She wondered if it were wise to knock at the countess's door. What if she woke her?

As she stood in the courtyard, hesitating, the problem was solved for her. Annora appeared at the entrance to the kitchen gardens. Her hair and clothes were rumpled again. Margaret was not as naive as her family imagined. How could she be? She had a good guess as to what Annora had been doing.

"Annora!" she waved.

Annora heard her and stopped. "Who is it?"

"Margaret." She came over to her. "Don't worry. I won't tell. When you didn't come in last night we thought something dreadful had happened to you."

"I'm fine," Annora said. "I spent the night at Saint-Etienne, praying for the soul of my sister."

"Oh," Margaret tried to keep the tone even. "Then you must be very tired. I'll let you go up to rest."

"Thank you." Annora unbent a little. "It was kind of you to be concerned. The meeting last night was very difficult for me. All the time I was safe with Countess Sybil, thinking my sister safe in the convent, Cecile was enduring so many horrors. Hearing about it was terrible. I couldn't help. I never knew. Now all I can give her are prayers."

Margaret felt ashamed of her suspicions although not entirely convinced they were wrong.

"When I pray for the soul of my mother, as I do each day, I'll add Cecile's name to my entreaties," she promised.

Annora thanked her and tried to continue up to their room. Margaret moved to stand in her way.

"Yes?" Annora asked wearily. "Is there something else?"

Margaret licked her lips. "Yes. I wasn't going to mention it, but my conscience won't let me stay silent, especially now that Gui has left."

"What? What are you talking about, child?"

"I'm not a child!" Margaret said instinctively. "I went to see Gui at the Temple. I had a brooch that was found when he was attacked and I thought it might be his. He said it was your grandmother's but that he had always wanted it. He seemed so sad. I gave it to him. I'm sorry."

Annora stared at her, not taking in what she was saying. She blinked.

"You went to see Gui?"

"Yes."

"You had a brooch you thought was his?"

"Yes, it was—"

"Gold, square, with topazes?" Annora asked.

"Yes, your grandmother's? He said you had it from Cecile when she left for the convent."

"No," Annora said coldly. "Cecile took it with her. She said it wasn't a piece of vainglory but a reminder of someone she had loved. It was the only possession she couldn't give up."

"But then how did it get into the garden here?" Margaret wondered. "I was sure Gui had dropped it."

Annora had paled. She was holding her mouth tightly, white to the lips, as if trying not to throw up.

"Whoever did"—she swallowed hard—"could only have taken it from Cecile. Sweet Virgin! The person who killed her was only a step away from me, and I did nothing! If I ever get that close to him again, I swear I will rip out his heart with my bare hands."

# *Nineteen*

A crowded beer stand, Reims. Thursday, 8 kalends April (March 25), 1148. Fifth day of the council. Feast of the Annunciation to the Blessed Virgin, nine months before the Feast of the Nativity.

*Cum ergo staret in conspectus concilii, interrogatus a summo pontifice quisnam esset, responit: "Ego sum Eun, qui venturus est juidacre vivos et mortuos, et seculum per ignem." . . . ad haec risit universa synodus, derisitque hominem tam profunde datum in reprobum sensum.*

And so, when he stood before the council and was questioned by the pope as to who he was, he answered, "I am Eon, who is come to judge the living and the dead and the world through fire." . . . At this the whole council laughed and derided a man so deeply disturbed in his mind.

William of Newburgh, *The History of English Affairs*

*I* was so sure Annora had dropped the brooch," Margaret said. "Gui told me it was hers!"

Margaret's teeth clanked against the rim of her bowl. She put it down, too agitated to hold it steadily.

"I've done something awful!" she went on. "You should have seen Annora's face when I told her I had given it to Gui. I might as well have stabbed her with the thing. Now how will we ever know who took the brooch from Cecile? For it must have been the one who killed her. Could it have been Gui?"

"I'm hoping for Arnulf," Astrolabe said.

"That would be nice, but he wasn't at the dinner where I found it." Catherine tried to envision the faces of the other guests. She had certainly had enough time to study them, since Gui had ignored her for most of the evening.

"Margaret, you mustn't feel bad about this." John patted her trembling hand. "Your impulse was generous."

"But stupid," Margaret sighed. "And I was positive that Gui had faked the attack. I must have been wrong about that, too."

"Astrolabe," Catherine asked, "could Gui have been among those who raided the Eonite camp?"

"I don't know," he said. "All I remember is a horde of men on horses coming toward me."

"But Cecile knew one of them," Catherine said. "We assumed it must have been one of the knights of Henri of Tréguier. What if she saw a family member, one she didn't trust?"

"Is there any way we can find out if Gui was in Brittany then?" John asked. "We don't have time to send messengers."

"We can't even find out if Gui is in Reims now." Astrolabe hunched over the table, his head in his hands.

"Then let's begin with what we can do," Catherine said. "John, will you come with me to the house where the bishop of Paris is staying? I want to catch this subdeacon Felix before he leaves for the council to see what he can tell us about Rolland's last night. You probably studied with him, or tutored him or drank with him at least. You can help me get information. Perhaps someone saw him leave for the toll booth."

"Certainly." John was on his feet at once.

"What can we do?" Godfrey asked.

"Find the other two," Catherine said. "Gui and Gwenael. None of you have told Gui that Cecile is dead, have you?"

Margaret shook her head vehemently. "He spoke as if he thought she was still at Saint-Georges."

"I said nothing," Astrolabe added.

"I think it's time to tell him," Catherine said. "If he's innocent of her death, then he may be willing to help us. If he is guilty, then he might well make a slip that will trap him."

"And Gwenael?" Margaret asked.

Catherine shook her head. "I have no idea what she's planning. But I'd feel better if she were under our supervision. Her wild ideas about Astrolabe could do as much damage as Rolland's rumormongering."

"What about those 'relatives' that came for Gui?" Astrolabe asked.

Catherine threw up her hands. "I'd forgotten all about them. Maybe the guard at the Temple can describe them? Someone will have to ask Annora what other family Gui has. Ow!"

She pressed a hand against her stomach. The others looked at her in alarm.

"Just a cramp," Catherine said. "This child seems to be playing crosses and naughts on the wall of my womb."

She adjusted her *bliaut*.

"Now, we all have a task," she said. "We'll meet back here at Nones. Is that agreeable?"

They all agreed. Catherine and John left on their errand. Astrolabe remained at the table with Godfrey and Margaret. Rather than leaping into action, as Catherine had hoped, all three seemed lost in their own thoughts.

Astrolabe sighed.

"Poor Eon is going to be brought before the council today," he said. "I can't help now in the way that I had hoped, but I still feel that I should be there to speak for him. Of course it might well make his case worse."

"Did it occur to you that you might be arrested before you had a chance to speak at all?" Godfrey asked.

"Oh, yes." Astrolabe rubbed his bare chin. "But I've waited long enough. I can't spend the rest of my life denying my name or running from faceless accusers. With all that's happened here, they may expect me to continue hiding. If I come before the council on my own, it may make their denunciations appear mere bluster."

"Perhaps." Margaret was doubtful. "But is it worth the risk? I don't mind going to observe the proceedings for you. I'd like to see this madman. I want to understand how he could inspire such devotion when his theology is so obviously preposterous. Even if he's condemned, you could plead for him privately later."

"Could you get me inside the cathedral?" Godfrey asked her. "It seems to me that we might begin there anyway. If Gwenael hasn't regained her senses and fled the city, then I'd bet she couldn't resist seeing her master again."

"I'm sure I could," Margaret said. "Astrolabe? Will you wait for us here?"

"No." Astrolabe got up. He squared his shoulders for battle, his hand automatically reaching for the sword that he no longer wore.

"I can't abandon Eon now," he said. "I'm sure he's frightened and confused. Someone must be his advocate. If I'm permitted, I'll speak for him. Compared to the bandits that roam the forest and the wandering preachers who incite riots, he's harmless. I've got to try to make the council understand that."

"And what if Arnulf takes the opportunity to bring his charges against you before the full council?" Godfrey asked.

"Archbishop Samson will see that he doesn't," Margaret said. "At least, I think he will. Anyway, Arnulf seems to be convinced that he's won. Why accuse him among so many of Abelard's old students and take the chance of swaying opinion in Astrolabe's favor?"

"Who knows what Arnulf might do? In his own way, that monk seems as mad as Eon," Astrolabe said. "Does anyone remember what monastery he said he was from? I'd like to know the abbot who would send him out on a mission like this alone."

"Good, they haven't left yet." John pointed at the sedan chair outside the house, ready for the bishop. "Now, to find Subdeacon Felix. Why don't you let me go to the porter first and ask for him?"

"Why can't I come with you?" Catherine asked.

John looked down at her. Catherine followed his gaze.

"Oh, yes," she chuckled softly. "Clerics do tend to panic when pregnant women show up at their door. Very well. I'll sit on the bench over there. Bring him out, though, if you can."

She sat down to wait. After a few moments the morning sun made her drowsy and she closed her eyes, leaning back against the rough wall in front of the house.

She was vaguely aware of people passing, but no one bothered her. Two men were conversing nearby in low tones. They must have moved closer to her for she caught a sentence that brought her suddenly alert. She forced herself to relax, keeping her eyes shut.

"Rolland never went to whores," one voice said. "Everyone knows that. And even if he did, he'd never go off to meet one in a remote place at night. He was slow but not stupid."

"I wonder if his death might have something to do with those questions he'd been asking," the other said. "Wanting to know about some priory in Brittany. Did he come to you? He seemed awfully agitated when I saw him."

"No," the first one said. "Why would he be interested in a Breton house? Do you think he finally realized that he had no hope for advancement? Even his family couldn't get him a better position in Paris."

"And so he decided to retire to the wilds of Brittany? Seems drastic."

"Oh, well." The men started to move away. "It doesn't matter anymore. The only position he has now is recumbent."

Catherine opened her eyes a slit. The men were walking away from her, toward the cathedral. She sat up. Interesting. Without any effort, she had overheard something useful. Assuming that she had no Latin, the canons had spoken without caution. After her wasted day as a beggar, she had decided that the plan had been foolish. She was astonished that it had worked after all.

John came out soon after with a boy who looked too young to be a student, much less a subdeacon.

"Felix?" she asked.

"Master John said you know my sister?" he asked in some puzzlement. "I'm not clear why she sent you to me. Canon Rolland and I weren't close."

"But you saw him just before he died," Catherine said. "Didn't you?"

"Oh, yes," the boy answered. "His appetite was the wonder of the table. He was in very high spirits."

"Did he say why?"

"No. He kept hinting that he had uncovered some serious malefactors who were threatening the body of the Church," Felix shrugged. "But none of us wanted to give him the satisfaction of asking about it. He was always boasting about something."

"Did he say anything about a Breton priory?" Catherine asked.

John gave her a look but didn't interrupt.

Felix scratched his head. "I don't think so. I know he'd been chasing some Breton heretic, a follower of this Eon, but I think that came to nothing."

"Did you see him leave the dinner?" Catherine asked.

Felix looked around to be sure none of his colleagues were nearby.

"As a matter of fact, I did," he said. "I'm afraid I also overindulged that evening. I needed to go out rather quickly. Rolland was talking with the porter when I came through. He was asking about a message. That's all I heard. I was in a *great* hurry."

"Of course," Catherine said. "But that's very helpful. And he was gone when you returned?"

Felix nodded. "You won't mention my gluttony to the bishop, will you? I'll confess it myself in Chapter, but I'd rather be the one to tell him."

"We understand completely," John told him. "Don't we, Catherine?"

"I won't say a word," she promised. "Especially to your sister."

The boy grinned at them. "I'm in your debt. Felicia would taunt me about it for years."

They gave him a coin for the poor and bid him good day.

"What was all that about a priory?" John asked after Felix had left.

Catherine explained. "I think Rolland may have become suspicious of Brother Arnulf's story about being sent by his abbot to chase heretics."

"I know I am," John said. "But Arnulf must have had a letter from someone of authority or Bishop Samson never would have given any credit to his accusations."

"One would think so," Catherine said. "Let's find out what the porter has to say."

The man who had been on duty that night wasn't there, but the day porter directed them to his home. They went down a damp alleyway behind the cathedral, coming out in a small square. Each building had a shop on the ground floor. The shutters were down to display ribbons, thread, gloves, trimmings, laces and cloth of all kinds.

"Which one did he say?" John asked.

Catherine had been momentarily distracted by the brightly colored patterns on a selection of hose.

"Over there, the ribbon seller's."

They asked the woman at the stall where they could find the porter.

"Upstairs asleep," she told them. "And he doesn't take kindly to being wakened before his time."

"It is urgent," Catherine said. "We need to ask him some questions. We'll pay for his trouble. It shouldn't take long."

The word *pay* changed the woman's attitude. She held out her hand.

Catherine dropped in a *solidus* of Paris. The woman bit it.

"That's worth him losing a bit of sleep," she said.

"Lambert!" She pounded on the ceiling with the pole used to open and close the shutter. "Get your ass up. Lady and a priest want to talk to you."

She gestured for them to go to the main floor. They climbed a narrow ladder in the corner of the shop that went up into the living area. As Catherine emerged, she gasped and looked away. Lambert quickly dropped a tunic over his head.

"Well, what do you expect, barging in on a man in his bed?" he demanded.

"I apologize," Catherine said. "I was just startled."

Lambert smirked. "That's what my wife said the first time she saw it, too."

Silently, Catherine climbed the rest of the way into the room, standing aside for John to ascend.

John explained their mission.

"Oh, sure, I remember him," Lambert said. "Big fellow, rude. I gave him the message and he left."

"Do you know who sent the message?" Catherine asked.

"No, the woman didn't say." Lambert scratched beneath the tunic. Catherine looked at the ceiling.

"Woman?" John asked. "It was a woman who brought the message?"

"Yes, what of it?"

"Did you know her?" John persisted.

Lambert shook his head. "Not local," he said. "She was foreign, maybe from the south or Germany, maybe Normandy. She talked with an accent, at least."

"What did she look like?" Catherine asked.

"Couldn't say," Lambert answered. "A bit shorter than you. She had on a heavy veil, covered most of her face."

"Do you remember anything else about her?" Catherine said, handing him a coin.

"No," he said. "I got the feeling she was a lady, though. She told me what she wanted and left. Didn't stop to talk or wait a bit in case there was a reply."

"She might just have been frightened or rushed," Catherine suggested.

"Don't know," Lambert said. "Just telling you what I noticed, like you asked."

They thanked him and left. John went down the ladder first. As Catherine descended, Lambert pulled off his tunic and got back into bed. She had no doubt that he'd be snoring before she reached the floor.

"A woman?" John said when they were out in the street again.

"Obviously the porter thought she was making the assignation for herself," Catherine said. "It does support the idea that Baldwin went out *d'amer fame vilaine.*"

"Except Lambert thought she was a noblewoman," John reminded her.

"Only because she wouldn't stay with him. She might just have wanted to get away before he demanded a sample of her wares," Catherine said. "I don't place much value on his judgment on that score."

"The information doesn't seem to help us," John commented.

"Not really," Catherine answered gloomily. "We only know that she didn't speak the way they do around here. I wish there had been some indication of who had sent her."

"Do you think she was involved in killing Rolland?"

"I don't know," she admitted. "She might have simply been selected to carry the message without knowing why. I certainly can't imagine the remnants of the Eonites being organized enough to plan an elaborate murder."

"But those were the people he was investigating," John said.

"No one else seems to have had a reason to want him dead, except Astrolabe."

"If someone else killed Cecile, and Rolland stumbled on the truth," Catherine insisted, "then that person would have a very good reason."

"Well, I hope Astrolabe is having more luck than we are in finding him," John sighed.

Archbishop Samson did not believe any of the stories about an army of demons coming to free his prisoner. Neither did he think that there were enough of Eon's followers in town to attempt a rescue, if any of them had enough wit. But he had seen Eon when he was brought in, and he decided that there was no point in humiliating him once more in front of an angry crowd. He gave orders to bring the man in to the cathedral through a side door to the palace and hold him in the vestry until called for.

He felt it to be a decidedly charitable act on his part, since he was certain that Eon was somehow the catalyst for this distasteful problem of politics and murder, even though he seemed far too simple to be the instigator.

Samson was growing weary of having to spend every day listening to the wrangles of his fellow bishops. His deacons complained that it made the seating charts impossible to make up. With all the traffic, the rushes in the cathedral had to be swept and changed daily instead of weekly. The expense in candles alone was more than he normally spent in the year. There also were not so subtle rumblings from the town that it was time to pay more attention to the concerns of the souls of Reims. Even opening the granary hadn't alleviated the food shortage. Families who had been forced to cede their houses to the visitors were becoming louder in their demands to return home. Samson didn't want to end up like Pope Eugenius, thrown out of his own city by its citizens. He had tried to hint as much but without success.

At least the pope had arranged to have the inquest into the work of Gilbert of Poitiers saved until after the main council.

Most of the bishops, abbots and their followers would leave before that. Only a few of them professed to be able to follow the arguments in any case. He certainly didn't pretend to.

Samson splashed cold water on his face. Time to pass another day in playing the gracious host. How did innkeepers stand it?

The crowd at the cathedral was the largest yet.

"There aren't usually so many people here," Margaret said as she, Godfrey and Astrolabe pushed their way up to the cathedral door. "Maybe you should each hold on to one of my braids so we don't get separated."

"Don't worry. We won't lose you," Astrolabe promised.

It was only because of the size of both men, one on either side, that Margaret managed to reach the portal. The guard barred the way.

"I'm Margaret of Wedderlie," she reminded him, "Count Thibault's granddaughter. Please conduct me and my men to his place."

The guard raised his staff. "Can't leave my post," he said. "But the count went in just a moment ago. You can catch up to him."

Margaret nodded and ducked under his arm. Godfrey and Astrolabe followed.

The crush was less severe inside, but it took them several minutes to work their way to the transept, where the count and countess were seated.

"Perhaps I should stand somewhere else," Astrolabe suggested. "Your grandfather may not want to be seen so close to me."

"I say the closer you are to someone powerful, the better," Godfrey declared.

"I'll ask him," Margaret said over Astrolabe's objection.

She wormed her way through to where Count Thibault was standing with Abbot Bernard. She waited until the count noticed her. He gave a wide smile and beckoned her forward. She bowed to him and then knelt to the abbot for his blessing.

"A lovely child," Abbot Bernard said as she rose. His eyes flickered over the scar and his smile became more gentle.

"I'm surprised to see you here again, my dear," Thibault told her. "I thought the debates had grown wearisome to you."

"I grieve that I haven't the learning to understand the arguments properly, my lord," Margaret spoke formally. "I must confess to you that I have come today to witness the questioning of the Breton, Eon."

"I trust your faith is not in jeopardy, my lady," the abbot said.

Margaret wasn't sure if he were teasing her or not.

"I pray not," she answered. "But my friend wished to attend and I agreed to bring him. I believe you know the abbess of the convent where I am a student, my lord abbot. Heloise of the Paraclete?"

"Yes, of course," he answered. "I have preached to the nuns there."

"My friend is her son, Astrolabe."

The smile grew more puzzled.

"He wishes to see a heretic tried?" the abbot asked.

"So he has told me, my lord."

Abbot Bernard looked to Count Thibault for clarification.

"He is his mother's son, more than his father's," Thibault said. "Eager to expand his knowledge rather than disseminate it. And he was raised among the Bretons. He may wish to familiarize himself with the forms their divergence from orthodoxy can take."

Bernard nodded. A moment later he excused himself to speak with the pope.

Margaret kissed her grandfather's cheek.

"Thank you, my lord," she whispered. "Hasn't the abbot heard the rumors in the town? I was certain he would say something."

"I would not repeat what was said in the meeting last night," Thibault told her sternly. "The abbot would have learned about Astrolabe's difficulty in no other way. He does not encourage those who gossip.

"I don't believe Heloise's son is a criminal," he added. "But that doesn't mean I can save him if the others judge him to be guilty. Nevertheless, he may stand with our party. No one will dare to attack him here."

"Thank you, my lord," Margaret said. "I'll fetch him."

"After you do, go over to stand by the countess," Thibault commanded. "She has missed your company."

Margaret went reluctantly, although she returned Mahaut's warm greeting. She felt guilty for avoiding the countess. The constant talk of her new life in Carinthia was too painful to face.

Mass was said. The business of the council resumed.

Engebaud of Tours intended to present Eon as but one more example of the disorder rampant in the land of northern Brittany under the care of Olivier of Dol. To this end he first gave a long explanation of the history of the conflict between Dol and Tours, a battle for supremacy that had been going on for more than fifty years.

Margaret felt her eyes drooping by the time that the archbishop asked Moses, abbot of Sainte-Croix, to relate the story of Henri of Tréguier. The old man gave a good account of how he and his monks had been driven from their monastery by Henri and his men.

"They have turned a place of chastity and prayer into a brothel!" he cried. "I begged the other lords in the region to help us. I pleaded with Bishop Olivier to anathematize these monsters. Nothing has been done."

There was a murmur of shock throughout the cathedral. Pope Eugenius addressed the abbot.

"I find it difficult to believe that any bishop could be so unmindful of his responsibility as to ignore such a clear affront. Are you certain there were no irregularities in your order that might have caused Bishop Olivier to ignore your plea?"

"None at all, your Wisdom," Moses said indignantly.

"Is there anyone else who can testify as to what happened?" the pope continued.

Beside her, Margaret could feel Astrolabe stir. Her shoulders tensed in nervousness.

"I can, my lord."

Every head turned. The speaker was a woman.

"My name is Marie," she said. "Abbess of Saint-Sulpice-de-la-Forêt, near Rennes in Brittany. I beg the indulgence of the council to allow me to give testimony in this matter."

She knelt humbly before the pope and cardinals, but her tone made it clear that she expected them to indulge her.

Her request was immediately granted.

"My lords," she began. "I have come to Reims specifically to complain about this very matter. Count Henri has not only evicted the monks of Sainte-Croix; he has also abducted professed nuns from Saint-Georges-de-Rennes to be companions for his mistress. I have good evidence that these holy women have been subjected to the most vile treatment. Abbess Adela is too infirm to travel, so I am here in her place to implore that Henri and all his lands be placed under anathema and that a troop be sent to rescue these poor women."

"Thank you, my lady Marie," Pope Eugenius said. "Has Henri of Tréguier come to answer these charges?"

"No, my lord."

"Then, until he does, this council will consider him outside the protection of the sacraments." Eugenius nodded to the clerk to add Henri's name to the list of those to be excommunicated at the end of the council.

"Archbishop Engebaud." Eugenius beckoned him to come forward. "I understand you have one more example that you wish to give us of spiritual laxity under the governance of the bishop of Dol."

"I do, my lord."

"I suggest that this assembly recess until after Nones," the pope said. "At which time you may bring your example before us."

While they were waiting for the council members to file out, Margaret decided to ignore dignity and sit on the floor. Astrolabe squatted next to her.

"You don't need to come back this afternoon," he told her. "You're clearly tired. I don't think we need to worry about Gwenael making a scene when Eon is presented. The guards would never let her past the door."

"If you are returning, then so am I," she said. "Was Arnulf here? I didn't see him, either."

"Neither did I," Astrolabe said. "He may not have had an important friend like you to get him admitted."

Margaret blushed. "The procession seems to have finally left. I'm terribly thirsty. Do you think we'll be able to get something to drink before they resume?"

"If I know John, he has a place ready for us," Astrolabe grinned. "I do hope he and Catherine discovered something useful. All we have to show for this morning's work are sore feet."

Godfrey reached the beer stand first, to find that Catherine and John had staked out a spot for them all. Catherine had bought some hard-cooked eggs and dried apples to sustain them for the afternoon.

"I didn't spot either Gwenael or Lord Gui in the cathedral," he told them. "With your permission, I thought I'd find out where Lord Gui was staying before he was taken to the Temple. He might have returned there with his relatives."

"He told me he was part of the entourage of Hugh of Rouen," Catherine said.

"I already asked there," Godfrey said, "but no one knew where he had gone. Still, he can't have slept with the beggars. He must have brought servants, at least a squire to tend to his horse. I can start at the stables and work from there, if I have to knock on every door in Reims."

"May you have better luck than we have," John said.

A few moments later Astrolabe and Margaret appeared. Their hopeful expressions faded with the news John and Catherine told them.

"The porter told us only that the messenger was a heavily veiled woman," Catherine said. "The way he described her, it could even have been a man in woman's garb."

"Now, I could see Arnulf doing that," John commented.

"Well, it's a possibility," Astrolabe said. "Shall we demand to go through his belongings for a veil and face paint?"

"If it comes to that, I wouldn't hesitate," Catherine said. "I keep thinking about how Rolland was killed, though. He was a big man and naturally belligerent. How could Arnulf have managed to get close enough to him with a knife?"

"He could have offered to shave him," Margaret suggested.

"In the dark?" Godfrey asked.

Margaret was momentarily crushed, but she continued.

"Cecile was unconscious when she was murdered," she said. "If I wanted to kill someone much stronger than I was, I suppose I would hit him from behind to knock him out and then slit his throat for good measure."

"Is that what they do in Scotland?" John asked, mildly shocked.

"No," Margaret answered primly. "No matter what you English think, in Scotland we usually give people a good meal, plenty to drink and then kill them while they sleep."

John gave a laugh that sent a mouthful of beer spraying across the table.

"My apologies," he said when he could speak again.

"Margaret has a point," Catherine said. "I've been wondering if more than one person was involved in Rolland's death. If someone lay in wait for him with a cudgel to knock him out, then even a weakling like Arnulf could have managed it. I wish I could see the body."

"What would that tell you?" Astrolabe asked.

"How the cut was made, of course." Catherine took her meat knife from the sheath at her belt and demonstrated on him. "You see, if I were facing you, then I'd cut across back to front, like this."

"Not too realistically, please." Astrolabe leaned away from her.

"But if you were lying facedown, then I'd reach around and pull the knife front to back, like this. The deeper part of the wound would be opposite to the first."

"You don't need to subject yourself to a rotting corpse, Catherine," John said. "I had it from the monks who washed the body. Rolland was found facedown, the throat cut just as you showed."

"Perhaps we should search Arnulf's boxes for a heavy veil drenched with blood," Margaret said.

"I think that would be a very good idea," John agreed.

Apart from Godfrey, who was determined to spend the afternoon tracking down Gui, they all returned to the cathedral. This time the guards had been doubled and it was harder for Margaret to talk her way past them with her friends.

"Samson is taking no chances," John said approvingly.

Even so, there were even more people in attendance, including several ladies. Catherine saw Countess Sybil, Annora at her side. She wondered what Annora's feelings were about the man who had sheltered her sister after she escaped from Count Henri. Which story about Eon did she believe?

After preliminaries and prayers, Archbishop Engebaud stood again before the council.

"Have the prisoner brought in!" he ordered.

There was a shuffle at the door to the vestry and Eon appeared, a guard on either side.

Catherine took one look and understood how, despite his insane claim, Eon could inspire such devotion. She had expected a ragged, dirty preacher like Henry of Lausanne or Robert of Arbrissel, wild-eyed and unkempt. Eon could have been a king. He was tall, with a finely chiseled face and strong chin. His eyes were large and penetrating. Despite his weeks in captivity he held his head high, moving smoothly as if his chains did not exist. Samson must have been a tolerant custodian indeed, for Eon's beard and hair had been trimmed and his robe was clean. He had even been allowed to keep his staff. That surprised her most of all. It wasn't as if he needed it for support.

Eon surveyed the assembly without fear. He even seemed amused by all the attention he was receiving. Astrolabe was right. There was something about him that radiated authority and kindness. There was nothing in his stance to suggest madness.

"Catherine, he's beautiful!" Margaret whispered in astonishment.

Catherine agreed. From the murmurs around them, others did, too.

Pope Eugenius did not appear impressed.

"You are here to answer serious charges," he told Eon. "First, state your name and your family."

Eon smiled. He seemed completely at ease.

"I am Eum," he said. "Come to judge the living and the dead and the world by fire, as my father has commanded."

There was a ripple through the room. The pope held up his hand for silence.

"And that staff you carry," he asked. "What is its significance?"

Eon stepped closer, as if confiding a secret. The guards yanked him back. He wasn't fazed. He held up the staff for all to see, a simple piece of wood, forked at one end like the tools used to load hay.

"There is a great and holy secret to this staff," he explained in a conversational tone. "My divine Father and I have an arrangement. When I hold my staff like this, with the two tines looking to Heaven, then God has control over two-thirds of the earth. But when I reverse it, like this"—he turned the staff upside down—"then two-thirds of the earth are mine to govern and only one-third is his."

He smiled as if everything were now settled.

There was a moment of silence, and then the whole assembly burst out laughing.

"This is your dangerous heretic?" Eugenius asked Archbishop Engebaud. "Would that all heresies were so foolish!"

"He has many followers," Engebaud said. "They have terrorized simple hermits and robbed the villages throughout the area."

"And no doubt outlaws and other villains have used him as a subterfuge for their own activities." Eugenius considered Eon. The Breton smiled again. He seemed completely unaware of the gravity of the charges against him.

"I should speak now," Astrolabe said.

"No," Catherine told him. "I don't think the pope means to

have Eon executed, or even insist on a profession of faith from him. Everyone can see that he's simple, just as you have always said. Wait!" She pointed. "That's Arnulf, over there, by the pillar. He's the one we need to be ready for."

The monk was trying to push his way to the front.

Eugenius consulted a moment with the cardinals. They all seemed to be in agreement. The pope stood to announce the decision.

"It is our opinion that this man is not in his right mind." He spoke loudly so that all could hear. "His heresy is not diabolical but the result of madness. However, since he has led others from orthodoxy to the peril of their eternal souls, we ask Samson, archbishop of Reims, to see that he continues to be held in custody for his own protection and the well-being of those whom he had led astray. He is not to be ill treated," the pope added. "It may be that one day Our Lord may remove the scales from his eyes and restore his senses."

"No!" a voice called out. "My lords, I beg you!"

Arnulf shoved aside all in his path without regard for rank.

"This man is dangerous, far more than you know." He panted as he approached the front. "He has led others to commit terrible sins! They kidnapped and murdered a noblewoman. He must be punished along with his most wicked disciple . . . Will you get out of my way, woman!"

Annora had been trying to see where the noise was coming from. She didn't realize that Arnulf was heading her way until he ran into her.

"How dare you!" she cried, grabbing at his robe to keep from falling. "Who do you think you are?"

She peered at him more closely as he frantically tried to release her grip.

"Arnold?" she said. "Is that you?"

# Twenty

The cathedral. The next moment.

*Quia etiam apostolica sedes quod rectum est consuevit
attenta consideratione defendere, & quod devium inventutur
esse devitare; praesentis decreti auctoritate praecipimus, ut
nullus omino hominum haeresiarchas & eorum sequaces, qui
in partibus Guasconiae, aut Provinciae, vel alibi
commorantur, mantenat vel defendat; nec aliquis eis in terra
sua receptaculum praebeat.*

Because it is the custom of the Apostolic See to defend what
is right with careful consideration, and since what strays
from it is found to be wrong, we declare by this decree that
no person should support or defend the heresiarchs and their
followers who are currently in Gascony or Provence, nor
should anyone offer them refuge on his or her land.

Canon XVIII
Council of Reims, 1148

*A*nnora pulled his face closer to hers.

"Arnold of Valfonciere, what are you doing here?" she demanded.

"My name is Arnulf, lady!" he snapped at her, struggling to break free. "Someone help me!"

"Arnold, the monastery promised they wouldn't let you go wandering off." Annora shook him. "We gave them tithes to make sure of it. Now, how did you get out and what have you been up to?"

"Anno . . . ra!" Arnulf whined. "I'm doing God's work here. Your behavior is most improper."

Annora suddenly remembered where she was. She let go of Arnulf's robe. He skittered back a few steps as people moved quickly to get out of his way.

Pope Eugenius leaned over to where his clerk was scribbling the events for the edification of posterity.

"This will not go into the records," he said. "Understand?"

The clerk smoothed over the previous two paragraphs in the soft wax. The pope rose in his chair.

"Who is this man?" he asked the world in general.

Archbishop Engebaud tried to retrieve command of the situation.

"Brother Arnulf is a monk of Brittany who has been aiding us in gathering information concerning the heretic Eon," he explained. "He was not authorized to speak today. I very humbly beg your pardon for his unseemly outburst."

He waved at his deacons.

"Remove him," he commanded.

"Just a moment," Eugenius stopped them. "What was he saying about a murder?"

Eon, momentarily forgotten, took a few steps toward Arnulf. "You are not one of my flock," he said. Then he spied Astrolabe.

"Peter!" he cried, grinning broadly. "I'm so glad you were unhurt by the devils who invaded our home. They martyred our beautiful Cecile, you know. But I can see her watching us all from Heaven. I shall join her soon."

Samson Mauvoisin covered his face with his hands. So much for taking care of matters in private. He approached the pope.

"If I may explain, your Ineffable Patience," he said.

The pope nodded with a sigh.

Samson related as much as he knew about the death of Cecile. Catherine had to admit that he did so fairly. She did note that he neglected to mention Rolland's death.

"It was Peter Abelard's son who killed her!" Arnulf screamed from where the deacons were trying to control him. "He told me so! He cut her throat and ran, but he can't escape judgment. There were witnesses!"

"Can you present them?" Eugenius asked sharply.

"The men sent by the archbishop of Tours!" Arnulf was pleading now. "The soldiers. They know. They told me who he was and then I followed him in Paris. He's friends with Jews! He's evil!"

Astrolabe felt it was time to speak. He came to stand next to Engebaud.

Eugenius stared at him, mouth open in amazement.

"No need to ask your name," he said. "You are my old master to the life. Amazing. Perhaps you would care to explain the accusations made by this monk? If it is true, as the archbishop of Reims has just said, that you were taken with the Eonites, then even my respect for your father won't be enough to keep you from censure."

"It is true that I was with them, my lord," Astrolabe admitted. "But I was not one of them. Eon's cousins asked me to convince him to return home. I was attempting to do so when the encampment was invaded."

"I see, and the woman, the one who was killed, was she one of them?"

"No, she was taken in by Eon after escaping from the horror of Sainte-Croix as Abbot Moses and Abbess Marie related," Astrolabe explained. "She was murdered after we were captured, I believe by one of the men in the raiding party whom she recognized."

"No!" Arnulf wept, pointing at Astrolabe. "He did it. The son of a cruel heretic, you can't let him go, my lord. He killed Cecile, my beautiful cousin. I saw her body. That's what happens when dissenters are allowed to run free. Please, my lord. He killed her. He has to burn!"

Samson had a whispered conversation with Engebaud. He then bowed to the pope.

"My lord, with your permission," he said. "This matter does not concern the church at large. Perhaps Archbishop Engebaud and I can interview the persons involved in this matter and report our conclusions to you at a later time."

"With pleasure," he said. "Abbot Bernard, Abbot Suger, this seems to involve monastic irregularities. Does either of you wish to be present for these interviews?"

Catherine hadn't noticed the tiny abbot of Saint-Denis before. Suger sat near the pope, as regent of France in Louis's absence, but he had said nothing during the proceedings. Nor did he now. He simply shook his head. Abbot Bernard did the same, adding that he trusted the sagacity of the two archbishops.

"I'm sure they will uncover the truth," he told the pope.

"Then I declare the session ended." Eugenius stood. "We shall convene tomorrow, at which time the canons of the council will be read."

Again there was a long wait while the dignitaries made their exit.

Catherine felt limp after the excitement. But there was one thing she had to know.

Annora was still standing next to Arnulf, now flanked by a pair of solid deacons who didn't seem inclined to let him leave. She was glaring at him in fury, but mindful of the place, she held her tongue. Catherine wasn't about to wait until they had left the cathedral. She took the woman's shoulder and spun her around.

"Why didn't you tell me that you couldn't see past the end of your nose?" she demanded. "Do you realize the trouble you've caused? You were there when Arnulf was giving his evidence Tuesday night. You should have recognized him then."

"I thought the voice was familiar," she admitted, looking ashamed. "But I hadn't seen him in years. I thought he was safe in the Norman monastery where his parents had placed him."

"And why was he placed there?" Catherine asked. "Is he insane?"

"Oh, no!" Annora said. "At least," she added, looking at him, still babbling to the deacons, "he wasn't when he entered. He did hear voices sometimes, warning him of enemies plotting against him. He was in constant fear and would accuse totally harmless people of trying to kill him, even me once. The story I heard was that the family thought he'd feel less frightened in the company of the monks."

"He must have thought they were against him, too." Catherine almost felt pity for Arnulf. "So he ran away. I wonder how he wound up in Tours."

Astrolabe had joined them in time to hear the last of this.

"What I want to know is who told him about me," he said.

Arnulf saw him and began screaming again.

"I don't think you're going to get it from him now," Catherine said sadly as the deacons dragged the monk off. "But I feel confident that you're not under suspicion anymore in Cecile's death."

Astrolabe gave a sad smile. "Perhaps not, but unless we find who really did it, there will be people who will always think that I was guilty but bought my exoneration from the bishop. And, there is still the murder of Canon Rolland. So far I seem to be the only one with a reason for wanting him dead."

"That's true. Arnulf was our best hope as an alternate suspect," Catherine sighed. "How did he see Cecile's body? At

Tours? He might have taken her brooch then. But I don't think he was present at the dinner where I found it. And there's no use asking you if he was, Annora."

"Don't be so resentful, Catherine," she answered. "Why should I tell anyone that the world beyond the end of my arm is nothing but a blur? A man doesn't want a wife who can't see clearly."

"I don't know," Catherine said. "I'd say most men would prefer it. I should have guessed it anyway, when you mistook Raoul of Vermandois for the pope."

The crowd was clearing. Catherine looked around for Margaret and John. She didn't see him, but Margaret was with her grandfather, waving for them to join her.

"Well, that was a fine show," Count Thibault greeted them. "I'm sure Sybil of Anjou will have a few things to say to you, young woman, about disrupting official synods."

"I am most mortified by my behavior, my lord," Annora told him.

"That's her affair, not mine," he waved off her apologies. "And you may have saved me another evening of listening to tedious narratives of crime.

"Now, Astrolabe," he continued, "I've spoken to Samson and Engebaud. Neither of them wishes to consider you a murder suspect any longer."

"I am relieved to hear that," Astrolabe said. "Thank you, my lord. But someone killed Cecile and Rolland, and is still free. I thought it was Arnulf, but now I'm not sure."

"I must agree," Thibault said. "He doesn't have enough *pendon*."

Countess Mahaut interrupted at this point.

"It's been a long day," she said. "Margaret's sister-in-law looks dead on her feet, if you'll excuse my saying so, my dear. Perhaps all of you could come to our chambers after dinner this evening. There are a number of questions that need answering. You, too, young man," she added to John, who had just arrived.

"Of course my lady," he bowed.

"Now, all of you go get some rest," she said, waving them

off. "I want a complete explanation of this by tonight. Margaret, you may stay. I want to introduce you to a few friends."

Margaret shot Catherine a look of panic but smiled at the countess and stayed.

Catherine shook her head. She had to do something to make Margaret take a stand against this marriage.

"I feel as if I'd been turned inside out, washed and laid out to shrivel in the sun," Catherine said as they left the cathedral.

"You need to sit someplace with your feet up and have someone bring you herbed wine and honey," Annora said.

"I'd be happy with water," Catherine said. "But both you and the countess are right. I must get off my feet before they explode. Astrolabe! What are you doing?"

"Getting you off your feet," he laughed as he lifted her into his arms. "Now, it's not an elegant way to travel, but it's not that far to Saint-Pierre. Catherine, you haven't been eating enough."

"Just be glad I'm no heavier," Catherine teased. "Thank you, old friend. The distance to the convent seems a hundred miles to me just now."

Astrolabe carried her to the gate of Saint-Pierre. She kissed him good day and went in immediately. "We will solve this," she told him before climbing the stairs. "No more rumors."

"Lady Annora." Astrolabe stopped her before she followed Catherine. "I know this has been a difficult time for you, too. But please make sure that someone sees to her. Catherine is not as strong as she pretends."

"No one could be," Annora said. "Except perhaps my lady Sybil."

"That was an interesting display," John told Astrolabe as they went back across the square. "I promised to write my friend Peter about the events at the council. I wouldn't know how to begin to tell this tale."

"John, you won't tell about what happened to me, will you?" Astrolabe said in alarm.

"Why not?" he asked. "You've been exonerated."

"But why have it known that I was ever under suspicion?" he said. "The fewer who know this, the better, to my mind."

"It will be difficult," he said. "But I don't suppose future readers will care about some *stultus* from Brittany too mad even to convert."

"Is that what you think of me?"

"Of course not," he answered. "I meant Eon, you dolt!"

Then he saw Astrolabe's face.

"Well, I'm glad you can still joke about it," he said. "Very well. I promise never to write a word of this episode. I'm more interested in the debate on the teachings of master Gilbert, anyway."

"Oh, yes," Astrolabe yawned. "I must confess I find Eon's beliefs more comprehensible than his. If the bishop's so important, why are they waiting until most of the council has left before they discuss him?"

"I don't know," John admitted. "Perhaps his opponents are hoping he'll die of old age before they have to face him."

"That old man may outlive all of his detractors," Astrolabe said. "I wish my father could have. Perhaps I should attend his trial, although I own I've had enough of heresy for a lifetime."

"Don't worry," John said. "I'll be there for all of it. When I write my report to Peter, I'll have a copy sent to you."

"Fair enough," Astrolabe said. "Shall we go meet Godfrey, or do you also need a nap?"

"You know what I need, *vieux compang*," John grinned, "and I'm sure your friend Godfrey will be happy to share."

They found Godfrey waiting impatiently. John's eyes lit when he saw the pitcher at his elbow.

"I found where Gui was staying," he told them even before they started to pour.

"Was?" Astrolabe asked. "Does that mean he's gone?"

"I don't know." Godfrey was clearly puzzled. "It seems he came back from the Temple, not much worse for wear but greatly changed in character."

"What about the people who were supposed to have fetched him?" John asked.

"No one has seen them," Godfrey said. "But the first thing he did when he got back to his room was give away his horse."

"What!" both men said together.

"Are you sure, Godfrey?" Astrolabe asked. "You must mean his packhorse or a mule."

"No." Godfrey shook his head slowly. "His best warhorse, the one that he won at a tourney in Bordeaux two years ago."

"But it must be worth more than all his land," John said.

"At least three hundred silver marcs of Troyes," Godfrey said. "I was told so several times. His friends can't believe it, either."

"But if he has nothing to ride, then he must still be in Reims," Astrolabe said.

"If so, none of his companions have seen him. He also gave away most of his clothes, all his gear and his weapons."

"He must have undergone some kind of conversion," John said. "It's the only explanation. Or he's atoning for some great sin."

"Like murder?" Astrolabe conjectured.

"I don't know," Godfrey told them. "His friends were completely stupefied by the change. Anyway, he gave everything away, went out the day before yesterday and hasn't been seen since."

"This is getting irritating," John said. "I'm not accustomed to people vanishing suddenly."

"It does sound as though he were going on a pilgrimage of expiation," Astrolabe said. "But I'd rather have a solid confession or certain proof of his guilt."

"You don't think he did it?" Godfrey asked. "Why not?"

"Because Margaret doesn't think he did," Astrolabe answered.

"But she was wrong about the brooch and the attack on Gui," John reminded him.

"I don't know that she was," Astrolabe said. "She's a remarkable person. She understands things without knowing them."

"I believe that is what Abbot Bernard says all of us should do," John said. "But in this case, Margaret must be wrong. It has to be Gui. Who else is left?"

"Me, I suppose," Astrolabe answered.

Catherine couldn't get to sleep. Her legs were throbbing, the baby was restless, and she had the uneasy feeling that she had overlooked something obvious.

She should have realized that Annora had poor vision. There had been any number of signs. But Annora had learned to cover them well. That sleepy, bored look that was really a practiced squint. The way she opened her eyes wide when addressed. The fact that she had been sitting directly across the room from Gui and not known he was there. How could she have missed all those clues? Catherine was beginning to doubt her own reasoning skills.

Annora wasn't the problem, though. Catherine was determined to find the answer, but she felt Annora wasn't the key to solving the murders.

No, it was something else, something she had heard and not paid attention to.

Now her head was aching as well as her feet. Catherine tried to relax, to think about nothing. She recited *Ave Marias* in her head, but other scenes kept disrupting the prayers: Arnulf in the cathedral, the saintly face of Eon, Gui's feckless grin.

Margaret believed that Gui had faked the attack on himself. It didn't make sense, but Catherine trusted her intuitions. Logically, all blame could be placed on Arnulf, or Arnold, as Annora had called him. He must have been in the raiding party, killed Cecile and stolen the brooch, then dropped it in the garden while trying to overpower his brother, Gui. He killed Rolland when the canon became suspicious of his motives.

It all fit together. But she knew it was wrong.

Catherine tried to view the problem objectively. The problem was Arnulf himself. The man didn't even have enough imagination to think up a proper false name. His lies very likely made sense in his own mind. It would have been so tidy if he were guilty.

Life was never tidy.

And yet, if Peter Abelard had taught her anything, it was that God didn't intend existence to be incomprehensible. If her intellect wasn't up to the challenge, then the fault lay in her.

She knew the answer was in her memory somewhere.

"Dear Saint Catherine," she prayed to her name saint. "You are wise as well as holy. Please help me to find the truth so that Astrolabe won't live forever with this shadow over him."

There was no blinding light of revelation, but Catherine was content. When logic failed, there was always faith. Perhaps with both a solution would appear.

Margaret came for her just before Vespers.

"Did you get a good rest?" she asked.

"Oh, yes," Catherine said. "But I can tell that you had none at all. Whom did the countess want you to meet?"

"German bishops," Margaret sighed. "There seem to be a lot of them here. These were related somehow to the man I'm supposed to marry."

"Margaret!" Catherine got up and started to put on her shoes. "You must end this marriage nonsense. Even if the countess is offended, you can't go off to Carinthia."

"I'm beginning to think I must," Margaret said.

Catherine dropped the shoe.

"You can't be serious. What would Edgar say?"

"He's not here, Catherine," Margaret told her. "And he has said nothing about arranging a marriage for me. I don't wish to take the veil, so a husband is inevitable. My grandfather has offered a noble dowry. If I disobey him, then that burden will be on Edgar. You know I have nothing of my own."

"You should," Catherine said, an old grievance surfacing. "Your brother, Duncan, has taken your father's title and land. He owes you a dowry, too."

"Only if I go back to Scotland and marry according to his wishes." Margaret shuddered. "At least Countess Mahaut is concerned with my happiness."

"Margaret, you're only fifteen," Catherine protested. "There's time yet to find you someone closer to home. I was nearly twenty when Edgar and I married."

"Catherine, the countess has worked very hard for my benefit," Margaret explained. "I don't feel I can betray her now."

Catherine had retrieved the shoe and was lacing it up. Now she stopped.

"Betray," she said.

"Yes, betray," Margaret repeated. "That's what it would be after she's been so kind."

"No. Wait." Catherine held up her hand to shush Margaret. "Betrayal. That's what she said. Margaret, we must find Astrolabe at once. If I'm right, he's in terrible danger. And then remind me to buy a candle for Saint Catherine."

They brushed past Annora on their way out.

"Catherine!" she called.

"So sorry," Catherine said over her shoulder. "We're in a great hurry."

"But I have to talk to you!" Annora followed them. "It's very important."

"Not now!" Catherine said.

"It's about Cecile." Annora trotted behind them. "I've spoken with Gui. He confessed everything."

Catherine stopped so quickly that Annora ran into her. Then a woman carrying a huge bundle of fresh wool on her back nearly bumped into both of them.

They were in the middle of the road. Catherine took Annora to one side. Margaret followed after helping the shepherdess to rebalance her load.

"He confessed?" Catherine said. "When? Where did you see him?"

Annora took a deep breath. "I was with him last night," she admitted. "He's going away. He says he needs to clean his soul."

"He killed Cecile and Rolland?" Margaret asked. "I don't believe it."

Annora stared at her. "Of course not. He loved Cecile."

"What?"

"I didn't know for certain until now," Annora said. "They seemed very fond of each other, but our fathers were always at dagger's point. Then she entered the convent and I thought that was the end of it."

Catherine was shocked. "But Annora, they are first cousins. That's not even consanguinity; it's plain incest."

"I know that," Annora said. "So did they. That's why Cecile went to Saint-Georges. But Gui told me last night that he couldn't accept her decision. He followed her. She refused to see him. When he heard that she had been taken to Sainte-Croix, he went to rescue her, only she had already escaped. He says that he hunted for her all winter. He joined the men hunting the heretics just to get a meal and a bed. He couldn't believe it when he saw her with them."

"Why didn't he tell someone who she was and have her freed?" Catherine asked. This story seemed stranger than Arnulf's.

"He wasn't very clear on this," Annora said. "I think he may have been afraid. He thought there would be time. She was unconscious so he had her put in the cart and wrapped her in his cloak. He came to check on her late in the night and found she was awake."

Annora paused, biting her lips to keep back the tears.

"She told him that this was her punishment for loving him, that he must take her back to Saint-Georges and never try to see her again. Then she gave him this."

She opened her hand. In it was a gold and topaz brooch.

"He promised to honor her request," she continued. "But when he came for her in the morning, she was dead and the other man in the cart missing."

"Why didn't he say then who she was?" Catherine asked.

Annora sighed. "There was a great hue and cry for the man who had escaped. Gui felt sure he'd be caught and hanged immediately and Cecile would be avenged. He was numb with grief. He still is."

"But he wasn't the one who killed her," Catherine said.

"Of course not," Annora said. "I've just told you."

"But he did pretend to be attacked?" Margaret asked.

"He did," Annora said. "He wanted to attract my attention while keeping up the myth that we were enemies. He always overdid things. He should have been born a *jongleur*. Idiot!"

"And you kept all of this to yourself?" Catherine wanted to shake her.

"I didn't know most of it until last night," Annora insisted. "And then Arnold appeared when he should have been behind thick walls. I was terribly confused. But Gui said he didn't even know his brother was here."

"And Arnulf wasn't with the raiding party?" Catherine asked.

"No, he was in Tours, running from the monks he thought were trying to kill him," Annora explained. "Just as he said. He stumbled on the heretics and Cecile. Her death only convinced him that all his fears were true."

Catherine rubbed her forehead. "And I thought my family was strange."

"Please don't tell any of this to Countess Sybil," Annora begged.

"I wouldn't know where to start," Catherine said. "Margaret, please, will you run and see if Astrolabe is still at the beer stand? I'll follow as quickly as I can. We've wasted too much time already."

"What is it?" Annora asked.

"I've been stupid," Catherine said, hurrying after Margaret. "It was never about your family. It was about a test of faith, betrayal and atonement. Please let Astrolabe still be drinking beer."

When they reached the stand, they found only Godfrey.

"Did Margaret find you?" Catherine asked.

"Yes," Godfrey told her. "I sent her on with John and waited here for you."

"On where?"

"Saint-Hilarius," Godfrey said. "Astrolabe wanted to light a candle for the soul of his father. He told us he'd never appreciated Abelard's travails until now."

Catherine leaned against the table to catch her breath.

"That should be safe enough," she said. "There will be other people around."

"What's the matter?" Godfrey asked. "I thought Astrolabe was out of danger now."

"Only from false accusations," Catherine said. "Not from Gwenael."

Godfrey's eyes narrowed. "Gwenael has been tormented enough," he told her. "She's deluded, but that's no reason to try to blame her for the murders. Both Arnulf and Gui are more likely suspects. Even Astrolabe. He could have been lying to all of us. You've settled on Gwenael now only because she's just a peasant woman with no family to protect her."

"No!" Catherine took his hands to keep him from leaving. "That was why I didn't even consider her. 'No one looks at a beggar.' Gwenael was always there. She followed Eon and the others when they were captured. She heard Cecile ask to return to the convent. It was she who found out who Astrolabe was and passed the information on, although I think it was unwittingly. She didn't want him harmed. She killed Rolland because he was going to prevent Astrolabe from saving Eon, and now she thinks that Astrolabe has betrayed her savior and abandoned him to his fate."

"I don't believe it," Godfrey insisted, pulling his hands away.

"Yes, you do," Catherine said softly. "We have to find her before she tries to hurt Astrolabe, too."

Annora had been listening to the exchange in growing fury.

"You mean this *bordelere vilaine* murdered my sister?" she cried. "And tried to put the guilt on my cousins? I swear I'll rip out her heart with my fingernails."

"Annora," Catherine spoke gently, "she will be punished. You need have no fear about that. As soon as John and Margaret return with Astrolabe, we'll go to Archbishop Samson to have the city searched for her. He and Count Thibault are expecting all of us this evening. We can enlist all their help."

"She's probably halfway back to Brittany by now," Annora replied angrily. "You were too busy slandering Gui and Arnold to even consider her. Too busy protecting your precious Astrolabe."

Catherine had no retort for this. Annora was right.

The bells began to ring the end of Vespers.

"What's taking them so long to find him?" Godfrey said. "It's not far to Saint-Hilarius."

Catherine felt an icy chill down her back.

"I think we should go find out," she said.

Margaret and John had arrived at Saint-Hilarius to find the church deserted.

"That's strange," John said. "Do you think we missed him?"

"There must be someone around to ask," Margaret said. "The sacristan, perhaps."

"I'll go look," John told her. "Wait here."

He went out to find a caretaker.

Margaret always loved small parish churches. This one was not much larger than their hall in Paris. It was a simple bare building with narrow windows that let in little light. The apse was barely an indentation in the far wall. The altar was only a stone box covered with a cloth. A few candles burnt before it. Margaret went closer.

That was odd. There was no cross, either on the altar or above it. Could the priest have taken it with him to prevent its being stolen? Or had some sacrilegious thief already stolen it?

Margaret went up to look. There was something on the floor between the altar and the wall. Someone had dropped his cloak. She bent over to pick it up and realized there was a body underneath it.

"Astrolabe?" she said as she bent over.

"Margaret!" John's voice echoed in the empty space. "Don't move. She's got a knife."

# Twenty-one

The church of Saint-Hilarius. The next moment.

*Et quoniam in multc locis non poterant victui necessaria reperiri, graviter afflictus fuit per aliquantulum temporis populus fame, et in une dierum, prout peccatis nostris exigentibus judicium divinum permisit, plerique ceciderunt de baronibus nostris. Fuerent enim mortui . . . consanguineus noster comes de Guarenna, Rainaldus Tornodorensis, Mannasses de Bulis, Gaucherius de monte Gaii, Evrardus de Bretolio et caeteri quamplures. . . . Et quonium pecunia nostra in multis et variis expensis non mediocriter imminuta est.*

And since in many places they couldn't find enough food to survive, the people were seriously afflicted by famine and in one day, as if divine judgment were permitting it for our sins, many of our barons perished. Among those who died were our relative, the count of Guenne, Raynold of Tonnerre, Manassas of Bulis, Walcher of Mongai, Everard of Breteuil and many others. . . . And so much of our money has been diminished by many and various expenses.

Louis VII, letter to Abbot Suger, from Antioch, the Friday after quadragesima (March 19), 1148

*M*argaret froze, bent over Astrolabe's body.

Gwenael paused, the knife in her upraised hand.

John came toward her slowly.

"You can't mean to hurt Margaret, Gwenael," he said quietly. "She's an innocent."

"She's one of them," Gwenael answered, and her voice held a world of hate.

"No, she isn't," John said. He thought, *She's not insane. I can reason with her. I can. I know I can. I hope I can.*

"Her blood is noble." Gwenael didn't turn her eyes from the cowering child. "They say it's different from ours, but it looks just the same to me. My Lord, my master Eon, told us that we were as good as all her sort. They drove us from our homes, burnt our fields in their stupid wars. She's always had it easy. Why should she live?"

"Had it easy? Have you ever looked at her face?" John asked. "Margaret, stand up very slowly. Push your hair back so Gwenael can see."

Margaret's hands were shaking, but she obeyed. The jagged line of the scar showed clearly in the flicker of the candles.

"There are others," she said in a small voice. "On my back, my stomach, my left shoulder."

"She was beaten by a mob and left for dead," John said. "A mob of people who were peasants like you. She had done nothing to them. Do you hate all peasants for what happened, Margaret?"

"No," she said. "A poor laundress found me. She saved my life."

Her deep brown eyes gazed pleadingly at Gwenael, who hadn't lowered the knife.

Gwenael didn't seem impressed. Her face was twisted in loathing. She pulled back the knife to strike. Margaret crossed herself and prepared to die.

"At least if you kill me," she said, "I won't have to marry a man I've never met in a country far from home."

She lifted her chin and steeled herself for the blow.

The knife wavered.

"Gwenael." John had crept closer while the woman was looking at Margaret. "Killing her won't save you. It won't buy Eon's freedom."

She suddenly realized how near he was. Her head turned.

As she moved to fend him off, John leapt for her, knocking her over and sending the knife clattering across the stone floor.

Margaret ran to pick it up.

"Help me!" John gasped.

It felt as if he were fighting the offspring of a snake and a tiger. Wasn't there something in the Book of Revelation about that? Gwenael bit, scratched and kicked all at once. John had meant only to subdue her, but now he was struggling to keep her from incapacitating him. Her knees knew where to jab.

All at once Gwenael went limp. Her wintry blue eyes glittered in revulsion but she didn't move. Cautiously, John drew away from her. Margaret was holding the knife at her throat.

"I know how to do this," she said conversationally. "I've seen my brothers kill deer and, of course, watched the villagers at home slaughter the pigs. I'd rather not. But you have just killed Astrolabe, whom I love dearly, so please stay still."

"That will do, Margaret." John put his hand over hers, taking control of the knife.

"He's not dead yet," Gwenael muttered.

"What?" John leaned to hear. "Margaret, would you check?"

"There's no blood," Margaret said, kneeling by the body. "Yes, I can feel the beat of his heart in his throat! Thank the saints! He has a bad bump on his head, though."

John felt light-headed with relief. He moved back so that Gwenael couldn't lunge for the knife again. Her eyes darted back and forth like a trapped fox, but he was blocking any way out. He wasn't sure how long they could stand like this. Where was the damn priest?

"I suppose I can understand why you wanted Canon Rolland to die," he said to keep her attention. "But why Astrolabe, Gwenael? Why Cecile?"

The woman wouldn't answer. Giving up on escape, she slumped down until she sat on the floor, head bent over her knees.

There was a creak as the door of the church opened.

"Finally!" John said without turning around. "Where have you been?"

"We came as soon as we could," Catherine said. "I see you found her. Don't let her go. She wants to kill Astrolabe."

"We know," John said. "Godfrey, could you run over to the Temple and see if they will send some men with a stretcher? Astrolabe has been knocked out."

It was some time before order was restored in Saint-Hilarius. Godfrey brought back the stretcher bearers who took Astrolabe back to the Temple infirmary. He also had the presence of mind to pick up a length of rope. They tied Gwenael securely. While waiting for him, John and Catherine had a great deal of difficulty keeping Annora from carrying out her own private justice.

"Would you have her death on your soul?" Catherine begged.

"Gladly!" Annora said, struggling in her grasp.

"We must take her to the bishop for justice," John said. "My lady Annora, if you don't stop trying to attack her, I'll tie you up, too."

"He will," Catherine assured her.

Reluctantly, Annora gave in. Catherine released her. "Stay back," she cautioned her. "One step toward Gwenael and I'll bind you with your own braids!"

Annora went to the other side of the altar. There she found Margaret, who had retreated to a corner while the men from the Temple were taking care of Astrolabe.

"Margaret? Are you all right?" she asked.

Margaret was trembling all over, her teeth chattering.

"I c-c-can't st-st-stop sh-shaking," she said.

"Oh, my precious, of course not!" Catherine went to her at once. "You've had a horrible ordeal. We're going right back to Saint-Pierre and getting you a hot posset."

"N-no," Margaret said. "Grandfather."

Catherine was aware that they were already late for the meeting before Count Thibault and Archbishop Samson. But even though they could now present them with the murderer, Catherine wasn't sure she wanted the count to know the danger his granddaughter had been in.

"Perhaps you should wait at the convent," she suggested.

Margaret shook her head. There was a set to her jaw that reminded Catherine uncomfortably of Edgar.

"Very well," she said. "We should all make ourselves more presentable after this struggle. But I would rather give Gwenael into the archbishop's custody at once than wait until I can appear before him with a clean face."

Godfrey took it upon himself to keep Gwenael in check as they made their way across town.

"I could have forgiven you, you know," he whispered to her, "until you went after Astrolabe. He wanted to help you. He did what he could to keep your heretical leader from death. How could you turn on him?"

"In the end, he betrayed us," Gwenael said in a flat voice. "They always do."

Twilight was fading as the strange procession made its way through Reims. Most people were on their way home or to the taverns. A few wondered why the woman was being dragged through the streets, but they were used to seeing criminals being taken and so thought no more about it.

A cluster of beggars was sitting at the steps of the cathedral. As she passed them, Annora stopped to drop a coin in an outstretched hand. Catherine was just close enough to hear her murmur.

"For Cecile."

She was startled when the man took Annora's hand and kissed it, even more that the woman allowed such familiarity. She was never sure afterward if she had really heard his reply.

"I shall strive to be worthy to join her in paradise. This is for a priest at Saint Gwenoc's."

Catherine thought she saw him pass her a purse. She told herself it was nonsense, that she was overwrought by recent events. But she couldn't quite shake the feeling that she had seen those beggars somewhere before.

Count Thibault was pacing the floor of the chamber when the group finally arrived.

"High time!" the count said. "The countess was about to have a search started for you. Where's Astrolabe? Don't tell me he's fled!"

Archbishops Samson and Engebaud did not seem concerned. They were at a table in a corner with a *tric-trac* board and their wine goblets. When everyone had entered they left the game, taking the goblets with them.

"We were hoping for an explanation," Samson said as he surveyed the assorted people before him. "I didn't expect a prisoner. What has she done?"

"This is a disciple of the heretic Eon, my lord," Margaret answered. "She is responsible for the deaths of Cecile of Beaumont and Canon Rolland. She also attacked Astrolabe in the church of Saint-Hilarius and threatened to kill me when we discovered her."

On hearing that, Count Thibault forgot ceremony. He embraced Margaret, holding her so tightly that the breath was knocked out of her. He hadn't realized until that moment how very much he had grown to love this newly found granddaughter.

Archbishop Samson continued the questioning. "Was Lord Astrolabe badly hurt?"

"He's still unconscious," John answered. "We won't know until he wakes."

The archbishop looked at John, his robe torn, hair wild and face scratched. His left eye was swollen nearly shut.

"You're tonsured," he commented, "and yet you seem to have been fighting."

Margaret managed to free her face from her grandfather's chest.

"Don't punish him, my lord," she said. "He saved my life."

John reddened under the gratitude the count poured upon him.

"I shall see that you are rewarded for your courage," Thibault said. "Although the price for Margaret's life is more than all my lands and property. Now, someone please explain what has been going on and how this woman was apprehended."

It took some time for the entire story to be told. John, Catherine and Margaret kept interrupting each other. Even Godfrey added his information. Only Annora was silent.

Archbishop Engebaud noticed this.

"My lady Annora," he asked, "are you satisfied that this is indeed the person who murdered your sister?"

"What?" Annora seemed not to have been paying attention. Catherine wondered if she were also deaf. "Yes, my lord. She has confessed. I have no reason to doubt her."

"Then you should have a say in what is now done with her," Engebaud said.

Annora shook her head. "I want nothing to do with it," she said. "I would have executed her myself, if Catherine hadn't stopped me. But perhaps a long and painful penance would be better."

"A penance can't be imposed until she repents," Archbishop Samson reminded Annora.

"Are you truly sorry for the horrendous sins you have committed?" he asked Gwenael.

Gwenael lifted her head and spat in his face.

When she woke the next morning Catherine felt as if she'd spent the past few days hanging over a precipice and, at the end, been dropped into a pit of mud. Annora refused to leave the bed. She covered her head with the blanket and then the pillow.

"Tell Countess Sybil that I will be here until she is ready to return to Flanders," she said through the bedclothes.

Catherine wished that she could do the same. She had no sense of victory. Gwenael was in the archbishop's prison until she could be turned over to the town authorities for hanging. Her last words to them had been a taunt.

"You're damned, all of you!" she had cried triumphantly. "You have no power over me. My savior will never let me come to harm. He shall rend the earth, crumbling it to dust under the feet of those who would destroy me!"

"That's the real danger in a madman like Eon," John had remarked to Catherine as they left the count's chambers. "He is nothing but a misguided fool. He has no wish to harm anyone. But he led Gwenael into a true heresy. And look what came of it."

Catherine didn't want to. She didn't want to think about what had happened. What she really wanted was to wash all over, her body, her hair, her spirit.

Margaret had stayed the night with her grandfather. She came early to the convent, though, bursting with rapture.

"Catherine." She kissed her good day. "I know I shouldn't be joyful now, but last night I finally told Countess Mahaut that I didn't want to marry her cousin. Do you know what? She said she was relieved to hear it. She had just learned that Lord Otto recently married a noblewoman of Poland. Isn't that wonderful? She had been worrying about disappointing me!"

"Oh, *ma doux*, I'm so glad," Catherine said. "It's wonderful to have something to celebrate. She doesn't have anyone else in mind for you, does she?"

"I told her I would like to pass another year at the Paraclete," Margaret said, "and suggested that she not exert herself on my behalf until then, in case I decided to profess as a nun."

"Well, it's not exactly the ringing assertion that I had hoped you would make," Catherine smiled. "But it does give us another year to find you a better fate. Now, would you like to come to the bathhouse with me?"

\*   \*   \*

They were cleaned, oiled, combed and dressed in their best by
Tierce. Catherine checked on Annora, whose only response
was to burrow farther into the mattress. Then they went to the
Temple to find out how Astrolabe was doing.

"We should have gone there first," Catherine admitted, "but
I just couldn't face any more problems with filthy hair."

Godfrey was talking to the guard when they arrived. He
greeted them with a disrespectful enthusiasm that scandalized
the old soldier.

"Astrolabe woke up just after dawn," Godfrey told them.
"His head feels like it's been cleaved by an axe, he says, but
otherwise he's fine."

"I want to see for myself," Margaret said.

She swept by the guard with queenly arrogance.

Catherine followed, happy to be in her train.

John was sitting next to the bed when they came in.

"You look worse than he does," Margaret said, studying his
scrapes.

"Gwenael is a fearsome opponent," John admitted. "But all
my scars are on the surface. They'll soon heal."

Astrolabe was pale, but his eyes were clear.

"Forgive me for not getting up," he said. "If I lift my head
even a fraction, the pain is blinding. But the infirmarian says it
will pass in a day or two. If you and John hadn't come looking
for me, Margaret, I'd be bled dry by now. I have no words to
express my gratitude."

"You're not supposed to be talking at all," John told him
sternly.

"We just wanted to see for ourselves that you were still
among the living," Catherine told him. "We won't tire you.
Margaret and I will come back this afternoon."

Astrolabe wasn't ready to rest.

"John has told me most of what happened," he said. "I can't
yet comprehend how Gwenael's devotion to Eon could have
warped her so."

"I don't think it was devotion, but guilt," Catherine told him.
"I think the first betrayal of Eon was hers. She said so more

than once, but I thought she only meant that she ran from the soldiers, like the apostles. But then I learned that she had likened herself to Judas. Judas gave Our Lord to the Romans. You told me it was Gwenael who warned the camp that the raiders were coming. She had seen them in the forest."

"That's right," Astrolabe said. "She was out gathering wood."

"I'm just guessing," Catherine went on, "but dawn is a strange time to go for wood. We usually wait until the sun has dried the dew. I suspect Gwenael met the men by arrangement and directed them to the camp."

"But why?" Godfrey asked. "I'd bet my mail shirt that her faith in him is total."

"I don't know," Catherine admitted. "Perhaps she didn't understand any better than Eon did. She may have felt that it was necessary for him to be captured so that he could prove his godhood. Whatever the reason, she soon regretted it. Her way of atoning was to remove anyone else who, in her eyes, threatened him."

Astrolabe started to shake his head, but a slash of pain stopped the motion.

"I don't suppose we'll ever know for certain why she acted as she did," he said.

"Abbot Bernard has asked to speak with her," Margaret said. "He says an iniquity this deep must be cleansed. He's managed to bring other heretics back to the faith."

"I don't think even Bernard of Clairvaux can penetrate Gwenael's convictions," John said. "But he's the only man who has even a chance."

"Oh!" Margaret said, "I almost forgot, John. Count Thibault wants you to come see him."

"If he wants to reward me," John told her, "please tell him that there's no need. Your life is precious to me, too."

"I don't think he was going to give you a bag of gold," Margaret said. "But I told him about your search for a position. I said that Catherine knew you quite well, that you had studied with every master in France and that you had a letter from Abbot Peter of Celle, whom he knows, of course, since it's not far from Troyes."

"Thank you, Margaret," John said, "but I don't feel right taking a benefice from a secular lord."

"I hadn't finished," Margaret said. "Grandfather said that these were all good recommendations and that he would ask Abbot Bernard to write you a letter of introduction to the archbishop of Canterbury. Is that all right, John?"

Even with a face full of scratches and one black eye, John's expression resembled that of a man who has just received a vision of paradise.

"My lady Margaret." He went down on one knee to her. "If ever I can serve you in any way, you have only to ask. I will come from the farthest corner of Christendom to repay you for your kindness."

He raised his hands to her in the gesture of fealty. Margaret placed hers around them.

Then she ruined the solemnity of the moment by grinning.

"Just do a good job and don't forget us when you become a bishop," she said.

"It seems odd to think that the council is still going on," Catherine commented as she, Margaret, John and Godfrey left the Temple. "And people here are going about their affairs as if they hadn't been certain three days ago that the world was about to end."

"Well, it didn't," Margaret said, as if that explained everything. "Countess Mahaut told me that at the end of the day, the pope is going to put King Stephen under anathema. She didn't seem very upset by it. She intends to be there. Do you want to come?"

"You might want to, Catherine," John said. "I have on good authority that Archbishop Theobald of Canterbury"—he let the name resonate in his mouth—"will make a plea for clemency in the case of the king."

"Really?" Catherine said. "That does sound interesting. Yes, I'd like to witness that. But even more, I want to see my children. Every minute away from them feels like an eternity. I didn't do what I was supposed to here, but Astrolabe is no longer in danger and there is no reason to prolong this visit."

"What about Arnulf?" Godfrey asked. "What if he continues to make those accusations?"

"He may, but only the monks of Marmoutier will hear him," John answered. "Archbishop Engebaud is having him sent back to Tours under guard. They won't allow him to leave again."

"Then, really, there's nothing more to do," Margaret said happily.

Now that Margaret was no longer threatened with a husband, she was animated once again. Catherine rejoiced at the change. Now if she could just grow out of her infatuation with Solomon, everything would be wonderful.

"That's right," she agreed. "And really, I don't think there were any real heretics at all. Even the council only thought Eon deluded, and Gwenael only believed in him, not in a new theology."

But for some reason her mind strayed to the lepers she had seen in town and then in the churchyard. Two women and two men who bore no marks of the disease. Yesterday there had been five beggars by the cathedral. Three men and two women. But they hadn't moved like supplicants. And one of the men had kissed Annora's hand.

The drama of the last-minute delivery of the king of England from excommunication had been very satisfying. The council came to an end, and most of the abbots, bishops, lords and their entourages prepared to return home. A handful stayed to present one more case before the pope. The bishop of Hereford had fallen ill on the first day and was not expected to live. The cardinals and the more scholarly of those present remained for the trial of Bishop Gilbert of Poitiers. If his opponents had hoped to weaken him through waiting, they would be disappointed. Catherine noticed him in the crowd at the closing processional and he looked, if anything, eager for the fight.

She wished she could stay for the debates, but the craving to hold James and Edana again was too great.

"Astrolabe won't be ready to travel for several days," she told John. "Countess Sybil is going back to Flanders. I know you are wild to get on a dreadful boat for England. There must be someone going in the direction of the Paraclete who would take me along."

"Godfrey is one of Edgar's men," John reminded her. "He'll accompany you."

"No, he needs to stay with Astrolabe," Catherine said.

"Margaret?" John suggested. "She has to get back at some point."

"I don't know," Catherine said worriedly. "The countess seems determined to see that she make the acquaintance of all the noble families of Champagne, Burgundy, France and beyond. The count is staying for the trial."

"So am I," John said. "I wouldn't miss it. So I can let you know if it's decided that the commentary on Boethius is heretical."

"You know, I don't care what the judgment is," Catherine said. "I've finished the book and know that Master Gilbert's orthodoxy is sure. The only thing he could be chided for is his abstruse syntax. John, I want to see my babies!"

"And you used to be such an ardent scholar," John said sadly.

Catherine was almost ready to send for her horse and start out alone when Margaret saved her.

"Countess Mahaut wants to return at once to Troyes," she told Catherine the next morning. "She has much to attend to. She'll take me to the Paraclete on the way. Can you be ready to leave tomorrow?"

"Margaret, I'm ready now."

The countess's party moved too slowly for Catherine, but she endured the journey, knowing that each day they came a little closer to James and Edana.

One day they went by a small group of pilgrims walking barefoot through the cold mud at the side of the road.

Catherine watched as the party gained on them. Three men and two women, all moving proudly, oblivious to the elements.

As she came up to them, one man held out his bowl for alms.

Catherine leaned over to drop a coin in. Instead of looking quickly away, she stared into the face of the pilgrim.

Gui looked back at her and winked.

The countess had sent messengers ahead to alert the convent of their arrival as well as give Heloise a report on the events, especially the complete exoneration of Astrolabe. So the party was expected, and by the time they reached the gates of the convent there was a welcoming party.

"Mama! Mama!" Two small bodies raced toward her.

Catherine almost fell from her horse in her haste to reach them.

"My precious Edana!" The child threw herself at Catherine with the force of a catapult, knocking her down.

Catherine lay on the grass being pummeled with kisses. James stood over her as Edana gave her a month's worth of affection.

"I can write my name, Mama," he said. "I can read a whole *Nostre Pere*. Sister Emily taught me. See, I'll show you."

He tried to turn her head so she could see the letters he was making with his finger in the dirt. Edana moved her sloppy kisses to the region of Catherine's ear.

"That's wonderful, darling!" she exclaimed. "I'm very proud of you. What have the sisters been feeding you? I'm sure you're taller."

"That's what Papa said," James finished the letters. "See? *Jacobus*. That's Latin for James."

"Yes, James, very . . . did you say Papa?"

"He did."

Edana was lifted off her. Edgar loomed above like the wrath of God, his face as stern. He held out his handless arm. She took hold of the sleeve and got to her feet.

"Edgar! What are you doing here?" she asked. "Is something wrong? Is Solomon safe?"

"Solomon was fine when I left him ten days ago," Edgar said, barely keeping the anger from exploding on her. "He told me it was easier to handle the trade on his own than put up with my constant worrying about you. I had a feeling that you were in trouble. It appears I was right."

"Edgar, I had to go to Reims," she started.

"You were supposed to watch over our family." His voice rose, despite knowing that people were watching. "I raced back here to be sure you were all well. Instead I find you and Margaret gone and our children being spoiled rotten by a houseful of nuns! How could you leave them, even to help Astrolabe? You knew there were men hunting him. How could you risk losing another baby? Judas's twisted neck, Catherine, you could have been killed!"

Catherine felt tears starting. Angrily, she wiped them away with her sleeve.

"James and Edana were well cared for here," she retorted. "They suffered no harm from my absence. Yes, I might have miscarried during this journey. There was danger, more than I expected. But that doesn't matter. I couldn't turn my back on a friend. It was my duty to aid him in any way I could. You know that. If I had refused to go, you might have felt it was the most prudent decision, but you'd have respected me less for being a coward. And I would have felt the shame of it the rest of my life."

Edgar continued to glare at her. Catherine glared back. In Edgar's arms, Edana tried to tickle both their faces but they ignored her.

Margaret felt it was time to intervene.

"Put away your anger, Edgar," she told him, putting her hand on his shoulder. "If Catherine had not taken on the burden of this journey, then a murderer would have gone free, Astrolabe would be forever branded a heretic and I'd be on my way to marry Lord Otto of Carinthia."

"What!" That got Edgar's attention.

"I'll explain later," Margaret said. "Now kiss your wife and make peace."

"Edgar, I . . ." Catherine began.

"Do you have any idea of how I felt when I arrived and learned you'd gone to Reims?"

His face told her.

"I thought I'd be back safely long before you returned," she explained. "You should have been gone at least another two months. Edgar, you trusted me to make the decisions. I acted according to my conscience. The safety of all of our children is the most important thing to me. You have to believe that and continue to have faith in me."

"I kept thinking there was a threat near to you," he said. "I couldn't throw off the feeling. Even when I realized what had started it, I still had to come back. It isn't a matter of faith, but fear."

"What was it that upset you so?"

"The hermits." He loosened Edana and let her slide down his leg. "The ones Solomon and I took shelter with. There was something wrong about them. I finally realized that they were just like those people in Trier, the dualist heretics. There were only three of them, but they must have been expecting more. That's why there were two buildings and an oratory. I knew in my head that they couldn't do you any harm. There was no likelihood that they would even cross your path. But something in me said they were a threat to you. I know it's foolish."

"No, not completely," Catherine said. "Two women and a man? Very thin and pale but straight limbed and vigorous."

"Yes," he said.

"They were in Reims," she told him. "But they posed no threat to us. They were on the edge of events. I could never decide if they were wraiths or angels or simply people who had no interest in this world and its cares."

She put her arms around him.

"But if it was because of them that you came back to me, I bless their names, whatever they are. I know you were more afraid for me than angry, *carissime*. There's only one thing you can do about that."

"And that is?" He bent to her upturned face.

Catherine looked into his sea-grey eyes. She wanted to

make him promise never to leave again. She bit her tongue to keep the words from escaping. It was an impossible demand and unfair.

"Just trust in me," she said finally. "As I do in you. And beyond that, we must both simply have faith."

Edgar kissed her gently.

"In this world," he admitted. "Faith is the only thing we can always hold on to. All the same," he added grinning, as Edana yanked on his tunic for attention, "I intend to hold on to you for quite a while."

Catherine grinned. She wanted to tell Edgar that she found his body much more comforting than faith. But that would be heresy, and of that, she had had quite enough.

# Afterword
## What really happened?

The Council of Reims in 1148 is one I have been investigating for several years. My research has been a detective story itself, complete with false leads, hidden agendas and red herrings. The following few pages are a summary of that search.

But first, I want to state that the part about a mini-riot fueled by a rumor of an invading army of heretics and demons is total fiction, made up by me for the story. For that episode I drew not on a medieval source but on the recent irrational stories involving the year 2000, along with various panics resulting from rumors spread over the Internet. Our credulity hasn't changed over the past thousand years, only the focus of our fears.

Now, who and what did I draw from historical records?

Astrolabe really existed. The son of Abelard and Heloise was born in Le Pallet, Brittany, at the home of Abelard's sister, Denise, who raised him. No one knows for sure what happened to him, although it is possible that he eventually became a Cistercian monk or a canon at Nantes in Brittany. There is a letter of advice from Abelard to him and evidence that Heloise tried to get a benefice for him so he must have at least been in minor orders. I invented everything that happens to him in this book.

Bernard, abbot of Clairvaux (1090–1152), we know better as Saint Bernard (*not* the one the dog is named for). He was arguably the most charismatic preacher and most influential man in Western Europe from about 1129–1149. Many blamed him for the failure of the second Crusade, which he preached. He was also accused of trying to influence the decision of the council of Reims in the matter of Gilbert of Poitiers (see be-

AFTERWORD

low). I have tried to fit him into several books, but he refuses to be caught. There are many biographies that try to explain the man who called himself "the chimera of his age." One of the most accessible and interesting is Brian Patrick McGuire's *The Difficult Saint*. And, yes, I did steal his title for an earlier book of my own.

Engebaud, Archbishop of Tours (d.1156), and his fight with Olivier, bishop of Dol (d.1153), was part of an argument between Tours and Dol that went on for almost a hundred years. It involved lots of name-calling, excommunications and trips to Rome. One of the times the bishop of Dol was excommunicated was at the council of Reims. It is my private belief that this is why Eon was brought to the council for judgment and this is what I've put in the book.

Eon, sometimes called Eon de l'Etoile, is an elusive character. The bare facts are that he was a Breton heretic who was brought before the council. He was deemed too simple to prosecute and was remanded into custody. After that the stories vary. I can find nothing written about him by someone who was actually at the council. The most complete story about him was written by William of Newburgh, some forty years after the council. William's account makes for great reading but can't be taken as fact. Otto of Freising's account is probably closest to the truth, but still secondhand as Otto was with Conrad on the Second Crusade and not present at Reims.

Eugenius III (d.1153) was born Bernard of Pisa and became a Cistercian abbot before being elected pope. He spent most of his time in office in France because the Romans had driven him from the city. He was a good friend of St. Bernard (see above) and also a former student of Abelard.

Gilbert de la Porrée, bishop of Poitiers (c.1075–1154), was a noted scholar and teacher before he became bishop of Poitiers. Most chroniclers of the council of Reims have concentrated on his trial for heresy there. I didn't show this trial because it's a book in itself. For those who are interested in the subtleties of his philosophy and the reasons why it was so important to intellectuals of the day, I can provide a reading list. Few modern readers will be surprised to learn that poli-

tics were involved in his trial. In essence, Gilbert was exonerated and remained bishop.

Heloise (d.1163/4) is primarily known for her love affair
with Peter Abelard that resulted in the birth of Astrolabe (see
above) and Abelard's castration by her angry relatives. Eventually, she became abbess of the Paraclete, a convent in
Champagne founded by Abelard on land given to him. She remained there for the next forty years. However, she did not sit
idly, but wrote, interacted with the community, and founded
six daughter convents. She was in contact with Abelard until
his death and he visited often. I am eagerly awaiting a forth-
coming biography of Heloise as abbess.

Henri, count of Tréguier, did everything I've attributed to
him. He installed his mistress in the abbey, throwing out the
monks. He was excommunicated but didn't seem to pay much
attention to that. At some point he grew tired of the mistress
and she married one of Henri's vassals. We have the whole
story from a letter Henri wrote to Pope Alexander III when he
was in his eighties. I have quoted from this at the beginning of
chapter seventeen.

John of Salisbury (c.1115–1120 to 1180) was at the council
of Reims and has left us the best firsthand account of it. In his
many books and letters, John gave a fascinating picture of the
world he lived in and of his own personality. At the time of the
council he was about thirty years old, had been studying for
most of his life and now couldn't find a job. (Of course no one
has this problem today.) Somehow, probably at Reims, he
managed to get a letter of introduction from Bernard of Clairvaux to Theobald, archbishop of Canterbury and shortly
thereafter became one of his clerks. John was a friend and
companion of Thomas Becket and present at his murder. He
ended his life as bishop of Chartres. Almost all of his work
has been translated and is well worth the read. There is also a
biography of John by Cary Nederman that will be out in 2003.
I have mixed feelings about using John as if he were a fic-
tional character but I like him and wanted to share him with
the rest of you.

Marie, abbess of St-Sulpice (1136–1181), was the daughter

of King Stephen of England. She probably wasn't at the council but I had to add her because she fascinates me and I read through her charters in the archives at Rennes. In 1160, Marie left, or was taken, from the convent to marry Matthew, count of Boulogne. After the marriage was dissolved, she returned to an English convent, where she resumed the religious life.

Petronilla of Aquitaine (c.1124–1151) was the younger sister of Eleanor of Aquitaine. At the age of seventeen or so, she fell in love with Raoul de Vermandois (c.1105–1152), count of Vermandois, cousin of the late king, Louis VI, married, and a good twenty years older than she. They arranged for friendly bishops to give him a divorce that most of Europe didn't recognize, were married and had three children. The pope finally granted the divorce at the council. I believe that the circumstances may have been much as I have written. Two of the children married children of Sybil of Anjou and Thierry, count of Flanders. The son of Raoul and Petronilla died a leper and their daughters had no children. At the time, many thought this was because of a prophecy (or curse) supposedly made by St. Bernard.

Sybil of Anjou, countess of Flanders (c.1110–1164), is one of the most remarkable women of the twelfth century. She was the sister of Geoffrey of Anjou, and the daughter of Fulk, who had become king of Jerusalem. She went to the Holy Land at least three times. The last time she remained, joining a convent. As related in this book, she governed Flanders while her husband was on crusade with King Louis. When the county was invaded, she directed the defense and earned much praise from her contemporaries. She did arrange a truce long enough to give birth, probably to her son, Peter.

There is no record of the name of the abbess of St.-Pierre-les-Nonnains at this time, so I have given her the name of an earlier one, Odile.

Any bishop or abbot mentioned in passing in the text did exist and was at the council.